PROMISED PROPHECY

ORACLE SERIES, BOOK 1

Jaemi Lee

Bamboo
Publishing

Promised Prophecy
Oracle Series, Book 1

First Paperback Edition: 2021

Hardback ISBN: 978-1-956501-00-1
Paperback ISBN: 978-1-956501-01-8
eBook ISBN: 978-1-956501-02-5

Cover art by Joshua Deni Prakoso (@jdprakoso)

The characters and events in this book are fictional. Any similarity to actual persons, living or dead, is purely coincidental.

To everyone who believed in me.

And to my younger self.

1
WARNING

Minari glided across the forest. He leapt, his body graceful and light as he went from tree to tree. Leaves barely rustled against the movement. His eyes scanned the darkness, looking for anything suspicious. Rowen, a fellow scout, had found a red, silk scarf not too far off from the village the previous night. It was unusual for someone to be that high in the mountains. Alder's powers protected their tiny village. Hidden away high in the mountains, the trees acted as a maze, fog as illusions. Anyone who wasn't an elf would find it impossible to pass through. For something that didn't belong to the elves, suddenly appearing so close to their sanctuary was worrisome.

The elf's stomach had tied in knots the moment he'd seen the piece of fabric draped over Rowen's hand. It had swayed eerily against the wind, and the atmosphere had seemed to freeze. Everyone had held their breath, the same thought racing through their minds.

The safety of Mistfall could potentially be breached. Whoever was looking for them knew where they were going.

Minari had finished his rounds a few hours ago but decided to double- and even triple-check the area. It was better to be safe than sorry. As a scout, it was his duty to protect Mistfall Village and what they hid away.

He jumped down, his boots barely making any noise. He only took a few steps before the snapping of a twig alerted him. He swiftly drew one of his daggers from his belt, the blade arching against his arm. He pivoted his foot, swinging his body around, ready to slash whoever tried to sneak up behind him.

Hands shot up, and the person following let out a squeak. A familiar shade of red hair caught his vision. Wide and frightened green eyes looked at him.

Minari stilled his body, pausing briefly before returning his dagger to its scabbard. He straightened his body and cocked his head to the side. His childhood friend and co-scout stood before him. "Lily, why are you following me? Shouldn't you be making your rounds?"

"I-I already finished." She lowered her hands, still shaken. She had nearly had her neck sliced.

Minari sighed. "If you're finished, why didn't you report straight to Commander Silas?"

Lily clasped her hands together and pressed them against her chest. "B-because I saw you were still here, and I know you always finish your rounds before anyone else does. I was just surprised to see you here . . ."

Minari cocked a brow. He knew the younger red-haired elf was hiding something. "And?"

"AndIwaswonderingifyoucouldhelpmegetElliottotal ktome?"

Minari blinked. He said nothing at first, still trying to decipher the spew of words that had quickly left Lily's mouth. He noticed the slight pink tinge at the top of her pointy ears. "Come again?"

Lily shuffled her feet, looking down. "I was wondering if you could . . . help me talk to Elliot."

"Oh." Minari ran his hands through his unruly, purple hair. He knew Lily had a crush on Elliot, but his childhood friend had gently turned her down. The three of them had grown up together, and the rejection had been awkward. It had been four months since then. "Maybe this should be a topic for another time. We should be looking for any intruders."

Lily's eyes widened. "You're right! I'm so sorry, Minari."

"It's fine. Did you at least finish your rounds before coming to me?"

Lily nodded. "Nothing out of the ordinary."

"Same. I'm practically done, so let's head back to Commander Silas." Minari and Lily made their way back. Minari kept his eyes and ears open as they returned, hoping he wouldn't see anything out of the ordinary.

"Minari, Lily, welcome back," Rowen said. The taller elf smiled at them. His sky-blue hair was ruffled from the search. Because he was a senior scout, he was tasked closer to the border, making his overall travel distance farther than either Minari's or Lily's. "Find anything?"

Minari shook his head. "Nothing on my end."

"Nothing here, either," Lily said.

Rowen crossed his arms and sucked his bottom lip. "Maybe it was just some traveler who got lost."

Minari frowned. "A traveler? I don't think a mere traveler would be walking up this high in the mountains. The person had to have known where they were going."

"I've talked with everyone else. They haven't found anything either. Their search came out clean. If it really was an intruder, they wouldn't have vanished in a day. They would still be around."

Minari knew that logic was right. If someone truly wanted to seek Mistfall out, they wouldn't up and leave. They would be persistent.

"What do you think, Lily?" Rowen asked. "Do you think it was a simple traveler, or could someone be trying to find us?"

Lily jumped at the sudden question. "Well . . ." She peered over at Minari. Her eyes met his, but Minari gave no indication of an answer he wanted her to share. Lily cleared her throat, her gaze shifting back to Rowen. "I think it was a traveler who came up here. Maybe they were curious and wanted to see what was up here. Alder's powers are enough to keep anyone away. They probably got lost in the fog and tripped, losing their scarf along the way."

Rowen nodded. "That seems like a plausible answer. Let us go with that for now. I'm going to meet up with Captain Errol and Commander Silas about all this. You two go on and rest. It's been a long night."

Minari and Lily went their separate ways, returning to their cabins.

Not having any further solid answers regarding the scarf or potential intruder didn't sit well with Minari. His stomach spun on itself as his mind replayed the image. Everything was pure speculation at this point, but he knew there wasn't anything else he could do but to keep a sharp eye out for anything that could lead to answers.

Minari opened the door to his home and let himself in, the wooden door softly clicking behind him. He trudged toward his room, exhaustion prevalent in his body. It was nearly four in the morning. After the meeting, he had made another pass around the perimeter of the village just to be positive he hadn't missed anything. Of course, nothing had turned up. He was so tired he barely noticed a presence in the kitchen.

"Minari." Her voice was sharp.

"Mother," Minari said. It didn't surprise him to see Mayleen waiting for him. She'd been the first to learn about the scarf after the scouts.

"You are home later than usual." Mayleen lifted her hand, motioning for him to sit with her at the kitchen table.

Wanting to get comfortable, Minari unbuckled his belt, which held a few of his daggers, and unzipped his coat. He placed the leather accessory on the table before slouching into the chair across from his mother. Mayleen pushed a mug across the table. He accepted it, thanking her before taking a sip. The tea warmed his body.

"Did you find anything else in regard to the potential

intruder?"

Minari shook his head. "No one discovered anything out of the ordinary. I surveyed the area multiple times and found nothing."

A shaky breath left Mayleen's lips. She clasped her hands together and pressed her forehead against her thumbs. Stray pieces from her otherwise neat bun fell across her cheeks. A faint line was starting to settle between her brows. Minari reached forward, tucking a few pieces of her amethyst hair behind her ears. "You didn't have to stay up waiting for me."

"I am worried, Minari," she said through her teeth. "Elliot turns sixteen today."

Minari frowned. He knew where his mother was trying to steer the conversation, and he wasn't in the mood for it. "Mother, the festival is next week. We should focus on that instead."

"Right; the villagers are looking forward to it. It's a celebration to show how far we've come since the terror that fell upon us."

"The 340th festival."

"A number we should be proud of, yet the history behind it is sorrowful." Mayleen looked straight into Minari's eyes. Her features softened. "Your eye . . . It never truly healed, did it?"

Minari looked down at his mug. He'd been born with purple eyes, but an unfortunate accident had left him blind in his left, ultimately shifting the orb to gray. He couldn't remember much of how it'd happened, as he'd been much younger than he was now, but he knew his father had lost his life. He'd been eight years old when Melvin died, thus forcing his mother to become the leader of the village.

Mayleen's role required her to attend meetings with the elders and Alder. She needed to ensure the villagers lived safe, peaceful lives in Mistfall without worrying about outsiders. It was regretful that the common elves weren't given the same extensive knowledge as Minari's family or the elders, but it was to ensure they lived blissful lives. A great deal of stress could be detrimental to elves. Those with strong wills were able to push through and survive, but it wasn't unheard of that elves could become shells of their former selves.

With Mayleen as the leader and his elder sister, Stella, tucked away in the Moon Shrine, he needed to be strong for his family, to be a pillar of support. He was eighteen years old—an adult.

Minari wrapped his hands around the smooth mug. The tea glimmered in the moonlight that spilled through the window. "Let's make the festival one that we'll remember."

Elliot dug his finger into the dirt. He dragged it across, creating circles, squares, triangles, and whatever else came to mind. The flickering fire illuminated his scribbles.

"What's on your mind?" A human male walked over, taking a seat on the log next to him. He didn't seem much older than Elliot, perhaps in his early twenties. His figure was a stark contrast to Elliot's. Elliot was slim, dainty, and small while the

human was tall with broad shoulders and a powerful chest. The man handed him a mug. "Careful, it's hot."

Elliot wiped the dirt off his fingers with his skirt. Wait. Why was he wearing a skirt? He accepted the mug and quickly took a sip. The man grabbed the mug away from his lips.

"I told you it's hot."

Elliot frowned. He hadn't felt any heat from the cup. He didn't feel much of anything. He pressed his fingers against his lips. They were puffy from the hot drink.

The man sighed, placing the mugs beside his feet. He turned toward Elliot, arms outstretched. "Come here."

Something tugged at Elliot, making him want to lean into the man.

So he did. He pressed himself into the man's embrace. Protective arms wrapped around him, pushing the two closer together. Elliot nuzzled against the man's chest, inhaling the faint aroma of bark and pine. It comforted him.

"Even after all this time, you're still the timid, little girl I found in the forest."

Had he just called him a girl?

The man pulled away and cupped Elliot's cheek. They locked eyes, speaking through their gaze. The man's lips parted slightly, and his eyes glazed over. Elliot's stomach fluttered. He wanted to be closer. He wrapped his arms around the man's neck, pulling him down to his lips.

A sharp poke on Elliot's cheek broke the elf from his dream. He flinched at the intrusion. He groaned, keeping his eyes shut. The unwelcome action continued. He swatted the hand, attempting to dispel the source of discomfort. He heard a flutter of wings before a soft breeze caressed his cheek. He rolled over, pulling his plush blanket over his head. His body relaxed. The strings of unconsciousness lulled him. Images of the dream came rushing back: the intimacy he'd had with the mysterious male, the kiss they'd shared. His eyes shot open. He jolted upward, sweat beading down his chin. Steadying his breath, he pressed a hand against his lips. "What was that?" he whispered.

"Good morning."

He jumped. By his bedside was Minari. He had pulled the chair from his desk and sat in it in a reverse manner. His wrists were crossed over each other on the backrest, and his chin rested against his hands. He cocked his head, a snide smile on his lips.

"Minari! How did you get into my room? Why're you here?" Elliot pressed a hand against his chest, attempting to calm his racing heart.

"Whatever do you mean?" Minari asked.

"Did my mom let you in again?"

"Miss Estelle is practically my second mom, Elliot. You should know that by now."

Minari's statement wasn't too far off. The two had grown up like brothers, and he'd become Elliot's confidant. They'd spent childhood days at each other's homes, playing games and telling each other secrets—whatever secrets child elves had, anyway. It was no surprise his mother would let Minari in. What surprised him was how *early* Minari had woken up. He couldn't remember a time Minari had been up before noon. It was barely eight in the morning.

A chirp pulled Elliot from his thoughts. Nestling into Minari's hair was a red songbird.

"So, are you going to tell me what kind of dream you were having? You were drooling into your pillow with a giddy look on your face." He lifted his hand, letting the songbird hop onto his finger. "Redd had a hard time waking you up."

Elliot turned away, attempting to hide his quickly flushing cheeks. The tips of his ears warmed. "It was nothing," he mumbled.

"You sure it was nothing?" He stretched his hand out. "I'm sure Redd here can pry the answer from you." Redd chirped and flapped his wings.

Elliot pushed Minari's hand away, careful not to disturb the small animal. "What are you even doing here, anyway? You aren't normally up this early," he said, changing the topic.

"I would never forget your birthday, Elliot." Minari's smile softened. "Happy sixteenth birthday."

For the second time that morning, Elliot's cheeks flushed. "Thank you," he mumbled. He had completely forgotten his birthday was today. He could remember Minari's, but for some reason he couldn't remember his own. He wasn't sure why; it was an odd quirk he was somewhat self-conscious of.

Minari swung his leg over, standing up. He pushed the chair back underneath Elliot's desk. "I can get Xeno saddled up while you get ready."

Elliot fiddled with his fingers. He knew Xeno, his ovis, would be excited to stretch his legs along the mountainside. It was a ritual to go out riding on the morning of their birthdays, but this would be the first time it would be just the two of them. He'd never made amends with Lily and had felt awful when he'd turned her down. He felt nothing for her other than sisterly love.

"What are you waiting for?"

"Um . . ." Elliot peeked at Minari. "Do you think Lily . . . ?"

"Do you want to invite her?"

"Well, I mean, I don't know."

"I can swing by her place and ask."

"If it's not too much trouble . . ."

"It's your birthday. I can at least do that." Minari smirked. "Now brush that silky hair of yours and get ready. The morning is slipping away, and I don't want to ride when it's hot!"

"Okay, you win. I'll get up now." Elliot swung his legs off his bed. He ran his fingers through his hair; not a single knot was in his pale green locks. He kept his head down, hoping Minari wouldn't notice the slight frown he was hiding. If Lily came, then he could make amends. If she didn't, then he would need to swallow the fact he'd lost a friend.

2
DISCOVER

Elliot patted his cheek dry before leaving the bathroom. He let out a sigh, enjoying the cleanliness of a freshly washed face. He slipped on his white stringed blouse and brown slacks. Reaching over to his desk, he grabbed his pouch. The pouch had two belt attachments, one that went around his hips, and a smaller one that went around his thigh. He slipped his boots on and quickly laced them up. He checked himself in the mirror one last time, making sure he didn't have bedhead before leaving.

He circled around his cabin, heading toward the stables. Minari was already there, finishing up saddling Xeno. Xander, Minari's ovis, was standing not too far off. Ovis could easily be mistaken for goats, but they were larger with stronger bodies. They had a deep connection with their owners and families.

The animals were mostly used for leisure riding and hauling crops. They were wild animals, native to the mountains, but occasionally one would seek the companionship of elves.

Elliot had run into Xeno while taking a walk with Minari and Lily when he was ten. They'd all been having a small picnic in the mountains when Xeno, appearing no more than one year old, had approached the trio. He'd eyed the food, and Elliot had offered him a baked potato, which Xeno had graciously accepted. He'd followed Elliot home, and they'd been bonded ever since.

Xander's tail swung side to side as he waited for his master to finish prepping the other ovis. Redd nestled in his brown fur between his horns. Xeno bleated when he noticed Elliot, shaking his large body.

"Hold on, Xeno! Let me finish strapping this on," Minari said, grunting as he connected the last clasp.

Elliot stroked the top of Xeno's head, right between his horns. He enjoyed feeling the fluffy fur against his fingers. "Morning, Xeno." He cupped his ovis's muzzle and pressed his forehead against Xeno's. "Ready for a morning ride?" Xeno snorted.

"Elliot," a soft voice called out.

Elliot stiffened. He hadn't heard that voice in what seemed like forever. The last time he'd heard it had been when he was confessed to four months ago. He slowly turned around. Lily had reins in her hands, her own ovis, Willow, trailing behind her. Willow's fur was the color of sand, and her horns were considerably smaller than Xeno's. As a male, Xeno's made a perfect arch, while Willow's barely showed above the tuft of fur on her head.

"Happy birthday, Elliot," Lily said. A small blush crept across her cheeks.

"Thank you." His voice was barely above a whisper.

"I . . . um . . . I got you something." Lily reached into her pouch and pulled out a necklace. She lifted it up. The string was made of dark brown suede. A wooden leaf pendant hung in the middle. "I made this. I hope you like it . . ." Her voice dipped lower after each word.

"You didn't have to." Elliot bit his lip. He was touched that Lily had bothered to make something even if she hadn't been sure they would talk again. He could sense the importance of their friendship through the gift.

"I—"

Minari smacked Elliot's shoulder. "Elliot! Just accept the present, will you? Lily worked hard carving the pendant for you."

Elliot opened his mouth, then closed it. He looked at the pendant and then at Lily. Her hand was still lifted, but her eyes had shifted downward. Her lips were pressed together, but he could still make out the gentle tremble. It would be harsh to reject the gift. Accepting the gift would be a good way to mend the bridge that had been abruptly torn down between them. "I love it. Will you put it on me?"

Lily's head snapped up, eyes wide. "Really?"

Elliot nodded.

Lily giggled. She unclasped the string and hooked it behind Elliot's neck. She placed her palm against the pendant and closed her eyes. "May Vylantra protect and guide you." She pulled her hand away and smiled. "Thank you for accepting my gift. I thought I'd never have the chance to give it to you, let alone talk to you again."

Elliot scratched the back of his head. "I guess things just got weird, huh?"

Lily slapped Elliot's shoulder. "That's because you got weird around me! I don't mind staying friends, Elliot."

Elliot rubbed his shoulder. It was the same one Minari had hit earlier. He was receiving a bit of abuse on his birthday. "Sorry."

Lily waved her hand. "The past is the past. Let's just look forward to the future. Now, are we riding or what?"

The trio gathered their ovis and made their way into the forest. They followed large boulders littered throughout the forest, which helped guide them, keeping them within their protected lands. Elliot was more than happy to have Lily back. It hadn't been the same without his figurative younger sister around him and Minari. They talked and laughed as if a single day hadn't gone by since they'd last seen each other.

It was nearing noon when Minari had them stop. They had been riding for three hours, and it was time to give their mounts a rest and head back. A small river ran nearby, and it was a good place to recuperate.

Elliot plopped down in the grass next to Xeno, who graciously drank the clear water. He patted the ovis. "Today's a good day, huh?" Xeno's ear twitched in response. Elliot looked over. Minari and Lily were talking a ways down from where he was. He knew Minari had kept in contact with Lily after the awkward confession. He'd repeatedly told Elliot the rejection didn't bother Lily, but Elliot hadn't been able to bring himself to face her. He remembered the night Lily had come up to him, how his voice had gotten caught in his throat when she'd confessed she liked him, how he'd only shook his head in response. He recalled Lily's furrowed brows as the tears welled up in her eyes and the forced smile across her lips, the way her voice had trembled when she'd insisted everything was all right and they could remain friends. The memory was painful and vivid, and he hadn't wanted to further break her heart by staying around her.

He propped his knees up and rested his elbows against them. He was curious to know what they were talking about, but they were standing out of earshot. Today was his birthday, so maybe they were planning a surprise. He took a deep breath.

And froze.

The sky darkened, and the water frosted over. Noise around him muted. Xeno was no longer next to him. Minari and Lily were no longer around him. The icy air bit at his skin. A powerful gust of wind roared. He lifted his arms to shield his face, shutting his eyes.

"Finally."

Elliot yelped. The raspy voice sounded right by his ear. It sent shivers down his body. He needed to get away from it. Now. So he ran, only to be greeted with a sudden rush of cold wetness.

"Elliot?" Minari called out.

Elliot sputtered, shaking his head. He blinked frantically. The water wasn't frozen. The sun was out. Xeno was next to the river.

Minari and Lily rushed to his side.

"Elliot, what are you doing? If you wanted to go for a swim, you should've at least taken your clothes off."

Lily shoved Minari's shoulder. He stumbled back but quickly regained his bearings to keep from falling into the river. Her cheeks were bright pink. "M-Minari! Don't say things like that! Elliot can't just u-undress!"

Minari rolled his eyes. "We used to swim together as kids."

"Yeah, but we aren't kids anymore!" Lily covered her chest with her arms. "We're adults, and we should act like adults."

Minari shrugged. "Sure." He held his hand out to Elliot. "You coming out?"

Elliot took Minari's hand, thankful for the help. His legs felt oddly weak, and he had to force them to stay still, or else they would be shaking. The mysterious voice still echoed in his mind. He looked around, making sure nothing would turn up.

"Are you okay?" Minari asked. "You look scared. Did something set you off?"

"Nothing strange happened, did it?" Elliot said.

Minari frowned, the corners of his brows twitching downward. "Strange in what way?" His voice was stern.

"Like . . . did it suddenly become night? And winter? The water froze over . . ."

"Nothing happened, Elliot," Lily said. The pitch of her voice was raised. "You were . . . dreaming. Right? Were you that tired when you woke up? Don't scare me,

Elliot."

Elliot pondered. Had it been a dream? Had he somehow dozed off and accidentally fallen into the river? It was possible. It wouldn't be the first strange dream he'd had. "Maybe?"

Minari sighed. "I didn't wake you up that early."

"If you woke up before me, I would consider that early."

"So you're saying I woke you up so early that you dreamed about winter nights and decided to fall forward into the river?" Minari deadpanned.

"Yep."

"I should get Redd to harass you."

Elliot gasped. "It's my birthday, and you're going to get Redd to make a nest in my hair?"

"What are you worried about? Your hair is so silky that it would be impossible to make a nest out of."

"Unlike yours," Lily said.

"Look, my hair has a mind of its own, okay? We should hurry back to Mistfall and get Elliot a change of clothes before he catches a cold."

"It's the middle of summer," Lily said.

"He can still catch a cold."

"It's the middle of summer," Elliot agreed.

Minari let out an exasperated sigh. He slid his hand over his face. "Fine. Fine. Young elves these days. Can't even listen to their elders." He grinned. "We should get back, anyway. Then we can have some real fun."

3
SECRETS

Elliot hunched over the wooden bench, pouting. His hair had stray pieces sticking up in different directions, and no matter how much he combed, he couldn't get them down. The sun had already set, and night fell upon Mistfall. Orange flames were lit throughout the village, giving his friends a warm glow that danced across their skin. Lily gave him a small smile, the corners of her brows lifted. Earlier that day, Minari had persistently tried to get Redd to make a nest in Elliot's hair. Lily did her best to protect Elliot, but they both couldn't stop Minari's persistence.

Elliot let out a sigh as he leaned against the wooden bench, his fingers still tangled in his hair.

"Are you still mad at me?" Minari asked. He was holding two loaves of sweet bread.

"Furious." He wasn't quite a vain person; he just

strongly preferred his hair to sit how it was supposed to sit.

"But you had fun, right?"

Elliot heaved another sigh. "Yeah, I guess." He couldn't stay mad at Minari for long, even if he wanted to. The entire ordeal had brought him and Lily back from their rocky relationship. Their friendship was solidified once again, and they were back to normal. Lily had left the two a few hours earlier. She'd apologized for leaving so soon, stating she needed to return home to help her mother prep dinner, especially since her younger brother, Galvin, was going through a growth spurt and ate like two full-grown elves.

"Good." Minari nudged the sweet bread into Elliot's face. "Now eat this while it's still warm."

Elliot took it, taking a quick bite. He paused. There was a gooey texture inside the bread. He peeked down. Inside the sweet bread was strawberry paste. Any last bit of anger he had toward Minari disappeared. Give it to his best friend to know what his favorite food was.

"Is it good? I made it myself, you know."

Elliot chortled. "You? Bake?"

Minari placed a hand on his chest. "Elliot! What are you insinuating? That I can't bake?"

"Basically." He took another bite. The sweet bread was delicious. It had the right amount of sugar, and the texture was perfect. The bread was soft, and the strawberry paste wasn't too sticky.

"Elliot," Minari said. His playful tone shifted to a serious one. "There's something you should know."

"Hmm?" Elliot shifted his eyes to Minari while his

mouth was still latched to the homemade dessert.

"Next week is the Bloom Festival."

Elliot hummed, waiting for Minari to continue.

"I know you're planning on performing the rite so you can become a keeper."

Elliot paused, pulling the sweet bread away.

"And I know you want to become a keeper so you can protect our oracle."

Elliot nodded. When Minari's older sister, Stella, had turned sixteen, a crescent moon scar had appeared over her wrist. It was a symbol of the oracle. Four years ago, the elders took her to the Moon Shrine, where she still resided. The keepers were guards, protectors tasked with guarding the oracle from any unforeseen danger. It was a necessary precaution even though Alder's power protected them. They didn't want a repeat of the tragedy that had occurred 350 years ago. The harrowing event was the root cause of why they lived deep in the mountains.

They had once lived in harmony with other races in the lower lands. But their precious oracle was murdered, and a civil war broke out. Ten years later, the elves, barely escaping by the skin of their teeth, retreated to the mountains. They took a heavy hit during the war. Many elves lost their lives, and they'd been close to getting wiped out. Since the elves were Alder's creation, he'd vowed to protect them, keeping them within his home. Their village was relatively small, and they still hadn't fully recovered from the devastating blow.

"What are you getting at, Minari?" Elliot frowned. "You're beating around the bush."

Minari bit his lip. He scratched his head and pulled at his hair. "I'm not sure you'll believe me if I tell you."

"I won't know until you tell me."

"You're sixteen now."

"Uh-huh."

"Actually, let me ask you this." Minari shifted, his body now facing Elliot. "What exactly happened earlier today when you fell into the river?"

"I guess I fell asleep." Elliot was unsure why Minari was asking him again. He wasn't even sure what had happened. Everything seemed surreal.

"I doubt that's what happened. Tell me the truth, Elliot."

"What does that have to do with anything?"

Minari sighed heavily. "I probably shouldn't be telling you this," he mumbled.

"What? Tell me. Minari, what's going on?" Elliot swallowed. He was on edge. Minari hardly ever spoke to him seriously. It unnerved him. His stomach churned, and his palms felt clammy. A sudden pressure on his shoulder startled him. He yelped and jumped off the bench, dropping the rest of his sweet bread.

"Elliot? What's gotten into you?"

"D-Dad!"

Errol stood behind the bench with a confused look on his face. He was a spitting image of Elliot if Elliot were twenty-two years older. Eye color was the only major difference between them. Elliot didn't have his father's sharp brown orbs. Instead, he'd inherited Estelle's soft blue eyes. Errol glanced over at Minari before shifting his attention back to Elliot. "I came to get you. Your mother finished preparing your birthday dinner."

"Oh. It's that late already?"

"Yes. Come, we can walk home together." Errol wrapped his arm over Elliot's shoulders. "Quality father and son time. We haven't had a heart-to-heart since you became a teen. Are you in your rebellious stage? Do you have a girl you like yet?"

"Dad!" Elliot's face flushed. He pushed Errol away. "Lily's just a friend."

"Oh? You made up with Lily? She's a nice girl, you know. Is that necklace from her? I can recognize that craftsmanship from anywhere."

"Dad!" Elliot covered his face with his hands. His ears heated with every second his father was talking. "Stop embarrassing me." His voice was muffled.

"Why are you embarrassed? Minari's been your friend since you two learned how to speak."

Elliot groaned. Errol never failed to tease him in front of Minari and Lily. He always asked questions that would be best suited to a private setting.

Minari chuckled. He stood and raised his arms in a stretch. "I should head back home too. Mother probably wants me to start planning for the festival next week."

"It's already that time, huh? I'm sure you'll do fine. Melvin would be proud of you," Errol said.

The corner of Minari's lips tugged into a weak smile. "Thanks. If he were still around, I'm sure he would be proud to see how far I've come. And on that note, I definitely need to leave before Mother gives me an earful."

"Don't give Lady Mayleen a hard time." Errol gave Minari a wave.

"Happy birthday, Elliot," Minari said. "I'll see you tomorrow."

"See ya . . ." Elliot's voice trailed off. He watched Minari turn and leave. The uncomfortable pit in his stomach was still there. What had Minari wanted to tell him before his father had interrupted them? Hopefully he'd find out tomorrow . . . if Minari remembered.

And when the next day came, Minari didn't remember what he'd wanted to tell Elliot. The younger elf shrugged it off. Perhaps something would happen to jog his memory. The next day came, and still nothing. With each passing day, Elliot soon forgot the weird dream he'd had the morning of his birthday and the strange vision he'd had at the lake.

4

MENACE

"Were you going to tell Elliot what he is?" Errol stood behind his desk, hands resting against the wood as he leaned forward. His eyes narrowed, and his gaze was focused.

Minari had been called into the captain's quarters right before he'd been about to leave for the weekly assembly. It'd been surprising when he'd opened his front door and found Errol waiting for him. He'd been promptly dragged into the captain's office.

It was a small cabin located three miles east of Mistfall, a thirty-minute walk for a scout. The furniture was sparse— only a desk and a chair. A few maps were littered across the wooden desk. The cabin was primarily used when Errol needed to hold private meetings with Silas and a few senior scouts. Minari was afraid the captain had overheard the conversation he'd had with Elliot a few nights ago, but it wasn't shocking how well the captain's hearing was.

"Don't lie to me, Minari." Errol's voice was curt. "I know that look. Don't even try making an excuse either."

Minari straightened his back. His hands were in fists pressed against the small of his back. "Captain, there was an event that occurred the day of Elliot's birthday. I suspected something might have happened."

Errol's expression faltered. The strong front cracked into a softer one. "What happened to my son? Tell me everything."

Minari explained Elliot's strange behavior during their ride, from seeming to gaze off into the distance to suddenly running into the river. He shared how Elliot had claimed it was winter in his dream and the waters were frozen. The oddest thing about it was that the rivers in the mountains didn't freeze; they always flowed, even in winter.

Errol cursed under his breath and sat down. He propped his elbows on his desk, then pressed his forehead against his hands and heaved a heavy sigh. "Time finally caught up to us."

"Captain, I apologize. I merely wanted to warn Elliot."

"You will do no such thing. He deserves to live a carefree life until his time has come." He ran his fingers through his hair. "He deserves that, at least."

Minari clenched his fists. "That would just cause more of a shock. If his role is cast upon him suddenly—"

"And telling him now wouldn't? Minari, I know you're smarter than that." Errol's eyes narrowed.

Minari shifted uncomfortably. He knew either way would shock Elliot, but maybe it would be easier for Elliot to swallow if Minari told him instead of one of the elders. Elliot didn't know that his family, the elders, Mayleen, and Minari knew his true identity. It had been difficult for Minari to withhold this secret from his best friend for all these years, but he knew it was something he had to do. It wasn't a choice.

Elliot didn't even know Minari was a scout. Even though Lily had no qualms letting Elliot know she'd become a scout, Minari had made Lily swear not to tell Elliot he was one himself. He didn't want Elliot to know his best friend had blood on his hands. He didn't want Elliot to know how fast he could take someone's life and how many lives he had taken. He didn't want Elliot to know the look of pure terror on their faces when they realize they had mere moments of life left. The number of intruders was steadily increasing, and the unknown scarf being so close to home set off warning bells in his head.

Whoever they were, they knew Elliot was drawing close to presenting who he actually was—*what* he actually was. It was only a matter of time before Elliot realized it himself. Minari didn't know how much time it would take for Elliot's powers to surface, and he just hoped Elliot could handle it when they did.

Minari had spent most of his life preparing for this time to come. Right before Melvin died, he'd enrolled Minari in the scouts. At the tender age of eight, Minari had learned how to move, how to fight, how to conceal himself, how to listen, and how to see. And soon after Melvin passed away, Mayleen had made him study every scroll and book in the hidden archives.

He'd studied every detail available regarding the lower lands. He knew he would eventually leave Mistfall, and it was important to have some knowledge of how people in the lands below behaved. The common elf knew of the three different races that lived in the lower lands: humans, nixen, and ethereals, but in comparison to the information in the hidden archives, it wasn't much. The hidden archives illustrated their different living habits, their magical abilities and weapons, and how they'd presented themselves during the war. He just hoped not much had changed in the past 340 years of separation.

"We need to expand our routes," Errol said. "We will widen our radius five miles. Go meet with the rest of the scouts. I'll make the announcement tonight before we begin."

"Sir." Minari bowed and made haste. It had gone better than he'd expected. Errol was strict as captain of the scouts. Nothing got past him. It had been unanimously agreed upon with the elders that they would tell Elliot who he was and the task he must fulfill. The only reason Minari knew was because he was next in line to become Mistfall's leader. Once he reached the age of twenty-five, his mother would descend to an elder and he would ascend to the leadership role.

In his hurried pace, he almost missed Lily trailing behind him. "How did you know I was here?"

"I saw Captain Errol at your house before I left for the assembly." She jogged to catch up. "What were you two talking about? What's going on with Elliot?"

"You shouldn't eavesdrop, especially around the captain's quarters."

"Sorry . . ."

Minari clicked his tongue. "It's nothing. Don't worry about it." It was only a matter of time before everyone knew what Elliot was. Telling her wouldn't change anything, and he knew better than to leak the information to Lily. They gathered with the other scouts. Only a few minutes passed before Errol arrived with Silas. The two leaders clasped their hands behind their backs and squared their shoulders, their expressions dark.

"Commander Silas just informed me he found another piece of suspicious evidence." Errol revealed a black, silk handkerchief. "I want everyone to expand their rounds by five miles. Leave no rock unturned, no leaves unchecked. Someone is looking for us, and we must do everything we can to prevent them from coming any closer."

Minari drew in a quick breath. There was no doubt in his mind that whoever was looking for them was aiming to find Elliot. He wanted to—no, he *needed* to—tell Elliot, warn him, bring him to safety. After he made his rounds, he would meet with Elliot. Even if it was in the dead of night, he'd drag him out of bed.

"Five miles? That's so much," Lily groaned.

"No one has ever alluded us for this long. We need to be diligent," Minari said. Lily's lax nature was gnawing at his nerves.

"I know! I was just saying . . . I mean, I can barely make my current rounds. Adding another five miles would kill me."

Minari shook his head. Lily's stamina left much to be desired. She was good at quick bursts of energy—if she found an intruder, she'd dispose of them within the blink of an eye—but make her run for a prolonged period of time and she would collapse long before the night was over. "I'll help. I'll take over half of your additional rounds."

"Really?" Lily clasped her hands together. "You'll do that for me?"

"Yes; I know you'll actually die if I don't."

"Thank you! You're the best. I'll meet you at Anchor Point after my rounds, then we can discuss where we split off." A bubbling sense of paranoia gnawed at Minari's gut as he watched her leave. It wasn't that he didn't trust Lily, but there were occasions when he wished she would take the potential threat more seriously. He shook his head, clearing his thoughts. He needed to focus on his task. Maybe it was better that he was the one who took her additional rounds. He would be able to thoroughly survey the area himself. He hoped taking the additional miles wouldn't take too much time. He'd have to quickly finish his own rounds plus the additional five before rendezvousing with Lily.

5
FATE

Elliot ran. He didn't know what he was running from, but the raw sensation of chase forced his body forward. His legs ached. His lungs heaved. His surroundings were pitch-black. It was so dark he could barely make out the trees surrounding him. The voices started to catch up. They vibrated around his head, screeching. He couldn't make out what they were saying, but he could feel the torment behind the cries.

Something encircled Elliot's ankle, pulling him to the ground. He yelped, using his hands to break his fall. A dark shadow coiled around his leg and slowly traveled up. His breathing was ragged. His chest tightened, his eyes wide in fear.

A roar broke through the abyss. The echo of galloping hooves drew near, and a small light grew in the distance. The voice called out again, and the restriction on his leg receded. The voice was familiar. He'd heard it somewhere. But where? And when? As the light drew closer, his vision began to swim.

"Elliot. Wake up . . . up . . . !"

Elliot stirred awake. His eyes snapped opened. It was still dark. He twisted his body, wanting to see who'd disrupted his sleep, but something was wrapped tightly around his left wrist. His heart raced. Was whatever had been chasing him earlier here? Had it followed him to Mistfall? How had it found him with Alder's powers protecting their village?

"Elliot, calm down. It's just me."

"Minari?" Elliot squeaked. He steadied his breathing. Relief washed over him. "What are you doing here?"

"We need to get out of here. It's not safe," Minari whispered, his voice rushed.

Elliot's stomach fell. Not safe? Why wouldn't it be safe in Mistfall? He scanned Minari's figure. He was wearing a scout's uniform: brown coat with daggers strapped around his body. The silver plating of his shoulder guards twinkled in the moon's rays. "You're a scout? When did—"

"Elliot, don't worry." Minari tightened his grip around Elliot's wrist. "I'll be with you the whole way. I can't say anything now, but we need to get to the Moon Shrine."

"What about the others? Mom? Dad?"

"There's no time." Minari tugged him up, still holding his wrist. "I promise I'll explain once we reach the shrine."

Elliot hesitated. The shrine was a place everyone knew to evacuate to if Mistfall fell into a dire situation. Images of his dream flashed before his eyes. His body shuddered involuntarily. Minari was a scout. He'd probably seen something during his rounds that had alerted him. Elliot closed his eyes and let out a steady breath. He nodded.

Minari slipped his hold from Elliot's wrist. Elliot laced up his boots in record speed. He was about to head out the door when Minari stopped him.

"Not that way. I came in through the window."

Elliot gawked at Minari. "Why did you come in through the window?"

Minari shied away. "Just . . . come with me, Elliot. I promise I'll explain everything."

Elliot followed Minari out the window. It was strange. It was almost like he was sneaking out of his house, but he trusted Minari. They walked briskly through the thick forest. Minari took the lead, guiding them through twists and turns, weaving through thick branches and bushes. Half an hour passed before an itch crawled up from Elliot's wrist. He put pressure against it, hoping to ease the irritated skin. But as soon as he did, a rush of pain shot up his arm. He yelped, and his footsteps faltered.

"Elliot? What's wrong?" Minari was by his side in an instant.

Elliot held his wrist. The initial pain subsided and was replaced with a constant throb at the base of his arm. "Something's not right. My wrist hurts." He rubbed his thumb over the source of the pain. There was a weird bump starting to form.

"Dammit," Minari mumbled.

Elliot moved to lift his sleeve. His skin was red and raw. He squinted to make out the shape of the bump, but Minari quickly pulled his sleeve down before he could see what it was.

"Don't look. Not yet." He peered down. "Bear with the pain for a bit longer. We're almost there. Promise me you won't look."

"W-why?" Elliot furrowed his brow. It was an odd request.

"There's something you should know, but I can't tell you yet. Not until we reach the safety of the shrine."

Elliot nibbled at his lip. Minari looked at him with hopeful eyes. Elliot had no doubt that Minari knew what was going on, and he couldn't do anything but put his trust in him. Elliot pushed the pain down and drew a shaky breath before nodding.

They continued. It was silent between them. Minari's pace slowed so Elliot wouldn't get left behind. The throbbing only increased as they kept walking, and the itch eventually returned. The urge to see what was happening was almost unbearable.

The branches closed in, and shadows grew. Minari's figure shrank and disappeared in front of him. Panic bubbled in Elliot's stomach. Had he been too distracted to notice Minari running off ahead of him? He gulped. He knew where the Moon Shrine was. He could easily make his way by himself, but why was everything so dark? Black crept in from the corner of his eyes, and soon he couldn't see the trees. He couldn't hear his footsteps against the ground. His breathing sounded heavy in the darkness.

A light caress against his neck startled him. He pressed his hand against his flesh, wanting to swat away whatever had blown past him. A low whistle reached his ears. It circled around him, starting at his feet, and spiraled up his body. A forceful grip enveloped him. He gasped, but air refused to enter his lungs. He struggled against the invisible hold, but the more he tried, the stronger it held him. He began to feel light-headed. His legs trembled.

"*There.*"

Before Elliot completely succumbed to darkness, air filled his lungs, and his limbs were freed. Color returned around him. But he was no longer standing. Arms were wrapped around his shoulders, and he was pressed against a warm body.

"Oh, thank Vylantra." Minari's eyes were full of worry. "You're back."

Elliot groaned. He was disoriented. His head was heavy. There was a dull ache in his chest, and his wrist itched even more. "Minari?" His voice cracked.

"How do you feel?"

"Like Xeno trampled me."

Minari let out a small laugh. "Glad you're still okay enough to make a joke like that. Xeno would be greatly offended if he heard you."

Elliot rubbed his fingers against his temple, closing his eyes. The pressure helped lighten the weight on his head. When he opened his eyes, his voice caught in his throat. His sleeve drooped down just enough for him to notice the red bump on his wrist had formed a scar.

A crescent moon scar.

The mark of the oracle.

"You have awoken, Oracle."

A voice drew him from his shock. A boy stood a few feet away. His body was petite and short, resembling a seven-year-old elf. His brown hair framed his round cheeks. He was bare, save the leaves, vines, and twigs that wrapped around his arms, torso, and legs. Two branches arched from the crown of his head. A familiar red bird rested on one of his branches.

"Alder," Minari said. He bowed his head slightly before lifting it back up. "Please, I can—"

"Minari, I understand what you were trying to do, but you cannot alter the course of his destiny. The prophecy foretold this."

"I was hoping I'd make it before they found him."

Elliot furrowed his brow. He looked between Minari and Alder. What was the demigod of earth doing here? He pushed out of Minari's arms and scrambled up. "What's going on? Why do I have this scar on my wrist? This has to be some mistake."

Minari frowned. He slowly stood and rested his hands on Elliot's shoulders, giving him a reassuring squeeze. "Alder stopped the tracking spell." His voice was barely above a whisper.

"Tracking spell? What tracking spell? What do you mean?"

"The Necromancers are after the oracle." There was a small quiver in Minari's voice. His eyes strayed away from Elliot.

"Stella!" Elliot tried to pry Minari's hands off his, but Minari's grip stayed strong. Elliot frowned. He took a step forward. "We need to hurry. If Stella is in danger, then we need to—"

"No," Minari said, shaking his head.

"What do you mean no?"

Minari gave Elliot's shoulders a squeeze. "Stella isn't the oracle." He sucked his lips before taking a deep breath and letting it out through his nose. His eyes met Elliot's. "Elliot, you . . . *you* are the oracle."

Elliot could only stare at Minari. His hands dropped limply beside him. His face ran, cold and his body stilled. He waited for Minari to give him a smirk, to tell him he was just kidding and say it was a trick he and Alder had thought up to give him a scare.

But none of that happened, and the silence between them was deafening.

6
ORACLE

Elliot remembered the day the elders had escorted Stella to the Moon Shrine. It had been a clear spring morning when word the mark of the oracle had appeared on her wrist had spread through the village. Leaves had sprouted, and buds had bloomed in bright colors. Oracles were presented once every fifty years, and the last oracle to have spoken to Vylantra had done so twenty years before. Once an oracle awakened to their powers, they had them for thirty years before they were cut off from the goddess. The period of silence had finally been broken with Stella. The entire village had cheered so loudly he could've sworn he'd felt the ground shake.

So when Minari confessed to Elliot he was the oracle, he couldn't believe it. The words were almost foreign to him.

Elliot shook his head, pulling away. He deeply wished for Minari's expression to crack—to show the slightest smirk, anything to prove that this was one cruel joke—but he knew it wasn't happening. He practiced the rite any chance he had. He was supposed to perform it during the Bloom Festival in three days. But it was all pointless now. His dream of becoming a keeper was crushed.

"Oracle, I am aware this must be an immense shock to you," Alder said.

"I'm not . . ." His voice quivered. "Don't call me that."

Alder pressed his lips into a thin line. "Oracle, you cannot deny who you are."

"No!" Elliot clenched his fists. "I'm not the oracle! I'm supposed to perform the rite for your festival in three days. Then I'll be a keeper. I'll stay with Stella, *the oracle*, in the Moon Shrine." His body was shaking. The Bloom Festival was a celebratory festival to thank Alder for protecting the elves during the war. He was so agitated he hadn't realized how improperly he was speaking to a demigod. "I'm not the oracle."

"Elliot—" Minari reached out to him, but Elliot slapped him away.

"How could you agree with him, Minari? Stella's the oracle. Remember when she revealed her scar four years ago? She was so happy. S-she's the real oracle. I'm not . . ." Elliot's voice trailed off. His vision blurred as tears welled up in his eyes. He couldn't—he *wouldn't*—believe it. He definitely wasn't the oracle.

A sudden prickle hovered over his head. Redd chirped, bouncing on Elliot's head. He plucked at his hair strands. All the strength in his legs left him. He collapsed to the ground and heaved. He pressed his fists against his eyes, wanting to hide his tears. He knew deep down Alder and Minari were telling the truth, but it was hard to agree with. For four years he'd thought Stella was the oracle. For four years he'd devoted himself to performing the rite when he turned sixteen so he could become a keeper. He'd lived a lie for four years, so how could a small animal break his resolve so easily?

Minari knelt down. He reached over and rubbed Elliot's arm. "Elliot, the dream you had by the river . . ." His voice was gentle.

"Was that them too?" he whispered. "The Necromancers. Were they tracking me then?"

"Probably."

"And you knew?" His voice cracked. "You knew I'd become the . . ." He couldn't say it.

Minari was silent for a moment. "Yes."

Elliot let out a breath he hadn't known he was holding. It hurt to learn his best friend had lied to him for so long. What other secrets was Minari keeping? Had he ever been true to him?

"I didn't want to keep it a secret. Please believe me. I just couldn't tell you."

Elliot chortled weakly and gave Minari a strained smile. "I believe you," he lied. In truth, he wanted to believe, but he couldn't bring himself to fully trust Minari. Not yet.

"C'mon. We need to get to the Moon Shrine." Minari helped Elliot up. Redd flew off his head and fluttered his wings in front of Elliot. He chirped, tilting his head. "Looks like Redd is telling you it's all right."

Elliot barely nodded. "Right."

"I will bring you to Mother," Alder said. "Please do not stray too far from me. I can shield you from the Necromancers' tracking spell, but only if you are near me."

Elliot followed them. He was numb, his body on autopilot as he weaved through the forest. Stella. Oracle. Necromancers. Tracking spell. What did any of this mean? He couldn't wrap his head around it. He didn't know what Necromancers were, but if he was in danger, then Mistfall would be in danger. The next safest place would be the Moon Shrine. Vylantra's powers encapsulated it.

"Oracle, before I lead you any farther, I must ask you this." Alder turned around. He tilted his chin up, looking at Elliot. "You are unaware of the prophecy, correct?"

"Nothing. I know nothing." Elliot glanced at Minari, clenching his jaw.

Minari flashed him an apologetic look.

"Do not blame Minari, Oracle. It was the elders who were tasked with informing you of your true identity. The mere action of bringing you to the Moon Shrine himself already breached the agreement."

Minari rubbed the back of his neck.

"Tell me about the prophecy." Elliot slouched his shoulders, exhaustion prevalent in his voice.

"The prophecy foretold you are Etheria's savior. You are the oracle who will prevent Father from destroying these lands my brother and sisters created."

"Your father?"

"Mykronos, known as the Dark God to mortals."

"Mykronos? Why haven't I heard of him before?"

"He isn't common knowledge to us. Not anymore," Minari said. He crossed his arms. "Ever since we escaped the lower lands, our ancestors wanted nothing to do with Mykronos."

"Why?" More secrets. It agitated him.

Minari leaned his shoulder against a tree. "Mykronos is the reason an oracle was murdered. His voice seeped into jealous humans and manipulated their negative energy. He convinced them to assassinate the oracle 350 years ago."

"The war lasted ten years. That was when they came to me, barely alive. It was painful." Alder pressed his hands against his chest. "The elves are my children. I created them with my powers. I planted seeds in the ground, and life blossomed. I protected them from harm. But there were repercussions." He stepped closer to Elliot. "The primary role of the oracle is to communicate with Mother. The oracle listens to the wishes of the people and conveys that message to Mother. In return, she casts her love upon them, granting them their desire. The people of Etheria are her grandchildren, and she adores them."

"And because we retreated to the mountains, there was no oracle for the people to confide in," Minari said.

"Why didn't Vylantra just pick someone in the lower lands to become an oracle?"

"Oracles can only be born from elves because elves came from Etheria," Alder said.

Elliot pinched the bridge of his nose. He wasn't any less confused. "That doesn't make any sense."

"I mentioned elves came from me. I planted seeds in the ground, and life blossomed in the form of elves."

Elliot desperately tried to grasp what he was hearing. He wasn't sure if he could handle anything else. But he still didn't know why there was a prophecy, nor did he know why he'd been chosen. What did he need to fulfill?

"As I mentioned before, Oracle, you must stop my Father from destroying Etheria. You must stop the Necromancers."

Necromancers. He still didn't know who or what they were. He wanted to ask, but his eyes were heavy. He wondered how late—or early—it was. He rubbed his hands over his face and shook his head, attempting to wake himself up.

"I apologize, Oracle. This is quite a bit to take in. I will let Mother explain the rest to you. Come." Alder held out his hands. "I can take us to Mother quicker than you two can travel."

Minari took Alder's hand. Elliot hesitated. He lowered his hand slowly. Alder reached for it and laced their fingers together. Alder closed his eyes, and the air was knocked out of Elliot's lungs.

7

SUPPRESS

Minari steadied himself. It wasn't the first time he had been transported somewhere with Alder's powers, but it didn't mean he was comfortable with it. The residue of magic tingled on his skin, and his head swam. His body felt featherlight until the familiar feeling of his clothes and weapons weighed him down.

Elliot was not holding the recent information down well. He was ghostly pale. His body made the slightest tremors. His shoulders were hunched, and he did his best not to look at Minari if he didn't need to. It twisted Minari's heart. He knew he'd lost some, if not all, of Elliot's trust in him. He'd feared this would happen, but it was inevitable.

Alder teleported them to the steps of the Moon Shrine. It was a tall, wide building with large arches. It stood in the center of a clearing. The white stones basked in the moonlight. It shimmered with millions of sparkles.

"You are safe now, Oracle. Here the Necromancers cannot reach you. Mother will protect you." Alder released Elliot's hand. "I will wait here until you return."

"Return? I'm not staying here?"

"Oracle, please understand you must fulfill the prophecy. You are the chosen one."

Elliot frowned. "Fine." He walked up the steps.

Minari followed him. Four flights of stairs separated them from the entrance. Each flight had a white statue of one of the four elemental demigods. The first was Alder, demigod of earth. Second, Ara, demigod of water. Third, Azar, demigod of fire. And at the top was Aapo, demigod of air. Each of them looked similar to Alder, small and childlike, but instead of earth characteristics, they had characteristics of their element. Ara had long wavy hair and scales that littered her body. Azar's hair was shorter and stood up. There were flames that danced around his body. Aapo's hair was similar to Ara's, but it floated upward. Her body was covered in clouds instead of scales.

Passing the statues made Minari wonder what personalities each demigod had. He knew Alder was serious most of the time, but he also knew the demigod enjoyed playing hide-and-seek with the villagers. It was an odd game for a demigod, but for whatever reason, Alder enjoyed knowing the elves were somewhere hiding in his mountain and he could easily tell where they were. A playful demigod, to say the least. Minari had played with Alder a few times in hopes it would help him conceal his presence during his rounds. Luckily, it had.

Mayleen was in front of the tall, arched entrance. Her hair wasn't in her usual bun. Instead, it was draped down to her waist. Her eyes were narrow, and her arms were crossed over her chest. "Minari." Her voice was laced with irritation.

Minari flinched. He knew that look. She would look at him with that expression when he did something he knew he shouldn't have. And the fact that he did it anyway gravely disappointed her. "Mother. Hi. Nice night we're having."

Mayleen was not amused. "Elliot, come inside the shrine. Stella is waiting. As for *you*, Minari, I have something to discuss with you."

Elliot walked inside, not even glancing at Minari.

Minari chewed on his lip. Watching Elliot's figure disappear into the shrine without acknowledgment broke his heart. When Elliot was out of earshot, Mayleen strode to Minari.

And slapped him.

Hard.

Minari's eyes widened. His neck snapped to the side from the impact. The skin on his cheek prickled and grew hot.

"How could you do something so foolish?" Mayleen seethed. "Did you not know how dangerous your actions were? What if Alder was not there? What if he didn't make it in time? You nearly jeopardized all of us!"

No words could convey how much he hated disappointing his mother. But he didn't regret taking Elliot. It had been a chance to bring him to safety before harm befell him, and he would gladly take that chance again.

Mayleen gripped the front of Minari's coat and pressed her forehead against his chest. Her shoulders shook. "*Never* do that again. I-I was so worried."

Minari placed his hands on his mother's shoulders and gently pushed her away. She took a step back. Tears silently fell down her cheeks. He held his breath. His stomach twisted. The last time he'd seen his mother cry had been the day she'd learned Melvin had passed away. She hadn't had a chance to mourn over his loss and had quickly hardened herself as the new leader. She'd had a new role. There were numerous things to learn and hold responsibilities for. He cupped her cheek, wiping the tears away with his thumb. "Mom . . . I'm sorry."

Mayleen smacked his hand away. She dabbed her cheeks with the back of her fingers. "Do not refer to me as 'Mom. I clearly instructed you to call me Lady Mayleen in public."

"Lady Mayleen." Minari frowned. First Elliot had refused his comfort, and now his mother. It tore him.

"You must look after him. You will do whatever you can to protect him."

"Of course. I'll risk my life to keep him safe."

"You will not forget your other duties. You are a scribe as well, and each detail must be recorded accurately. I will not tolerate it if you miss the smallest detail, whether it's about the weather or the color of an object. Each hour of the day will be recorded. Every day."

Minari nodded. He had read many books from scribes before him and knew how detailed their recordings were regarding the oracle. Who saw them? What did they look like? What day was it? What was the weather like? What did they ask of the oracle? But this would be the first time a scribe ventured out of the shrine. He would need to be diligent with every detail because this would be the first time elves stepped into the lower lands in 340 years.

"I want you to send me a report every week using Redd."

Minari looked over his shoulder at where Alder stood waiting. Redd was perched on one of his branches and was resting peacefully. Redd was Alder's familiar. Traveling between Mistfall and wherever he ended up shouldn't be a problem.

"If I hear nothing from you at the end of every week, then I know the worst has come and will prepare accordingly."

"That won't happen. I promise to fulfill my duties and make a report every Saturday until we return when the prophecy is completed."

"Do not make promises you cannot keep." Mayleen took a deep breath and let out a shaky sigh. Her hard eyes softened. She reached for Minari's hand. "Melvin would be proud of you, Minari. Proud to see how brave and strong you've become."

Minari didn't respond. Mayleen's hand was warm. He wanted to drown himself in it. The brief comfort ended too soon when she pulled away.

"Head back. Rest for the remainder of the night. In the morning I want you to prepare for your departure. You will leave in two days."

"You want us to miss the festival?"

Mayleen shook her head. "I've spoken with the elders. There will be no festival this year."

8
DESTINY

Elliot walked through the long hallway. Torches hung off the walls, lighting the corridor. He slowed his pace, boots clacking against the stone floors. This was supposed to be his life—being surrounded by tall stone walls and Vylantra's magic, being around Stella and protecting her. Being a keeper, not the oracle. It stung. His dream had been ripped from under his feet, and there was nothing he could do about it. He wanted to know why Stella had been taken to the Moon Shrine as the oracle. If she wasn't, how had she fooled everyone for four years?

The dark path finally ended. He took his first step into the large, open area and gasped. His eyes widened as he took in the tranquility of the room. Tall trees lined up against the walls, their branches reached toward the sky, spiraling up. Two parallel rivers ran across the sides, creating a clear path forward. Stella stood in the center of the room, her keepers standing in a wide circle around her. She was as beautiful as he remembered, if not more.

"Oracle, welcome." She smiled. She was the spitting image of Mayleen. There were fewer lines across her features, but her sapphire eyes shone just as brightly. Her indigo hair was pulled into a ponytail and adorned with flowers.

Elliot was taken aback. Even Stella was referring to him as the oracle. It didn't sit well with him. Stella seemed to have noticed.

She held her arms out, ushering him forward. "Shall I call you Elliot instead?"

"Stella, I'm not . . ." Elliot shook his head. There was no point denying it. "Elliot is fine." He stepped forward, and she took his hands into hers.

"I have missed you, Elliot. I have not seen you in four years. You have grown quite handsome."

Elliot flushed. "Thank you . . ."

Stella smiled warmly. "Come, we must get you to Vylantra quickly." She turned and led Elliot farther into the shrine, holding his hand in hers.

Stella walked down another corridor, one that could've easily been missed. It was hidden behind a thick layer of vegetation, and the walls surrounding it were covered in vines. "Careful. It is dark, and there are stairs."

Elliot placed his hand against the wall as they proceeded. Stella took each step down the stairs slowly, and he was grateful for that. He could barely see anything in front of him. He heard a soft click, then the creaking of a door.

An iridescent light spilled through the darkness.

The room was round and spacious. A large tree was planted right in the middle, surrounded by luscious green grass and vibrant flowers. Stella pulled Elliot out of his trance as she dragged him forward and closed the door behind him. She took both of his hands into hers and squeezed them. "Elliot, I know you're scared. Surprised too, probably."

Elliot blinked. Her tone had changed. It was less formal and more similar to how they used to talk. He was about to respond when she placed a finger against his lips.

"You don't have to say anything. I know how scary it is to suddenly be pushed into a role you don't want."

Elliot stared at Stella. Had she not wanted to become the oracle? Had she not wanted to come to the Moon Shrine? But she looked so happy. "Why are you here, Stella?"

Stella placed a hand on Elliot's chest. "I'm here because I had to be. I had to be the fake oracle to protect our real one. The only people who know of my true identity are the elders, your family, and my own. Although it was tricky to pretend I knew how to talk to Vylantra, after some time I got used to it." She gave Elliot a reassuring smile before continuing. "I did it to protect you. You may not know this, but there have been people lurking around the mountains in search of the oracle."

Elliot's jaw dropped. Stella had gone through so much for his sake, and the possibility of risking her life just for him shook him to his core. Why was he so important that he needed her protection? "Why?" he whispered.

"Why?"

"You're the chosen oracle who will fulfill the prophecy, the one who will stop the Necromancers and stop Mykronos. It has to be you."

"But why? Why does it have to be me? Why do you need to risk yourself for me? What if something happened to you?" Elliot couldn't see. His stomach twitched in painful knots. No one should've had to sacrifice their freedom for his sake.

Stella grabbed Elliot's hand again and led him forward. "Nothing happened to me, Elliot. I've been safe here." They stopped at the base of the tree. The large bark pieces stuck out in jagged directions and were rich with mahogany. "This tree is Eekruce. You'll be able to speak to Vylantra through it."

Elliot had ripped his gaze off the tree as soon as Stella mentioned its name. If he spoke to Vylantra, he would be admitting he was the oracle. He wouldn't be able to keep denying it. He'd have to accept it—accept the role, accept the prophecy.

And he wasn't sure if he was ready for that.

Stella placed a hand against his cheek. He leaned into the warm touch. "You have nothing to fear. This is your destiny. You're strong, Elliot. Stronger than you think. You can do this."

Her words eased his nerves. It was just enough for him to swallow his fear and momentarily accept his destiny. "I can do this," he whispered.

"Yes. Yes, you can do this. I believe in you." Stella separated from Elliot and took a few steps away. "Call out

to her from your mind when you're ready. I'll be here waiting."

Elliot took a deep breath. He pushed his lips together
in the shape of an O and breathed out. He could do this. He
was brave. Stella believed in him. He glanced at Stella one
last time, and she gave him a nod. He turned to fully face
Eekruce. He patted his hand against his pant leg before
placing it against the rough bark. He closed his eyes and
pressed his forehead against Eekruce. "*Vylantra.*"

The back of his eyes flashed white, and a warm blanket wrapped around his body. His body felt light, like he
was floating. He opened his eyes. The ground beneath him
was the sky. The sky above him was the ocean. He took a
step forward, and ripples vibrated away from his foot. He
took another step. Then another. There was nothing
around him. It was pure emptiness, yet it was tranquil. He
was no longer worried or anxious about his newfound
identity. He was calm, yet he also felt nothing. It was odd,
but it didn't bother him.

"Greetings, young Oracle."

Elliot spun around. A woman floated toward him.
Her white hair ribboned from her head, flowing behind
her, and sheer fabric draped over her body. Light bounced
off her creamy skin, making her glow. Her long, slender
legs landed in front of him. Her feet were planted firmly on
the ground, but her hair and the fabric continued to flow
around her. Her white eyes twinkled at him.

"Vylantra?"

"Yes." Vylantra smiled. "It pleases me to know you
are unharmed, young Oracle. Alder quickly alerted me

when you were targeted by the Necromancers."

"I was . . ." Vylantra's beauty allured Elliot. He wasn't sure where to look.

"You are here because of the prophecy, young Oracle. The soul of Myru—a past oracle who stood against my brother and protected Etheria from his wrath—dwells inside you."

"I'm—" Elliot choked. "I'm what?"

"There is something you must know about us divine gods, young Oracle," Vylantra said, ignoring Elliot's confusion. "We originally held no emotions. We felt nothing but emptiness. When my brother and I created Etheria, we created Alder, Aapo, Azar, and Ara, and in turn, they each created mortal life. From there, we learned how to feel. While I absorbed the light, happiness, and warmth, my brother took the burden of darkness, anger, and coldness. And that was when he became corrupted."

Elliot knew he should be worried—should feel *something*—but oddly enough, he stayed calm.

"A destructive plague wreaked havoc upon Etheria 320 years ago," Vylantra continued. "It did not affect the elves, only those in the lower lands. The plague took the lives of many, and my brother bathed in the sorrow and woes of our grandchildren. As a result, he became corrupted. He wanted to break the only rule we gods have, and that is to never walk upon the world. If we do, it will throw the flow of life off-balance and the world will be destroyed."

"How bad was the plague? For a god to become corrupted?"

"The plague devastated Etheria. It was known as Death's Kiss. Those who suffered under the illness lived their lives in hallucination and pain. They could not decipher reality from falsehood. They suffered for a week before they eventually passed."

"A week of suffering," Elliot repeated. "There was no cure?"

"At the time, there was none." Vylantra waved her hands. The surroundings suddenly morphed into large buildings. They were burning, and people ran from the fires. He could see their torment and fear as they tried to escape, but he couldn't hear. The visions were muted.

"Destruction moved through small towns and villages. My brother sent his whispers into the dreams of mortals. He commanded them to burn, to kill. He told them if they destroyed everything, the plague would vanish. They believed him. His voice reached five humans, and they agreed to make a pact with him. He promised to eradicate the plague, freeing them from Death's Kiss. He transformed the humans into monsters, forcing magic cores into them, thus giving them the ability to wield the dark arts. They became Necromancers—pure, devoted worshippers of Mykronos. They could no longer see reason through their madness."

Five hooded figures cloaked in black appeared, encircling them.

"They each needed to collect the souls of one thousand people by drinking their blood and devouring their flesh. This way, their bodies would become strong enough to host my brother's divine soul."

Elliot's head was spinning. Mykronos sounded horrifying. Why would anyone worship a god who wasn't Vylantra? Vylantra was gentle, warm, caring. Motherly.

"But because humans were not made to wield magic cores, it slowly destroyed them, draining their souls. But even if their bodies were empty shells, they kept moving, kept killing, kept devouring. I had to do something. I had to stop my brother's insanity. So I asked Myru to stop him."

"But why would he want to destroy Etheria? He created this world with you."

Vylantra's expression faded. "Yes, we both created this world. Do not underestimate the strength of corruption, young Oracle. It can change even the strongest of hearts." Vylantra flicked her wrist, and the vision vanished. "Stop the Necromancers, young Oracle. That will stop my brother and cure him of his corruption. That is your prophecy."

"You said Myru stopped the Necromancers. If they were stopped, how are they back?"

"Though Myru and the other warriors succeeded in stopping my brother from stepping into Etheria, they did not quell his darkness. They reduced it, but it eventually grew, and now the Necromancers' souls have returned, along with Myru's."

"Warriors? There are others?"

"There were four others who fought alongside Myru. She also had a keeper, her most trusted companion. You must find all five of them. Only the originals can stop the Necromancers."

"But how do I—"

Vylantra placed a finger on Elliot's forehead, silencing him. "Your souls are linked together. They will reach out to you. Now, young Oracle, I beseeched you with my powers. We can no longer talk once you leave Eekruce, but you will have the ability to use some of my magic. It will prove helpful on your journey."

She gave him a gentle push, and Elliot fell backward.

Back to reality.

His eyes shot open, and he took a few steps away from Eekruce. He took gasps of air. He looked at the tree, then to the left and right, until he remembered Stella had said she would wait for him. He twisted around and found her still waiting. She hadn't moved.

"Welcome back, Elliot."

"Stella. I-I just . . . Vylantra . . . she . . ." Elliot couldn't form sentences. He was still panting. His chest ached like he was holding his breath. A rush of emotions came crashing down.

"She told you about the prophecy."

Elliot nodded.

"I see." Stella took his hands into hers. "Then you know what you must do. I will take you outside. Alder is still waiting for you, right?"

"R-right."

Stella gave his hand a reassuring squeeze. "Don't worry. You won't be going on your journey alone."

9

PROMISE

Two days passed quicker than Minari would have liked. It was the last night he would be staying in Mistfall. He hadn't spoken to Elliot since the entire ordeal. He had stayed awake after getting home, hoping to spot Elliot when he returned with Alder. But as soon as he'd spotted Elliot, Alder had shot him a disapproving look. Elliot hadn't left his house since. By now, word had circulated throughout the village that the Bloom Festival was canceled. Many questions popped up, but the elders easily dismissed them, claiming Vylantra had told Stella not to host one this year.

What a big lie that was.

The villagers didn't know Elliot was the oracle. They were supposed to sneak out in the morning while Stella continued to pretend to be who she wasn't.

Minari collapsed on his chair, the wooden legs scraping the floor. He pulled his hair, glancing around his room. There was a worn desk pushed against the wall and a small drawer where he kept his clothes. It was sparse since he spent most of his time with Elliot and Lily, and if he wasn't with them, he was buried nose-deep in the hidden archives or fulfilling his scout duties. His eye caught the shine of his daggers. They were scattered haphazardly across his desk. Heaving a sigh, he stood and gathered them. He'd sharpened them earlier but had been too dejected to put them away.

His daggers had been with him throughout his entire journey as a scout, and his daggers were going to be with him on his journey with Elliot. They protected him from danger—protected Mistfall from danger—and now he was about to use them to protect Elliot. It was ironic. The inanimate objects had been by his side almost as long as he'd been in Elliot's life. But now the younger elf probably wanted nothing to do with him, while his blades were going to stay by his side until the day he died.

He wished it were the opposite.

He picked up one of his daggers. There was a hole at the end of the hilt, and the blade was sharp and narrow. He stuck a finger through the hole, twirling it before sinking the tip into his desk. He'd give up his weapons if it meant having Elliot trust him again. He'd give up his role, give up everything he'd trained to do. But he knew that would be impossible. He was allowed to be with Elliot because of his vigorous training. He'd begged and pleaded with his mother to let him leave with Elliot when the time came. In exchange, he'd thrown away his innocence and naive view of life. He'd prepared himself for the prejudice they'd face when they reached the lower lands. He'd protect Elliot from the truth and the ugliness of the world. He'd hide him from it all. It was a foolish wish, but he at least wanted to keep Elliot smiling.

Even if he would never trust him again.

The door creaked open, and soft footsteps made their way over.

"Minari," Mayleen said.

"Yes, Mother?" Minari turned, leaving his dagger impaled in his desk.

She held a book and a pen in her hands, offering them to him. "You will fulfill your scribe duties in here. I had Alder cast it in illusionary magic. Anyone who isn't you cannot read the pages."

Minari nodded, taking the book from Mayleen's hands. He ran his fingers across the dark brown leather cover. In the middle was an engraved leaf. He flipped it open. The pages were a pale, faded yellow.

"Are you ready to leave when morning comes?"

Minari snapped the book closed and placed it on his desk. "Yes, I've already prepared all the saddlebags. The only thing I need to do is saddle them on Xander, and we'll be ready to leave in the morning."

Mayleen hummed in response. She moved to sit on Minari's bed. "I hear Elliot is not taking this well."

Minari winced. He dearly wished he could be there for Elliot. He wanted to soothe his worries and make sure he knew he wasn't in this alone.

"Estelle tells me he barely eats and does not get out of

bed. As far as I know, he has made no preparations for his journey."

"I should prepare for him then, at least have Xeno ready," Minari mumbled. He moved to leave his room.

"What will you do if he never forgives you?" Mayleen's voice stopped him.

Minari's shoulders stiffened. His chest ached at the simple thought of their friendship remaining distant. "I promised to always be with him. That hasn't changed. Whether or not he forgives me . . . that's his own decision. I'll respect whatever he chooses."

"Just remember to take care of yourself, Minari."

That was enough to bring a sad smile to Minari's face. "I will, Mother. Thank you."

Minari made his way down the familiar dirt path with flowers sprouting at the edges. They were closed, only blooming when the sun was out. He quietly entered the stables, careful not to squeak the hinges. His legs froze. Someone was leaning against the sleeping ovis, oblivious to the unwelcome guest. The figure had green hair.

He crept closer, his footsteps silent. Elliot was sleeping against Xeno. His usually smooth hair was ruffled, and there were wrinkles across his shirt. Minari just looked. Elliot seemed peaceful, even if his complexion was slightly sallow. Right now he was away from reality, in a world where he wasn't the oracle, where he didn't have to fulfill the prophecy and could spend his days together with Stella in the Moon Shrine. He knew that had been Elliot's dream: to stay by his sister's side and protect her.

Elliot shifted, and Minari froze. He furrowed his

brows before opening his eyes. He slowly blinked a few times before rubbing the tiredness away. Minari stood incredibly still, hoping Elliot hadn't noticed him while at the same time hoping Elliot would acknowledge his presence and talk to him.

Elliot slowly tilted his head up, his eyes widening. Minari felt like he couldn't breathe. Should he say something or wait for Elliot to make the first move? It was bad enough he'd walked in when the younger elf was in such a vulnerable state, especially since Elliot didn't trust him anymore.

"Minari." His voice was barely above a whisper. Xeno's ears twitched but otherwise made no movement.

"Elliot." Minari shifted uncomfortably. "How are you doing?"

He looked away from Minari. "Fine."

"I haven't seen you since—"

"I've been fine."

Minari chewed his lip. The atmosphere was rigid. "I came to prepare Xeno for the journey . . ."

"I don't need your help. I can do it myself." Elliot stayed seated, making no move to get up.

It was silent between them. The slightest noise or movement threatened to break the thick, heavy air.

It was suffocating.

"We leave in the morning. Before sunrise," Minari said.

"We?" Elliot looked up at Minari, confusion in his eyes.

"We. Me and you. I'm going with you."

"Oh . . . I didn't know." Elliot glanced down at his hands. They were clasped together in his lap as he rubbed his fingernail against his thumb.

Minari moved to sit in front of Elliot. He crossed his legs, placed his hands on his knees, and bowed. "Elliot, I'm sorry. I'm sorry for taking you out in the middle of the night. I'm sorry for placing you in danger. I'm sorry for not telling you anything. I'm sorry for keeping secrets. I'm sorry—" There was a hand on his shoulder. He looked up slowly. Elliot shook his head.

"I should be the one to apologize." Elliot retracted his hand. "I . . ." He swallowed. "I don't really know how it feels to keep everything to yourself, but I can imagine how much of a burden it was. And I'm sorry I lashed out at you. I was . . . surprised to learn I was the oracle."

Minari punched Elliot's shoulder playfully. "Just surprised? If it were me, I'd be so shocked I'd probably faint."

"I practically wanted to. Honestly, when you showed up in my room wearing a scout's uniform, I didn't know what to think. I had no idea you were a scout, and Dad never told me."

"I had Captain Errol keep it a secret—even made Lily promise not to say anything."

"But why?"

"I . . ." Minari trailed off. He contemplated how much he wanted to tell Elliot. No. He needed to be honest with him. Keeping secrets was what had caused the rift in the first place. "I didn't tell you because I didn't want you to know that I've . . ." He took a deep breath. "That I've killed people."

Elliot flinched.

Minari placed a hand over Elliot's clasped ones. "Elliot, please understand I did it because I had to, not because I wanted to."

"But Lily's never mentioned anything, even after I've asked. And Dad . . . he says nothing really happens."

"Well, let's just say you don't want to be between Mistfall and Lily. Bluntly speaking, Lily probably gets possessed when she assassinates someone. She gets into this mood and sort of forgets it happened. As for Captain Errol, he's at another level."

Elliot frowned and cast his eyes down. "So you guys didn't tell me because you thought I couldn't handle it?"

Minari squeezed Elliot's hand. "No. We didn't want to worry you." He removed his hand and stood. "Anyway, I came here to prep Xeno for the journey. Mother told me you probably didn't prepare anything."

The tips of Elliot's ears turned pink. "No. I guess I was too busy moping. But it's good to know you're coming with me. Stella told me I wasn't going to be alone. I never thought it was going to be you."

"Who did you think was going to come?"

Elliot shrugged. "No idea." He stood, brushing hay off his pants. "I'm glad it's you though."

Minari smirked. "With me around, you have nothing to worry about."

"Cocky, aren't you?"

"Confident." Minari's gaze met Elliot's. "I promise I'll keep you safe. As long as I'm alive."

"You sound like a keeper." Elliot smiled, the sparkle

reaching his eyes.

"Guess that's what I am, huh? I'll be your keeper until we finish this prophecy. I still need to take over Mother's role, after all. Then she can retire as an elder and never worry about me again."

Elliot laughed—a genuine laugh. He hunched over, pressing his hands against his stomach. The sound destroyed the weight on Minari's chest. He could breathe again. He felt lighter. Relieved.

"I doubt Lady Mayleen will stop fretting over you." His laughter slowed, and he straightened back up. The smile was still on his lips. "I trust you, Minari. Because I know you never break your promises."

10
JOURNEY

Elliot lay on his back, arms outstretched. He stared at his ceiling. There were only a few hours left before he needed to leave. He'd been anxious at first. The unknown had torn through his stomach, and dread had filled his every thought. He had sought refuge with Xeno earlier, hoping the animal would comfort him. It had helped. Slightly.

He'd somehow ended up falling asleep in the stables. It had been a restless sleep, and he hadn't dreamt. He'd been lulled out of slumber upon feeling a presence by him. To his shock, Minari had stood a few feet away. He hated himself for lashing out at Minari a few nights before and had been ashamed to face him, but when Minari had said he would be with him, all the apprehension he'd felt had vanished. His best friend would be with him, and that was more than what he could've asked for. Minari had always

73

promised to protect Elliot when they were growing up. He'd assumed it was typical brotherly love, but now he knew he'd actually meant it. Minari had promised to keep him safe as his keeper.

And Elliot believed him with all his heart.

The air was still and silent. Elliot opened his eyes. He must have fallen asleep without realizing. There were muffles at the other side of his door. A soft, orange light seeped through the crack. He sat up and tried to listen to what the voices were saying.

"... not ready."

"We ... lieve in ..."

"... just ... boy."

"You ... and!"

The sound of chairs scraping the floor stopped the muffles. Elliot gripped the bedsheets. At the other side of the door were his parents. This would be the last time he would see them, hear them. He didn't know how long he was going to be gone for.

Or if he was going to return at all.

He lazily swung his legs off his bed and took a deep breath. He laced up his boots and clasped his belt pouch on. His hand was on the handle of his door. He paused. He wouldn't be able to say goodbye to Lily. His stomach dropped. She didn't know he was the oracle. He had shut himself in his room without saying anything to her, and they had *just* rekindled their friendship. He shook his head, pushing back the tears that threatened to fall. Remembering the birthday gift, he ran his fingers across the leaf pendant. Even if he couldn't say goodbye, at least she'd be with him on his journey.

Steeling his resolve, he opened the door.

There was a candle lit on the kitchen table. Errol and Estelle turned their heads.

"Elliot!" Estelle's blue eyes were puffy and red, and tears stained her cheeks. Her hair was pulled back in a messy bun. She ran and embraced him. "Elliot," she sobbed.

Elliot's lip quivered. He couldn't hold the tears back. His chest tightened painfully. He wrapped his arms around Estelle and buried his face into her shoulder. She held him tighter.

"Estelle," Errol said. He put a hand on her shoulder, gently pulling her away.

"No!" She shook her head vigorously. "You can't leave! Forget the prophecy! Just stay here, Elliot. Stay home. Don't leave." Her voice waned. She cupped Elliot's face in her hands. "Forget everything. We can run away. Hide from this."

"Mom . . ." Elliot's gut twisted. Seeing his mother sob made him second-guess his destiny. Could he run away and forget the prophecy? Nothing was forcing him to fulfill it, right?

"Estelle, you must let Elliot go." A figure stepped from the corner of the kitchen. Her back was slightly hunched. She held a mug in her hands. "You know he cannot defy destiny."

"He's just a boy, Mother. How can you just let him go? He's your grandson!"

"Estelle, you are one of the advisors. You already knew this would happen," Lyla said.

"Elder, I apologize for this. I hoped she was more prepared for this day," Errol said.

"One is never truly prepared to let their child leave the nest." Lyla frowned. "Errol, please take Estelle into the room. At this rate, our oracle will never leave, and he must leave before sunrise."

"Of course." Errol looked at Elliot and gave him a sad smile. "Come, Estelle." He pulled the crying elf away with more force, successfully unlatching her from Elliot. Estelle flailed, attempting to claw back to Elliot.

"Let me go! Let me go! Elliot, don't leave! Elliot!"

Her screams shook Elliot's core. It took all of his willpower to stay still. He watched his father practically drag his mother away. Errol had his arms wrapped around Estelle's waist, holding her back. She struggled against his hold. Her nails dug into his arm, drawing blood. Her feet pounded the floor. But her attempts were futile, as he eventually led them to their bedroom and slammed the door closed.

"Elliot," Lyla said. She pushed the mug into his hands. "Drink this."

Elliot looked at the orange liquid. Estelle's cries and the pounding on the door slowly died down.

"Chamomile. It will help you relax."

Elliot held the mug under his nose, appreciating the floral scent. He sipped it at first but soon chugged it down. He felt the comforting liquid pass through his stomach, warming up the rest of his body.

Lyla took the empty mug from him. "Minari is waiting for you in the stables. He has Xeno ready for you."

"Can I—" Elliot glanced over at his parents' bedroom door. It was eerily quiet. "Can I say goodbye?"

"Unfortunately, that would not be wise."

Elliot tucked his head. "Right."

"We will await your return, Elliot." Lyla smiled warmly. She placed a hand against his lower back, leading him outside.

The sky was barely painted red, the sun threatening to rise. Lyla followed him down to the stables, ensuring he made it to his destination and didn't wander off.

Minari was waiting for Elliot, clad in his scout uniform. He smiled briefly before putting on a stoic expression. He bowed his head. "Elder Lyla."

"Minari, I trust everything is in order."

"Yes, I've saddled both Xeno and Xander. We are ready to go in a moment's notice."

"Perfect. Elliot, quickly now. Before anyone wakes up." She ushered him forward.

"Wait." Minari reached into one of Xander's saddlebags and pulled out a dark green cloak. He moved the fabric over Elliot, wrapping it around his shoulders and securing it with a bronze clasp. "Now you're ready."

Elliot took one last look at his grandmother before taking Xeno's reins and leaving the stables. The two moved quickly through the village. No one had left their cabins yet, but they were cutting it close. Right when they were about to reach the gates, a voice called out to them.

"Elliot! Minari!" Lily ran over. "Wait!"

"Lily?" Elliot's eyes widened.

Lily slowed to a stop, planting her hands on her knees as she took gulps of air. "I made . . . it just . . . in time." She straightened. "You're leaving?"

"How did you know?"

"I overheard. I can't believe you're—" She glanced around, making sure no one was near. "The oracle," she whispered.

Elliot sucked the side of his cheek and nodded. "Yeah . . ."

"Oh my gosh." She pressed her hands together and pushed them against her nose. "Okay. Okay, you're the oracle. No big deal," she blurted. She reached into her pouch and pulled out a dagger. "Here. Take this."

"You're giving him one of your daggers?" Minari asked, cocking a brow.

"Just because you're going doesn't mean I can't protect him too." Lily shoved the sheathed blade against Elliot's chest. "It was my first dagger. Well, the first dagger that I . . . Anyway, just take it. For good luck. Get Minari to teach you how to use it."

Elliot looked at the dagger in his hands. The scabbard was curved, the leather was worn, and the hilt had dents. He curled his fingers around it. "Thank you, Lily. I still have the pendant with me."

Lily instantly turned red. "Oh. Oh, right! Um. Then you have two good luck charms."

Minari cleared his throat. "Lily."

"Oh, right." Lily took a few steps back. "May Vylantra protect and guide you." The corner of her lips curled.

"I'll be waiting for you two to return. I'll keep Mistfall safe while you're out."

"I'll take your word for it." Minari smirked. "Let's go, Elliot."

Elliot took one last look at Lily, then at the village. The red spread farther in the sky, spilling bits of blue. He didn't know what the journey had in store for him or how the prophecy would unfold, but knowing his two best friends were with him calmed his nerves and put him at ease.

He wasn't alone.

He nodded at Lily, giving her one last smile. "Let's go."

He didn't turn back.

11
BEGINNING

The two trotted at a decent pace, not wanting to tire their ovis too early. They were still surrounded by Alder's magic, but the edge was drawing near. The morning sun was at its highest point. They'd been riding for five hours straight, longer than usual. Another hour and the afternoon heat would hit them. The looming trees provided shade as they traveled, but it was a wonder how the weather would treat them once they reached the lower lands.

Minari had taken the lead, riding Xander through the thick fog. It progressively thinned out as they descended. The vapor did little to hinder their travel.

The more they distanced themselves from Mistfall, the stronger the jitters in Elliot's body became. He chewed at his lip and picked at the skin around his fingernails. He'd never left home before; no one had left home before. What ordeal would they face when they left Alder's protection? The thin veil separating them from safety and the outside came into view.

"Are you ready, Elliot?" Minari asked. He pulled Xander to a stop and turned him. "Once we pass the veil, that's it. We'll have to travel down another twenty-five miles before we reach the lower lands. If you're tired, there's a clearing around here with a pond. We can rest there before passing through."

"Y-yeah. That sounds good," Elliot mumbled. He kept his eyes lowered. His thumb was red and raw. Thin pieces of skin stood up.

Minari moved Xander so he could be next to Elliot. "Nervous? I'll be with you, you know. Along the whole way."

"I know."

"Come, follow me. We can rest for an hour before heading out again."

Elliot followed. Minari kept the conversation going. He told him about when he'd enrolled as a scout, about how scary Errol had been and how he'd wanted to drop out. He told him about the first time Lily revealed she liked Elliot and how she wanted to confess her feelings. Minari had thought it was a bad idea since he knew Elliot had a crush on Stella, but he hadn't been able to bring himself to mention it. Elliot's cheeks warmed at the thought of Minari's older sister. She'd looked beautiful wearing the oracle's attire. The long, indigo robes had wrapped around her body, complementing her mature figure, and the fabric had draped across her arms gracefully.

Minari was distracting Elliot from what was to come, and he appreciated that. He needed it.

An hour ticked by, and they were off again.

Right before they passed through the veil, Redd flew off of Minari's head and onto Elliot's shoulder. He chirped and fluffed his feathers. Elliot scratched Redd's chin, not thinking much of it, but accepted the new companion.

When they crossed, Elliot wasn't sure what he expected. The dense forest looked exactly the same; it had the same green leaves, colorful flowers, and forest critters. He relaxed. If the lower lands were like Mistfall, he could get used to it.

"Another four hours and we'll reach the bottom. Do you think you can handle the rest of the ride down?"

"Maybe we can rest after two more hours?"

Minari nodded. "That should give us enough time to find shelter once we reach the bottom. Two hours, then a half hour break."

The sun beamed down on them harshly as soon as they entered the lower lands. Off along the horizon was a thick layer of trees—another forest. Unfortunately for them, at the base of the mountain was barren land. A large body of sand stood between them and the cool shelter the forest would provide. The heat from the sun burned through their clothes. Minari dabbed the sweat off his forehead.

"Unless you want to stay here, which I doubt you do, the forest looks about fifty miles away . . ." Minari trailed off. "We'll be riding into—"

A deafening screech exploded in their ears.

Elliot flinched and pressed his hands against his skull. Redd burrowed his head under the folds of Elliot's cloak.

Xander and Xeno reared back onto their hind legs.

Minari twisted his body as he pulled the reins. Soothing words left his lips as he tried to coax Xander. His eyes caught something off in the distance. A large, dark shape was drawing near, kicking up dirt as it moved. It started out as a small dot but quickly grew in size. His blood ran cold. The hairs at the back of his neck stood. "Elliot—" His voice hitched. "Run. Run as fast as you can."

An animal was charging toward them. The longer he looked, the more he realized it wasn't a normal animal. It was an enormous scorpion. Its bright crimson eyes leered through the dark clouds. Its eight long legs dug into the ground, pushing it forward.

"Elliot, go! I'll take care of this." He kicked Xander's sides, and they darted forward. He'd known they would be attacked as soon as they left the mountains; he just hadn't thought it was going to be this soon.

The closer he got to the beast, the more hairs on the back of his neck stood. Its glossy, black body was littered with tiny spikes. The joints of its legs held larger ones. He didn't know how he was going to fight the enormous beast, but he would die before harm befell Elliot.

The pounding of Xander's hooves centered him. They were thirty feet away. Twenty-five. Twenty. Fifteen. Ten. Minari lifted his body off of Xander, planting his feet against the saddle before launching himself in the air. He drew a long dagger from the sheath strapped around his thigh. With all his might, he drove the blade into the scorpion, right between its eyes. The shell cracked underneath the pressure. He kicked off, swinging his body upward, landing on top of its head.

The scorpion let out a howling shriek. It stumbled, but it wasn't deterred. It rose back up and swung its head around.

Thick, black gunk oozed from the cracked shell. It traveled up the blade onto the hilt, getting onto Minari's hands. The gunk was slimy, and it was proving to be more difficult to keep his hold. He drew another dagger from his other thigh and drove it into the beast's head. Letting go of the original dagger, he reached for one that was attached to his belt. With a flick of his wrist, he threw it into the beast's eye.

The scorpion let out an ear-splitting wail. Pure, white pain shot through the center of Minari's skull. He covered one of his ears with his free hand, but it did little to lower the noise. The scorpion's tail vibrated, aiming for the dazed elf.

Sensing the shift in the beast's muscles, Minari released the grip on his dagger and rolled out of the way. The tail attacked nothing, hitting the air. Minari dug his fingers into the folds of the hard shell on its back, careful to avoid the many spikes. He pressed one of his knees down, balancing himself. Ideas were running through Minari's mind as fast as he could think. His daggers weren't nearly long enough to deal any actual damage to the giant scorpion. The most he could do was blind it, and that alone wouldn't guarantee their safety.

The scorpion dug its pincers into the ground and leaned forward, then launched itself into the air. Minari held his breath and crouched. He braced for impact as the scorpion landed. His entire body shook, and his grip slackened. The scorpion jumped again, and this time Minari wasn't sure if he could hold on.

A tuft of brown fur caught the corner of his eye.

Xander was galloping nearby. He moved close to the scorpion, but not so close that he would get trampled—just close enough for Minari to jump.

Right before the scorpion landed, Minari kicked off its back and into the air. Xander followed suit, taking a gigantic leap. Minari grabbed the reins first before moving his legs over Xander's sides.

The scorpion landed, and a large cloud of dust enveloped it. Xander circled around the beast. It was still, appearing to make no movements. But Minari saw its red eyes. They followed him, stalking him like prey.

One pincer rose and dove. Minari quickly steered Xander out of the way, narrowly dodging the attack. Another pincer attack landed in front of them. Minari didn't react fast enough, and Xander couldn't control his speed quick enough to avoid collision. They slammed into the shell. Minari rolled as he landed on the ground, tucking his head into his arms.

He quickly stood, coughing and waving his hand in front of his face. Dust and dirt had been kicked up into the air, and it was difficult for him to see. He glanced around, desperately looking for his companion. He spotted Xander.

He was on his side, legs kicking as he tried to get back up on his feet. Minari dashed toward him. Xander was nearly within reach when Minari sensed a change in the air. There was movement from above and it was coming right at him. The beast's tail was mere moments from colliding with Minari.

Xander bleated, urging for his master to move, but Minari was frozen. Was this how he was going to end?

A sheer dome suddenly wrapped around him. It blocked the attack, shattering upon impact. Minari raised his arms, covering his eyes from the light. The force pushed him, and his back collided with Xander. He didn't have time to consider what had just happened. He scrambled to his feet, quickly pushing Xander back onto his hooves. One of his horns was broken.

"Minari!"

He looked around for the source of the voice. The sound of Xeno's hooves drew closer. Why was Elliot here? He'd told him to get to safety. Minari didn't know how to fight this giant scorpion, and he couldn't risk Elliot getting hurt. "Elliot, stay back!"

The scorpion raised its pincers again. Minari was still getting Xander situated back on his legs. The ovis was somewhat dazed from the collision. Minari didn't have time to move, and if he did, he would be leaving Xander alone to fend for himself.

Everything seemed to happen in slow motion. The pincer moved terrifyingly close, and the back of Elliot's head came into view. Minari flinched as a burst of white light blinded him once again.

When Minari opened his eyes, the same sheer dome surrounded him. Elliot had his hands up as if he was controlling the shield.

"Elliot. You . . . you used magic." His eyes were wide as his gaze landed on Elliot's back. He'd known the younger elf would be able to use some sort of magic as the oracle, but it was still surreal to see.

Elliot grunted as another attack came. His shoulders and arms shook, but he kept his arms up. The beast was relentless with its attacks. One after another, it kept punching. Cracks formed in the shield. Minari didn't know how much longer Elliot could hold out for. He needed to figure something out.

Fast.

Two bright beams zipped past them. The beast's pincers landed on the ground with a loud thud. It shrieked the same bloodcurdling scream that had split Minari's skull in half. Another beam flew past them, this time severing the scorpion's tail. The beast immediately stilled. Slight tremors wracked its body before it viciously vibrated. Its legs began to crumble into black dust, and its body soon followed, completely disintegrating.

Elliot lowered his arms, and the shield disappeared. He clutched the front of his shirt and turned to Minari. Sweat rolled down his temples. He was flushed. "Are you all right?"

Minari gaped at him. "I should be asking *you* that."

"I'm fine."

Minari frowned. He didn't look fine at all. There had to be repercussions for using magic.

"Don't move, both of you!" a girl's voice called out. A figure came rushing to their side. Her curls bounced as she ran. She was considerably shorter than them; the top of her head barely reached Xeno's or Xander's chin. She had milky brown skin and bright pink locks. There was a red choker around her neck with a round opal in the middle.

A nix. They were cave dwellers with the ability to use magic.

Before Minari could answer, the girl had a pink barrel pointed at him. There was another one pointed at Elliot. It was short and rectangular—a pistol. He had read about them during his studies within the hidden archives. Her red eyes narrowed at him. "Hands up. Which one of you summoned that monster?" Her voice was threatening.

"What?" Minari said.

"I said hands up."

Minari eyed Elliot. He slowly raised his hands, and Elliot did the same.

"Oh, so you two can understand common tongue. Good. I wonder if you can speak it." Her face twisted in disgust. She tightened her grip on the pistol. "Don't try anything funny. If I see either of you try to summon another monster, I'll shoot you where you stand, *elf*."

12
TRUST

The girl kept her eyes on Minari. She wasn't bluffing. Her finger rested on the trigger, and the barrel was pointed at his forehead.

"Minari . . ." Elliot started.

The girl quickly shifted her eyes. "I said don't move, or do you want to see what happens when I let Rose loose?"

"Hurt even a hair on his head, and I swear on Vylantra that I'll cut you down," Minari warned. At first, he hadn't wanted to create a scene. He didn't know if this girl was acting alone or not, and he didn't want to draw too much attention to them. They were elves, and elves were practically extinct to anyone who lived in the lower lands. But if she was a threat to Elliot, he would kill her.

"Vylantra?" the girl scoffed. "Disgusting elf. You dare threaten me? Do you even know who I am?" The girl didn't wait for a response. "I doubt savages like you would. Why do I even bother?"

"If you were paying attention, maybe you'd have realized we were the ones being attacked," Minari spat. His blood was boiling. "Or maybe you were too short to notice."

The girl spewed a slew of sounds. "Y-you *dare* insult me?"

Minari lowered his hands. He took a step forward. The girl quickly shifted the pistol that was pointing at Elliot to Minari, both weapons now directed at him. "What do you think you're doing? Didn't you hear what I said? Do anything funny and I'll shoot."

"Shoot me with what, your toy pistols?" Minari mocked. He didn't care how riled up the girl got. He had to distract her somehow so Elliot could at least get out of here. He didn't want to spill blood in front of the younger elf. "I thought they were real until I saw how disgustingly pink they are."

The girl flushed in anger. Her stance faltered, mouth opening as if she was about to say something, and that was the opening he needed. Minari lunged forward. He swung his leg and kicked one of the pistols from her hand. He grabbed her other wrist and stretched her arm upward. He drew a dagger from his belt and pressed the blade under her chin. The girl gulped, her neck pressed against the blade.

"Elliot, get out of here. I'll catch up with you after I'm done with this girl," Minari said. His tone left no room for negotiation.

"Are you going to . . . ?" Elliot's words were soft.

"Don't worry. I'll keep you safe."

The girl chuckled. "Typical elves. First your kind ran away with your tails between your legs, and now you summon monsters and threaten to kill innocent, little girls? Savages."

Minari pressed the blade closer, drawing a thin line of blood. "Watch it."

"Minari, don't. Please don't kill her."

Minari's grip faltered, but only slightly. It wasn't enough for the girl to notice. "She's a threat to us, Elliot."

"But she saved us."

What? What was Elliot saying?

Elliot dismounted from Xeno. He picked up the fallen pistol and walked over to the two. "I'm not sure what these are, but she saved us with these. These are called pistols?" He put a hand on Minari's shoulder and softly tugged him back.

Minari hesitantly released his grip on the girl's wrist and withdrew his dagger. The girl backed away but made no attempt to threaten them. She'd probably learned her lesson. Minari was quick, and she knew it.

Elliot moved to stand in front of her. She took a step back for every step forward he took. Elliot smiled, and he held out the pink weapon. "You saved us, right? Thank you."

The girl looked at him with cautious eyes. She glanced at Minari, then back to Elliot. She moved forward, just enough to snatch the pistol out of Elliot's hand, and retreated.

Minari clicked his tongue. "If Elliot doesn't want me

to hurt you, then I won't. You don't need to act like a pathetic, scared forest animal. I hate to admit it, but you probably did save us from that thing." He recalled one of the books he'd read explaining the magical weapons different races used. Nixen were able to transfer their stamina from their magic cores into the weapons, allowing them to project energy beams. The girl probably had good control of her powers considering her beams had been strong enough to sever the scorpion's giant pincers and tail. Though how had she known to aim for those?

"I'm Elliot, and this is my friend, Minari."

The girl pressed her lips into a thin line before answering. "Chloé."

"Thank you again for saving us, Chloé. Minari and I just left our tiny village. We've dreamed about going on an adventure together and were curious to see what the lower lands were like."

Minari stared at the back of Elliot's head. He was making up a lie. He mentally smirked. He hadn't thought Elliot would be able to change the narrative of their journey as quickly as he had.

"And you expect me to believe you?"

"You have your weapons back now, so I'm at a disadvantage. There's no reason for me to lie."

"That purple-haired elf . . ." Chloé mumbled.

"He won't do anything. I already told him not to hurt you."

Chloé shifted, blinking a few times as she looked at Elliot. Her eyes widened briefly before turning away. She placed her two pistols in the lace-covered holsters on her thighs. "I believe you, but I can't let you two go."

"What?" Minari said. "What do you mean you won't let us go?"

"You two are coming back to the city in the caves with me. I want to make sure I can trust you before I let you go."

"You can't be serious."

"There's an agreement between the three races that we nixen keep the mountains in check. We make sure the elves stay within their territory, ensuring our safety in the lower lands."

Was Chloé insinuating that the elves would come storming down from the mountains and create another war? There was no chance of that ever happening.

"If it'll help us pass through, then we'll go with you," Elliot said, turning to Minari. "Plus it'll be a good idea to take a look around. We could replenish our supplies while we're there."

Minari gaped. "And are you assuming she'll allow us to wander freely?"

"She wants to make sure we aren't a threat."

"And you trust her? She could be lying, waiting to toss us into a dungeon!"

"I will keep an eye on you two for a week. During your stay, I will accompany you wherever you need to go. That should give me enough time to evaluate if you are a threat to us or not. Although, I will have to keep you in a dungeon cell at night." Chloé paused before continuing. "If at the end of the week I find you harmless, I will need to brand you." She lifted her left wrist and pointed at the underside of it. "Right here. It's to prove that I have fulfilled my duty and confirm you are no threat to us. Without the brand, you may as well be tossed into a dungeon by someone else."

"Okay. I agree to that." Elliot nodded without missing a beat.

"Elliot! You what?" Minari was baffled Elliot hadn't even tried to talk to him about it. Being followed around by a nix wasn't something he was keen on doing. They would need to be extra cautious since he wasn't sure how the cave dwellers would take to two elves suddenly appearing within their territory.

Elliot glanced over his shoulder, giving Minari a reassuring smile. "It'll be okay. Trust me."

Minari couldn't believe what was happening. He sighed and shook his head. "If you insist." He would play the part of the lie they were stringing along.

It was a lie he trusted Elliot to lead.

He was the oracle, after all.

13
BARS

Chloé had the two elves walk behind her. Their giant goat animals trotted slowly behind them. She peeked over her shoulder. They were talking in hushed voices, making it hard for her to hear what they were saying. Other than the purple-haired elf, they didn't seem to be threatening. Actually, the green-haired elf seemed gentle. The way he looked at her made her feel oddly calm. She didn't want to admit it, but she'd been beyond frightened when the dagger had been pressed against her throat.

She led them three miles west. An hour later, they were in front of a cave. The entrance was covered with vines from the mountainside. She turned around and gestured at the two goats. "I don't know what animals those giant goats are, but they can't enter, so send them back or something."

"You want us to send them back?" Minari asked. He looked at her like she'd grown an extra head.

"Can't you just send them up the mountains?"

"We've been traveling since morning. I doubt they have the energy to make it back home," Elliot said.

Chloé put her hands on her hips. "Well, do something about them because they can't come in." She pointed at the small, red bird on Elliot's shoulder. "The bird can't come either." She wasn't sure if the small animal was a messenger of sorts, and she wasn't about to take the risk. "Like I said, you'll be staying here for one week. Unless you don't mind if they end up wandering off, I don't care. If your belongings get stolen, I don't care."

Minari frowned. "You can't be serious."

Chloé crossed her arms. "I'm one hundred percent serious. Oh, and I'll be taking your mini knives." She made her way over to Minari and held her hand out. "Hand them over. All of them."

Minari clicked his tongue. "They're daggers." He unbuckled the belt that held his smaller daggers, then moved to unlatch the holders that sheathed his longer ones to his thighs. He handed them to Chloé before reaching behind and under his coat, removing another belt that held two of his curved blades.

Chloé cocked an eyebrow. "Do you really need seven?"

"Yes," he responded plainly.

"Barbaric," Chloé mumbled. Minari rolled his eyes. She held them close to her chest. "You're not hiding anything else, are you?"

"No."

She narrowed her eyes at Minari, studying his blank expression. She turned on her heel. "Okay. Have you decided what to do with your goats?"

"They're ovis," Minari said.

"Fine. What are you going to do with your ovis? And your bird?"

Elliot was stroking and patting his ovis's head, whispering something to the animal. He gave one last pat before shifting his attention to Chloé. "They'll be okay if they stay here. Nothing will harm them, right?"

Chloé shrugged. "If travelers pass by and see these animals, I can't say they won't be curious, especially if they're unattended and with saddlebags."

"I think they'll be okay alone. Redd'll watch over them, right, Minari?"

Minari looked at Elliot, giving him a look like they were talking with their eyes. "He will."

"Redd?"

The small bird on Elliot's shoulder chirped. Elliot poked his index finger against the animal's head. "This little guy's Redd."

Chloé squinted her eyes at Redd. How would a bird watch over two large animals? She shook her head. She didn't have time to think about that. She had a meeting to get to. "Whatever. Just follow me." With one hand, she pushed the vines to the side and entered the cave.

The air was thick with humidity. Chloé had long since gotten used to the moisture and welcomed it against her skin. It was far too hot and dry outside. This year's summer was harsh. The bottom of her heels clicked loudly against the ground, echoing off the walls. The sound of water dropping from the ceiling onto the stalagmites comforted her. It was progressively getting darker as they proceeded. She heard shuffling of feet and Elliot's grunt.

"Sorry," Elliot said. "I can't really see."

"Hold on to me," Minari said.

Chloé looked over her shoulder. Minari was helping Elliot off the ground. He placed Elliot's hand on his shoulder, guiding him through the darkness. She turned her attention forward. So, one of them could see in the dark and one couldn't. It was an interesting fact to know. It was clear to her that the purple-haired elf had combat experience while the other didn't. They made an interesting pair.

The darkness eventually faded, and light shone through the end of the tunnel.

They stood at the edge of Blanc Grotto. The cave walls stretched high, forming a large, circular opening. Even though the evening sky had already settled in, the full moon illuminated the city with a blueish light. They proceeded down, stepping onto the wooden platforms. The city was above water that spilled from the Great Etherian Ocean. They passed many stone buildings and houses before they reached their destination: Gemme Hall. The large, gray building acted as a courthouse for the nixen. Chloé mainly used it when she had to attend important council meetings with the other nixen, one of which she had in about thirty minutes. Licht and Emilee were traveling from Lapis Grotto, and it was important for her to get ready.

She pushed the double doors open and led the two elves inside.

"Milady, welcome back." Cecilia bowed. She was Chloé's trusted maid. Her dark blonde hair framed her small face. "Lord and Lady Azure will arrive shortly. Which tea would you like me to brew for them?"

"Black is fine. Add lemon."

"At once, milady." Cecilia's tangerine eyes landed on the two elves that stood behind Chloé. "Milady, I apologize for intruding. Why are there two elves behind you?"

"I found them by the mountains. I'm taking them to the dungeons. Oh, could you take care of these for me, Cecilia?" She spilled the many daggers from her arms into Cecilia's. "Make sure no one takes these . . . or even sees them."

"At once, milady. Do you need me to accompany you down to the dungeons?"

"I'll be fine. They're harmless without their knives."

Cecilia looked at Elliot and Minari dubiously. "If you say so, milady."

"Send one of the guards down to watch them. I don't care which one."

"Yes, milady."

"You're dismissed. I'll be back before the meeting starts."

Cecilia bowed. "Milady." She disappeared down the hall.

Chloé walked down the opposite hall. She removed a lit torch from the wall before stepping down into the spiral stairwell. She was honestly surprised the two elves followed her without much of a fight. She had thought elves were crude, ill-behaved savages. On the contrary, they were docile. At least, Elliot was. The purple-haired one was definitely hotheaded.

Once they reached the cells, she turned to them. "One week. I'll have a guard deliver two meals a day—one in the morning and one in the evening." She unlocked the cell door. "I'll come by to pick you two up after breakfast."

Elliot entered first, seemingly not having a problem with being in the dungeon. Minari followed shortly, but not before shooting a glare at Chloé. She slammed the bars closed, locking it. She tucked the bronze key into her bosom. She didn't spare a glance before walking back up the stairs, leaving them in complete darkness.

14
WAITING

Elliot shrank down into the farthest corner. The sudden events came crashing down on him as soon as Chloé left. With the only source of light gone, his emotions let loose. He clutched his knees close to his chest, burying his face in them. He let out a shaky sigh.

He felt Minari sit next to him, draping an arm over his shoulders. "If you ever change your mind, let me know. I'll get us out of here."

"It's not that." Elliot untucked his head from his knees. "I think there's something about her."

"Does it bother you? All the stuff she said about . . . us."

"It's inevitable, right? To be hated." Elliot didn't want to admit it, but it had become painfully obvious how bad of a light elves were under. Chloé's view of them couldn't have been more opposite. The way she spoke about her keeping watch over the mountains like the elves were a threat had been shocking, especially since he knew they did everything to prevent anyone from entering Mistfall. It was like they were protecting themselves from each other. The more he thought about it, the more he believed there had been some miscommunication.

Elliot heard a curse beside him before Minari groaned. "I forgot my book with Xander. Mother is going to murder me."

"Book?"

"Mother also made me your scribe." Elliot couldn't see, but he could tell from Minari's muffled voice that he had his hands pressed against his face. "Dammit."

"Alder knows. I heard his voice earlier."

"What? When?"

"When we were outside the cave," Elliot said. He leaned his back against the cold wall. Minari withdrew his arm. "I heard him through Redd."

"You're able to talk to him through Redd?"

"I think it has to do with the fact I'm the oracle. I wasn't able to hear him before now."

"That makes sense. So, he told you he'd watch over Xander and Xeno?"

Elliot nodded. "He told me not to worry. He'll make sure they're well taken care of while we spend our time here."

"Hopefully he also tells Mother that I'm stuck inside a dungeon with you, therefore I can't write."

Elliot chuckled. "Sorry about that. I kind of decided

that on my own."

"It seemed like you had a plan. You thought up that lie earlier."

Elliot adjusted himself, crossing his legs and putting his hands over his lap. "Actually, I wanted to tell you something." He paused. "When we were talking to Chloé earlier, I felt something. Like . . . a memory."

Minari didn't answer right away, but Elliot could sense his eyes on him, waiting for him to continue.

"I don't really know how to explain it. There was a shock when I looked at her, as if I'd met up with a long-lost friend."

"I doubt you have a friend you've known longer than me," Minari joked.

Elliot elbowed Minari's side. "I don't. I'm just letting you know how I felt."

Minari hummed. "Well, at least I didn't try to blow your head off upon first meeting."

"I kind of felt like she wouldn't hurt us, no matter how much she threatened."

"Well, I'm trusting your judgement on this."

They sat in silence. Elliot's eyes never adjusted to the complete darkness. He would lift a hand and stare at it, but no matter how much he stared, he couldn't see any of his fingers. He jumped, suddenly feeling a weight on his shoulder. He let out a sigh of relief when he felt the slight tickle of hair against his cheek. He heard Minari's light snores and smiled softly. Minari deserved the rest, but he wished he could have been in a comfortable bed.

Elliot thought back to when they'd first reached the

lower lands. It was hot. Hotter than he thought it would be. His skin felt like it was on fire as soon as the sun hit. When he first saw the giant scorpion, he was frozen in fear. No amount of heat from the sun could thaw him. He'd never seen anything so monstrous. He watched Minari fight the beast. He knew Minari was trained and could handle himself, but it was terrifying when he hit the ground. Elliot's body instantly thawed and acted on its own, rushing toward him.

Something inside him snapped. The veins in his body began to pulsate, sending waves of warmth through his body. He could feel thin strings tug from the center of his chest. They wrapped around his arms and fingers. And like an instinct, he knew what he needed to do.

He tapped into his center core, calling forth his magic. Another wave of warmth surged through him as power swirled inside him. It coursed through his veins. He projected that power into a wall of energy from his hands, sending it to Minari. It was just enough to block the attack, but it was only a matter of time before another one came.

He pushed Xeno, pushed him to run as fast as he could. He barely made it in time, putting himself in front of the pincer and Minari. He forced a larger amount of energy out, successfully creating a more robust shield. Each attack from the scorpion felt like a stab in his chest. He had choked and gasped for air every time the scorpion had brought its pincer down. The pain had only increased.

Maybe it was luck that Chloé had been there when it'd happened. She'd known how to handle the monster, as if she'd fought them before. Those in the lower lands were surely more accustomed to seeing things like that. Large monsters were probably a common occurrence.

At least Elliot hoped so.

He closed his eyes, resting his head against Minari's.

The rattling of the cell door drew Elliot from his slumber. He rubbed his eyes, letting out a yawn. He pushed himself off of Minari's shoulder, attempting to massage the kink from his neck.

"Morning. The guard just brought breakfast," Minari said.

The guard was leaning against the wall, arms crossed. A torch was lit beside him, illuminating the dungeon enough for them to see. Two metal trays had been pushed into the cell, each with a cup of tea and a loaf of bread.

"This girl is going to starve us to death," Minari mumbled.

Elliot went over to the food. The bread was still warm, and so was the tea. "It's fresh."

Minari scoffed. "At the very least."

The two ate in silence. It wasn't enough to fill their bellies, but hopefully their dinner meal would be bigger. It wouldn't surprise Elliot if Chloé had offered a lighter meal for breakfast.

Footsteps echoed down the stairwell as they were finishing up their meals.

"Ah, so my ears don't deceive me," a nix said. There was a smile on his face as he approached the cell door. His skin was the same milky brown as Chloé's, yet he looked older and had wavy, red hair framing his face. There was a twinkle in his wide eyes that made Elliot's skin crawl. "Interesting to see what cute, little Chloé caught. I never imagined I'd lay my eyes on an elf, let alone two."

"Who are you?" Minari asked. Elliot could feel Minari's body grow tense beside him.

The man tilted his head. "Oh, and they speak common tongue! How exciting. I wonder if Chloé would let me run tests on you," he said, as if talking to himself. He turned to the guard. "They've been down here since last night, yes?"

"Correct, Lord Azure."

"Please, do not call me Azure. It makes me feel so old."

"Lord Licht."

"Better." Licht turned back to them, his eyes studying them closely. Elliot couldn't help scooting closer to Minari. Unlike with Chloé, Elliot didn't get a sense of comfort or longing when this nix was around—only suspicion and fear.

"One of them seems to be . . . tamer than the other. Interesting. Very interesting indeed," Licht said. "The one with green hair would be easier to experiment on, but the one with purple hair looks very interesting with those eyes. Could it be heterochromia iridum? I must ask Chloé when she gets down here. When did she say she was coming?"

"Lady Chloé did not tell me a time, only to deliver the food before she arrived."

"Well it seems they already ate, so it won't be long. The anticipation is killing me." Licht reached into his coat and pulled out a pistol that looked similar to Chloé's, except it was covered in blue gemstones. He pointed it toward Elliot. "Do you think they bleed the same as we do? Chloé wouldn't mind if I take a peek, would she?"

The guard didn't answer, probably aware that Licht was mainly talking to himself.

Minari moved in front of Elliot. "Hurt him, and I will kill you."

"Threatening me, are you?" Licht's lips curled. "I say that is enough for me to open fire. As a precaution for my own safety, of course." The pistol in his hands started to glow.

Elliot braced himself. He tapped into his core, ready to pull his magic out into a shield.

"Don't," Minari whispered. "We can't let them know you use magic."

"But—"

"Don't worry."

Elliot bit his lip. He knew where Minari was coming from. It was a risk to reveal who he was to people they couldn't trust. He relaxed his shoulders, releasing the flow of magic and allowing it to return to his core.

"Licht," a voice called out. It was Chloé.

Licht lowered his pistol, the glow disappearing. He turned away, attention now on the other nix. "Ah, Chloé! So nice of you to finally arrive."

Chloé stood at the base of the stairwell. Her hands were in fists as she marched over to Licht. "Dare I ask what you are doing here, Licht? You do not have clearance to wander into my dungeon without seeking me out first."

Licht tucked his pistol into his coat. "I couldn't find you, and I couldn't withhold my curiosity. After our meeting yesterday, I heard whispers of you bringing back two elves. I had to see for myself. I hope you weren't planning on keeping them to yourself. You didn't mention them in our meeting yesterday."

Chloé pressed her lips into a frown. "It is our duty to make sure they aren't a threat to us, so I brought them down here. And since they haven't done anything, I figured there wasn't a point in mentioning it."

"The topic of potential threats in the lower lands should always be mentioned."

"I disarmed them, and they are here in my dungeon. As of right now, they are no threat."

"Your proficiency is admirable. However, I would like to take one of them with me to experiment on."

"No," Chloé said, narrowing her eyes.

"Chloé, you know we need to work together in order to keep the lower lands safe. If I'm able to study the elves, I can see what sorts of weaknesses they have. It would help with our defenses."

"I have not yet deemed them a threat to us."

Licht chuckled. "And how do you go about seeing if they are a threat? Keeping them in the dungeon proves nothing. If anything, they should already be seen as a threat simply because they are elves."

Chloé heaved out a sigh. "Licht, I will allow it, but only if I deem them a threat. If I do, I will send one over to your manor in a week's time," she said, ignoring his initial question.

Licht hummed and turned back to look at Elliot and Minari. "I will allow you to have your fun for a week then, but if something happens earlier, I want them sent over immediately."

"Of course."

"Perfect. I trust you, Chloé, so please do not disappoint me."

Chloé nodded once before moving out of the way, allowing Licht to travel back up the stairs. When the sound of his footsteps disappeared, Chloé let out a frustrated groan. She turned her attention to the guard. "Give me the keys."

The guard cocked an eyebrow. "To the cell?"

"Yes. I can handle myself. Give me the keys, and you are dismissed until later tonight when you deliver their dinner."

The guard hesitated momentarily before unhooking the key ring from his hip and handing it over to Chloé. He gave her a small bow before ascending the stairwell.

"That Licht, acting like he can do whatever he wants," Chloé mumbled. She inserted the key and unlocked the door. It creaked as it swung open. "As promised, I will allow you to roam the city, but only under my watch. If I see you two acting suspicious, I won't hesitate to throw you back in here."

Elliot nudged Minari forward when he didn't move. He knew Minari was still wary of Chloé, but Elliot had already established his trust in her. He hoped it was only a matter of time before Minari trusted her too.

15
KNIFE

Elliot and Minari followed Chloé out of the dungeon and into the open air of the city. The smell of salt reached Elliot's nose, and there was a cool breeze. The shadows in the city were soft, indicating it was still early morning. The city was surprisingly large, taking into consideration it was inside a cave. In comparison to Mistfall, it seemed to be four times its size.

"What is this place called?" Elliot asked.

"Blanc Grotto," Chloé said, pausing before she continued. "There are two major grottos, this one and Lapis Grotto."

Elliot nodded. He briefly glanced at Minari. He knew Minari wouldn't be caught asking Chloé questions, so he would do his best to gather information for him. "Is there anything more you can tell us?"

Chloé chewed on her lip. "No. It is best if you know little of this place, at least until I give you clearance." Another pause. "You mentioned you two needed supplies. I don't know what two elves would need, but I can show you around the plaza."

Chloé led Elliot and Minari around Blanc Grotto. They gazed into storefronts that sold different arrays of clothing and food. It was the first time Elliot had seen food consisting of meat. It didn't sit well in his stomach, and he could tell the aroma was affecting Minari as well. The hunger that had been creeping in vanished. Chloé didn't seem to take notice, her eyes wandering over the food.

The different types of clothing and fabrics were different than those in Mistfall. They were silky and soft to the touch. They were light, not thick like the cotton he was used to wearing.

They weren't able to buy anything due to the unfortunate fact they didn't carry any coin. Mistfall operated on trade and the goodwill of other elves rather than using coin for goods.

The murmurs and stares grew as they progressed. Nixen stopped in their tracks, pointing and whispering amongst one another. Though they showed politeness to Chloé, they showed none to Elliot or Minari.

The sun was beginning to set when Chloé announced she would be taking the two back to the dungeon. Even though it was the first day under her watch, Elliot hoped it had showed her that he and Minari weren't threats. The day passed by without any problems. Minari had stayed quiet, silently keeping watch over Chloé's actions.

There was suddenly a scream from behind them. Elliot jumped at the sudden noise. He turned around, only to be shoved away by Minari.

A boy ran toward them, but Minari intercepted, grabbing the small nix by his wrist and lifting his arm up. The boy yelped, a knife clattering to the ground.

"Barbarians! Savages! What are you doing down here?" the boy screamed. He struggled in Minari's grip, which only tightened, causing him to wince. "I'm not scared of you! I'm going to protect Mom, and Dad, and Molly!"

"You're just a kid," Minari mumbled.

"Stop!" A man held a pistol in his hands, pointing it at Minari. His arms trembled. "L-let go of my son!"

"Dad!" The boy clawed at Minari's wrist.

Elliot looked over at Chloé. She had her lips pressed into a thin line, her eyes never leaving the event as it unfolded before her. Was she just going to stand by and watch? Could this be a test? Elliot needed to dispel the hostility before it was too late. Elliot put a hand on Minari's arm. "Let him go. They won't hurt us if we stand down."

Minari's eyes narrowed. He shoved the younger boy back. The boy stumbled, landing on his back. "Do that again and you won't like what happens. Now go back to your dad."

The boy's eyes widened, tears beginning to well up.

"You filthy savage. How dare you hurt my son! I'll kill you where you stand!" The man's pistol glowed before a beam shot out of the barrel.

Minari tugged Elliot out of the way and dashed forward. He pushed the nix onto the ground, forearm pressed against his neck. "This is your last warning. I won't hesitate to kill you if you and your son don't leave."

Chloé quickly drew one of her pistols and pointed it at Minari. It briefly glowed before a pink beam grazed the side of his arm. Elliot scrunched his nose. It smelled like burned flesh.

Minari cursed, pushing himself off the man and applying pressure to his arm. He glared at Chloé. "What was that for?"

Chloé pressed her other pistol against Elliot's side. "Don't move." Chloé's voice was cold. "Put your hands up or I will shoot him."

Minari peered at Elliot, frowning before raising his hands. Elliot followed.

"Back to the dungeon. Keep your hands where I can see them." She pressed her pistol harder against Elliot's back.

"Lady Gemme," the man whispered.

"Hurry home," Chloé said before shifting her gaze to the younger nix. "I'll take care of this."

The boy nodded, scrambling up and grabbing the fallen knife before reuniting with his father.

Elliot knew this didn't bode well.

Elliot and Minari were shoved back into the dungeon. There was a small sore on his back where Chloé had pressed her pistol against him. The cell door closed loudly, echoing off the walls.

"I don't need to tell you anything for you to figure out this isn't looking too good for you," Chloé said.

"You're going to take what happened and see it as us being a threat?" Minari seethed. "That kid was coming at us with a knife, and his father had a weapon!"

"It was for self-defense. It should've been obvious that your presence would put people on edge," Chloé said.

"Self-defense?" Minari moved toward the bars. He paused when Chloé raised her pistol.

"Don't move any closer. Come any closer and I will shoot you."

"What makes you think how I reacted wasn't for self-defense also?"

Chloé pressed her lips together.

Elliot reached for Minari's wrist and pulled him back. "Minari, calm down."

Minari whipped his head back to Elliot. "Calm down? Elliot, you know we can't stay here. The sooner we leave, the better."

Elliot shook his head. He needed Chloé to trust them. He deeply desired having the nix by his side, and he couldn't bear the thought of her turning against them. "Is there a way for us to make up for it?" Elliot asked Chloé. "As Minari said, it was for self-defense."

Chloé was silent. She shifted her weight before crossing her arms. "Elliot, if you two can prove to me you aren't a threat without leaving this dungeon, then I won't see you as a threat. But because of the stunt earlier, I cannot allow you to leave. Word spreads fast, and I'm sure the two of you didn't notice the small crowd that was accumulating."

Minari scoffed. "Let them look. Everyone who thinks of harming Elliot will meet the end of my—"

Elliot elbowed Minari, silencing the sentence. "So if we stay in here peacefully, then we can leave?"

"After I brand you, yes. There's no doubt the people would wonder why I let you two go freely. I'd need to think of something and release a public announcement."

"Thank you, Chloé. I'm sorry for what happened," Elliot said.

Minari gawked at Elliot. Elliot gave the older elf a reassuring smile.

"The guard will arrive with your dinner later." Chloé turned to leave, but not before giving Elliot one last glance. "Until then . . ." She disappeared up the stairwell.

Minari cursed under his breath and sat down. He winced as he brushed his fingers across his wound. It was red and raw, skin blistering. The edges were singed black. It was a severe burn, and they didn't have anything to soothe the skin. "I can't believe she actually shot me. And you said you trust her."

Elliot nibbled at his bottom lip. Chloé had opened fire and harmed Minari, but he couldn't fault her. He knew it had been meant as a warning shot to show that Chloé had the situation under control, to show that even though they were hostile, she was able to quell the situation. Still, it pained him to know Minari had gotten hurt and would end up with a scar because he'd wanted to visit the grottos; he was the one who'd made the decision to follow Chloé and wander around town.

The undeniable trust he felt for Chloé was still there,

and he just hoped he hadn't made the wrong decision.

Elliot nibbled at his meal. It was his tenth one, marking the end of the fifth day confined in the dungeon. They hadn't seen Chloé since the incident four days ago. The wound on Minari's arm was still raw and blistering. The food they were given was the same each time: a piece of bread and tea. Finishing up, he pushed the metal plate against the bars and heard a thud.

Minari had collapsed on the floor, unconscious. Elliot's eyes widened. He scrambled to Minari's side and shook his shoulder. "Minari?" He tapped his cheek, but there was no response. "Minari!" His gaze landed on the nearly empty plate. He squinted at it, furrowing his brow. Was it something he'd eaten? But Elliot had eaten the same meal. Though, when the guard had pushed their evening meals into the cell earlier, Minari had quickly grabbed a plate before Elliot. It had been a little odd, especially since he always let Elliot pick whichever plate he wanted even though they were identical.

Elliot pressed a finger underneath Minari's nose. He let out a sigh. Minari was still breathing. Relief filled his nerves. Chloé hadn't decided to end one of them after all.

He was about to reposition Minari so his head would rest on his thighs, but a familiar clicking of heels stopped him. He glanced over at the bars. Chloé stood, blocking the small torch that hung on the wall. It cast a shadow against her features, making it difficult for him to read her expression.

"That didn't take long at all," she said. She stuck her hand out to the guard. "Key. And don't ask questions. I can handle the green-haired one myself." The guard didn't hesitate, quickly removing a key from a ring and handing it to Chloé. She unlocked the door. "You're coming with me. Leave the purple-haired one in here."

16
QUESTIONS

Elliot hesitated. His hands were still under Minari's head. He didn't want to leave Minari alone, especially since he didn't know if he would be all right. Chloé must have sensed his uncertainty.

"He's just sleeping. You don't need to worry about him."

Elliot unclasped his cloak. He folded it and tucked it underneath Minari's head, hoping it would be enough to keep him comfortable.

They walked up the spiral stairwell. Chloé wasted no time, practically hopping between the steps. She led him down a corridor. Then another one. And another. Elliot's hope of memorizing where the dungeons were located slowly fizzled. Chloé led him through a set of double doors and into a library. It was filled to the brim with bookshelves, all housing hundreds of books. Even the archives in Mistfall didn't have this much reading material.

"I released an announcement yesterday," Chloé said.

Elliot followed her, waiting for her to continue.

"It wasn't easy, but I released a public announcement stating that you two acted out of pure self-defense. Unless provoked, you're harmless. It was a natural reaction anyone would have."

Elliot mentally sighed in relief. He and Minari would be able to leave the dungeon soon. "Thank you."

Chloé hummed in response, her fingers gliding along the books. She then stopped and pulled one out. She flipped through the pages, her back still facing Elliot. "Elves: a misfit race that once lived in the lower lands," she began. "They traveled in large packs, raiding and burning down small villages, leaving nothing in their wake. They thrived by slaughtering. They bathed in blood. They ate flesh straight from the bones of the dead, completely raw."

Elliot froze. The way the book portrayed the elves was far from the truth. It was completely wrong. Elves were peaceful. They didn't even hunt animals. Their diet was comprised of grains, fruits, vegetables, and berries. The only time elves would kill was when a scout found an intruder, and Elliot couldn't imagine it was that many.

Chloé snapped the book closed. She tucked it back into the shelf before pulling out another one. "Year 1010 EA. The civil war between the elves and the humans, nixen, and ethereals finally came to an end. The elves stole many lives, but they were eventually defeated. They retreated into the mountains, where Alder keeps them. It is unknown when they will return to the lower lands and brew destruction. The three races focused their remaining energy and resources on rebuilding what was destroyed during the war." She then flipped through the pages. "Year 1030 EA, Etheria was plagued with an unknown illness. It was named Death's Kiss."

Elliot snapped out of his shock. He couldn't believe the things the book said about elves during the war. It didn't sound accurate at all, especially since Alder himself had told Elliot what had happened. But he remembered the term "Death's Kiss." Vylantra had mentioned it. The Necromancers had been born because of the illness.

"Mysterious cloaked figures appeared out of thin air. They held their hoods over their faces so no one could see their identity, but it was rumored and later proven they were elves. They descended the mountains twenty years later only to terrorize the peaceful lower lands, burning and killing in excessive amounts. They did not stop. They did not sleep. Nine months later, their horrific antics were put to an end by Leonard Valentine, a human warrior. Because of his heroism, the three races agreed to make him their king. He became the first ruler of Etheria." She closed the book. The slam echoed through the empty library.

Elliot stared at the back of Chloé's head. Everything she'd just said was false. It had to be. Vylantra had told him humans caused the destruction. They were the reason why Myru, one of the previous oracles, had set off on a journey to stop them. They were the reason *he* had to fulfill a prophecy. His body refused to move, and his mind was dizzy. The center of his chest felt cold.

Chloé spun, the book still in her hands. "Now you understand why I had a difficult time persuading the nixen that you two elves aren't a threat. Everything I just stated is what we all believe in. I pulled you out here because, frankly, I don't trust the purple-haired one. The more time that passes by, the less likely I see it being that you two left the mountains for the sake of traveling. Why are you two down here? I want honest answers only."

Elliot opened his mouth, wanting to deny everything in the books, but he stopped. Even if he said it wasn't true, the likelihood of her believing him was slim to none.

"Honestly speaking"—Chloé drew him away from his thoughts—"I don't sense any hostility from you. The other one, I do. His weapons prove my suspicion."

"We don't mean any harm," Elliot said. At least that was the truth.

"If you don't, why did the other elf have seven mini knives? It is quite obvious he's had combat training."

"Uh . . ." Elliot searched his brain. How could he make it sound like it was normal for Minari to have daggers? He reached into his pouch—the one Chloé surprisingly hadn't confiscated. She might not have seen it under his cloak. He pulled out Lily's dagger. "I have one too. It's a normal elf thing, similar to how you have pistols." He eyed the two weapons against her thighs.

Chloé pushed the book back onto the shelf. She took a deep breath before quickly drawing one of her weapons and aiming it at Elliot.

Elliot flinched. He shut his eyes and turned away.

"You say it's a normal elf thing, but you don't even

know how to use one," she said plainly. "Look at me."

Elliot slowly opened his eyes and peered over. Blue met red, and he drew in a breath. He had the sudden urge to rush over to the smaller girl and wrap his arms around her in an embrace. Chloé took a step back, lowering her arm. Her lips were quivering.

"How?" she said. "What are you doing? Is this some sort of trick?"

"What do you mean?"

"Don't mess around!" She lifted her arm again. "How come when I look at you, into your eyes, I . . . I just . . ." She turned away and held herself.

"Chloé?" Elliot took a step forward.

"Don't! Don't come near me." Her shoulders started to shake. "Why is it when I look at you . . . it's like I've known you my whole life?"

Elliot barely caught what she'd said. His eyes widened. "Like a long-lost friend?"

She looked at him, eyes wide and mouth agape. "How did you know?"

"Because I feel it too." Elliot pressed a hand against his chest. "I have this ache in my heart like I've known you for a long time and we've been apart. Now that we're to-gether . . . it's like seeing a long-lost friend."

"So you are doing something to me."

Elliot shook his head. "I'm not." He put Lily's dagger back into his pouch. "I don't know why." He bit his lip. Vylantra's words echoed through his mind. There were four warriors. Their souls were linked with his. They would reach out to him. Had Chloé saved them because her soul was drawn to his?

"I've missed you," Chloé whispered. "I feel like I've missed you, but I don't know why. We don't even know each other, and this is the first time I've ever seen elves."

Chloé's reaction pulled at Elliot's heartstrings. He didn't want to see her conflicted. Confused. "Chloé."

She turned, her arms still wrapped around herself. Elliot opened his arms. Something seemed to snap within Chloé. She ran toward him and leapt into his arms. He held the smaller girl close. The feeling of longing subsided. They held each other for a while until Chloé abruptly pushed away. The tips of her small, pointy ears were a deep shade of pink. "Sorry, I don't know what came over me," she blurted.

Elliot smiled. "It's all right. Do you feel better?"

Their eyes met again. This time there was no longing—there was trust. Elliot knew for a fact Chloé would never hurt him, even if she pointed one of her pistols at him. She was someone he could trust his life with.

"You promise you aren't doing anything? No weird elf tricks?" Chloé turned her eyes away.

"Nothing."

"You still have to go back into the dungeon until the full week is up, even though I know you're practically harmless. Couldn't kill an ant even if you saw one."

Cold realization slammed into Elliot. Minari was still in the dungeon. Was he okay? Was he still asleep? How would he react knowing Elliot was missing?

Chloé frowned. "You look like you just saw a ghost."

"Minari. I can't believe I forgot."

"The purple-haired elf? I told you, he's just asleep. I put valerian root in his tea."

"For how long?"

Chloé shrugged. "A few hours? Maybe the rest of the night? I don't really know. We sometimes drink it with our tea to help us sleep. I just put in four times the amount I would normally use on myself. I figured it would be all right since he's so tall."

Four times? That had to be an overdose. Elliot didn't know what the normal amount was for one serving, but if it was anything similar to lavender back in Mistfall, that would still be too much.

"I'm sure he's fine. We can head back so you can see for yourself."

"But before that"—Elliot pointed to his left arm—"you shot him, and it hasn't been healing. Do you have any ointment?"

Chloé's eyes widened. "What? It never healed? I thought you elves had the ability to regenerate. That's why I thought it was okay to nick him."

Elliot was at a loss for words. His mouth hung open, unable to produce a reply. He didn't know what was more bizarre—the fact that everyone in the lower lands believed they slaughtered meaninglessly or they could regenerate wounds.

"Judging by your reaction, I guess that's wrong too. I'll bring some aloe ointment later tonight. It should patch him up," Chloé said.

Elliot blinked, snapping out of his stupor. "Thank you."

When Elliot returned to the cell, Minari was still snoozing away, unaware that Elliot had been gone.

17
OUT

Chloé tossed and turned before furiously ripping her blankets off. She sat up and huffed. Almost a week ago, Licht had gone down into the dungeons and seen the two elves. She had promised to send them his way if anything were to happen, and something *had* happened. She hadn't accounted for anyone trying to attack the elves—not when she was there with them. She had assumed her presence was enough to put the nixen as ease, to show she had them under control.

She'd been mistaken.

The day after the incident, she'd made her way to their house. She'd recognized them immediately. They were members of the Jasper family. They didn't hold much power in society, but they were still a respectable family of miners. They frequently visited the same seamstress as her.

She talked to them whenever they crossed paths. It shouldn't have surprised her that they would try to keep her out of harm's way. If they could prove to her they were a formidable family to ally with, they would move up the chain. Instead of miners, they could become artisans.

She questioned them regarding why they'd done what they had, and they insisted they saw the way the elves were looking at her—eyes gleaming with malice and a snicker across their lips. It was only a matter of time before they struck and attacked her. They wanted to protect Chloé before it was too late. The child had wanted to show his bravery. He was a proud miner and wanted to show his strength to his father.

The child was indeed brave. Chloé shivered, remembering the time she'd clashed with the purple-haired elf, the way his cold eyes glared at her and how quickly he'd disarmed her. She could only hope he hadn't shown the same gaze to the smaller boy.

After thanking the Jasper family for looking out for her, she explained the elves meant no harm. Whatever they'd seen was probably built out of paranoia. She left the house determined to set the record straight. Something about Elliot drew her in. She wanted to know more about him, yet at the same time felt like she knew all there was to him. It was an odd feeling, one that contradicted itself.

Chloé met up with the Onyx family. They were in charge of releasing the daily press. She wanted to make sure she set the story straight. She made sure the article was as detailed as possible, depicting the elves as harmless and acting out of self-defense. They were new to the lower lands, so they were not aware of the possible hostile nature of the nixen. It had been an honest mistake. Anyone who had an issue with Chloé's announcement was to see her personally.

Luckily, she hadn't received any complaints. The murmurs and whispers about the elves had disappeared. Blanc Grotto was quiet once more.

Chloé drew her knees to her chest and rested her chin upon them. There was still the potential that Licht had caught wind of what had happened. The other council member was sharp—nothing could sneak by him. She could only hope that she'd quelled the situation before word could reach him.

She thought about all the books she had read while growing up. Pictures in the books had illustrated the elves grotesquely: fangs, ashen skin, a slight hunch in the back. The only reason she'd recognized the two as elves had been because of their ears. Nixen were the only other race with pointy ears, but they were smaller and pointed to the side while elves' ears pointed up. She'd initially thought they were younger than all the drawings she'd seen. Their skin didn't wrinkle and wasn't sunken in.

The facts she'd learned about elves while growing up didn't add up to what she saw in Elliot or the purple-haired elf. She was so caught up in her emotions that she'd forgotten to pinpoint why the two of them were in the lower lands. It didn't seem like they were trying to start another war. But what were they planning? What did they intend to do? She couldn't let them walk free and alone with no supervision.

She decided wherever they went, she went. This way

she wouldn't have to resort to branding them. She shivered, thinking how disgusting the smell of burnt skin was. She didn't want to bring them any harm. Yes, this was better. She could tag them with an opal instead, claiming them as her property. She would need to make up an excuse the next time she saw the Azure family, but she would worry about that later.

Chloé hopped out of bed, making her way to her vanity. She pulled open the top drawer and pulled out a square box. She ran her fingers across the crimson, velvet material before popping it open. Inside it were round opals. They didn't shine as brilliantly as hers, but it was enough to show which family the two elves belonged to. She placed the box onto the counter before digging deeper into the drawer. This time she pulled out a rectangular box. She took two black chokers from it. The design was plain, not as intricate as hers, but it was a given considering the two would pose as her property. They didn't have a right to something as delicate as lace or frills.

She placed the two chokers flat on the counter, then chose two opals and set them in the center of each. She placed her hands over them and reached into her core, sending a steady flow of magic into the two items. The opals embedded into the chokers. Once she attached them on, no one could remove them but her—a contract bound by magic. She would meet with them tomorrow before their last day.

They had no choice but to agree to pose as her property or return to the mountains.

Chloé took a seat in her kitchen, allowing Cecilia to tuck the chair in. Everything inside her home was accented with gold trim. Delicate lines ran through each piece of furniture.

"Milady, Lord Azure has sent a message. He wishes to return for another brief meeting regarding the elves," Cecilia said.

Chloé pressed her lips into a thin line before taking a sip of her afternoon black tea. It had a hint of lemon, just how she liked it. "When?"

"He will arrive here tonight."

Chloé placed her teacup back on its saucer. She leaned against the round, glass table, propping her chin against her hand. It was no surprise Licht had heard what had happened six days ago. She crossed her legs. She would need to sway him to leave the elves alone. "Did he mention anything specific?"

"No, milady."

Chloé hummed. "Cecilia, I'm going to tell you this now. I plan on placing my council duties on hold. I may not return home for some time."

Cecilia's usual apathetic expression turned into one of shock. It was a brief moment before her features returned to normal. "Milady, is there a reason?"

"I plan on making the two elves my property. I also intend to figure out the reason they're down here in the first place. Wherever they plan on heading to, I'll be going with them. They'll be under my supervision."

"They are property, yet you are following them, milady?"

"I am supervising them, Cecilia." Chloé took another sip of her tea, this time flashing her eyes to her maid.

Cecilia seemed to have understood what she'd meant. She bowed her head. "Of course, milady. I will watch over the manor and courthouse while you are away."

"Thank you, Cecilia."

Chloé spent the rest of the remaining day brewing up a lie Licht would believe. He was considerably older than her, sitting at ninety while she was only eighteen. She'd inherited the position in the council when her mother passed away and her father went missing. Because of the longevity of his absence, they'd deemed him dead. Though she was only eight when it happened, she hadn't needed to attend meetings until she was fourteen. It wasn't easy listening and trying to understand the politics behind everything, but she'd somehow managed. Four years later, she definitely wasn't the same naive girl.

Chloé waited in the meeting room, a book propped open in front of her. She sat alone at a long, rectangular desk. It was made of dark polished wood and was large enough to seat ten people. It was usually only her and the Azures. There had once been a time when the other council members would venture to Blanc Grotto, but ever since Chloé had become part of the council, they'd shifted their assemblies to Valquent. Now only the nix members used the large room.

A knock came against the door, and it opened.

"Ah, Chloé. You're here already. I hope I didn't keep you waiting long," Licht said, a smile on his face. With better lighting in comparison to the dungeon, Licht didn't look like he was aged past thirty. Nixen generally stopped aging physically once they reached thirty to thirty-five. At ninety, his skin was still tight, his back straight, and he had a full head of maroon hair. He quickly made his way over, taking a seat across from Chloé. His wide eyes landed on her.

Chloé closed the book. "I wasn't waiting too long. I was too engrossed in reading."

"*Records of Etheria, Volume Three.* I believe this one talks about the elves during the war?"

"It does. I quite enjoy history."

"That you do!" Licht grinned.

"May I know why you traveled all this way to speak with me, Licht? We just had a meeting the other day. Surely it isn't so important that it couldn't wait until next month."

"Ah, that's the thing. It couldn't have waited." He pulled out a black cloth pouch and placed it on the table. He pulled the tie, revealing its contents. There was a pile of black dust. "I found this while I was heading home with my dear Emilee. I know we talked about those enormous beasts that ran rampant around two weeks ago. I find it curious that you picked up two elves around the same time these furious monsters appeared."

Chloé leaned back against the armchair, crossing her legs. The first beast she'd run into had been a giant salamander, its body pitch-black and littered with spikes. The long tail had had a ball of spikes at the tip, and it had used that to attack. Only after severing the tail from the rest of its body had Chloé realized in order to kill the mysterious monster she had to remove its method of attack—in the case of the salamander, its tail. In the case of the scorpion, it's pincers and tail. "So you think there's a connection between the two elements?"

"I do. This is something the rest of the council members should know. King Leonard VI, especially. Another war could be upon us."

"What idea do you have in mind?"

"I know what happened here, and I am willing to postpone my experiment. Drastic times call for drastic measures. We should push the meeting in Valquent up. Instead of having it two weeks from now, we should have it next week at the latest."

"It already takes us one week to reach Valquent from here." Even though Licht was willing to hold off on getting ahold of the elves, Chloé didn't like where the conversation was going. She was about to place her duties on hiatus. It would look extremely poor on her part if she were to put a hold on her duties right before an assembly.

"That it does. You know I can use my magic to send a message quickly. It'll reach them by sunrise."

Chloé tapped her finger against the armrest. "I have a better idea."

Licht raised his brows. "Do tell, Chloé."

"I trust you, Licht." She knew buttering him up usually placed her on his good side. "You are more than adequate enough to attend the assembly yourself. You and Emilee both represent the nixen."

"Go on." Licht was looking at her with his full attention.

"I plan to take a brief break from my council duties. Just temporary. You see, I've been doing this basically my entire life, and I feel like my youth was practically stolen from me. I want to travel and explore Etheria. I already informed Cecilia, and she will take care of matters for me."

Licht watched her, as if searching for a lie in her statement. Technically, she wasn't lying. She had spent most of her life being part of the council. In actuality, she wasn't supposed to have been part of it until she reached forty, at the very least. The only reason they'd forced her into the position was because she was a Gemme, a marchioness. Licht too was a marquess, thus making him and his wife part of the council.

Licht smiled. "Chloé, if you really feel that way, I completely understand. But may I ask how long you plan on taking a hiatus for?"

"No more than a month."

"So you will be back in time for the next assembly?"

"Yes. Just inform Cecilia of the date, and I will be there."

"Wonderful. I will let the rest know you caught a terrible summer cold and couldn't make it to the assembly." Licht tied the pouch back up. "Because I am covering for you, Chloé, I would like compensation. At the end of the month, the elves are mine."

"Agreed," Chloé lied. "I will keep them in the dungeon and transfer them to you once the king is notified of the potential threat."

"I am delightfully excited to dissect the specimens."

Licht's smile never left. "It's giving me goosebumps."

Chloé uncrossed her legs. She leaned forward, lacing her fingers together and balancing her chin against them. "Licht, please keep your excitement to yourself. I'd rather not know how you plan on treating them." The way Licht's eyes twinkled made Chloé's stomach turn. She couldn't imagine them being in his hands. She would do everything she could to prevent it. "Actually, I would like to have some fun with them before I transfer them to you."

"Oh?"

"I'm going to make them my property. It'll show just how powerful we nixen are. The elves pose no threat to us if I can prove how easily they are tamed."

"I find it interesting that you would take on barbaric savages as your property."

Chloé bit the inside of her cheek. Agitation stirred in her stomach at the insult directed at Elliot and, surprisingly, the purple-haired elf. "They are interesting . . . specimens."

"Specimens? Are you thinking of dissecting them?" There was an eerie sparkle in Licht's eyes. "I knew you'd come around with my methodology of experimenting."

"No." Chloé closed her eyes. She willed herself to calm down, to stop the rage that stormed inside her.

"And what have you learned so far?" Licht leaned closer, enamored. "You've had them for nearly a week now. How did they act after the incident in the city? I read the article, though I hardly believe it's true."

"The article is as true as it gets."

Licht flashed a look of disappointment. "Oh."

"If you have nothing else to discuss, I would like to

retire for the night and rest."

Licht hummed. "No. I guess there's nothing else." He stood, tucking the pouch against his waist. "I will see you next month, Chloé. Hopefully there isn't another war upon us."

"I hope for that as well."

Licht left, leaving her alone with her thoughts. She had a month to find out what Elliot and the purple-haired elf were hiding and what their goal was. She hoped that was enough time.

But something in the back of her mind told her she would be gone longer than a month.

18
ONE

Minari listened carefully to everything Elliot told him. It was difficult. His mind was foggy, and his body was lethargic. When the guard had pushed their meals in and he'd smelled the strange aroma, he'd taken the plate before Elliot could. He'd drunk it, not wanting to worry him. As soon as the liquid had passed through his lips, his body had felt heavy. His vision had blurred, his eyes drooping. Darkness had swept him away almost immediately.

Minari let out an aggravated sigh. He had asked Elliot to repeat the same sentence three times already, but no matter how much he tried to listen, his focus faded. He pressed his fingers against his temples, rubbing them. "Sorry, Elliot."

"Are you sure you're feeling okay?" Elliot had his cloak back over his shoulders. Minari had insisted he didn't want to keep lying down. He needed to force himself to wake up. Luckily, the wound on his left arm had stopped aching. The injury had been treated with aloe ointment sometime during his sleep. It soothed the burn.

"Great. Just great." He closed his eyes, and they wanted to stay closed. He shook his head, forcing them open. He stared at the burning torch. Squinting his eyes, he tried to focus on the flames, but his vision kept blurring. "This girl must be trying to sabotage me."

"There was valerian root in the tea. She said she put four doses in it."

"Right. You did mention that, didn't you? How long was I out for, anyway?"

"A day and a half. You missed breakfast earlier. Our last meal here should come sometime soon."

Minari had been asleep for at least thirty-two hours. Valerian root was by far more potent than lavender. If he had four times the amount of lavender, he wouldn't be out for longer than twelve hours. "Tell me again, Elliot. What did Chloé want with you?"

Elliot started over, and this time Minari willed himself to listen, forcing his mind awake. The knowledge base in the lower lands regarding elves wasn't surprising to Minari. The winners were the ones who wrote history, after all. The scrolls and books within the hidden archives dated back to before the war had started, so he knew they were true. The oracle had been murdered, and that had caused the Civil War. The major concern would be traveling through the lower lands with the negative stigma. It wasn't going to be easy for them.

"I think Chloé might be a warrior."

Minari was more alert now. "Did something else happen?"

"When we were still in the library, there was a connection between us. A spark."

Minari didn't answer right away. "What are you hoping will happen when we get out of here tomorrow morning?" He readjusted himself, propping up one knee and resting his arm against it. That was something they needed to consider. When they ran into the warriors, how would they tell them? They lived in two different worlds. They knew they had a mission to fulfill, the others didn't. They couldn't rip them away from their day-to-day life without an explanation.

"I don't know, but I do know I don't want to be apart from her."

"We can't stay here, and whether she comes with us is up to her."

"I'm sure if we explained the situation to her—"

"I don't think we should tell her our mission unless we can absolutely trust her." Minari glanced over at the guard. He was slouched in the chair, arms crossed. His head had lolled onto his shoulder. It was fortunate he didn't seem to care to watch over them. "Remember, Elliot, there are those out here who wouldn't hesitate to kill us, Necromancers or not. We need to be careful."

Elliot frowned, his expression sunken. He slouched and leaned back against the wall. "You're right. Sorry. It's just . . . I really think she's a warrior." He shook his head. "No, she *is* one. I know she is."

The conversation ended there. Minari didn't know how much time passed. Elliot dozed off occasionally, waking up when his head drooped too low. He offered the tired elf his shoulder, which he accepted. Being confined in the cell didn't do well for either of them. Elves loved being out in the open air. Minari ached to be outside, to feel the warm sun against his skin. He knew Elliot felt the same way, even if he was quiet about it. Minari arched his back and stretched one of his arms, mindful of Elliot on his shoulder. Soft footsteps reached his ears. Someone was approaching. No, it was a pair of footsteps. It wasn't more guards. Their boots didn't make the high-pitched click. As the footsteps drew closer, he recognized the pattern. He'd only heard it once, but it was the same footwork as Chloé's.

Chloé stopped in front of the sleeping guard with Cecilia right behind her. Drool dripped from the side of his mouth. She stared at him before kicking his shin. The guard sputtered, quickly wiping his chin.

"Lady Chloé! To what do I owe the pleasure?"

"Hand me the keys. You are dismissed."

The guard unlatched the ring from his hip and placed it in Chloé's hand before scurrying off.

Chloé walked to the bars. "Is Elliot asleep?"

"He is."

"That's unfortunate. I was hoping to speak to him."

"About what?" Minari put his guard up.

"Well, for starters, your week is up."

Minari cocked a brow. "Oh? We haven't had our last meal yet."

"Whether you have your last meal is entirely dependent on what you decide." She wrapped a hand around a bar. "Could you wake him up?" she asked gently.

Minari looked at Chloé, and she looked back at him. He debated whether he wanted to deal with whatever she wanted to offer. He still had his doubts about Chloé, but Elliot was willing to take the risk. "What do you want to ask him? I'll relay the message."

"There's no time for that."

"Then tell me what you want." His voice was curt.

Chloé pressed her lips together, a slight scrunch on her face. "I need to ask him something important."

"And that is?"

Chloé clicked her tongue. "Elliot!" Her call was enough to bring Elliot out of his slumber. He jolted, eyes opening.

He glanced at Minari before turning his attention to the waiting nix. "Chloé?"

"Sorry to wake you up, but there's something important I need to ask you before I can let you two go."

"What is it?"

Chloé opened her palm. Cecilia draped two slim, black pieces over her hand. "In order for me to free you from here, I'm going to have to claim you as my property."

If Minari had been drinking his tea, he would have spat it out. Being claimed as a nix's property was the same as slavery. They didn't have the right to anything. They always needed permission to talk, eat, even sleep. "No."

"You didn't even let me finish." She glared at Minari.

"There is no way on Vylantra's name we're going to be your property."

"You aren't letting me finish." Chloé scowled.

Elliot placed a hand on Minari's shoulder. "Let's hear her out."

Minari silenced himself. He narrowed his eyes at the nix.

"The reason I need to claim you two as my property is because I will be supervising you."

Minari was about to yell again, but Elliot pulled his shoulder back, shaking his head.

"I believe this is a better alternative to branding. If anyone gives you a hard time while you are in the lower lands, I can easily step in. If you still don't want to become my property, I'm going to have to force you two back into the mountains." Chloé shrugged. "Or I can keep you here and let you two starve to death. I have no reason to keep you alive."

Minari was seething. If Elliot weren't so adamant that Chloé could be a warrior, they wouldn't still be locked up. He could have easily picked the lock and gotten himself and Elliot out of the dungeon before Chloé could have the time to consider starving them to death.

"What would we need to do if we became your property?" Elliot asked.

Chloé's expression softened. "You wouldn't actually be my property. You can act freely, but there are some rules when we're in public. You must stay behind me with your heads down. Speak to no one unless I allow you to." She brought her hand forward. "These chokers are a sign that I'm your owner. They will be magically bound to you, so no one but me can remove them."

Elliot looked at Minari, hope clear in his eyes. Minari was reluctant to be her property, even if it was an act. He was a proud elf, a proud scout. But he knew this was exactly what Elliot wanted. They hadn't even needed to explain themselves, and she was willing to come along with them. He was surprised but didn't like the circumstances it came with. "Up to you, Elliot."

Elliot smiled. He turned to Chloé. "We accept those terms."

Chloé brightened. "Good!" She unlocked the door. "I'll attach these onto you, then we can have dinner back home."

Elliot went first. He bent over, allowing Chloé to wrap the choker around his neck. Her fingers emitted a soft glow as she pressed them against his nape. Chloé did the same for Minari. A warm sensation seeped from Chloé's fingertips as she pressed them against Minari's nape. The collar tightened slightly around his neck as it began to fill with her magic.

"By the way," Chloé said, "if you do anything I find threatening, like put a dagger up to my neck, I can make these collars constrict and suffocate you. So, do be careful." The warning was directed at Minari.

She had to have been joking. The fact that she was specifically outing him made him unbelievably agitated. But he would handle it. Elliot truly believed Chloé was of importance and a warrior. He would endure her antics for Elliot.

19
START

Elliot inhaled the fresh air, letting it fill his lungs. His skin soaked in the sunlight, appreciating the warmth after being tucked away in the darkness for so long. Xeno, Xander, and Redd weren't at the entrance of the cave. Minari seemed to take notice immediately. He pressed two fingers against his lips and whistled. They waited, and soon enough, Xander came running back with Xeno and Redd following behind him.

Elliot grinned. He'd missed his ovis dearly. He nuzzled against the animal's snout and stroked his fur.

Minari made sure everything inside the saddlebags was accounted for while Redd found his home back in Minari's purple locks. "Looks like everything is still here." He patted Xander's large body. "What have you been eating? It looks like you gained weight." Xander snorted, twitching his ears. Minari tugged at the saddle straps. "Yep, you definitely gained weight."

Elliot examined Xeno. He also looked a little plumper than he remembered, but that didn't bother him. He readjusted the straps so they wouldn't dig into Xeno's skin.

Chloé cleared her throat. "Are either of you going to tell me why you're down here, or am I going to have to keep guessing?"

Minari glanced at Elliot but made no movement to answer her. He must have wanted Elliot to answer the question. Elliot considered Minari's warning: only those they trusted should know of the prophecy. He agreed, but he believed Chloé wouldn't betray them. It was a chance he was going take. "I'm the oracle, and I came down here to fulfill a prophecy."

Chloé stared blankly at Elliot. A pause stretched between them. She chuckled, then laughed. She pressed her hand against her horse's side, hunching over. "You . . . you've got to be kidding me! You? The oracle? Do you . . . do you even know what that is?" she asked between gasps of air.

Elliot frowned. What was so funny? Did she not believe him?

Chloé wiped the corner of her eyes and straightened back up. "You're going to have to try better than that. Even a child could think of a better lie."

"I don't understand. What's so funny about it?"

"Well, for starters, the oracle is supposed to be the leader of the elves—someone tyrannical, someone strong. Someone who isn't you."

Elliot wasn't sure if that was supposed to be an insult or not. Did Chloé really mean she didn't see him as strong? It was true he didn't know how to fight, but he had Vylantra's powers within him. He knew she didn't know that, but was that enough? Would he eventually be a hindrance to Minari?

"There's no reason for the oracle to be down here." Chloé's smile vanished. "Unless you mean to start a war."

"No! That's not why we're down here."

"She's not going to believe anything we say, Elliot," Minari said. "You either come with us, or I kill you and we leave without you."

Chloé's eyes narrowed. "Threaten me again and I will suffocate you faster than you can draw your mini knives."

"Want to make a bet? First one to die loses."

"It won't be me who dies, elf."

Elliot stepped between them, his hands outstretched. "Chloé, can't you just take us to the nearest town? We just want to travel Etheria and update our books back home," he blurted. It was a poor lie, but he had to think of something before they killed each other. Minari's expression was dark, and Elliot could tell he fully intended to slit her throat. Chloé's eyes watched Minari for any sudden movement.

It was silent for what felt like an eternity. No one moved. Eventually, Minari and Chloé relaxed. Elliot let out a breath he hadn't realized he'd been holding.

"I guess since your kind has been cooped up for so long, the information you have is outdated," Chloé said, her gaze still locked on Minari.

"Please forgive us for making you worry. Our goal is

completely innocent," Minari said sarcastically, mismatched orbs still on the nix.

Chloé scoffed. "Elliot I can trust. But I have my eyes on you, Purple Hair."

"You are *not* calling me that."

"You seem to have forgotten something important: I'm your master. You're my property. I may call you whatever I please." Chloé crossed her arms and tilted her chin up. "You are Purple Hair. Elliot is Elliot. Question me again and I will punish you."

Minari groaned. "Whatever." He placed his foot in the stirrup, mounting Xander. Elliot followed suit, and Chloé got on her gray mare.

"If you want to get to the nearest town, we head north. Venin's about a two-day ride."

"What kind of town is Venin?" Elliot asked as they began their journey with Chloé in the lead.

Chloé hummed. "It's kind of small. Nothing much goes on around there. It's a peaceful town. Everyone kind of knows everyone. But the night market is nice." She brightened. "The townspeople hold musicals and dances in the town square. The food is good, and they sell fairly decent clothes. Of course, nothing beats the quality my personal seamstress makes."

Elliot listened to Chloé ramble. Being around another girl who wasn't Lily was a different experience. While Lily was tomboyish and practical, Chloé seemed to enjoy feminine things like dressing up. Her clothes were more intricate than their own and had frills and lace. She wore dresses and shoes that made her appear taller. Compared to the simplicity of elven clothing, there was no practical reason for the attire. It was purely aesthetic.

They reached the dense forest by nightfall and settled down in a clearing. The temperature dropped from uncomfortably hot to pleasantly cool. Chloé was already asleep. She snoozed lightly, lying on top of the blankets they'd brought with them.

Minari had left to survey the area, leaving Elliot alone with the sleeping nix. He fumbled with his pendant as he sat by the campfire. His arms rested on his knees. The orange light was mesmerizing. He watched the flames flicker up, swaying side to side from the slight breeze.

He wondered how his mother was doing. They hadn't had a proper goodbye, and he still regretted it. Thinking back to her tear-streaked face and puffy eyes created knots in his stomach.

He wondered how his father was doing. Was he managing the scouts well? Had they lost a valuable scout because Minari had to go with him?

He wondered how Lily was doing. Was she handling herself all right? Maybe she had to pick up Minari's duties now.

And, at last, he wondered how Stella was doing. Everything had seemed normal when he'd seen her in the Moon Shrine, but how much longer could she keep a smile on her face as she pretended to be the oracle?

A soft whimper broke Elliot from his thoughts.

Chloé was turning, her body getting tangled in the blankets. She was mumbling, a sheen of sweat on her forehead, her brows furrowed. She tossed around, and her arms began to thrash.

Elliot quickly made his way to the distressed nix. He grabbed one of her hands and sandwiched it between his. "Chloé," he said.

Chloé didn't wake. She continued to stir and pull at her arm. Elliot kept his grip on her hand. He called out to her again, louder this time. Her movements slowed, but her expression was still strained.

"Daddy," Chloé whispered. "Mommy . . ."

Elliot's breath caught in his throat, and he tightened his grip. She missed her family. He ached to see his too, but he didn't have a choice. Chloé had left her home to follow Elliot and Minari. She was a warrior, but she didn't know that. She could've lived a normal life if it weren't for him. He pressed her hand against his chest, hoping the beating of his heart would calm her.

After a few moments, Chloé's breathing relaxed. Her eyes blinked open.

"Hey," Elliot said softly.

Chloé's eyes widened, and she yanked her hand away. She sat up, pulling the blankets over her body. Her cheeks flushed. "E-Elliot! Wh-what are you doing here?"

"You were having a nightmare. I tried waking you up, but it didn't work. So, I just held your hand."

"Y-you held my hand!" Chloé turned away. "You held my hand . . ."

"Sorry if that was overstepping." Elliot frowned. Had he done something wrong?

Chloé shook her head. "Thank you," she whispered. "It was just a bad dream."

Elliot sighed. Relief washed over him. "I'm glad I could help. Do you want to talk about it?"

Chloé lowered the blanket and began playing with the seams. "I don't really know what it was about, but I was running through the hallways at home. No one was around, and I was alone. It was like I was lost in a maze with no exit. Every door I open created a fog of darkness, and I eventually couldn't see anything. That was when I heard a soft beating. It was comforting through the silence. Then there was a light." She peeked shyly at Elliot. "It was probably your warmth that brought me out. So . . . thank you, again."

Elliot couldn't stop himself from smiling. "I'm sure you'd do the same for me. If I ever get lost in a dark and scary maze, you'll get me out."

"Of course!" Chloé turned her body to face Elliot, but her eyes were lowered. "We're friends . . . right?"

Elliot took Chloé's hand in his. "Why wouldn't we be? Friends help each other out, right?"

Chloé's eyes met Elliot's. She beamed. "Yes! Friends help each other out." She suddenly frowned. "I'm really sorry about making you my property, even if it's just an act. I hope you understand I can't let you two walk freely. I have an image as a council member to upkeep . . ."

"I'm sure if there was another way, you would've taken it, Chloé. Although I'm sure Minari would've loved not having to do this." Elliot chuckled.

Chloé slouched and pushed out her bottom lip. "Purple Hair can stay my property. He's not as nice as you."

"I'm sure you two will get along. Eventually."

Chloé hummed. "Maybe. Only if I have to."

Chloé had fallen back asleep when Minari finally returned. Minari raised an eyebrow, and Elliot gave him a small smile. He was still holding onto Chloé's hand, making sure the nightmares didn't find their way back to the sleeping nix.

20
NEW

Elliot and Minari traveled the remaining road on their feet when they were ten miles away from Venin. Chloé didn't want to risk any travelers seeing them riding their ovis. Property wasn't supposed to have that luxury, after all. Minari had stripped his daggers and hidden them inside one of Xander's saddlebags. A long rope attached Xeno and Xander to Chloé's mare. The two elves walked behind them.

The golden light splashed across the town, bouncing up the walls of the brick buildings. They followed Chloé, keeping their heads down. Whispers and murmurs reached their ears. Elliot couldn't make out full sentences, but he would occasionally hear "savages" and "barbarians." Some townspeople wanted to make sure they heard them.

"Wait here." Chloé's words were sharp. She entered a building. Elliot looked at his boots. He swallowed the urge to look up to see the town. He'd only seen the entrance briefly before Minari had reminded him to keep his head low. Luckily, no one had seen the blunder.

It wasn't long before Chloé returned with another figure.

"These three?" he asked.

"Yes. I expect them all to be well fed and kept for the duration of our stay," Chloé said.

"Guaranteed, Miss Gemme. Would you like me to bring the luggage into your room?"

"Yes. I will head over there first with my property." Chloé turned her attention to Elliot and Minari. "You two come with me." She used the same curt tone as earlier.

Bursts of laughter and conversation filled the inn. Though Elliot couldn't see it, he knew the inn was bustling with people. The atmosphere was jolly, and he found himself hoping to one day be a part of the event. But for now, he needed to keep this farce.

They proceeded up the stairs, their heads still kept down. Chloé unlocked one of the doors in the hallway, and the three of them entered.

As soon as Minari shut the door behind them, Elliot took a glance around the room. It was larger than his bedroom. There was a wooden dresser, a desk, and one bed. There was plenty of floor space because of the minimal furniture.

Chloé collapsed on the bed with her arms outstretched. "Finally, a bed."

"You only slept on the ground for a day," Minari said. He put his hands on his hips and looked around. "And I take it we're going to be sleeping on the floor."

"You're property. At least it's clean."

Minari pressed his shoulder and twisted his arm. "How long are we staying here?"

"I booked this room for five nights. That's enough time for you to gather information, right?" Chloé leaned up, her attention now on Elliot. "Sorry you have to sleep on the ground again. I really can't do much about it."

"It's not a problem." Elliot flashed a smile. A week in the cramped dungeon and a day and a half of traveling had taken a toll on his body. He ignored how much his lower back ached and how stiff his shoulders were. Sleeping on the hardwood floor wasn't appealing, but he needed to get used to it.

There was a knock on the door. "Miss Gemme, I've brought your luggage, but there seems to be a problem," said a muffled voice.

"Sit on the floor and face the wall," Chloé whispered. Elliot and Minari scrambled to a corner. "Come in," she called.

The door opened. Redd's chirping filled the room as he flew in.

"Miss Gemme, I apologize. Your songbird refused to stay with your mare and goats," he said. His feet shuffled against the floor as he dragged the saddlebags in.

"It's all right. Just leave my stuff there. I'd like to request three orders of your specialty for tonight. And some plain bread and water for my property."

"Three orders?"

"Did I stutter? I am famished from my journey."

"N-no. Your order will be ready in an hour, Miss Gemme. That is when dinner hour starts."

"That's fine."

The man clicked the door behind him.

Elliot found it difficult to sleep on the floor. Even with his cloak acting as a pillow and the blankets acting as a makeshift bed, his clothes didn't provide enough warmth. He turned to Minari, wondering how he could fall asleep so easily. He was on his back, his hands clasped over his stomach. Unlike Elliot, he had no pillow or blankets. The hard floor pressed uncomfortably against Elliot's hip through the shallow cushioning. He turned onto his stomach and tucked his arms underneath the cloak. He closed his eyes, willing his body to sleep.

He didn't know how long he lay there before he realized sleep wasn't coming to him anytime soon. He got up and made his way to the window. The room was on the third floor, allowing him to see parts of what he assumed was the town square. A few torches were lit around it, and merchants moved around, packing up their stalls for the night. The people were taller than Chloé but shorter than him or Minari. The tips of their ears were rounded. They were humans.

Elliot watched them put their belongings away in wagons and drape tarps over their tables. The torches were eventually put out, and soon the square was lit only with moonlight. He looked up at the sky. Bright stars glimmered against the black night, and the moon was a waning gibbous. His stomach grumbled, indicating he had been up for too long. Even though Chloé had ordered three meals and given two of the three to him and Minari, the portions weren't large. He assumed since Chloé was a nix, the innkeeper prepared the portions accordingly. Chloé was smaller than either of the two elves, so it made sense for her to need less food.

He sat next to Minari, about to lie down. Minari jerked up. Elliot flinched at the sudden movement. "Minari?" he whispered.

"Shh."

Elliot didn't move; he didn't even breathe. He stayed completely still. A chill ran up his spine as he gulped. He couldn't hear anything, but Minari's eyes were darting across the ceiling.

Minari grabbed his curved daggers and jumped in front of the window. The pane shattered, sending shards across the floor. A figure swept in through the exposed window. The intruder's golden eyes pierced through the night, his slate-colored cloak draped over half his body. Both of his hands gripped the hilt of a rapier.

21
WHO

Chloé jolted awake from the sudden crash. She reached under her pillow and pulled out her pistols.

"Who are you?" Minari demanded.

Chloé scrambled off the bed and pointed Prim toward the intruder. If she wasn't careful, there would be major repercussions. Her beams were too wide to use in an enclosed space.

There was stomping and loud voices coming from down the hall.

"Wait! Please! You can't go down there!" It was the innkeeper.

"A chimera has been spotted snooping around here. We have the right to survey the area," a female voice said.

Chloé focused on the unknown figure's ear. He had an intricate piece on his left ear, contrary to the plain bronze cuffs chimeras wore.

"Please! A council member is in there—"

"A council member? Then we must hurry." There was an obnoxiously loud banging against the door. "I'm very sorry to disturb you, but we heard a loud noise from inside your room. If you do not answer within three seconds, I have no choice but to tear this door down."

Chloé couldn't risk them seeing Minari with his daggers out. She didn't want to resort to this, but there wasn't much of a choice. She turned her palm toward the elf before squeezing her hand closed.

Minari released his daggers and dropped to one knee, clutching the collar. The door slammed opened. The intruder glanced past them before he turned and leapt out the window.

Chloé relaxed her hand. Minari choked and coughed, gasping for air. She bit the inside of her cheek. She hadn't meant to use that much magic.

"Dammit, he got away," the female said. Her hips swayed as she strode into the room and peered out the window. There was a silver bow strapped against her back. "We barely missed him. Looks like he's heading north."

"Excuse me," Chloé said. "Care to explain what's going on?" She needed to take the attention away from Elliot and Minari. The others with the woman stared at the elves with curious, disgusted eyes.

"Ah, I'm sorry." The woman twirled. Her beige trench coat swayed from the movement. There was a brooch over her left breast. It was a silver oval with a straight line running across horizontally. "I'm Charlotte, an officer from Oasis."

Oasis was an official guild of hunters in charge of capturing chimeras who were seen trespassing into human towns and cities. The difference between an official guild and a nonofficial guild was that they had the approval of the council to perform their duties. They worked alongside law enforcers but didn't receive the same training as them.

The innkeeper rushed in. "Miss Gemme, I deeply apologize for the ruckus this late at night. Please allow me to relocate your room so I can clean this mess up."

"Wait," Charlotte said, lifting a hand. "Miss Gemme and these two . . . *elves* are valuable witnesses. I want to know what happened. Every detail."

The innkeeper rubbed his hands. "I'm sure this can wait until morning."

Charlotte crossed her arms. "No, it's best to ask when details are still fresh within their memories. Can these two speak common tongue?" She motioned toward Minari and Elliot.

"There's no point in speaking with them. They're just property," Chloé said.

"Witnesses are witnesses, Miss Gemme, whether they are property or not. I'm sure you can understand that. It's important that we keep the chimeras in check."

Chloé didn't like the stern voice Charlotte was using. She refused to be swayed. "I, and only I, will speak to you regarding this matter. If you do not accept these terms, then leave my room. I may have been killed if it wasn't for my property. Actually, I probably would have been killed."

Charlotte raised her brows. "That's what property is

for. Why do you make it sound like they are important?"

Chloé mentally cursed. She hadn't meant to make it appear like she was thankful toward them. She needed to twist the narrative. "Yes, that is what they are here for, but these two are elves—a rare commodity. They cannot be easily replaced."

Charlotte hummed. "True. I can agree with you that they are indeed a rare commodity." She shifted her attention to the innkeeper. "Could you provide us a private room?"

He looked over at Chloé, who nodded in return. "Yes, yes, of course. Please come this way."

Chloé placed Prim in her holster before reaching under the pillow and tucking Rose into the other. "Keep everything here. I want nothing moved without my supervision."

"At least allow me to clean the glass shards."

"Only that."

The innkeeper led Chloé and Charlotte to a room on the second floor. It was half the size of her rented room, with a smaller bed and a single desk. Charlotte motioned for Chloé to sit in the only available chair after flicking the oil lamp on.

Chloé crossed her legs and her arms. "Well, what did you want to ask?" She hoped the interrogation wouldn't take long.

Charlotte placed her hands on the edge of the table and leaned forward. "What happened first?"

Chloé cocked a brow. "First? Well, first I was sleeping."

"And then?"

"I heard the window shatter. Next thing I knew, the chimera was in my room."

"Anything else?" Charlotte leaned even closer.

"No. That's all until you barged into my room with all your men." Thievery was common in cities far away from the capital, and Venin was the farthest away. It wouldn't be shocking if the chimera had been lurking in the shadows when they'd entered the town. The color of her mare was a dead giveaway for who she was since the king gave council members gray mares for their travels. With the addition of two ovis, both with saddlebags, it was obvious they would be targeted. The chimera thief probably hadn't accounted for Minari's abilities.

"Well, that's unfortunate." Charlotte pushed herself off the table. "We've been trying to capture that chimera for a while now. There have been reports of him ransacking homes and shops."

"Just him?"

"Yes. He's a pretty slippery fella." Charlotte looked at her nails. "He's been giving us the runaround for a month or so."

"What kind of chimera is he?"

"A snake. I guess that's why he's so slippery to catch, huh? The thing keeps slithering away." Charlotte's eyes widened, and a quiet gasp left her lips. She leaned back against the desk. "Wait. Was he wielding a weapon?"

"Two rapiers."

Charlotte cursed under her breath. "The damn thing actually has the nerve to use a piece of history." She scrunched her face. "His most recent acquisition was a set of rapiers used by one of King Valentine I's knights."

That was odd. Why hadn't such an important piece been kept in the kingdom's treasury? "How did he get that?"

"It was being transported to a well-known blacksmith in Trox. His name slips my mind. King Valentine VI wanted to repair it. Prince Alexander is adamant about learning how to dual wield and wanted to use the same weapons as the knight from the first king's era."

Chloé's eyes narrowed. "You seem to know a lot about this."

"Ah, that's because my brother was in charge of transporting the rapiers. His carriage was ransacked during the journey. I have a personal grudge against the chimera, you could say."

"Your name is Charlotte, you said?" Chloé was skeptical. What kind of person was her brother if the king had trusted him with such an important piece?

"Oops, I didn't mention my family name, did I? Truth is, my men don't know which family I'm from. I kind of hate the formalities." Charlotte tucked her blonde hair behind an ear and extended her hand. "Charlotte Hawthorne. It was a pleasure to meet you, Miss Chloé Gemme. Though I wish the circumstances had been better."

Chloé blinked, accepting the hand. She hadn't expected the woman to be a Hawthorne. They were an aristocratic family with close ties to the knights. "I find it hard to believe a chimera would rob the Hawthornes."

"He only strikes when he knows everyone should be dead asleep. My brother wasn't expecting the attack. The chimera singlehandedly wiped out his men and stole the rapiers. My brother was lucky he made it out of there alive." Charlotte frowned. "He's no ordinary chimera, and he's a threat to us. They should've kept to themselves when King Valentine III set them free from our ownership. I know King Valentine VI is very close to taking their freedom away."

Chloé shrugged. That was a topic discussed occasionally during assemblies. "Why hasn't he? The chimeras were meant to be our property in the first place, so why not?"

Charlotte raised her hands. "That's exactly it! I feel the same. Our ancestors created them, so why can't we use them for ourselves? King Valentine III must have had a soft spot for those mutts."

Not wanting to stay any longer, Chloé stood. "If there's nothing else you want to ask me, I should get back to my room."

"Oh. We went off topic, didn't we?" Charlotte gave a crooked smile. "One last question."

"Yes?"

"Why do you have elves as your property? And how come the one with purple hair has daggers?"

Chloé's blood ran cold. She'd hoped to avoid the question. She hadn't expected Charlotte to be observant enough to have noticed the daggers. "I found them by the mountains on one of my patrols. I took them in and forced them to be my property."

"Right. Nixen have binding collars. That would

make sense."

"I went through the long ordeal of punishing them and breaking their will. They won't defy me."

Charlotte's eyes never left Chloé. Her brown orbs ran up and down. "All right. You've had them for some time then. That's reasonable. I can't imagine it was easy breaking the will of savages."

"They're useful," Chloé said, avoiding the open-ended statement.

"Oh, absolutely. The elf protected you from the chimera, after all. Anyway, sorry for keeping you, Miss Gemme. I hope the rest of your night is pleasant. And sorry again for the ruckus."

"Thank you. I don't know how much help I provided, but I hope you catch the chimera soon." Chloé took her leave and traveled up the stairs back into her room.

The glass had been cleaned up, as promised. Elliot and Minari were sitting on the floor by the bedside, whispering to each other. "Did the innkeeper say anything to you?" she asked.

Elliot shook his head.

"Did you really have to do that?" Minari sneered. "I thought my neck was going to snap in half."

Chloé frowned and moved to sit on the bed. "I had to do something fast. I couldn't let them barge in and see you with your daggers. You're supposed to be property. I had to make up some lie to Charlotte."

Minari shot her a side-glance, his eyes dangerously narrow. "If you jeopardize my duty to protect Elliot again, I *will* kill you."

"Minari, it's fine. No one got hurt," Elliot said, placing a hand on Minari's shoulder.

"It's not a guarantee there won't be casualties next time. I need to be there to protect you."

"I could've handled the situation fine without you," Chloé said.

Minari snorted. "We would have all been dead if I'd left it to you. You were still asleep when the intruder broke through the window."

"You just have freakish hearing." When Minari didn't retort, Chloé thought she'd won the battle, but a knock told her otherwise.

"Miss Gemme, I've prepared another room for you. You can move over there now, and I'll take your luggage," the innkeeper said.

She realized Minari had heard the innkeeper come up the hallway and had silenced himself. It wasn't that she'd won the argument. Instead, Minari had plainly proven his point. The way he could probably hear a pin drop made her glad she was on his side of the fence rather than the opposite, even if they had their disagreements.

22
GONE

Elliot and Minari spent the next three days at Chloé's heel. They behaved as property in front of the public eye. The only relief from the act was when they were in the privacy of the inn.

Minari was still furious from two nights prior. The collar around his neck had constricted him so much he hadn't been able to take in a single breath. A burst of pain had shocked his entire body, briefly immobilizing him. He had never experienced that amount of pain before, and it had made him feel powerless.

It was their last night in Venin, and so far Minari couldn't care less what happened in the small town. Based on what he'd observed just from hearing and quick side-glances, only humans inhabited it. They would often throw words at him and Elliot, but for the most part it was harmless. There'd been times in the night market when some who'd had a little too much ale would try to get physical with them, but Chloé quickly dispelled such situations.

Minari wasn't going to risk running into someone who was far too drunk to notice Chloé was a council member. He secretly buckled the belt that held his curved daggers under his cloak before leaving the inn. They had finished dinner, so it was going to be the last night in town.

Chloé led them straight to the town square.

"There's supposed to be a performance from a traveling band called Minerva," Chloé said. "I've heard of them but have never seen them in person. I'll let you two watch." She raised her voice at the last statement, making sure those around them heard her.

It was a signal giving Elliot and Minari permission to raise their heads.

They settled near the front of the forming circle. The band was composed of three violinists and a dancer. People packed in, excited to see the traveling performers. Minari bit his lip, not wanting to snap every time someone bumped into either him or Elliot. The two of them were eventually pushed to the far back. Chloé was too engrossed to notice being separated from them. There were three taps, then the group performed their first piece.

"Inconsiderate piece of—"

"Minari," Elliot whispered. "It's fine. We can still see the performance."

No one paid any attention to them. The band drowned their voices.

"I don't see why we have to stay here."

Elliot gave Minari a sheepish smile. "Sorry you have to put up with me."

"It's not you, Elliot. It's Chloé."

"Well, we're with Chloé because I want her to be with us."

"It still amazes me she believes we want to travel around the lower lands but doesn't believe you're the oracle." Minari crossed his arms. "The lies they put in the books down here . . ."

"I hoped having her with us would make our journey easier."

"It does. That's what bothers me. We have to rely on her sass to get us anywhere."

Elliot elbowed Minari. "Remember, she was the one who saved us from the giant scorpion."

Minari rolled his eyes. How could he forget? It slightly wounded his pride, but he was grateful she'd saved them. He couldn't deny their journey could've been cut short if not for her. Maybe putting up with her antics was another method of repayment.

"Let's make the most out of this journey. I know I still have to fulfill the prophecy, but it would be nice to at least experience life down here; plus, meeting Chloé set aside some of my worries."

"Nice to know you were still worrying even with me at your side."

"You know I didn't mean it like that."

Minari didn't answer. It eased him to know Elliot was less anxious with the discovery of one warrior, but he still didn't trust Chloé to protect Elliot.

It was his duty to keep him safe, and he intended to keep it that way.

Minari stifled down a yawn. They'd been watching the performers for what felt like hours. The townspeople were still as captivated as when they'd first started. Elliot's eyes never left them either. He was completely enthralled. His eyes sparkled at the dancer. Her movements were fluid like water. Her body swayed in unity with the strings.

A shuffling of leaves caught his attention. It sounded forceful, different from how a simple breeze would graze them. He peered over his shoulder, eyes narrowing. He scanned the bushes and heard the sound again, but there was no movement. His senses gnawed at him, and his skin prickled. He looked over at Elliot, who was still watching the performance. The noise happened again. Minari reflexively reached for his daggers.

"Elliot," Minari said.

Elliot hummed, eyes still forward.

"There's something around here. I'm going to scout the area. Stay here, and don't move." Minari hoped whoever was lurking in the shadows would be too intimidated to do anything out in the open.

Minari slipped away. He walked in long strides, eyes darting toward every corner. Out of habit, his own footsteps didn't make a sound. He tuned out the music, the conversational buzz, and the laughter. The only noise that reached his ears was his own breathing. He made multiple rounds around the town square, not wanting to stray too far from Elliot.

And then a scream. It came straight from the heart of the crowd.

"Chimeras!"

"Catch them!"

"They stole my bracelet!"

"My bag!"

The crowd dispersed like an unorganized stampede. People ran in different directions, tripping over one another. A group of figures clad in black clawed and grabbed anything they could get their hands on. The band stopped playing, already running through the chaos.

Minari rushed back to Elliot, sidestepping through waves of people. Instead of finding Elliot, he spotted Chloé. She was frantically looking around. Her eyes widened when they landed on Minari.

"Where's Elliot?" Chloé asked. "How come he isn't with you?"

Minari's body ran cold. Images of the intruder from the other night flashed before him. Was the intruder after Elliot? "I have to find him."

"He should be around here. He's an elf; he's hard to miss."

Minari glared. He didn't appreciate Chloé's lax behavior. It was true it should be easy to spot Elliot in a sea of humans, but that was precisely why worry filled his every nerve. He didn't think humans were going to provide the same hospitality as Chloé.

There were much worse things than being locked up in a dungeon.

"I have to find him," Minari said. "He might still be around."

Chloé grabbed his arm. "You can't. It's already bad enough you're wandering around without me."

Minari pulled his arm out of Chloé's grip. "Forget the property act. You think I'm going to worry about that when my best friend is missing?" His blood boiled. It took everything he had to keep his body from shaking.

"You know I can force you to come with me, right?"

Minari snapped. He hadn't regretted listening to Elliot until now. The fact that he'd let Chloé place this magic collar around his neck was a mistake. But he couldn't back down. He needed to show her that he wasn't afraid of her. He stepped into Chloé's personal space. He looked at her, eyes narrow. "You do that, and I *will* kill you." It wasn't a threat. It was a promise.

Chloé's bottom lip quivered ever so slightly, and her shoulders stiffened at the proximity. She was scared, as she ought to be. He was faster than her, and she knew it.

Minari took a step back. "Don't get in my way. I will find him." He paced around where he'd last seen Elliot, hoping to find any clues. His eyes caught something on the ground. He quickly bent down, picking up the fallen item. He looked at it with shaky hands.

It was the pendant Lily had made.

The string was snapped, clear that it had been forcibly taken off.

Minari's ears buzzed, and his body went cold. His mouth felt incredibly dry as he tried to swallow. The world spun around him.

This couldn't be happening.

Elliot was gone.

23
THREAT

Lily jumped through the trees, her feet featherlight against the branches, which barely swung as she leapt off. It had been two weeks since Elliot and Minari had left. She wondered how many places they'd already visited and how many different kinds of people they'd met.

Mistfall was peaceful, but she felt like it was the calm before the storm.

The villagers had started to take notice of the two missing elves. They often asked Lady Mayleen and Errol where they were. The lie they'd come up with was they were training in private within the Moon Shrine. If there was a reason as to why they couldn't know the truth, she didn't know it.

Lily had learned about Elliot's true identity out of pure coincidence. The night she'd followed Minari and Errol, she'd overheard Errol scolding the younger elf about what Elliot was. She hadn't understood it until a couple nights later.

She hadn't been able to sleep on that particular night. She'd been staring out the window, looking at the moon when she'd seen Minari leading Elliot somewhere. Considering the direction they were going, it had looked like they were moving toward the Moon Shrine.

Luckily, Lily had still been in her scout's uniform. She knew she wasn't going to sleep anytime soon, so she hadn't bothered to change. She'd hurried out the door and followed.

It hadn't taken long for Lily to lose sight of them. She mentally cursed. She really had to start working on her stamina. Slowing to a stop, she leaned against a tree to catch her breath.

That was when things got weird.

Dark shadows appeared in the forest. They floated, unattached to a physical body. Lily had to blink a few times and rubbed her eyes to make sure she wasn't imagining it. Then they spoke. At first it was gurgled noises, but eventually she was able to make out what they were saying.

"*Oracle.*"

"*Awake.*"

"*Him.*"

"*Must.*"

"*Now.*"

The words were broken up, but it was clear to her that Stella was not the oracle. Based on observation alone, it was Elliot who was the oracle. Minari must have known.

Errol must have known. The conversation in the captain's quarters made sense. Errol wanted Elliot's identity kept a secret until his last moments of being a normal elf. But that made little sense. Why keep it a secret?

Lily's head spun with all the questions. She continued to walk toward the shrine, and the shadows followed her. After a few moments, she stopped, and the shadows stopped. As odd as the transparent figures were, she didn't feel threatened by them. Were they messengers of sorts? Could this be Vylantra's doing?

Before she could go any farther, Alder appeared before her. His eyes narrowed and glowed red. The shadows evaporated, and so did her consciousness.

The next thing Lily knew, she was waking up in her bed. The morning sun hadn't cracked yet. Her clothes had somehow been changed from her scout's uniform to her casual wear. Her gut twisted. Something told her she needed to hurry or she would be too late. She grabbed one of her trusted daggers from her desk and rushed out.

Elliot and Minari were nearing the gates. They were leaving. She called out to them, and fortunately they stopped. They shared their goodbyes, and she gave Elliot her dagger. She didn't understand the situation fully, but she at least wanted to be a part of Elliot's journey.

They'd left, and Lily had been left feeling empty. She was alone now.

But she had a job to do.

They would have a home waiting for them when they returned.

In the midst of reminiscing, Lily missed her footing

on a branch and went tumbling down. She cried out as she landed. She rolled onto her back, clutching her throbbing shoulder. Part of her was glad Minari wasn't around to ridicule her for making such an amateur move. One of the first rules of being a scout was to have a clear mind and always be alert.

Lily lay on the grass, her eyes trained on the stars. She controlled her breathing, in and out. With a forceful grip on her shoulder, she popped the dislocated joint back into its socket. She bit her lip, attempting to hold back a yell, but she couldn't stop a strained groan from escaping. "I'm never going to do that again," she mumbled to herself.

The sound of rustling leaves caused her body to freeze. She swallowed, forcing it down as it was getting caught in her throat. There shouldn't have been anyone near her. Captain Errol and Commander Silas had organized the scouts so their paths wouldn't overlap.

The pain now forgotten, she got up and hid within the shadows. The noise wasn't too far. Her eyes scanned the area. It was silent. The wind picked up, brushing the branches and leaves together. Lily pushed her hair out of her eyes and tucked it behind her ear.

"Excuse me."

Lily's body jerked. Her heart was beating painfully against her chest. There was someone behind her with a voice she didn't recognize.

And she hadn't even heard them coming.

Lily turned, hands inching toward her daggers.

A woman. The top of her head reached Lily's chest. Her clothing was strange, full of frills and lace. It wouldn't have been practical if she'd worn the attire while climbing up the mountains. Her footwear arched her feet onto her toes, making her appear taller than she actually was. Her complexion was a soft brown, and she had deep maroon hair. The unknown woman wrapped a curl around her finger. She smiled at Lily.

"Hello there. Could you help me?" she asked.

Lily struggled to respond. Her throat was tight. She spewed out incoherent words before answering. "Where did you come from?"

The woman blinked. She tilted her head. "What do you mean?" She pointed to her left. "I came from down there."

"How did you get here?" Lily's fingers wrapped around her dagger behind her back.

"I walked." She let go of the curl she was playing with. "Could you help me? I got lost while looking for items I misplaced."

Lily pressed her lips together. Lost items. "What did you lose?" She held her breath.

"I lost my scarf and my handkerchief."

Scarf.

The red scarf Rowen had found.

Handkerchief.

The black, silk handkerchief Commander Silas had found.

The person in front of her was the intruder.

Lily unsheathed her blade, and within the blink of an eye she'd slit the intruder's throat.

The woman's mouth gaped, gargling noises escaping

her lips. She fell to her knees, then onto her side. Her eyes stayed wide open as she lost the spark of life. Blood gushed from her neck.

There was no doubt in Lily's mind that this woman was the intruder who had been lurking around Mistfall. The items she'd lost were the same exact ones that'd been found weeks prior. She brought the curved blade to her lips, and her tongue slid across the warm liquid.

The threat had been eradicated.

Mission complete.

24
MISSING

Chloé nearly collapsed to her knees when she saw Minari gripping Elliot's pendant close to him. She knew what it meant. He wasn't here. He was missing. She steeled herself when she heard shouting. It was Oasis, and they were clearing out the town square. Chloé pulled Minari off the ground. "We have to get out of here."

"Elliot. Elliot, he's—"

"Don't. Let's just get out of here." There were too many people around. The chaos was suffocating. She needed to get them back to the inn where it was safe.

Chloé did her best to lead Minari back to the inn. He was in a stupor but seemed to snap out of it when townspeople began to throw slurs at him, calling him a barbarian, a savage. Minari disregarded their property protocol completely. He sneered and glared at anyone who bumped into him or even tried to say something. It was exhausting, and Chloé didn't have the energy to even try to stop him. Everything had been going so well too . . . and then this happened.

Chloé slammed the door shut when they returned to the inn. She took a deep breath, trying to calm herself down. "Could you at least be a little less conspicuous? You're supposed to be my property." She couldn't hide the slight quiver in her voice.

Minari had his back to Chloé. "I already told you. I. Don't. Care." He began picking up the rest of his daggers.

"What are you doing?" Chloé's voice cracked.

"I'm going to find Elliot. What do you think I'm doing?" Minari's voice was clipped.

Chloé paced over. "You can't just leave."

Minari didn't stop. He was being rash. The townspeople were already on high alert because of the chimera raid. They wouldn't appreciate another outsider wandering around their grounds.

Chloé grabbed his arm for the second time that night. She needed him to stay. "I want to look for Elliot too, but nothing good will happen if you go out there. The townspeople already don't like you, and you wandering out there after the recent event will only aggravate them more. Wait until the morning."

"*Morning?*" Minari scoffed. "You want me to wait until *morning* to look for Elliot? You are out of your mind." He jerked his arm away. "Stay here if you want. I'm leaving." He shot Chloé a look. "And *do not* stop me."

Minari had already attached all of his daggers back

on. Any wrong move and she didn't doubt he would stab her.

An emptiness had filled her chest when she hadn't been able to find Elliot. Dread had overflowed when she'd spotted Minari alone. She'd finally found someone she wanted to call a true friend, and he'd been ripped away from her, just like her parents had been removed from her life ten years ago.

Chloé had grown up believing she could only rely on herself. It was only her and Cecilia in the Gemme manor. She had dismissed her other servants, as they'd only been there with the intention to take advantage of the child master. Cecilia was the only one she could trust. She was the closest to a companion Chloé had.

When she'd met Elliot, she'd been so overwhelmed with warmth that she'd let herself trust him. She'd let her guard down, thinking Minari would keep him safe and she wouldn't lose anyone important again.

"I'm worried about him too," Chloé whispered.

Minari made a noise between a chuckle and a gag. "You're worried? If you're so worried, why not do something about it instead of returning here? Sitting here isn't going to bring us any closer to finding Elliot!"

"I told you, right now isn't a good time to leave! I may be a council member, but that doesn't mean I can waltz my way around places without considering how the townspeople feel. It's bad enough you two are elves, and everyone hates elves!"

"If your reputation is so important, then drop it. Drop us. Pretend you never associated with us."

Cold. Chloé felt cold. She didn't want to be alone. Not again. "No!" She yanked Minari's sleeve. "I want to find Elliot too, but please understand now isn't a good time. The town is in disarray, and you stick out too much." She tightened her grip. "Please stay here." With the townspeople on edge, it wouldn't be a good look for her if she was wondering out with an elf.

Minari didn't jerk his arm away. She felt his shoulders relaxing. "Sitting here isn't going to help either. The longer we wait, the farther away he gets."

"I know that. I'll help you look." Chloé began to shake. "Just don't leave me," she whispered. Her vision blurred as tears threatened to fall.

Minari was silent, and Chloé thought maybe Minari would stay. She let go of his arm.

"I'm not staying here."

His words cut through her core.

"It's my duty to protect Elliot. I have no obligation to listen to you." Minari glanced around the room. "Redd isn't here."

The situation was so chaotic that Chloé hadn't noticed the absent songbird. The door and window were closed. How had he gotten out? Had someone entered their room while they were gone? But none of their belongings had been moved.

Minari didn't seem bothered by the missing bird, already making his way to the door.

There was a sudden knock.

Minari's hand was on the door handle. He paused before opening it.

The dancer from Minerva stood on the other side, though her attire differed from what she'd worn before. Her costume had been replaced with black, leather boots and a black, leather coat that reached her knees. Her black hair was tied in a ponytail.

"Good evening." She smiled. There were freckles across her cheeks and bright red lipstick on her lips.

Minari didn't return the greeting. He sidestepped and pushed forward.

"Wait," she said. "You're looking for your friend, right?"

That stopped Minari. "Do you know something?"

"I got a glimpse of him during the commotion," she said. "We should take this inside, no?"

Minari pinched his lips. He glanced at the dancer, then at Chloé. There was hope written in his eyes. The eye contact between them was brief before he turned away. He shifted where he stood before walking back into the room. The dancer followed, closing the door.

Minari crossed his arms. "Well?"

"I saw him being taken away by a few chimeras," she said.

"The ones who were stealing from the townspeople?" Chloé asked. She furrowed her brow. How had she noticed that in the midst of the chaos? She glanced at Minari. He had his full attention on the dancer. Though they didn't know who she was, listening to what she had to say could prove to be useful. They would need to trust her for now.

"Yes. He put up a fight, but it looked like they drugged him, then they hauled him away."

"Did you see where they took him?" Minari asked.

"I saw them leave Venin and head north."

Minari reached for the door again.

"You're going to go after him now?" the woman asked.

"They took him north, so that's where I'm going."

"Chimeras are extremely fast. Even if you left now, you wouldn't be able to catch up to them."

That didn't deter Minari. His hand was already on the handle.

"I can help you. Hear me out."

Minari let out an aggravated sigh. "What? What could you possibly offer that I can't already do myself?"

"I can help you locate your friend, and I can do it quicker than you can, especially as an elf." When Minari made no move to leave, she continued. "I'm the leader of a guild called Nighthawk. We gather intel and trade that intel for coin. I'm willing to bet my men already have information regarding your friend. The information could prove valuable during your search. What do you say?"

"How much?" Chloé asked. Coin was no problem for her, and if it helped rescue Elliot, she'd spend as much as she needed to.

"The payment is something only you can do, Miss Gemme." The dancer turned her attention to the nix. Her amber orbs landed on Chloé's red eyes. "In return for providing intel on your missing property, I want you to disband Oasis. As a council member, you can persuade the table and have them formally gone."

Chloé frowned. It was an odd request. As far as she

knew, Oasis abided by the law and worked to enforce it. They kept chimeras in check, making sure they stayed within their lands. The council had approved them, naming them an official guild, and it would be difficult to persuade them to revoke the approval.

"You are wondering why, aren't you? I can tell by your face."

"Well, frankly, yes. If it were coin, I could easily give you what you want, but this is something I can't guarantee."

The dancer smiled, a slight glint in her eyes. "I believe this is something you can do, Miss Gemme. You have the ability as a council member. But if you don't think you can do it, then I'm afraid I won't help. My services aren't free."

"I . . ." Chloé glanced at Minari. He stared at her, almost hopeful. He wanted her to take this offer. Any lead on Elliot would aid in the search for him.

"If you're worried about a deadline, don't be. As long as it happens within your lifetime. But I will know if you do not attempt to disband them. Remember, I have eyes and ears everywhere."

Chloé had to accept this offer. She couldn't let Elliot slip through her fingers. She wouldn't be alone. Not again. Not ever. "Okay, I accept."

The dancer clapped her hands. "Wonderful! I believe I owe you an introduction. My name is Bunnie."

"You already know who I am," Chloé said. It was common knowledge to know who the council members were.

"I do, but I don't know the name of your property."

"I'm Minari, and the friend I'm looking for is Elliot. Please, if you have any information, tell me." Minari's hard demeanor had disappeared. It was soft, frantic, and desperate, like this was his only chance left without running into his search blind.

"Like I said, I saw the chimeras heading north." Bunnie placed a hand on her hip, popping it to the side. "If you want detailed intel, it will have to wait. I will meet with my men when I'm done here. We can gather downstairs in the dining hall no later than ten in the morning. How does that sound?"

"We'll be there," Minari said.

"Ten sharp," Chloé added.

They would find Elliot. Chloé would make sure of it.

25
LOST

Elliot's body ached with a thrumming soreness. His joints cracked as he moved his arms and legs. His hands ran across cold grass. The scent of soil filled his nose. He opened his eyes and stared into the blue sky. A wave of memories surged through him.

The town square.

Minerva.

The dancer.

Shouting.

Black cloaks.

Darkness.

He jolted up, and the world immediately spun. He gripped his head, shutting his eyes. A familiar chirp reached his ears. It was Redd. He opened his eyes and almost lost his balance. Relief washed over him as the world stabilized.

"Hey, Redd."

Redd flew into his lap, chirping wildly.

Elliot heard a voice and the crunching of grass. Someone was approaching him. He twisted his body and came face-to-face with a tall, broad-chested male. His hair was a reddish brown, and he had deep brown eyes. There was a bronze cuff on his left ear. The cloak around his shoulders was like the one the intruder from a few nights ago had worn.

Elliot's blood ran cold. He scurried up, backing away. He was shocked to see the man was taller than he was.

The man spoke. The tone he used was gentle, and he didn't appear hostile. Elliot slightly relaxed but still kept his guard up. "I don't . . . understand what you're saying."

"Ah . . . common tongue?" the man said. "I've never seen someone like you around here before. I thought you were a new chimera the kingdom had concocted."

"Chimera?" Elliot dug through his memories. He'd heard the term before, once at the inn and once in the town square.

The man cocked his head. "You don't know what chimeras are?"

Elliot shook his head.

"Chimeras are . . . well, simply chimeras. We're half-human, half-animal. That's all you need to know."

Elliot's eyes widened slightly, but he didn't pry. He knew chimeras weren't a race mentioned in any of the records, but to find out they were half-human and half-animal wasn't something he would've thought. The man before him certainly looked human. Yes, he was taller and broader than the typical human, but Elliot didn't think too much of it. Mentioning he was half-animal made some sort of sense. Whatever animal he was half of probably gave him the larger physical stature. "Where am I?"

"We're in Scarstone Forest."

Elliot realized how pointless that information was. He had no idea where that was or how he'd ended up in the forest. He looked around. There was no one but the two of them in the clearing. "Where are the others?"

"Others? You mean the chimeras who kidnapped you?"

Elliot's eyes widened. His stomach dropped. Had he been separated from Minari and Chloé? "I was kidnapped? What do you mean?"

The man frowned. "The Outlawers kidnapped you. Probably wanted to trade you in for some coin or whatever they get from humans."

Outlawers? Trade? Elliot's stomach churned. He wanted to throw up. He was separated, lost in a forest, and together with a stranger.

"You're not from around here, are you?"

Elliot couldn't confess that he was from Mistfall, but he also knew nothing about the lower lands. He didn't know the names of any places except Blanc Grotto and Venin. He also couldn't just make up another place without sounding like an obvious fake. "No, no, I'm not from around here. I came from across the mountains."

"Across the mountains? I didn't know there was any-thing across the mountains."

"There's an island. I'm from a village called Rainwell." Elliot furrowed his brow. Rainwell? He'd made the name up, but it felt familiar. Had he read it in a book?

"Oh. That explains why the Outlawers wanted you then. You're definitely exotic, and the humans would've loved to have their hands on you."

Elliot was glad his lie had worked. He must've had a knack for creating believable lies, but he needed to get back to Minari and Chloé. "How far are we from Venin?"

"Venin?" The man pressed a finger against his chin. "Venin . . . I want to say four days away at your speed. If you walk as fast as a human, anyway."

"Four?" Elliot gaped. Just how long had he been out for?

"For us chimeras, that's about a day. We intercepted the Outlawers pretty early if you came from Venin."

"So . . . I haven't been out for long?"

"No, just about a day. We cured you of whatever poison they used to tranquilize you. Cleared your system of it."

"We?"

"Yes, I'm with someone else, but he's hunting right now." The man grinned. "It's his turn. His catches are usually very meaty."

Elliot's stomach did somersaults. The idea of meat made his body feel gross. "I should get back to Venin." A growl then emitted from the same organ that was revolting against the offered food.

"We don't mind if you have a meal with us. I don't know why, but my partner has a fascination with you, so I can't let you leave." The man's friendly demeanor shifted. "I can easily outrun and overpower you. You're pretty lanky, so I doubt you'd get far, anyway."

Elliot swallowed, slightly relieving his parched throat. He moved his hand over his pouch. He still had Lily's dagger. He could at least put up a fight if anything happened. He also had Vylantra's power. Maybe he could make a getaway. Maybe Redd could distract them too. Surely Alder could see the danger he was in, right? He took a step back. "I really need to get back to my friends." He tried to steady his voice, but it still came out with a slight quiver.

"I'm sure you do, but for now you're staying with us. Until I figure out why my partner is so interested in you, you are staying right here." The man crossed his arms. "You don't seem to have the same disgusting scent as humans. You don't smell like a nix or ethereal either. Tell me, what are you? What kind of people live in Rainwell?"

Elliot blinked. Was the man unaware of elves existing? If that was the case, then maybe it was safe to mention it. "I'm an elf."

"Elf?" The man looked Elliot up and down. "You do have a particular scent to you. Very . . . foresty. You smell of fresh, morning leaves. Rainwell is all elf then?"

"Elves. Yes, there are only elves there."

"What brought you and your friends over to this side? I can't imagine this place worth visiting."

Elliot used the same lie he'd told Chloé: He and his friend wanted to travel and see what the rest of Etheria was like. Living in a small village for so long had piqued their curiosity about the larger continent.

Relaying stories about Mistfall, even under the guise of Rainwell, to the taller male helped to alleviate the tension in his nerves. The man had saved him from the Outlawers, and he was grateful for that, but being kept in their custody still didn't sit well with him.

Elliot's mind flashed to Minari and Chloé. Minari was probably tearing Venin and any nearby area apart just to look for him. His chest tightened at the mere thought of his friend being tormented by his absence. Chloé had to be worrying too. Were the two of them getting along? He knew Minari only controlled himself around Chloé for his sake, and he hoped the older elf hadn't done anything he'd later regret. He'd told Minari that Chloé was a warrior, but he knew the scout wouldn't mind defying the prophecy in order to find him.

Elliot held himself as the chilly evening breeze brushed past him. He didn't have his cloak. He had left it in the inn when they'd gone to watch the performers.

"Cold? I can start a fire."

Elliot nodded. "That would be nice. Thank you."

The man knelt down to a stack of charred lumber and twigs. There were stones around the edges. He grabbed a pair of smaller ones, striking them together until he made a spark. The man sat down next to the fire and motioned for Elliot to join him.

Elliot sat but kept a reasonable distance from the man. Redd was silent the whole time. He was perched on Elliot's shoulder, observing.

"I never told you my name, did I?"

"No."

"Name's Sage. My partner's name is Mimi. Speaking of Mimi, he should be back anytime now."

"I'm Elliot." He tucked his knees against his chest.

"Do all elves have birds with them, Elliot? The red bird you have there has been with you the entire time. Never left your side."

"Not exactly. Redd is a special case." Elliot wasn't going to tell Sage the bird was actually a demigod's familiar.

"The bird has a name?" Sage's eyes widened. "Elves are interesting. I'd like to travel to Rainwell someday. Do you know if chimeras are welcome?"

"Are you not usually welcome?"

"Around these lands? No." Sage's features turned solemn. "We're not welcome anywhere."

Elliot understood what it meant to be unwelcome. Elves were in the same situation, confined in the mountains for the foreseeable future. He would never have known the truth if he'd stayed up there. He hadn't enjoyed the slanderous words the townspeople had said to him and Minari, but he'd done his best to ignore it. It hurt to know his kind was seen so negatively. He hoped things would be different once the prophecy was fulfilled.

Elliot reached for his pendant, but he only felt skin. He gasped and frantically patted around, but he couldn't feel it. He scanned the grass. His heart raced as his head darted in different directions.

"Looking for something?" Sage asked.

"I had a pendant around my neck," Elliot blurted. He was crawling, hands roaming the green blades.

"There was nothing around your neck when we found you. Maybe you lost it somewhere?"

No. No. No. This couldn't be happening. The pendant was important. It was a memento from Lily, a sign of their mended friendship. He couldn't lose it. Tears threatened to fall as he thought of it being lost forever. His chest tightened painfully. A choked sob left his lips. He dug his fingers into the dirt, shutting his eyes.

"Hey, are you all right?"

Elliot felt a hand on his shoulder, and he flinched. He slowly opened his eyes. He was still in Scarstone Forest. It wasn't a dream. He wasn't in the comfort of Minari's and Chloé's presence. He was with Sage. Alone. It was suddenly too cold. "The pendant is important," he whispered. "It was a gift from a dear friend."

"Is this something you can get another of?"

Elliot shook his head. How was he supposed to face Lily after losing something so important?

"Look, I know you're sad and all, but I'm sure you'll feel better with a warm belly of food." Sage patted his shoulder. "Sit up. No point in being on all fours crawling through the grass looking for something that isn't there."

Elliot blotted his eyes and sat back down. He pursed his lips and took a deep breath, willing his heart to calm and his nerves to settle.

"Look, Mimi's back. And he brought a tasty-looking boar."

Elliot looked over to the edge of the clearing. A smaller chimera was making his way through the trees. He was pulling something behind him, dragging it across the dirt. When he came closer, Elliot went cold. It was the intruder who had barged into their room.

That explained it. They hadn't saved him—they were

after him.

26
MEET

Elliot wanted to run. Every nerve in his body was telling him to get away. But his limbs refused to move. He could only watch as the smaller chimera entered the clearing, large boar in tow. A line of blood trailed behind him. The boar's tongue stuck out of its mouth, its eyes completely gouged out. It made Elliot's stomach churn. He covered his mouth, urging the bile back.

Mimi said something, and Sage responded with an enormous smile on his face. Mimi blew his pale, sand-colored hair out of his eyes and glared at Sage. He said something again, and Sage shook his head.

"He's not a chimera. We'll need to speak common tongue," Sage said.

"Oh." Mimi frowned. "Well, are you going to help me, or are you going to sit there and stare? I'm tired, and this boar isn't exactly small."

"Okay, okay." Sage got up, patting his pants as he made his way over.

Elliot watched them in disbelief. He knew Mimi was the one who'd broken into the inn, but his eyes were different as he interacted with Sage. They were warm and filled with affection. The eyes before had been cold, hard, and empty. Elliot's hand inched toward his pouch as Mimi walked toward him. Sage threw the boar over his shoulder and carried it back.

"How are you feeling?" Mimi asked.

"Fine."

Mimi grunted. "Back to normal then?"

"As normal as I can be."

Mimi nodded. "Good. Then I extracted everything from your blood." His face scrunched. "Whatever they used, it was human made. It tasted gross." He took a seat next to Elliot. He stretched out his legs and leaned back against his hands. Neither of them spoke.

Sage dropped the boar near the fire. He reached behind his cloak and removed a knife. "We having it charred?"

"Yes. We carry whatever we can bring with us and leave the rest for the vultures."

"That seems like a waste." Sage began carving the meat. It made an awful squishing noise. Elliot had to turn away.

"What's wrong? Can't eat meat?" Mimi asked.

Elliot shook his head. He clasped his hand over his mouth and nose again. He'd have rather starved than eat the dead boar.

"Can you eat berries? I brought some back."

Elliot hesitantly looked at Mimi.

Mimi removed a handful of blueberries from his pouch. He outstretched his hand to Elliot. Elliot stared at the offered food. "Why did you help me?"

"Sage saved you, said the Outlawers kidnapped you. We thought you were a chimera at first. We've never seen someone who looks like you before." Mimi nudged his hand forward. "Eat. We can help you get back to wherever you came from, but you need energy first."

Elliot took a berry. He couldn't hold back a moan as the sweet texture met his tongue. The soup he had at the inn in Venin was bland in comparison to the bright flavor.

Mimi grabbed Elliot's wrist and dumped the rest of the berries from his palm into Elliot's. "I need to help Sage cook. He'll probably end up overcooking and burning the boar if I don't watch him."

"I can hear you, you know," Sage called out.

"Good. Since you heard, maybe you can become a better cook." Mimi made his way over, the grass crunching loudly beneath his sandals. He picked up a few longer sticks and stabbed the sliced meat pieces with them before propping them against the fire. He did that for a few more pieces Sage had already cut before turning around. "Aren't you going to eat? Your bird is going to eat it all."

Elliot looked at his hand. Redd was sitting on his palm, a blueberry in his mouth. "Redd," Elliot mumbled. Redd chirped and flew off his hand, but not before eating the stolen berry.

Elliot was silent. He watched the two chimeras talk with one another. They reverted back to their native tongue, and he couldn't understand them anymore. Their interaction reminded him of himself and Minari—how much Minari would tease Elliot because he was two inches shorter. How they'd learned to bake in Minari's kitchen. Minari was usually the one making the mess, and Elliot had to clean up after him. A smile found its way onto Elliot's lips. The strawberry sweet bread was probably the best thing Minari had ever baked. Anything before had been a complete disaster.

Night finally settled in, and all three were gathered around the warm fire. Both Sage and Mimi had eaten a large amount of the boar. Elliot was shocked to see there were leftovers. Mimi had given Elliot the rest of his blueberry stash, which had surprisingly been enough to fill him up.

"My name is Mimi," Mimi said. "Sorry, I never introduced myself. I got distracted."

"Elliot."

"Sage tells me you're trying to get back to Venin."

"Yes! My friends are probably looking everywhere for me."

Mimi hummed. "It's not that far from here, but probably far for you."

"Four days of travel, but one day for . . . chimeras." Elliot wasn't sure if it was all right for him to refer to the two as their race. It had sounded negative back in Venin, and Sage hadn't seemed proud to say what they were.

"You don't need to worry about calling us chimeras,"

Mimi said. He must have picked up on Elliot's hesitation. "That's what we are, what we will always be." Mimi reached for another stick and took a bite of boar.

Elliot looked away. He still couldn't stomach watching someone eat meat. "What's so bad about being a chimera?" he asked. Even though he'd somehow gotten used to the grotesque sound of chewing meat, he would've rather heard something than only listening to that.

"There's nothing wrong with us," Sage said. "The other races just treat us like dirt. We gained our freedom three kings ago, but we were given nearly unhabitable lands. It took our ancestors years to make it work, make it so anything could grow in it. We had to travel far to hunt, and we'd get punished if we 'trespassed.'" He scoffed. "Humans are by far the worst. Think they're at the top of the food chain."

Mimi chucked the empty stick into the fire. "Sage and I left the village. We wanted to find a new place to call home."

"Somewhere the kingdom doesn't have reach," Sage added.

"The land that was given to us shrinks with each passing year. We're overcrowded, and it's difficult to live and feed everyone."

"So when you asked me about Rainwell, you wanted to know if chimeras could live there?"

"It would help us if we could live there," Sage said.

"We'll help you return to Venin if you help us reach Rainwell," Mimi said.

"R-Rainwell is on an island," Elliot stammered.

"We'd have to cross the mountains if you wanted to reach it . . ." There was no way he could bring the two of them to a place that didn't exist.

"You've crossed them before. How hard could it be?" Sage asked.

"I had help from my friend. I didn't do it alone. And it's not like we can return now. There's something we need to do here."

"What do you need to do?" Mimi asked.

"Um . . . I can't say . . ."

Mimi placed an elbow on his thigh and leaned his chin against his hand. "Well, we can't really slow our search down. You'll have to return to Venin on your own then."

Sage said something to Mimi, and Mimi just shook his head. Sage looked at Elliot and then back at Mimi. He spoke once more, and Mimi shrugged.

"We'll part ways in the morning," Mimi said. "You can stay here with us for tonight, but don't be surprised if we're gone in the morning."

"Could you at least give me directions?" Elliot blurted. It would've been nice if he hadn't spent his whole day with Sage and Mimi. The reason he'd stayed was because Mimi was interested in him, but it was apparent it was because Mimi had wanted to know where Elliot was from.

Mimi pointed past Elliot. "Head south. There should be a road if you keep going that way. Follow the signs that lead to Venin, and you'll be there in four days."

"Thanks." Elliot frowned. He scooted away from Sage and Mimi before lying on his side. He used his arm as a pillow and closed his eyes. He would return to Minari and Chloé whether he was alone or not.

There was a weight on top of Elliot. He moved his elbow, attempting to push whatever was on top of him off. The weight didn't move. Instead, it shifted. He groaned, cracking his eyes open. He froze as he came face-to-face with cold, golden eyes.

Mimi was hovering over Elliot. Mimi's hands were beside Elliot's shoulders, his knees beside Elliot's hips. His gaze was locked on the elf.

Elliot shoved Mimi off, but the smaller male immediately latched back on. Elliot winced at the strong grip on his shoulders.

"He's been like this since we saw you in Venin," Sage said. He stood close by, arms crossed.

Elliot's eyes widened. "You were with him in Venin?"

"I was." Sage frowned. "Mimi started acting weird in the dead of the night. It's like he's possessed. He doesn't realize what he's doing, nor does he remember. At first, I thought you'd worked with Oasis to bewitch him or something. They're after us because of a stunt Mimi pulled a while ago, so I was sure you were trying to do something. But after seeing you get dragged away by the Outlawers, I knew I was wrong."

Elliot pushed Mimi away. He peeled Mimi's grip off his shirt. He sat up, keeping his hands on Mimi's shoulders. Having any sort of physical contact seemed to work. Mimi was only staring at him now. "So you knew Mimi broke into the inn I was staying at?"

Sage nodded. "I followed him and made sure there was a getaway route when I saw Oasis."

"Well, I can assure you I'm not with them."

Sage tilted his head. "It's still strange Mimi behaves like this when he's around you. Do you have any idea why?"

Elliot looked at Mimi. The golden orbs stared at him. They caught the moonlight, making them shine. He had a hunch as to why Mimi was clinging to him, why he was drawn to him, but he didn't know how to explain it.

27
TOGETHER

Minari watched Bunnie lay out a large map on one of the inn's dining tables. She placed empty mugs over the corners, preventing it from rolling back up. She removed a pen from her pocket.

"We are here," she said, circling a drawing of a town labeled "Venin." She drew a line. "My men saw Elliot get taken around here. But remember, chimeras are fast, so the men who saw them take off couldn't catch up."

Minari frowned.

"But," Bunnie said, "I have my men scattered all around Etheria. There was another group that saw them here." She drew an X.

From her original marking, it looked like Elliot was already one town over. The city they'd passed was labeled "Lonin."

"They proceeded north." Bunnie drew another line. "This is where the trail runs cold." She drew another *X*. The nearest location to the mark was Scarstone Forest. Bunnie tapped her pen over the latest *X*. "This is a four-day journey by foot. We can cut it at least in half by traveling by horse."

"So we should go now," Minari said.

"Yes, we *should* go now, but it's a question of can we." Bunnie leaned against the table and placed a hand on her hip. "Oasis wants to interview *everyone* in this town since there was a chimera raid last night. They closed the exits earlier this morning. No one can enter or leave. Chances of us leaving today are slim. Earliest would be to-morrow."

"We don't have time for interviews." Minari seethed.

"Do you know if Charlotte is here? I can probably talk to her," Chloé said. There was a mug filled with tea in front of her, but she hadn't touched it.

"Charlotte . . ." Bunnie pressed her lips together and shook her head. "I don't remember seeing her. But since she's one of the captains, she might be around. If not, then there's probably another one you can talk to."

Chloé stood from her seat. "I'm going to prepare for the day. Thank you for the information, Bunnie."

Bunnie smiled. "Of course, Chloé."

Minari blinked. That was the first time he'd heard anyone who wasn't Elliot call Chloé by her first name. Chloé didn't seem to mind. She left her untouched tea and made her way up the stairs.

"Aren't you going to follow her?" Bunnie asked.

"I will, but I want to ask you something first."

Bunnie moved the mugs and rolled up the map before taking a seat. She gestured for Minari to join her. "Come and sit. We're equals here."

Minari was already getting stares from other patrons and didn't care if he got more for sitting on a piece of furniture. He took a seat across from Bunnie, which so happened to be the same seat Chloé had used.

Bunnie laced her fingers together and balanced her chin on them. "What did you want to ask?"

"How did you know we were looking for Elliot?"

"We Nighthawks gather intel wherever we go." Her lips curled. "When I dance, I'm not just dancing. I observe and gather information all around me. My eyes and ears are open to changes. My body already knows how to move with the music, so I don't need to focus on my performance. Two elves standing at the back of the crowd are hard to miss. You two were interesting, so I kept watch. Even if you thought it was boring, Elliot seemed to thoroughly enjoy the show."

The mention of Elliot's brightened face as he watched the performance pulled at Minari's chest. It was the last he'd seen of Elliot.

"Don't worry, we'll find him. I'll be going with you guys. Information changes constantly, so it's best if I'm around to give you two updates."

"You don't have an ulterior motive, do you?" Minari narrowed his eyes.

"My motive is to get Oasis disbanded, and I can only do that with Chloé. It must be fate that we ran into each other, hmm?"

"Fate, huh?" Minari looked into Chloé's untouched tea. It was chamomile instead of her usual black tea.

"It would be a waste. Why not drink it?"

Minari held on to the mug. Elliot would drink chamomile whenever he was stressed or anxious over something. It was ironic that Chloé had picked the same tea. The connection they had . . . perhaps she was a warrior. He could afford to trust her. Maybe. Just a little. He drank the tea, finishing it in gulps. It was warm after sitting on the table for so long. It didn't have the same warming effect, but it was enough to relax Minari. They had a lead. He knew where to look for Elliot, and he would find him.

When Minari returned to the room, Chloé was sitting on the bed, her pistol in her hand. She held a white handkerchief in the other, absentmindedly polishing the weapon. Chloé seemed to snap out of her silent thoughts when Minari drew closer. She looked at him with wide eyes. Minari was taken aback. Her eyes were puffy and rimmed in red. She quickly turned away and used her forearm to wipe the unshed tears.

"Are you . . . okay?"

"Fine," Chloé mumbled. "Just something in my eye." She sniffled.

"Dust makes you snotty too?"

"Allergies."

"Right." There was an awkward pause. Chloé was still turned away from Minari.

"I miss him," she whispered.

Minari sighed. "I miss him too. We won't be separated for long. We'll find him."

"But what if . . ." Chloé hunched over. She clasped her hands together and leaned her forehead against them. "What if we don't find him? What if he's never coming back? What if he's . . ." Her voice quivered, and she inhaled a shaky breath.

Minari placed a hand on Chloé's shoulder. "We'll find him, even if it's the last thing I do." He gave her shoulder a soft squeeze. "Don't worry. Elliot won't die. Not on my watch. Not as long as I live."

Chloé suddenly stood, her pistol dropping to the floor, clattering away. She buried her face in Minari's chest and wrapped her arms tightly around his body. Her small body shook as her muffled voice wailed.

Minari contemplated if he should wrap his arms around her or just let her use him as a handkerchief. She was behaving out of the norm, and it had taken Minari by surprise. He was used to her being sassy and snarky, but the Chloé in front of him was a lost, frightened girl. After juggling the thought for a few seconds, he settled with hugging her back. He bent over and wrapped his arms around her shoulders.

They stood in silence. Chloé cried and hiccupped against Minari. He didn't let her go until she pulled away. She sniffled. Her entire face was puffy, and her cheeks were streaked with tears. The front of his coat was damp, but he could live with that for now.

"Thank you," Chloé said. "Sorry, I dirtied your coat."

"It's fine." Had Chloé just apologized to him?

Neither of them moved. Chloé shifted her weight,

eyes looking down. She then looked up at Minari. Without a word, she reached behind his neck, and Minari felt a warm pulse. The collar unclasped, and Chloé removed the black fabric. "No more pretending," she said. She pulled the white stone off the collar. "I want to start over. I know we had a rocky start, and I probably said some cruel things to you, but I just want you to know I'm really sorry." She bit her lip. "But I can understand if you don't trust me or hate me . . ."

Minari finally understood. He understood Chloé wanted to find Elliot as much as he did. She would throw away her perfect image so they could come together to find him. He wouldn't be doing this alone. "We can start over." Minari held out his hand.

Chloé took his hand, and they shook. A bright smile broke through her features. "I still get to call you Purple Hair though."

Minari sighed. He couldn't win with this girl, could he?

28
CLEAR

Chloé and Minari walked through the streets of Venin. Whispers, stares, and gossip followed them. She didn't care for any of it. She was side by side with someone she could trust, someone who wouldn't take advantage of her because of her wealth or her status, someone who, like her, had a mutual longing for a certain elf.

A disgruntled woman approached them. She was large and had a white apron tied around her wide waist. "Miss Gemme, excuse me, but could you please explain what's going on here? Are you being threatened by this savage?"

Chloé threw on a smile. "Whatever do you mean?"

"Why is this *thing* walking next to you? Doesn't he know his place?"

"I will not tolerate you speaking to my companion in

such a way." Chloé's smile disappeared. "He has been more civil than anyone else in Venin. He deserves as much respect as any of you."

The woman gaped at Chloé. "Miss Gemme, have you completely lost your mind?" Her stubby finger pointed at Minari. "This fiend, what did he do to you? Please come back to your senses! This is nonsense!"

A crowd slowly formed around them, wanting to see what the commotion was about. They whispered amongst themselves, nodding toward Chloé and Minari.

"I am completely sane," Chloé deadpanned. "If there's nothing else you need to say, *we* have places to be."

"Miss Gemme! What happened? You were normal yesterday."

"She probably got threatened by one of them!" a man yelled. "She had two yesterday, and now she only has one. Maybe the other one got shanked."

Chloé clenched her fists. She'd known this would happen. What she was doing was practically seen as unethical by others. She needed to remain calm. There was no point creating a scene. She inhaled through her nose and exhaled through her lips. "As far as I can see, I have no business talking to you any longer. Now, if you'll excuse *us*, we have places to be." She pushed past the woman and ignored all the incoming looks.

"You handled that pretty well," Minari said.

"I don't have spare energy to spend on her," Chloé grumbled. "I need to find Charlotte or another captain. I want us to leave here sooner rather than later."

"I'm going to assume the captains wear the coats."

"Yes. The regular members just wear the normal uniform."

"In that case, we should split. I haven't seen any, and it'll be faster if we cover the grounds separately."

Chloé frowned. "I don't want to say it, but you do know how difficult it would be to get them to talk you, right?"

"I can handle myself."

"It's not that I don't think you can . . ." Chloé paused. "I just don't want anything to happen to you. Elliot's already missing, and I . . ." She didn't want to lose Minari too.

"I guess it would be hard to find you. All these humans tower over you." Minari smirked.

Chloé pivoted and pushed Minari's chest. "I'm not short. You're just freakishly tall!"

"Your shoes cheat your height. I know you're not this tall." Minari pressed a hand across his chest, right where the top of Chloé's head would be. "Right now you're here." He lowered his hand by three inches. "In reality, you're actually here."

Chloé's cheeks warmed. She crossed her arms, puffing up her cheeks. "In reality, you're stupidly tall and have purple hair, Purple Hair."

Minari shrugged. "At this point, you're just stating the obvious."

Chloé fumed. "Hmph." She walked ahead of Minari, not waiting for him. But it didn't take much time for his long strides to catch up to hers.

They circled around Venin twice and still couldn't find Charlotte or anyone who appeared to be a captain.

There were two Oasis members stationed at each exit, and none of them allowed them to pass. Even though Chloé was a council member, bypassing an official guild order was out of the question. Her position allowed her to approve new laws and guilds and voice the concerns of the people. It didn't allow her to jump through hoops. She had hoped if she found Charlotte the captain would allow her through. They'd had an interview together a few nights ago, so there wasn't a reason to have another one. And if that wasn't acceptable, she would have Charlotte interview her right there and then, then proceed to leave the town.

It was well into the afternoon now, and a hot day at that. Fatigue chewed at her limbs. It frustrated her they weren't any closer to Elliot. And on top of it all, she wanted to get her feet out of her heels.

Chloé was about to turn into the inn when Minari grabbed her shoulder and pulled her back. She nearly stumbled. "What was that for?"

The double doors swung open, and a man walked out.

He was wearing a beige coat.

For once, Chloé appreciated the elf's freakishly good hearing. He must have heard the footsteps approaching the doors.

The man paused, noticing Chloé and Minari. "Sorry, did I almost swing the doors into you?"

A gasp escaped Chloé's lips, and her eyes widened as she saw just *what* had passed through the doors. The man's straight, silver hair flowed down to his waist. His eyes were purple, but not the same shade as Minari's. It was light, pastel. Lavender. There was a set of small, light blue feathered wings on top of his head. The man was an ethereal. Ethereals rarely left their snowy sanctuary, finding the hustle and bustle of towns tiring, so it was strange to find one so far away from their home, let alone a captain of Oasis.

"You're one of Oasis's captains," Chloé blurted.

"Yes." The man blinked. "I'm sorry, Miss Gemme, but I am not holding interviews."

"I'm not here for an interview. I need you to let me out of this town."

The man raised a brow. "I cannot allow you to leave, Miss Gemme. Please do not attempt to abuse your position."

"Luka, is something the matter?" Another figure left the inn. He wore the same beige coat. He had the same set of wings on his head, though they were gray instead of pale blue, and the feathers were more pressed together rather than spread apart. His eyes sparkled blue. His light gray hair was cut short and tied back into a high ponytail.

"Miss Gemme and this . . . elf apparently want to leave Venin," Luka replied. "I was just informing them they can't."

"I already had an interview with Charlotte the other night," Chloé said. "A chimera broke into our room, and she was there to intercept him."

"Basically, we don't want to waste our time with another interview. Let us leave," Minari said.

Luka's eyes flashed curiously at Minari when he spoke. "Owen and I are not the ones holding interviews . . . but we can make an exception for you." He turned, reentering the inn. "There are not many patrons in the dining hall right now. Why not continue this discussion there?"

Luka chose a round corner table. Chloé and Minari settled in the seats across from him and Owen. Luka waved down a server and requested water for the whole table.

"Lemon in my water, please," Chloé said. It wasn't tea, but she would make do.

The server rushed with the order, probably because there were two Oasis captains and a council member all at one table.

"This chimera you encountered in your room, did he have light hair and gold eyes?" Luka asked.

"Yes," Minari said. "Light hair, gold eyes, slate cloak, and two rapiers."

"Interesting." Luka leaned back. He crossed his legs, placing his intertwined fingers over his knee. "We've been looking for him for a while now. It's interesting he would appear here with you."

"Charlotte told me he stole the rapiers from her brother," Chloé said.

"Yes, he stole them from Aiden as he was transporting them from Valquent to Trox. Alvin was tasked with bringing them back to their original condition, but they never made it to his shop."

"I assumed he broke into my room to steal from me," Chloé said.

"Perhaps. That is a very likely possibility. It's vital we retrieve the weapons soon. Prince Alexander was not pleased when he learned he needed to wait longer than the desired promised time."

"Did you see him during the raid incident?" Owen asked. "The chimera who broke into your room."

"I didn't, no," Chloé said.

Minari shook his head.

"Hmm. So he wasn't around when it happened. Interesting." Luka swirled his drink before taking a few sips. "You mentioned you already spoke to Charlotte about this matter, correct?"

"Yes."

"Then I suppose it will be all right for me to issue a release for you two. Charlotte should have all the information we need."

Chloé let out a sigh. She slouched in her seat. Finally, progress.

"But the earliest I can let you leave is tomorrow morning."

"What?" Minari exclaimed. "You just said you'll let us go."

"Yes, but we just issued the lockdown for another day. I would be allowing you two to leave a day early."

"Why did you extend it?" Chloé asked.

"Some interviews are taking longer than predicted. And we still haven't spoken to everyone."

"It's not like you know how many people are here anyway, so why bother being so precise?" Minari asked.

"Even if we don't get to everyone, the more information we have, the better precautions we can take so this doesn't happen again." Luka stood up. "Meet me at the southern exit at seven in the morning. I'll be there to clearance you out."

Chloé watched the two ethereals leave. She sighed and pressed her forehead against the table. It wasn't the answer they wanted, but it was the answer they got. They were going to have to wait another half a day before leaving.

Minari kicked the underside of the table, startling Chloé. "That was annoying. We were basically led on."

Chloé couldn't help but agree. What did Luka have to do to get them permission to leave? Couldn't he just walk down there with them and let them go?

"I'm going to saddle Xander—and Xeno—tonight. They'll be ready in the morning." Minari let out a soft chortle. "Xeno's going to be so excited to see Elliot when we find him."

Chloé nodded. She was going to be right behind the ovis. "I'm going to ask the innkeeper for another room for tonight. One with two beds."

29
ANSWER

Elliot could feel Sage's intense gaze on him. He ran through his thoughts at the speed of light. There had to be an excuse he could give Sage without revealing what he was. But what could he say? He was coming up blank with ideas.

"If I discover you're actually bewitching Mimi, it won't be a good time for you," Sage said.

"I . . ." Elliot wracked his brain. There had to be something he could say. "Maybe my scent attracts him? You said you've never smelled someone like me before, so maybe Mimi . . ."

Sage's frown deepened. A faint line appeared in the center of his brow. "If that's the case, we may have a problem. I can't have my partner rubbing against you every night."

Elliot became flustered. Were the two of them in *that* kind of relationship?

Mimi pressed forward, arm outstretched. He brushed his fingers against the collar around Elliot's neck.

"This?" Elliot whispered. Chloé's magic was inside the fabric. Was Mimi drawn to the accessory as well?

Sage knelt down. He placed a hand on Elliot's shoulder and pressed his nose against his neck. He immediately pulled back, face scrunching. "What are you? The thing around your neck smells of nix, but everything else about you doesn't."

"I . . ." Elliot stammered. If he'd had any hope of making up a lie, it was gone. His mind was completely blank.

Sage narrowed his eyes. His hold on Elliot's shoulder became painful. Elliot winced. "If you've been lying to us, you're a dead elf, Elliot. Tell me, are you working with Oasis? Did you get the Outlawers to fake a kidnap so you could draw us out?"

Elliot frantically shook his head. "No! No, nothing like that at all! This was given to me by another friend."

Sage's grip tightened, bruising Elliot's shoulder. "Why are you friends with a nix? Pick your words carefully. They may be your last."

Elliot scolded himself. He'd forgotten the chimeras didn't have a friendly relationship with any other race.

Mimi wrapped his hand around Sage's wrist. His gaze now rested on the taller chimera.

"Mimi?" Sage asked.

Mimi pulled Sage's hand off of Elliot. Elliot rubbed his aching shoulder. He pulled the fabric of his shirt back slightly and grimaced at the purple skin.

Once Sage's hand was away, Mimi let go and brought his attention back to Elliot.

Sage let out a frustrated sigh. "I get the message. Looks like Mimi doesn't want me to lay a finger on you. I don't like whatever hold you have over him, but I won't go against Mimi's wishes." He turned away. "Even if he won't remember this in the morning." He continued to grumble, but Elliot couldn't make out what he was saying.

Elliot felt bad for the chimera. He wished he could tell him what was going on, but that wouldn't fix Mimi's behavior. He knew why Mimi was behaving like this, but he didn't know how to change it.

Elliot didn't sleep much the rest of the night. If he fell asleep and his hand slipped off Mimi, the smaller male would close the distance between them, disrupting his rest.

When morning finally came, Elliot woke up alone. Redd was sleeping a few patches of grass away. It was up to him to make it back now. He patted his clothes as he got up. His shirt clung to his skin from the morning dew. Redd woke up from Elliot's movements. He chirped and found his way to Elliot's shoulder, luckily his right one, which wasn't bruised.

Elliot walked in the direction Mimi had instructed. He found the trail and followed it. He reached a fork in the road and proceeded in the direction of the arrow that was labeled "Venin."

It was unfortunate he hadn't been able to persuade Sage and Mimi to come along with him. He was certain Mimi was a warrior. The way he was drawn to him and the collar around his neck proved it, but it was odd that there was no connection, no sense of longing like he'd had with Chloé. There was a possibility he could be wrong. Maybe Mimi was drawn to him for a different reason.

As Elliot trudged along the path, a fog began to roll in. The farther he walked, the thicker the mist became. He was trying to decide between slowing down so he wouldn't walk into anything or running so he could get out of the fog faster. He opted to quicken his pace. His long legs moved him forward. Sweat collected at his lower back. His nerves were on high alert.

The sun was now entirely blocked out. The mist was dense. Elliot couldn't see the path. The hairs on the back of his neck stood, and goosebumps covered his skin. This fog wasn't normal. Redd was eerily quiet. He tried calling out to the bird, hoping to get a conversation going so he wouldn't feel alone, but the bird remained silent.

There was a sudden pull in his chest, in his core. The sensation tightened around his ribs. He stopped in his tracks and gripped his shirt. He was going in the wrong direction. The sensation he was feeling . . . It was trying to lead him somewhere.

Elliot closed his eyes. He could see glowing vines in the darkness. They were loosely wrapped around his body and looked like they were originating from his left. He needed to divert from his path. He opened his eyes and ran. The vine's pull urged him through the maze of trees. The hold lessened with each stride.

The sound of a thunderous roar and clashing metal caught his ears. The noise grew with each step. Then he heard voices. Shouting. They were familiar. They belonged to Sage and Mimi. Elliot ran faster. His blood ran cold at the thought of what the two chimeras were facing. The ground rumbled, and there was another roar.

Faster. Faster. Faster. He pushed his legs faster. His lungs burned with each gasp, but he ignored it.

He made it to a clearing. The fog lightened, allowing him to see. Gray spikes were scattered across the ground. They tore through the dirt, and black goo seeped from the overturned soil. A monstrous toad was seated in the middle. It was as large, if not larger, than the scorpion. Its body was folded in wrinkles with pores the size of craters. There were spikes on its back. Sage was on top of the beast. His fists were pounding against the spikes. They cracked from each hit. Mimi was balancing on top of the spikes with his rapiers out. He leapt through them, avoiding the sea of slime.

The toad slid out its tongue, which had smaller spikes scattered across the surface. It swung its head, whipping the muscle for an attack. Mimi pivoted to his left, attempting to dodge the incoming blow, but he wasn't quick enough. His body still collided with the spikes. His weapons flew out of his hands as he fell to the ground. A long gash ran across his right arm.

Sage yelled. He jumped off the toad's back and ran toward the fallen chimera. He cradled Mimi in his arms, grimacing at the wound.

The beast did not wait. Its eyes rolled, locking on the still targets. It lifted its head and roared before its tongue lashed out once again. If this attack hit, they wouldn't survive.

Elliot dashed. He was mindful of the spreading goo on the ground. He tapped into his core. The same surge of magic he'd felt when he'd wanted to protect Minari kindled inside him. He threw a hand out, sending a wave of magic toward Sage and Mimi. The invisible wave projected out of his fingers, forming a dome around the two chimeras.

The tongue collided with the shield, shattering it upon impact, but the force was enough for its large body to stumble backward. A sudden wave of pain coursed through Elliot's body. He staggered, but it didn't stop him from pushing forward. He needed to reach Sage and Mimi.

Sage's eyes were wide. He glanced over at Elliot like he'd just grown another set of arms. "What are you doing here? Did you just do that?"

"I don't have time to explain," Elliot said. The throbbing in his chest continued to ache. He gripped the front of his shirt. "That thing is no ordinary monster."

"You've seen something like this before?"

Elliot nodded.

Mimi separated himself from Sage. He winced as he tried to move his arm.

"You can't fight like that," Sage said.

"I can still fight," Mimi said. He pressed a hand against the gash. He bit his lip, but a hiss still escaped. He furrowed his brow.

The toad regained its balance. It loomed over the three of them. Its crimson eyes shone through the fog. Its wrinkled body edged closer and closer to them.

Elliot tapped into his core again and created a shield around them. "Sage, take Mimi away. I'll hold it off for now."

Sage quickly took the reluctant chimera in his arms. He hooked his arm underneath Mimi's knees and held him close to his chest. He darted, leaving Elliot alone.

Elliot braced for the impact. The attack wasn't enough to break the shield, but the force still sent daggers of pain into his chest. He knew he couldn't stand still. He had to keep moving. He glanced over, getting ready to pull back his shield, and Mimi's discarded rapiers caught his eye. He could at least use those to damage it.

The attack that came crashing down was stronger than Elliot had expected. It shattered the shield, throwing Elliot backward and knocking Redd off his shoulder. He gasped as he landed hard on his back. His chest felt like it had been stabbed repeatedly. He staggered back to his feet. Each breath felt like a million glass shards embedding themselves in his lungs.

Elliot pushed past the pain and quickly retrieved the weapons. As soon as the hilts reached his hands, the blades glowed. The once dull and rusted metal sparkled, transforming into pristine steel. The silver surfaces shone through the fog. The rapiers felt light in his hands. His body moved on instinct, as if he knew how to wield the paired weapons. He changed his grip, the blades now pointed downward.

The toad shot a spike off of its back. Elliot rolled out of the way, dodging it. His lungs suddenly felt clear. There was no pain with every breath he took. The beast rolled its tongue out. Elliot took the opportunity to strike. He focused his magic around his feet. He willed it to launch him into the air.

Elliot pushed himself from the ground, and he flew. With the rapiers held tightly, he pulled his arm through the grotesque muscle. The silver blade cleanly severed the tongue from the toad's mouth. He landed on the grass, using a bit of magic to cushion his landing.

The toad stilled, its mouth now hollow. It let out a bellow before viciously shaking and disintegrating into black dust. All the spikes and goo on the ground dissolved into the same black dust.

The fog immediately cleared up. Redd suddenly came to life. He chirped and flapped his wings. He zipped around Elliot before landing on his shoulder. Elliot glanced at the rapiers. The left one was drenched in black liquid. His nose scrunched from the offending odor. He glanced around, hoping to find Sage and Mimi.

Sage wasn't too far off from the edge of the clearing, but instead of walking forward, he was walking backward.

"Well, well, well. What do we have here?" A woman stepped forward. There was a group of men behind her.

He recognized the voice, the sway of her hips, her long blonde hair.

It was Charlotte.

"I knew there was something suspicious about you, *elf*." Charlotte smirked. "You're working with the chimeras who stole kingdom property and conjured up a monster." She tilted her head and tapped her bow against her shoulder. "If I didn't know any better, I'd say you're trying to start a war. I can't have that happen now, can I?" She snapped her fingers. "Get them."

30
SNARE

Mimi swung his arms. Kicked his legs. Bared his fangs. Oasis had fired tranquilizer darts. Two had hit Sage in his thighs, and he'd immediately fallen under. Mimi didn't know how many had hit Elliot, but the elf had fallen soon after. One had found its way into Mimi's arm, but the toxin didn't affect him. He was a snake chimera, and not an ordinary one.

His body carried the abilities of the Colorless Snake.

The term mainly came from his distinct appearance. Snake chimeras typically had dark shades of green or black hair with tan skin, but Mimi was different. His hair and skin were pale, almost colorless. Being the Colorless Snake meant his body was immune to most toxins. His blood acted as an antidote. He could even save someone from the brink of death if he wanted to.

Elliot had been feverish when Sage had saved him from the Outlawers. His body had been having a negative side effect to the tranquilizer they'd used on him. Mimi had bit into the elf's shoulder to draw out the poison. Luckily, it had worked.

Large hands bound Mimi's arms behind his back and pushed him to his knees. He struggled. He refused to be captured. There was so much more he and Sage needed to do. He also needed to repay his debt to Elliot. The Rainwell elf had saved their lives instead of returning to Venin. And because of the detour he'd taken, he was now at Oasis's mercy.

A needle was stabbed into his arm and another into his other arm. More came. More injected him with an unknown fluid. They disregarded the large wound, ignoring the way Mimi hissed and flinched.

His mind was starting to cloud. Noise became muffled. His heart painfully raced against his chest. Blood pounded in his head.

"Keep going. We should have enough to put this one under," a voice said. She had to be the leader of the pack. The corner of her lips curled. She knelt down and took a handful of Mimi's hair into her hands, jerking his head back. "I've finally caught you, you piece of shit. I'll make sure you pay for embarrassing my family." She reached into her coat pocket and pulled out a glass vial. The liquid was pitch-black. It swirled as she tipped it in front of his eyes. "A gift from a colleague." She popped the lid with her thumb and shoved the contents in Mimi's mouth. Once the vial was emptied, she pressed her palm against Mimi's mouth and pinched his nose.

The liquid was viscous. The taste was unbearable. It attacked his tongue like a million different spices. He wanted to gag, but he couldn't. He was forced to swallow. It burned his throat as it traveled down.

The blonde woman released him, and Mimi's head fell forward. Colors began to fade. His body was freezing and burning at the same time. The hands that held him down sent waves of pain through his body. His chest tightened. It was hard to breathe. He gasped for air. He wanted to claw his throat. Everything was excruciating. Something smashed into his temple, and his world turned dark.

Hot.
Cold.
Dizzy.
Pain.
Suffocating.
Elliot was in so much agony when he came to that he nearly cried. He rolled onto his side. The hard floor bit through his clothes, making him shiver. The surrounding air was frigid. He couldn't decipher which direction was up or down. He stared at the stone walls, watching them spiral around him. A torch off to the side was softly illuminating the dark room.

He didn't know how long he stared at the spinning world, didn't know how much time was passing. Panic built up inside him, but he felt so weak he could barely lift his head when he heard footsteps.

The orange light crept closer. A set of feet appeared in front of him. One boot lifted, digging into his shoulder, and rolled him onto his back. Elliot cried out. The movement jarred his body, sending waves of agonizing pain through him. Mustering up the energy, Elliot peered up at the man. He had a wide grin. Multiple teeth were missing from his mouth, and a black eyepatch covered his right eye.

"Finally awake, eh? I was hoping to pour water over you to get you up," the man said. "But I guess there's nothing stopping me from doing it anyway."

Ice-cold water drenched Elliot. He gasped, his mind no longer in a confused haze. The figure gripped his arm, tugging him up. Elliot tried his best not to trip over his own feet, but the man didn't seem to care. If Elliot fell onto his knees, he just got dragged back up.

The dungeon was more humid than the grotto. Elliot's wet clothes hugged his feverish body, causing uncontrollable shivers. His legs and shins had to have been thoroughly bruised by the time they reached their destination. The man dragging him up had not been too kind when he'd tripped climbing the stairs.

The room was completely dark save for the small candle sitting in the middle of a table. There were two wooden chairs, one on each side. The man shoved him into a chair. He took Elliot's wrists and bound them behind the backrest. Without another word, the man left, slamming the door behind him.

Elliot tugged at the binds. He winced as the rough edges of the rope bit into his skin. Water dripped from his hair into his eyes. He blinked and lightly shook his head, attempting to clear his vision. He tried to level his breathing, tried to calm his body from the shivers. The violent movements were causing him to feel nauseous.

The door creaked open, and Charlotte stepped inside. She was holding a scroll and a pen in her hands. The door clicked behind her. She took a seat across from Elliot and straightened the scroll on the table.

"So, elf," she said. "Care to explain what you are doing out of your cage?"

Cage? What did she mean? He opened his mouth to respond, but Charlotte lifted a hand.

"You left your cage, also known as the mountains, to start a war. I already know that. Don't even bother trying to lie." She scribbled something on the scroll. "Now, tell me why you are working with the chimeras."

"I'm not." Elliot's voice cracked.

"Hmm . . ." Charlotte tapped the back of the pen against her shoulder. She tilted her head and smiled. "You wanted to rally them against us. I can see how that could help you. They multiply like roaches, honestly. Disgusting." She wrote something else down.

Elliot's eyes widened. His mouth went dry. Charlotte wasn't interested in anything he said. She wasn't interested in learning the truth. She was *lying*. She was writing down whatever answer made sense for her narrative.

"Miss Gemme told me she'd trained you. I am terribly surprised you would defy her like this. This is practically treason. If she couldn't prevent you from colluding, then she is to blame as well."

"No! Chloé has nothing to do with this." Elliot coughed. His throat was parched.

"That's interesting. She wants to overthrow the king, you say? I knew that kid was up to no good." Charlotte shook her head. "A shame, really. Once King Valentine VI hears about this . . ." She continued to write. "It won't be pretty for you or her, you know."

Was Chloé going to take the blame for something that wasn't even true? No, this couldn't be happening. He had to do something. "Please."

Charlotte hummed. She looked at him after finishing her last sentence. "Please what, elf?"

"Chloé has nothing to do with this."

"You sure? That isn't what you said earlier."

"She doesn't know."

"Oh, I see. What you're telling me is you're doing everything behind her back."

Elliot nodded.

Charlotte smirked. "You're quite clever. You must have purposely gotten caught by her when you left your cage."

Elliot nodded again.

"Must be convenient for a council member to catch you." Charlotte made her way across the table. She lowered her lips by Elliot's ear. "I want to know how you summoned the monster. You tell me how you did it, and I'll keep your treason a secret," she whispered. "Miss Gemme will be spared from your antics."

Elliot sucked in a breath. She'd seen the toad and thought he was the cause, just like Chloé had believed he and Minari had been the cause of the scorpion when they'd first met. But something told Elliot he wouldn't be able to persuade Charlotte otherwise.

Charlotte snaked one hand over Elliot's shoulder and another over his chest. "You can use magic, elf. I know you can. Tell me, do you feel anything in your core?"

Elliot froze. He'd been so disorientated earlier he hadn't realized the feeling of emptiness. He tried to tap into his core, but he felt disconnected, like a cut string.

Everything came crashing down. He was at the mercy of Oasis. Charlotte knew he could use magic. The Necromancers could've been anywhere, could've been anyone.

And he was alone.

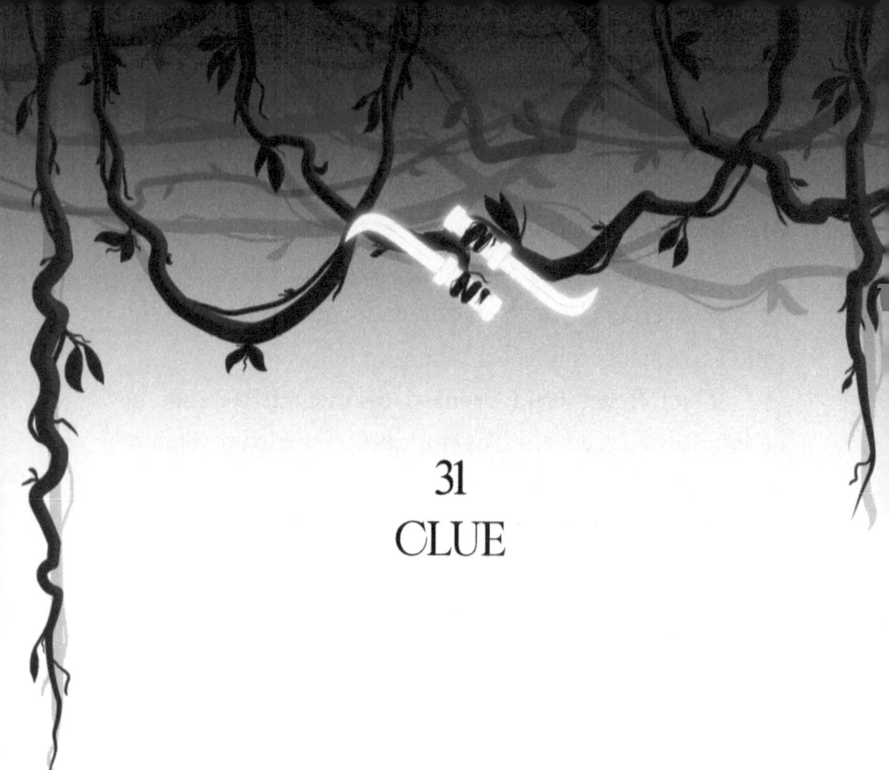

31
CLUE

Minari stroked Xeno's fur. The ovis was restless. Elliot wasn't with him, and it didn't sit well with the animal. "Hey, don't worry, Xeno. We'll find him. Don't you worry," Minari said. Xeno pulled back against the reins, grunting. "Xeno, come on. Don't worry. It'll be okay." Minari tried coaxing the distressed ovis again. Xeno eventually conceded, but he didn't look too happy leaving without Elliot.

Minari saddled Xander and Xeno and attached the saddlebags. He double-checked to make sure everything was in place. Looking into one of the saddlebags attached to Xeno, he frowned at the sight of Elliot's cloak. The pendant was pressed against it. His chest twisted, and his stomach knotted. He closed his eyes and took a deep breath. Reopening them, he tied up the saddlebags.

The next time he saw the cloak and the pendant, they'd be on Elliot.

Minari tied a rope to the two ovis and attached them to Chloé's mare. The nix's horse was surprisingly well-behaved. She didn't seem to mind a stranger handling her. Taking the rope, he led all three out of the stables.

The morning sky was gray. Storm clouds blocked the morning sun. Chloé was waiting by the inn's entrance, and she wasn't alone. As promised, Bunnie was there, a red crossbow tied against her back and a brown mare by her side.

"I'm glad you two found an officer to help," Bunnie said. "I was just informing Miss Gemme that I'd be coming along."

"He said he'd meet us at the south exit. Let's go," Minari said.

The streets were mostly empty. The only townspeople bustling in the roads were the ones setting up their shops for the day. There were a few Oasis members walking about the streets, but none paid any attention to them.

Luka was at the southern exit. He was talking to one of the two Oasis members standing watch. His attention shifted to them once they were within earshot. "I see you made it."

"You said seven in the morning, so here we are. It's seven in the morning. Let us out," Minari said.

"Damn, savage! You dare speak to Officer Luka like that?" the Oasis member scoffed.

"Be grateful he's even letting you through," the other member said. "If it were up to me, I'd break your legs for speaking out of place."

"Dustin," Luka said. "These three will pass through. Be sure to let the other members know they are free to leave Venin. If I find any one of them is mistreated because you failed to follow orders, there will be consequences." He narrowed his eyes. "Do I make myself clear?"

"Y-yes, sir." Dustin lowered his head.

"Now open the gate and let them through. I'm sure they have a busy day ahead of them."

Dustin unlocked the gate and pulled up the latch. He pushed the giant doors open.

"Thank you," Chloé said. "Sorry, I don't think I've properly caught your name."

"Apologies. The way we met was indeed rather sudden." Luka placed a hand over his chest and bowed. "I am Luka Yunmei. My partner's name is Owen Ko. Fourth and fifth officer, respectively."

"You have quite the manners," Bunnie said.

"It's only proper. Those who deserve respect will receive respect. As far as I'm concerned, Miss Gemme and this elf have done nothing to offend me in such a way where I shouldn't give them a proper introduction."

"And here I thought all the captains of Oasis were haughty," Minari said.

Luka chuckled. "Do not let Charlotte hear you say that. She wouldn't take the offense lightly."

With parting words, the three trudged on. The heavy gates of Venin closed behind them.

Bunnie mounted her horse. "From what my men have told me, Elliot still hasn't appeared from where his trail went cold. Our best bet is to head over and see if we can find any clues."

Minari untied the rope that attached all the animals together. He rolled it up and shoved it into one of Xander's saddlebags. The air smelled sweet and fresh. "The rain is probably going to hit us before we get there."

Chloé swung her leg over her mare's back. "We should get a move on then. Rain can wash away clues."

Minari settled himself on Xander. He turned to look at Xeno. The ovis still didn't look happy but understood he had to follow.

The rain crashed into them after three hours of travel. Their clothes were drenched and clung to their bodies. The wind blew hard, making it difficult to see. Bunnie was leading the way, but the initial momentum from earlier was gone.

Minari peeked back to make sure Chloé was still following. The nix's expression was pure horror. She held on to herself, covering her body as much as she could. It could have been from the harsh weather or the simple fact her dress was mostly white. Though the road was bare except for the three of them, Minari could understand why she would feel embarrassed.

He was a male, after all.

He brought Xander to a slower trot, matching Chloé's speed. She looked at him curiously, bringing her arm closer to her body. Minari unbuckled his coat. He slid it off and tossed it over her shoulders.

"What . . . ?"

"You looked cold," Minari blurted. He looked away,

wanting to show decency. "It's not much, but I thought it'd help more than what you have on right now."

He heard Chloé adjust the large coat, covering as much of herself as she could. "Thank you."

Minari grunted, bringing Xander back to their original position.

Unfortunately, the weather had significantly slowed them down. Nature wasn't on their side, and they needed to succumb to defeat and stop earlier than they would've liked. They hadn't traveled as far as planned. They were probably behind by a day. The closest to shelter they found from the storm was under a thick bundle of trees. The branches and leaves created a canopy, blocking some rain out.

Bunnie had gathered twigs and stone to make a fire. It had been difficult at first, but eventually a spark was made and a flame was lit. Minari hoped the fire would survive the night.

Xander and Xeno looked like they'd seen better days. Their once fluffy fur was completely soaked and sagged straight down like a wet mop. Xander nibbled Xeno's head, attempting to soothe the distraught animal.

"So," Bunnie said. "We're all soaked to the bone, and I know I shouldn't have to say it since we all know this, but . . . we're going to have to dry out our clothes."

"No!" Chloé's face turned incredibly pink. She tightened her grip on Minari's coat.

"If we don't, we're going to catch a cold." Bunnie frowned. "We won't be able to save Elliot if we get sick."

Chloé shook her head. "I won't catch a cold."

"They say idiots don't catch colds," Minari said. He was lifting his shirt when Chloé shoved him. He stumbled but quickly caught himself. "What was that for?"

"W-why are you undressing? Show some modesty, would you!"

Minari cocked a brow. "So you're okay with me saying you're an idiot, but you aren't okay with me drying out my clothes?"

"I'm not okay with either!"

Minari's shoulders sagged as he sighed. "Would it be better if I was elsewhere?"

"We probably shouldn't get separated," Bunnie said. She was already halfway undressed, hanging her clothes on a makeshift rack she had made.

Minari hadn't realized she had begun shedding her clothes and abruptly turned away. He tried to wipe the imagery from his memory. Bunnie was a beautiful woman with mature and stunning curves. But those were facts Minari shouldn't have been focusing on. Facts he shouldn't have been thinking about. He felt his cheeks flush. He couldn't decide if it was from the chilly wind or the detailed memory he couldn't seem to erase from his mind.

Chloé had a deep scowl on her face. She stared at Minari as if he were a dirty mongrel.

Her assets were significantly less voluptuous compared to Bunnie's.

Minari needed to push those thoughts away and never think about them again.

"Miss Gemme, I have some blankets we can use to wrap ourselves in while our clothes dry," Bunnie said.

After a few reluctant moments, the nix shuffled her way to Bunnie.

Minari kept his back turned to them. He didn't have any plans to look at either of them for the rest of the night.

The skies cleared up in the morning. Their clothes were slightly damp, but they were good enough to wear.

"We're here," Bunnie said. "This is where my men lost track of Elliot."

They were on the side of the road. Minari dismounted and examined the area. The dirt was still slightly damp from the rain.

He knelt down, eyes scanning. There were footprints that led straight down the path. Then another set came in from the side. It looked like there had been a struggle. The dirt was kicked up, and the prints were messy. Then a pair of feet walked deeper into the forest. Minari furrowed his brow at the size of the footprints. They were larger than his own. Whoever they belonged to, they weren't human.

"Well?" Bunnie asked.

"A set of footprints lead that way," Minari said.

"Then we go that way."

The trail led them to a clearing. There was an abandoned fire in the middle and half a boar carcass. Minari scrunched his face at the foul stench. He covered his nose. Someone had set up camp here. Minari ran his hands across the grass. Three people. There had been three people here.

Minari squinted at a particular pair of footprints. He gasped. A curvy *E* had been etched into the soles of Elliot's boots when he'd had them made, and the footprints had the same curvy *E*. He followed them, ignoring the calls from

Chloé.

He nearly ran, afraid the trail would suddenly go cold. They followed a trail that led toward Venin but suddenly diverted and entered back into the forest. The distance between the feet was wider now. Elliot had probably started running.

Minari followed Elliot. The footsteps he'd left behind led to another clearing, and the elf's breath caught his throat. There were craters scattered across the entire clearing with a larger one in the middle. He walked slowly, looking around. Could Elliot have run into another one of those giant beasts? Minari knew nothing normal could have created this much damage at this magnitude. If there had been any black dust left, it would've been washed away from the rain.

Something on the grass caught his eye. His stomach immediately dropped.

"Redd!" Minari picked up the small bird, cradling him in his hand. Dread filled every nerve in Minari's body. Redd had been with Elliot the entire way. But now he was here, and Elliot was nowhere to be found.

32

VANISH

"Purple Hair!" Chloé called out to Minari multiple times, but he didn't respond. He'd left in a hurry, leaving both her and Bunnie behind, along with the two ovis.

"Looks like he found a lead," Bunnie said. She stood from where she'd been kneeling by the carcass.

Chloé sighed. She patted her mare before making her way to the abandoned animals. She recalled the names Minari used to address them. One of them was Xander, the other Xeno. They were calm when she approached them. She put her hand under Xander's chin, scratching him. Xander licked her arm.

"Miss Gemme."

Chloé shifted her attention to the female, her hand still on the ovis.

"There's something I want to discuss with you."

Chloé blinked curiously. "What is it?"

"Minari. He isn't your property anymore?"

Chloé frowned. "No." She didn't want to have this conversation. It was controversial, and she knew it.

"What made you decide to release him?" Bunnie's voice held no malice. Her expression was unbothered.

Chloé relaxed the tension in her shoulders. Bunnie didn't appear to be judging her. She was probably curious. Her desire to disband Oasis made Chloé believe perhaps Bunnie wasn't like the others, wasn't blinded by the information that had been shoved down their throats at a young age. But she wasn't sure if she could trust the older woman quite yet.

"You don't need to tell me now if you aren't ready," Bunnie said. "Just wondering is all."

Chloé returned her gaze to Xander, who was still licking her arm. "He's not as bad as I thought."

Bunnie hummed. "It was tough for you, wasn't it, Chloé? Growing up alone."

Chloé blinked. How did Bunnie know she had grown up alone? Before she could ask, Bunnie began walking down the same path Minari had left for.

"We should catch up to him. I can kind of make out the faint footprints."

Chloé's mind wandered. It wasn't uncommon for others to know her parents had passed away, but no one knew she had grown up alone in the manor. Other than Cecilia, no one else had raised her. The only other person she could think of who knew this information was Licht, but he wasn't one to gossip. There was no reason to openly reveal how Chloé had grown up. Few humans traveled down to the grottos, so she would've remembered seeing one down there.

Chloé was drawing a blank.

The sun's rays weren't enough to dry out the dirt. Brown stuck into the bottoms of Chloé's pink heels. She grimaced at her dirtied footwear. She considered mounting her horse, but she didn't want to appear too vain. Bunnie was trudging along, analyzing the ground. She held her horse's reins in her hand, and her boots picked up the same wet dirt. She hadn't been bothered by undressing in front of Minari. She wasn't afraid of insignificant things. There was a clear goal, and she went for it, uncomfortable situations be damned.

The female nix wanted to be independent like her.

The path Bunnie walked down would have led them back to Venin. Had they just passed Elliot? Where had he stayed during the storm? He didn't have his cloak with him. Was he sick?

Bunnie changed direction. She left the trail and headed into the forest. Chloé furrowed her brow. So they hadn't missed each other.

The nix followed, the three animals trailing behind her. Xeno abruptly galloped, passing her and Bunnie.

"Hey! Wait!" Chloé yelled. Xeno didn't stop. He disappeared into the thick trees.

"He must've picked something up. Let's hurry," Bunnie said. She broke out in a light run.

It amazed Chloé how fast the large animal could weave through the trees. She had to watch her step carefully, or else she would trip. She was losing sight of Xeno, but Bunnie didn't show any signs of stopping. She saw the older woman glance from the ovis to the ground, then back up. Chloé realized she was following Xeno's hoofprints.

They led to another clearing. Chloé's eyes widened, and she held in a breath. There was clear evidence of a giant beast. That meant the reason Elliot had shifted paths was because he'd known. Had he fought it alone? Did either he or Minari even know how to fight it? They'd been struggling the first time she'd run into them.

Minari's knees were on the ground. Xeno was pressing his muzzle against the elf's cheek, but he wasn't responding.

Chloé approached him. "Purple Hair?" She couldn't keep her voice from shaking. She was worried beyond belief. Minari's shoulder jerked, but he still kept his back facing her. "Purple Hair?" she called out again. When she was close enough to see what Minari was holding, she gasped. It was the red songbird that was always around either Minari or Elliot.

"Elliot isn't here," Minari whispered.

"What about . . . ?" She hoped the poor animal was all right.

"He's okay. Redd's fine." Minari tucked the bird into his coat. There was an unreadable expression on the elf's features, almost as if he was torn. Minari cursed under his breath as he stood up. "Bunnie, do you have any new intel on Elliot?"

"I would have informed you if . . ." Bunnie paused and cleared her throat. "Because of the storm last night, I didn't receive anything." She placed her hand on Minari's shoulder. "I'm sure I will get something tonight."

"So our trail runs cold here," Minari said.

"Unfortunately. Until later tonight. You have my word."

Chloé watched Minari. He was chewing his lip, and the way he spoke to Bunnie was uptight. His tone was curt. He was shifting his weight between his feet and looking at Xander and Xeno. "What's wrong?" Chloé asked.

"Nothing."

A clipped answer.

"There's no sign of Elliot here, which is good." Minari turned his attention to Chloé. "You're thinking what I'm thinking, right? There was a monster here."

Chloé nodded.

"But Elliot isn't here. Which means he probably killed it." Minari placed his hands on Chloé's arms. "He's fine."

Chloé nodded. "He's okay." With how quickly Minari was speaking, Chloé could tell he was anxious and just wanted to hear anything that could possibly mean Elliot was alive. A sign of hope. That's why he asked Bunnie about Elliot, knowing full well Bunnie would have told them if she had news on the other elf.

"Elliot must be strong if he defeated something that could cause this much damage at such a massive level," Bunnie said. "And there's no body, so he either dragged it away or it's still alive."

Minari gripped his hair and let out a frustrated moan. "No. Elliot is okay. I'm sure of it."

"He's okay," Chloé said, repeating Minari, hoping it would help calm his nerves. "We'll find him.

Minari covered his mouth, letting out a heavy sigh through his nose. His eyes shifted away.

Chloé followed his gaze. She didn't see anything peculiar in the direction he was looking. There was a heavy silence in the air. No one spoke a word, and Minari's gaze didn't change. She was about to draw the elf's attention away when she realized just what lay in that direction.

The mountains. But why was Minari so intent on staring at them? Did he think Elliot had gone home? Chloé's chest twisted. That couldn't be it. She'd promised herself she would see Elliot again. They were friends. She knew he wouldn't abruptly leave.

Right?

33
IDENTITY

Mimi couldn't believe he'd fallen into their trap. The giant beast must have been set up by Oasis. There was no other explanation. They'd been waiting. They'd been there right when the giant toad had been killed. If only he weren't weak. If he were stronger, he could've defeated the beast with Sage, and they could've escaped before they'd gotten surrounded. If he were stronger, Elliot wouldn't have needed to help. The elf could've been in Venin, but instead he had gotten captured with the two of them.

The metal tore through Mimi's wrists. He wiggled his arms, attempting to loosen the bite, but his attempts were futile. The binds were locked tightly around him, preventing movement. He let out a frustrated huff and let his arms relax against the cold table. Though he'd barely struggled, he felt lethargic.

There were fixed times when an Oasis member would enter the room and draw vials of his blood with a needle. It was possibly every twelve hours, but the snake chimera's sense of time was beginning to muddle. At first, they'd taken five vials. Then it had doubled. Mimi was positive no one knew of his special blood. If he had to guess why they drew so much at a time, it would be because they were selling it in the market.

The door opened. It was sooner than he'd expected. His blood had been drawn not too long ago.

The figure who approached him differed from the others—an ethereal. His hair was silver with small, light blue feathered wings on the crown of his head. He wore the same coat as the pack leader from the forest. There was a clear vial with black liquid in his hands.

"I'm going to need you to drink this," he said. He held the vial over Mimi's face. "You can refuse and put up a struggle, but I can assure you this will enter your body one way or another."

Mimi shot the man a glare. "*You think you can do whatever you want to us chimeras?*" he said in his native tongue. "*You're lower than the dirt beneath my feet.*"

The figure didn't seem fazed by the insult. Probably because he didn't know what Mimi had said. "Are you done gibberishing? I'd like not to waste my time here any longer than I need to."

"*Once I get out of here, I'll make sure to kill every last one of you shitters.*"

"A lively one, aren't you? Even after all the blood we drew from you . . ." The man ran his fingers through

Mimi's hair.

Mimi jerked away. It was an intimate gesture for chimeras. He didn't appreciate anyone touching him in that manner if they weren't Sage. He gave the man another glare. "Don't touch me."

The figure pulled away. "So you can speak common tongue."

"Just because I can doesn't mean I'll speak it with you," he said, shifting back to the chimeran language.

The man hummed. He put the vial on the table. "Since I feel sorry for you, I'll allow you one question."

Mimi scoffed. As if he needed this man's pity. He was a Lykrine, son of the Lyeokee of the entire chimera tribe. His father was a powerful leader who wouldn't bend his will for anyone, and Mimi would be the same.

"You know, Lady Namir wouldn't appreciate me talking to a prisoner, but it's not like you'll remember anything anyway. I'll give you one last chance to ask me a question of your choosing."

Namir? Mimi felt like he had heard that name before, but where?

The man picked up the vial. "Time's up."

"Where's Sage?" Mimi blurted.

"Sage?" He tilted his head. "The ox chimera, I assume. He's with all the other chimeras."

The reply hardly answered Mimi's question. He gathered all the saliva in his mouth and spat at the man. It didn't quite reach his face, but it did land on his chest.

The man pressed his lips into a thin line. His brows furrowed, and there was a slight scrunch in his face. He bent over, and his fingers wrapped around Mimi's left ear. "This is an intricate cuff you have, chimera. It's different from what the others used to have. Why is that?"

Mimi froze. The earpiece he wore was a symbol of the Lykrine. It was a family heirloom, passed down from since the chimeras had obtained their freedom. They'd come as a pair—one for the Lykrine and the other for the Lyeokee. His father's was gold, while his was bronze. It was irreplaceable.

"What happened to all the bite you had?" The man traced his fingertips across the surface of the accessory.

"Don't." Mimi kept his body still. He wanted to sink into the table and be away from the unknown man as much as possible.

The man leaned down. His breath tickled the side of Mimi's ear and neck. "Oh, I think I will." He tore the earpiece off of Mimi's ear.

Mimi cried out. His ear was hot. Warm blood dripped from the tear in his ear. He couldn't stop his body from trembling. His chest closed in, and his stomach churned. He wanted to vomit. The precious earpiece was the last thing his mother had given him before she'd died. She'd gotten entangled in a poacher's trap and had barely escaped, making it back home. Her wounds had been too severe to heal. She'd been gone from his life before he'd been able to learn about his powers. If he would have known, then he would've done everything he could to save her.

The man caressed Mimi's cheek. "Don't worry. You won't remember anything after this." He popped the cap off the vial and tipped the glass tube over Mimi's lips. Mimi allowed the thick liquid down his throat. It was tasteless. Unlike the first one he'd been forced to drink, it didn't burn his throat.

The man removed something from his coat. It looked like a long, curved tooth from an animal. He pressed a hand on Mimi's chest, moving around as if he was searching for something.

Mimi's body quickly numbed. Whatever was flowing through his body, it was taking away his senses. He couldn't feel the dryness of his mouth. He couldn't hear the shuffling of the man's clothes next to him. He could still see, but just like before, the colors began to fade. The pressure of the man's movements was there on his chest, but he couldn't feel his hand.

Mimi saw the man's lips move. He gave Mimi a sly smile before positioning the point of the tooth in the middle of his chest. He pressed the tooth down. It pierced Mimi's flesh slowly. It was an odd sensation. The pressure increased as the tooth pressed deeper and deeper.

And then pain.

Searing hot pain.

The pain was unbearable.

Mimi screamed at the top of his lungs. He tried to pull his arms and legs from the binds, but it was futile. It felt like his chest was being split open. He could feel every nerve, every muscle, every bone crack and creak apart. Sparks popped at his joints as he arched his back off the table.

Mimi didn't know when he was left alone. He somehow ended up on his side, unbound. His eyes glossed over his raw wrists. There were deep cuts and bruises over the pale skin. He winced as his body twitched and spasmed. The motion happened every few minutes. The pain had mellowed out, but it flared up every time his body moved.

Why did his body hurt so much?

Where was he?

Why was he here?

What was he?

Who was he?

34
SAVIOR

Charlotte circled around Elliot. Her boots echoed against the stone walls. There was a torch in her hand. Elliot's knees dug into the hard ground. His arms and hands were bound behind him. The bindings he'd had earlier had been redone, and the rope bit into his skin painfully. He had lost all track of time. It felt like it had been so long since he'd seen the sun. Clear, blue skies were a faraway memory.

When Charlotte asked him about his magic, he didn't answer. He could deny it, but she wouldn't believe him. Her story was set in stone, and she would see it to fruition no matter the cost.

Charlotte had dragged Elliot into a different room. There was no fire, no light source. Elliot was stuck in complete darkness. They must have had a way to watch him. Every moment the elf was about to fall asleep, he would be jolted away by a kick to the stomach. He never knew who had done it because they left right afterward. Elliot would be in too much agony to fall back asleep. And when he had the sweet relief of slumber, it wouldn't be long before he was forced back awake.

Elliot's body shivered from fatigue. His mind was muddled. His eyes drooped closed. Sleep almost engulfed his body.

"You're not allowed to sleep," Charlotte said.

Elliot's eyes snapped open. The room spun, and he almost fell forward.

"You still haven't answered my question from a few days ago."

Days? Just how long had he been here?

"I wanted to be nice to you by leaving you alone to think about the answer you'll give me, but I see it didn't work." She stopped in front of him. "I told my friends to keep you company. They were to make sure you didn't miss a beat."

Elliot remembered every time they'd jostled him awake. A kick to the stomach or a bucket of ice-cold water had been poured over him.

"They're giving you supplements, right? We don't have food to give to your kind, so whatever they inject will have to do."

Elliot knew. He was awake for the torment whenever he was injected with the so-called nutrition. His body felt like it was on fire, and everything was painful. It surprised him when he didn't pass out from pure exhaustion. His core still felt detached. Whenever he started feeling the strings pull together, the injection would rip them apart.

"Let's play a game," Charlotte said. "You answer my question, and I decide if I like the answer or not. If I do, we move on to the next question. If I don't like it . . ." She smiled. "You'll see when it happens."

Elliot nodded weakly. He forced his eyes to remain open, but his vision refused to focus.

"Question one: How come you can use magic?"

"I can't." Elliot's voice was weak, barely above a whisper.

Charlotte hummed. She moved the torch close to Elliot's face. He moved back from the heat. "This is a warning. Answer me again. How come you can use magic?"

Elliot shook his head. "I don't . . . know how to."

"Okay." Charlotte pulled the torch back.

Elliot sighed in relief. She'd taken the answer.

Charlotte reached into her coat. Elliot's eyes widened. It was Lily's dagger. She held the blade in the flames. She moved the blade away and waved it in front of Elliot. "Wrong answer." She pressed the hot metal against Elliot's collarbone.

Elliot cried. He jerked away and fell on his shoulder. He whimpered. The burn was agonizing. He could feel the skin flare up.

"I'll ask again. How come you can use magic?"

Elliot closed his eyes. This had to be a dream. A nightmare. And he desperately wanted to wake up, to be back in Venin with Minari and Chloé.

"I hope you're thinking of an answer," Charlotte said. "I'll give you five seconds. Five . . . Four . . . Three . . .

Two . . ."

"I was . . . born with it," Elliot said, opening his eyes.

"Interesting answer!" Charlotte tucked the blade away. "Second question: How can you, an elf, be born with the ability to use magic?"

"Vyl . . . Vylantra . . ."

"Vylantra?" Charlotte chuckled. "A dead god?" She shuffled toward Elliot. The flame was now inches away from his face. "I'll let you choose where I give you your punishment for giving me a wrong answer. Right or left hand?"

Elliot didn't want to think about what Charlotte was imagining. He shook his head. "Please. It's the truth."

Charlotte only smiled. "I don't think so. Dead gods don't just give cores to elves." She pushed Elliot to his stomach. "Since you didn't respond . . ."

Elliot felt the tip of the flame tickle his fingers. He tried pulling his hand away, but Charlotte held him down by his shoulders. Searing pain ran up his hand to his arm. He tried to kick his legs, flip himself over, but Charlotte kept the torch close to his hand. Tears spilled from his eyes. "Please! Please stop!"

Charlotte held the fire for another few excruciating moments before pulling away. His entire right hand throbbed. He couldn't move a finger without feeling pain.

"Last chance. How can you be born with a magic core?"

Elliot tried to control his breathing and choked back sobs.

"Five . . . Four . . . Three . . ."

"I'm the oracle . . . I was born defective, so they deemed me the oracle," Elliot lied. He spewed the first thing that came to mind, anything that would get her to stop.

Charlotte's eyes lit up. "The *oracle*? I have the actual oracle here? Leader of the savage elves. This is rich." Her expression suddenly darkened. "If you're the oracle, then I would be greatly rewarded if you told me where your pitiful kind live. Wiping out all the savages would purify all of Etheria."

No. That wasn't something Elliot was going to reveal. If he told Charlotte, there was no doubt in his mind that she would send an army into the mountains. The scouts wouldn't stand a chance against a force that large. Mistfall would crumble to ruins in an instant.

"Did you not hear me? I asked where the elves live."

"No . . ."

Charlotte frowned. "No?"

"No."

"All right. Since I knew you weren't actually going to answer it, I'll give you a free pass for now." She set the torch down in its sconce on the wall. She grabbed Elliot by his arm and dragged him across the room.

The bindings around Elliot's arms were cut. The relief from the uncomfortable position was short-lived; the sound of chains reached his ears. His arms were pulled above his head, and cold metal clasped around his wrists. The chains were yanked upward, forcing Elliot to stand.

Charlotte tapped his cheeks. "Time unfortunately is up for me, but I can't wait for our next meeting. This game is fun, isn't it, elf?"

The torch was taken away when Charlotte left, leaving Elliot in complete darkness. He let his head drop. He needed to protect Mistfall. He was the oracle. It was the least he could do. If he had to endure the painful torment, then so be it.

The humans would never reach the elves.

35
TIME

Torn. Minari's heart was torn in two. His mind had wanted to stop functioning as soon as he'd seen Redd on the ground. He'd known the bird was fine. It wasn't like Alder's familiar could be injured or killed. The unresponsive bird meant only one thing.

Alder's attention was compromised.

Something must have happened in Mistfall.

Part of him wanted to rush back home to make sure his mother and sister were all right, but he knew he couldn't. He needed to find Elliot. The oracle was top priority over everything else.

Minari had to believe Elliot was all right, that he was still alive. If Minari lost both Elliot and his family, he wouldn't know what to do. There would be nothing to return to. No Mistfall. No family. No Elliot.

Minari mindlessly followed Chloé and Bunnie from the destroyed clearing. Xander tried to bring the elf out of his woes, but his mind refused to work. He stroked Xander's head and mounted.

Night settled in, but Minari didn't know when. A fire was made, and Minari didn't know when. They settled around the warmth. Minari didn't know when. He was leaning against Xander. The ovis's soft brown fur brushed against his cheek. He felt Chloé's eyes on him, but he couldn't bring himself to have a conversation.

Bunnie was standing away from the fire. A leather glove was slipped over her arm. A great horned owl came swooping down. Its large wings were nearly silent as they flapped, and it settled on her arm. There was a piece of paper tied around its leg. The brown bird twisted its head and pecked at its wings.

Bunnie slipped a finger under its chin and rubbed the animal. The owl's feathers flared from the sensation. "Hello there, Ginger. I've missed you," Bunnie said. She untied the paper, and the owl took flight once again. She returned to the fire and took a seat next to Chloé. She unraveled the note, and her eyes darted across the paper.

It felt like long, anxious minutes. Minari wanted to know what it said. Where was Elliot? Was he okay? Bunnie's growing frown didn't soothe his worries. His stomach turned the longer he waited.

"Well," Bunnie said. She rolled the paper up and tossed it into the fire. "Good news and bad news."

"Where's Elliot?" Minari blurted. It was the first thing he'd said since they'd left the clearing and settled down.

"Elliot is . . . alive."

"But?" Chloé asked.

"Elliot was with two chimeras—one snake and one ox. It looked like the three of them were fighting a giant toad." Bunnie rubbed her fingers against her temples, shaking her head. "I find a giant toad hard to believe, but it's not like I could be convinced otherwise with the amount of damage."

"Snake? The one who broke into our room?" Chloé asked.

"He was wearing a slate-colored cloak. Both the chimeras were."

"Oh, no." Chloé pressed a palm over her mouth. "Is he okay?"

"Like I said, he's alive. The three of them are, but that isn't what we should be worried about."

"Elliot and the chimeras. Were they working together?" Minari asked.

"It appeared like they were. There wasn't a report on them being hostile."

Then it was no coincidence the chimera had appeared before them in Venin. Minari knew he'd probably been drawn to Elliot's oracle powers. For them to meet again may have been a good sign. If the chimera felt anything like how Chloé felt toward Elliot, then that was one less worry for Minari.

"The bad news is . . . Elliot and the chimeras were captured by Oasis."

"What?" Chloé's eyes widened. "Oh, Mykronos. Please no . . ." she whispered.

"Unfortunately, my men lost sight of them shortly after. They believe Oasis has taken them to a secret location. They didn't return to HQ in Valquent."

Chloé's head was shaking. "No. No. No. Why was Elliot taken by Oasis? He's marked with . . . with my collar. They should've returned him to me."

"So I take it you know what happens to chimeras who get taken into custody by Oasis?" Bunnie asked.

"I only know what they report to the council. Each month they disclose how many chimeras they took into their custody. They keep them in cells and try to reform them. It isn't against the law, but . . ."

"You don't know what it means to 'reform.'"

Chloé shook her head. Her fists were clenched tightly over her skirt. "Elliot isn't a chimera though. He's an elf . . ."

"You should know elves don't have the same rights as we do. If anything, they may be lower than chimeras."

"But the collar." Chloé bit her lip. "The collar was for his protection."

"Miss Gemme, I'm sorry to say this, but if you have any hope of finding Elliot, we need to find their hideout. But that is going to have to wait. I have my men surveying the different parts of Etheria for anything unusual."

"So . . . we wait," Minari repeated. "We wait like sitting ducks while who knows what happens to Elliot." Minari's world was crumbling apart. He hoped with all his heart that Elliot would be okay, but this recent information told him otherwise. He didn't want to know what it meant to be reformed. He didn't want to imagine what the younger elf was going through.

"He'll be okay," Chloé said. She put a hand over Minari's and gave him a comforting squeeze. "We'll find him."

"But we need to wait," Minari said.

"It shouldn't take long," Bunnie said. "I'll be getting updates each night, so we won't be waiting in the dark."

"Where should we go while we wait?" Chloé asked.

"My home is in Lonin, which isn't too far from here. A day's ride. I wouldn't mind taking you two there. I have a stable where I keep Lightning. There is enough space to keep the other animals as well."

"Thank you, Bunnie. We appreciate it. I promise I'll do whatever I can to disband Oasis."

Minari tuned the two out. A steady buzz rang in his ears. Wait. He would have to wait. How long did he have to wait for? Anxiety swirled in the pit of his gut. He didn't want to wait. There was no time. Mistfall could be in danger, and Elliot was nowhere to be found.

Minari was pulled from his slumber. His nerves alerted him someone was nearby. Chloé and Bunnie were resting, wrapped warmly in blankets. The fire was out, probably having been blown out by the wind. He leaned forward, a blanket slipping off his shoulders. He moved it off and quickly stood. Whatever was coming was approaching fast.

Minari dove into the trees. He traveled through the shadows, listening for any change in movement from the unknown figure. Whoever it was, they kept a steady pace.

Minari was sent sprawling onto his back. A blade pressed against his throat. His eyes widened. "Captain Errol?" What was he doing here?

Errol was above him. His arm dug into Minari's chest. "Minari. It's just you." The blade was removed from his throat. Errol offered a hand. "I didn't realize it was you."

"Captain, what's going on? What are you doing here?"

"Never mind that. Where's Elliot?"

Minari's body ran cold. Of course Errol wanted to see Elliot, but what could Minari say? What would he be able to say? "He's . . ."

"Tell me." Errol's eyes burned through Minari.

"He's not here."

"What do you mean?" Errol grabbed the front of Minari's coat, pulling him up to eye level. "Where is he?"

"I can't say where, but I just know he's not here."

Errol released Minari, shoving him away. "Is he safe?"

"Yes," Minari blurted. He didn't know if it was true, but for now he had to believe he was.

"As long as he's safe . . . that's fine." Errol paused. "I need you to return home. I've come to bring you back."

Minari's stomach dropped. "Why?"

"There was an attack. Luckily everyone made it to the Moon Shrine, but Mistfall is in ruins. I need all the scouts I can get."

Minari became aware of Redd's still body pressed against him from the inside of his coat. He grabbed Errol's arm. His hand shook as he tried to control his breathing. "Is Mother all right? Stella? Lily?"

"They're fine, Minari. But like I said, I need you to return with me. As long as Elliot isn't here . . . he'll be safe."

Mayleen, Stella, and Lily were safe. Elliot would be safe the farther he was from Mistfall. Minari needed to return. He nodded. "Let me gather Xander and Xeno. Then we'll return."

36
OPEN

Chloé glanced around. The morning sun cracked, a golden hue illuminating the trees. The fire was long cold, probably blown out in the middle of the night. Bunnie was still tucked away in her blankets. Their two mares were still slumbering. But there was something missing. Or rather, someone.

Minari wasn't with them, and neither were Xander and Xeno.

Chloé scurried out of her makeshift bed. "Bunnie! Bunnie, wake up!" She rocked her sleeping companion.

Bunnie moaned. Her eyes cracked open. "Miss Gemme? What's wrong?" she said, voice deep and groggy.

"Purple Hair isn't here."

"Purple Hair?" Bunnie mumbled. "Morning calls?" She closed her eyes.

"No! The ovis are gone too. Everything." It was as if he'd never been there to begin with.

Bunnie opened her eyes and sat up. She looked around but didn't seem to be bothered by the missing elf. "I don't believe he would be rash enough to look for Elliot himself, but what do you think, Miss Gemme?"

Chloé knew Minari would do anything to save Elliot, so the first thing she'd thought of was that he'd indeed gone to find the other elf. He'd been keen on leaving Venin the moment Elliot had gone missing, but that had been before Chloé had opened up to him, before they'd formed a friendship. She trusted Minari to stay with her and not to leave her alone, but maybe it was wishful thinking.

"I don't think he would leave without a good reason," Bunnie said.

"But where is he? Why did he leave? He didn't even leave a note."

"Let us focus on the goal, Miss Gemme. We need to locate Oasis's secret hideout and find Elliot. Do you agree?"

Right. The goal. Chloé nodded.

"Good. Since we're already up, why not begin our journey? The sooner we reach Lonin, the better for our backs. We ladies need a nice warm place to sleep, don't you agree?" Bunnie smiled.

"Yeah," Chloé said. A hole formed inside her heart. She deeply wished Elliot would stay by her side as a trusted friend. She hoped Minari would be another friend she could put her trust in. Both elves had been torn from her too soon. Just like her parents.

They folded the blankets and placed them inside

Lightning's saddlebags.

Chloé and Bunnie rode into the day, following the trail leading to Lonin. They took four breaks throughout the ride. Not wanting to spend another night outside, they pushed through the dead of night. Camping outside reminded the nix too much of the two elves. Once they reached Lonin, Chloé would make sure she rewarded her mare with the juiciest apple she could find.

Lonin was larger than Venin. While Venin was a small town lit by gas and fire, Lonin was a full-size city powered by electricity. Stores and booths filled up many sections of the town. It was second largest to the capital in terms of purchasable goods. Though there was Solime, it was used mostly for trade rather than purchasing.

The only places that were open when they arrived were a few bars. Drunk patrons shouted and laughed, slapping one another on the back and clashing pints together.

Bunnie led her deeper into the city, past the midnight buzz.

"This is where I live," Bunnie said. Her home was a brick apartment building hidden in an alleyway. "I can take your mare to the back. You can make yourself comfortable while you wait." Bunnie reached into her coat and unlocked the door. She flipped the light switch before taking the reins from Chloé's hands.

Bunnie's house was bare compared to Chloé's lavish home. It had a single bed, a circular wooden table, and a bookshelf. The kitchen was in the corner without walls separating it from the rest of the room. The ceiling fan turned slowly, giving the room a small breeze. Chloé wondered how Bunnie could own her own stables if she lived in an apartment. Did the other tenants have horses also?

Chloé glanced at the books. They were volumes on Etheria's history, common in any household. She stepped away from the bookshelf when she heard the door click open.

"Sorry, hope I didn't keep you waiting for long." Bunnie shut the door with her hip. She held blankets in her arms. "You can have the bed. I don't mind sleeping on the floor."

Chloé shook her head. "No, this is your home. You should take the bed."

Bunnie's eyebrows rose. "If you insist. Let me lay these blankets down for you, at least." She flattened the plush material against the wooden tiles.

Chloé was taken aback by her own response. It wasn't like her to reject a bed. She was usually the one to claim it first. With her status, it was only right for her to be comfortable.

"Do you want some tea before you sleep? Chamomile, maybe?" Bunnie asked. She patted the blankets one last time before standing up.

"Sure." Chloé slipped off her heels, placing them by the blankets before settling in.

Bunnie took a kettle and filled it with water before putting it on the stove. She removed two mugs from the cupboard and placed a tea bag in each of them. The room was silent until the kettle hissed. Bunnie shut off the stove and poured water into the mugs. She held on to the handles and settled on the floor next to Chloé. She set them on the floor. "They're still hot. Let's wait for it to cool off first."

Chloé nodded. She tucked her legs under her chin. Even with the company of the other female, she still felt alone. Elliot and Minari had sparked something in her, and it had changed her. She could hardly fathom how she used to believe everything written in books. How they slandered elves. How they described how disgusting and rotten they were. They were all lies. But did that mean the war was a lie too? What had really happened?

"I can hear you thinking from here," Bunnie said. She held her mug under her lips, blowing the steam before taking a sip.

Chloé took the untouched mug and took a sip. She immediately pulled the hot drink away, sticking her tongue out.

Bunnie chuckled. "It's still hot. Did I trick you by drinking mine? I tend to like my drinks more on the hot side."

Chloé set the mug down. "Do you have lemon?"

"I don't. I'm not usually home for long periods of time to keep food around."

Chloé stared at the burnt orange liquid. It was quiet between them again. The only noise was the ticking of the clock and Bunnie's sipping.

"Do you think you're ready to tell me why you freed Minari?" Bunnie asked, breaking the long silence.

Chloé untucked her legs from her chest and folded them underneath herself. She laced her fingers together. "He doesn't deserve to be anyone's property." She opened up. She didn't want to keep the truth to herself any longer.

"Elves aren't what we think they are. They don't mindlessly kill, and they don't eat flesh. If anything, they're vegetarian."

Chloé recalled the night before they'd left Venin. They were sitting in the dining hall. She had ordered two specialties, one for each of them. When the food arrived, Minari paled so much he looked like a piece of paper. That was when he admitted he couldn't eat meat, let alone stand to be near it. She realized she hadn't eaten meat in front of either him or Elliot since they'd met. During their travels they'd had bread and whatever berries they'd gathered. At the inn, each specialty she ordered was some sort of soup, and that night was the first time she'd had meat in a while. She'd had the waiters take back her original order and had reordered potato soup for the both of them, which Minari had graciously eaten.

"I had a feeling," Bunnie said. "The two of them didn't have any hostile energy. Well, except when I first met Minari, but that was probably because Elliot had just been abducted."

Chloé picked up her tea and took a sip. This time it didn't burn her.

"I feel the same when it comes to chimeras." Bunnie set her empty mug down. "They shouldn't be treated so poorly just because humans created them. They deserve as much freedom as we do. They're living and breathing beings."

"If you'd told me this a month ago, I would've thought you were crazy." Chloé's lips slightly curled. "But now I think I know what you mean. We don't choose how we are created, and we all deserve to live a life without fear of segregation and prejudice." She matched her gaze to Bunnie's. "They deserve equality as much as we do, and for that to happen, Oasis needs to go."

37
GIFT

Chloé ran through the halls. The carpet was hot beneath her bare feet. Red footprints were left in her wake. The sound of snarling sent shivers down her spine. She pushed herself faster. It was chasing her. It had eaten her parents.

And now it wanted to eat her too.

She saw the monster. It looked like a three-headed dog. It was hunched over, teeth ripping Elizabeth apart. Her body was sprawled on the floor, painting the carpets crimson. Her eyes were wide open, staring at Chloé. Gerald's body wasn't too far off, mutilated beyond recognition.

No matter how far Chloé ran, the walls remained the same. It was like she was running in circles. No matter which door she went through, which stairs she climbed, she always ended up passing the same room her parents were in.

The snarling was getting louder. She could feel its breath running down her neck. Panic bubbled up in her stomach. She squeaked, urging her legs to move faster. She turned at a corner and the floor disappeared, replaced by a staircase. She felt herself fall forward.

Chloé jolted upward, throwing her blankets off. Her body was trembling and drenched in sweat. She took deep breaths as she tried to calm her racing heart. The sunlight spilled through the small window, casting a morning shadow throughout the room.

"You're finally awake."

Chloé jumped. She jerked her head to the side. Bunnie was sitting at the edge of the bed with her brows laced together. There was a mug in her hands. She handed it to Chloé.

"I tried waking you up, but you wouldn't no matter how hard I tried," Bunnie said.

Chloé accepted the mug. The familiar aroma hit her instantly. Black tea with a hint of lemon.

"I figured this would help calm you down."

"Thank you." Chloé took a sip, relieved it was cool enough for her to drink. "What time is it?"

"Just past eight in the morning." Bunnie's voice was gentle. "How are you feeling?"

"Better." Chloé took another sip. The tea settled in her stomach, warming her body. She did her best to push the images of her parents' mangled bodies from her mind. There had been so much blood. The taste of iron suddenly reached her tongue. She looked into her cup. Her stomach immediately dropped. She threw it away. It shattered, ceramic pieces scattering across the floor. Blood spilled from the broken mug.

"Chloé?" Bunnie placed a hand on Chloé's shoulder.

Chloé swatted the hand away, shrieking. She threw the blankets at the older human and crawled away. She hunched over, clutching her head. She clenched her eyes shut. She imagined herself anywhere but here. She wanted to be in the forest, camping with Elliot and Minari, eating warm bread and drinking tea.

"Chloé?"

Chloé flinched. She recognized the voice. It was Bunnie's. She opened her eyes. She was in Bunnie's apartment. She peeked over her shoulder. Bunnie was looking at her while gingerly picking up the broken mug. Tea sputtered across the floor.

"Chloé, are you all right?"

Chloé nodded once. "Y-yeah . . . sorry. I think I was still dreaming. I saw something and got scared . . ."

"As long as you're okay." Bunnie tossed the broken pieces and grabbed a rag, wiping the floor.

Chloé watched her quietly. She appreciated the silence. It helped soothe her frazzled nerves and racing heart.

"Are you calm now?" Bunnie asked.

Chloé nodded. "Thank you."

"No worries, Chloé." Bunnie threw the soiled rag into the sink. She turned the water on and began rinsing.

"You occasionally call me by my birth name. Why is that?" Chloé asked. It was unusual for someone she didn't know on a personal level to address her as such. It was always "Miss Gemme" since she was part of the council. Normally, Chloé would've been annoyed someone would address her so casually, but it felt familiar when Bunnie called her by her name.

Bunnie's hands paused momentarily before continuing rinsing the rag. "I guess it's time for me to tell you, huh?" She turned the sink off. "Follow me."

Chloé and Bunnie left the apartment and circled around behind the building to where the wooden stables were. Bunnie ushered Chloé inside.

The stables held eight stalls. Chloé spotted Lightning and her gray mare. There was one more horse at the end, away from the other two. It had a shiny, black coat and bright eyes.

They passed the familiar horses and ended up in front of the unknown horse. Bunnie stroked its muzzle.

"Her name is Windfall," Bunnie said. "A gift from your father."

Chloé's eyes widened. "Father . . . ?" Her body wouldn't move.

"Yes, Gerald Gemme, your father."

"How do you know my father?"

"My adoptive grandfather was good friends with both Gerald and Elizabeth Gemme." Bunnie unlatched the door. "Come inside. There's something I want to show you."

The horse flicked its ears, gaze locked on Chloé.

There was a small chest at the back of the stall. It was white with gold trim. There were a few scuffs on the surface, but other than that it was in pristine condition. Bunnie knelt down and reached into her bosom, pulling out a golden key. She popped the lock off and pushed the lid open. She lifted a hand, beckoning Chloé closer.

When Chloé's gaze landed on the contents of the chest, she lost her breath. Inside was an intricate neckpiece large enough to wrap around a horse's nape. Gold lines twisted and turned in a floral pattern. In the middle was a gold plate with the most brilliant opal she had ever laid eyes on. It reflected the light, and gold and blue specks glimmered across the stone.

"Uncle Gerald never intended for you to become part of the council at this young of an age," Bunnie said. "He wanted you to have your freedom, to travel Etheria." There was a pause. "The reason I call you Chloé is because we've met before. Of course, you wouldn't remember. You were still a newborn."

Chloé was lost for words. She'd never imagined she would meet someone who'd known her parents besides Cecilia.

"I think to attract the least amount of attention during our search, you should take Windfall."

Chloé nodded. It made sense. If she was riding her gray mare, it would definitely attract unwanted attention, especially since she had informed Licht she would be putting her council duties on hiatus. It wouldn't make much sense to be riding a council mare. "Would you . . . would you tell me about my parents?" she whispered.

Bunnie smiled. "Of course, but maybe another time, Miss Gemme. We have a lot on our plate right now."

"Chloé. Call me Chloé." Chloé bit her lip. "Please," she whispered.

"Chloé." Bunnie smiled, opening her arms.

Chloé rushed forward. She buried her face in the other woman's chest. Tears spilled from her eyes. Her shoulders shook as she let out her sobs.

Gerald had wanted her to be a free spirit before council duties tied her down. He'd wanted her to travel Etheria and explore. Perhaps it had been the last wish he'd had for her before he'd passed away. She would fulfill it. She would take Windfall all around Etheria and explore what the world had to offer. She would do it with Elliot and Minari at her side.

Chloé needed to focus on the goal. She would work together with Bunnie to find Oasis's hideout and bring back Elliot.

Hopefully Minari would be there when it happened.

38
SURPRISE

Minari had quietly roused Xander and Xeno from their slumber. He was lucky Chloé was a deep sleeper, but he couldn't hide his departure from Bunnie. She merely looked at him and didn't ask questions. She gave him a single nod, as if she understood. Minari knew she didn't know why he was leaving, but it relieved him when she quietly let him go without needing to explain himself. He took the two ovis' reins in his hands and left, making sure he didn't leave anything behind.

Errol refused to ride the ovis back to the mountains even though it would've expedited their journey, and he refused to answer why when Minari asked. He insisted that they needed to keep the ovis rested in case anything happened. On top of the strange decision, Errol led them through detours. He took curved paths that swung around the forest. It appeared he was doing everything he could to slow their journey down. The captain had made it seem like he was in a hurry when they'd collided, so why the sudden slowdown?

The talks they had were short-lived. Errol never gave concrete answers to Minari's questions and left no room for further conversation. So far, the only things Minari knew were that everyone was safe in the Moon Shrine, an unknown attack had destroyed Mistfall, and Elliot would be safest away from it all, which wasn't any different from when they'd first talked. The older elf refused to go into further details beyond that.

Minari counted the days they spent traveling. It was nearing a week and a half, and they weren't as close to home as he would've liked. The travel back should have taken no more than seven days with the ovis.

Evening fell on the tenth day, and Minari was restless. He couldn't quell the anxiety bubbling in his stomach. He couldn't quell the jitters in his legs. He *needed* to be home. He *needed* to be sure Mayleen, Stella, and Lily were safe.

Minari wandered away from the campfire. The tree branches loomed over his head. Clouds hid the moon and stars, but it didn't stop Minari. He was accustomed to walking in the dark. If the two of them continued on their current track, they would probably reach home in another week. That was too long for Minari. What was Errol hiding?

The elf's mind drifted to Chloé and Bunnie. Had they been able to locate Oasis's hideout? Had they gotten Elliot out of there? Was Elliot okay? Did Elliot need him? Minari didn't like being separated, and it ate away at his heart every day. They'd always been together, and now they'd been forced apart.

On the thirteenth night, Minari couldn't keep it down. He approached the older elf. It was disrespectful to go against Errol since he was the captain of the scouts—that was why he'd waited so long to approach him—but he needed answers. He wasn't going to postpone this any longer. Errol's unusual behavior was clawing at his nerves.

Errol was sitting crossed-legged by the fire, a dagger in his hand. He held a sharpening stone and brushed it against the already-sharp blade.

"Captain," Minari said.

"What is it, Minari?" Errol responded, not taking his eyes off his task.

"We've been traveling by foot for two weeks. We should've been back in Mistfall by now, so why aren't we?"

"As you can see, we aren't back yet because we're still traveling to get to Mistfall."

"We should've been back a week ago!" Minari raised his voice. He was showing a significant amount of disrespect to the older elf, but he couldn't bring himself to care.

"Minari," Errol said.

Minari clenched his fists. "Why aren't we riding the ovis back home? Why are we taking detours?" The sight of Errol ignoring his questions made his blood boil. Errol kept to his task. Every night he sharpened his blades. Every night he refused to give Minari a proper response. He wasn't going to waste any more time. If he rode Xander back to Mistfall, he would arrive in two days. The only reason he'd taken Xeno with him was because he'd had the intention of Errol riding him back. If Errol would not ride Xeno, then he would have the ovis follow him home. Once he made sure everyone was accounted for, he would descend the mountain and search for Elliot.

The scout turned on his heel, heading straight to the resting ovis.

"What are you doing?" Errol called out.

Minari didn't answer. He patted Xander's back, motioning for him to stand. He did the same with Xeno. Luckily, both animals had plenty of energy to spare. Trotting at the slower pace of the elves hadn't worn them out in the slightest.

"Minari, what are you doing?" Errol asked again, his voice stern. He stood and made his way over.

"Follow me, okay, Xeno?" Minari whispered to the ovis. He patted his muzzle before mounting Xander.

"Minari, we shouldn't separate," Errol said, now standing next to the younger elf.

"Captain Errol, you told me the situation at home is dire. The fact you've taken us on detours and have refused to travel by ovis proves to me you aren't in the right state of mind to be making any calls. I will return to Mistfall and the Moon Shrine on my own and assess the situation. I will report to Commander Silas when I arrive." With a kick to Xander's sides, they departed. He ignored Errol's calls.

The initial sprint eventually died down to a steady trot. They traveled throughout the night, only resting when the morning sun cracked on the horizon.

Traveling alone made it considerably quicker. Minari

took a straight path back to the mountains.

It took the lone elf two days to reach the base of the mountain. He was about to ascend when he sensed movement beyond the trees. He pulled Xander to a halt.

An elf stepped forward. His teal hair was a tousled mess. A patch covered his right eye and half his cheek. He crossed his arms and leaned his shoulder against a tree. "Welcome back, Minari."

"Commander Silas," Minari said. He tried not to react to Silas's messy appearance. The elf never would've been caught seen so ruffled up. His coat was tattered, and his boot laces were partially undone.

"What are you doing here?" Silas asked.

"I could ask you the same question. Shouldn't you be in the shrine?"

Silas frowned. His brows pressed together, forming a thin line. "Where is Errol?"

"Not . . . with me. I left without him."

Silas heaved a sigh. He ran a hand through his hair. "Follow me. We shouldn't be out here for too long."

Minari followed Silas up the familiar path. He noticed there was a slight limp whenever Silas placed weight on his left leg. What exactly had happened?

"Did the captain say anything to you? Anything strange?" Silas asked.

"He said Mistfall was attacked."

"Unfortunately, that's true," Silas hissed. He stopped, rubbing his left leg.

"Commander, why not ride Xeno?"

Silas shook his head. "I don't have the right to ride

Elliot's ovis." He paused. "Wait, where is Elliot? He's not with the captain, is he?"

Minari gripped the reins. "No. No, he's not." He hoped Elliot was with the others. Surely enough time had already passed for the Nighthawks to gather intel.

"Good. I don't think the captain could handle seeing him right now." Silas squeezed his leg once more and continued forward. "Now, why isn't the captain with you?"

"I came into contact with the captain about two weeks ago. We should've arrived back here last week, but he refused to mount Xeno. He had us take unnecessary breaks and circle around trails when we should've gone straight. He wouldn't answer why we weren't hurrying back."

"Captain Errol—"

"Silas. Minari."

Both Minari and Silas froze in their tracks. Minari turned. Errol was standing behind them. His brown eyes pierced through the dark night.

"Captain Errol," Minari whispered. It should've been impossible for Errol to keep up with the pace of an ovis, no matter how fast he was. "How did you get here so fast?"

"Captain," Silas said, not giving Errol time to answer. He moved to stand between Minari and Errol.

"Commander," Errol said. "I trust you've been holding down the shrine since I've been gone?"

"Captain," Silas said again.

There was a long pause. The tension in the air was so tight that Minari almost forgot to breathe.

"Captain Errol, you were not in the right state of

mind to leave the shrine."

Errol's eyes narrowed. "Watch your tongue, Silas. You are speaking to your captain."

"With all due respect, Captain, your state of mind isn't in the right place. You should return to the shrine immediately."

"That was where I was taking Minari. He is to return to us. You know we need all the scouts we can manage."

"No, Captain. Did you forget why the two of them departed in the first place?"

Minari blinked. When had Silas learned the truth? He was sure the elders had fabricated a lie. The only ones who should've known were him, Lily, Mayleen, Stella, Elliot's parents, and the elders. All of them knew to keep it a secret . . . except Lily. It hadn't occurred to him to warn the younger elf not to spread the information, but he'd trusted her to make the correct judgment.

"I didn't forget, Silas. My son has to fulfill a prophecy. It has nothing to do with Minari."

"Minari is the oracle's scribe. He *has* to be there," Silas snapped.

"How did you find out?" Minari asked. "Commander, how did you know?"

Silas peeked over his shoulder. "Errol . . . wasn't in the right state of mind after the retreat to the shrine. He started spurting words. The elders couldn't keep the lie any longer. Everyone knows that Stella isn't the true oracle."

Minari gulped. "Is she . . . Is she okay?"

"She's fine," Silas said quickly. "We have it under control."

Minari sighed in relief.

"Minari may be Elliot's scribe, but we need him back at the shrine. We need to strengthen our defenses. We don't know when there could be another attack."

"We have the culprit in the shrine's basement. There won't be another attack."

"You can't know that for sure."

"We've been interrogating—"

"And what have you learned, Silas? She could've been lying the entire time, just like how she fooled us all."

"What happened during the attack?" Minari asked.

"Minari, I don't think now is a good time to answer that question," Silas said.

"No. I want answers. Tell me." Minari didn't want to be given the runaround any longer. "As the scribe and a scout, I have the right to know."

Silas's shoulders tensed. He had his hands in fists. But he didn't say anything.

"Minari," Errol said. "You'll learn this sooner or later, but the reason I didn't want to hurry back is because . . ." He paused, looking over at Minari as if waiting for a response.

Minari met his gaze, waiting. He was finally going to know the reason for the delay. He bit the inside of his cheek. Errol was hesitating. "Because?"

Errol took a deep breath. "Because the one who attacked Mistfall is Lily."

Minari's entire world stopped. The trees around him began to disappear. He couldn't hear the rustling of the leaves. A chill ran through his entire body, biting through every nerve.

The one answer he'd never expected to hear had come through Errol's lips.

And he was about to return home and pick up the pieces.

39
ATTACK

Eighteen days earlier . . .

Errol placed a plate in front of Estelle. Estelle had gotten alarmingly thin since Elliot had left. She barely ate, barely spoke, barely bathed. She was bound to their home, hardly leaving the bedroom. The only time she would leave was to sit in the kitchen for dinner before Errol left to tend to his scout duties.

Her once bright emerald hair was now dull. Her sparkling, blue eyes were sunken in. Her pale complexion had become sallow. She had gotten so thin that her clothes looked like they were engulfing her.

"Estelle, please take a couple of bites. I promise I made this potato soup edible," Errol said, attempting to lighten the mood.

Estelle stared at the plate with empty eyes. Her hands were still in her lap, shoulders hunched over.

Errol placed a gloved hand on her delicate shoulder. "Estelle, please eat something. You wouldn't want Elliot to worry, right?"

There was the slightest movement in her eyes at the mention of their son's name. "Elliot?" she whispered.

"Yes, Elliot!" Errol grinned. Was she finally coming around?

"Where is Elliot? How come he isn't down here for dinner?"

Errol's shoulders sagged in defeat. She still didn't remember, or rather refused to acknowledge Elliot had left because he was the oracle. "Love, he's not here because he's the oracle, remember? He left on a journey. He's been gone for about two weeks now."

The light in Estelle's eyes disappeared. She shrank back into her shell.

Errol sighed. He made his way over to the stove, taking his own bowl and scooping himself a serving.

A deafening, high-pitched shriek rattled the windows.

Errol's hold on the bowl faltered, and it shattered upon impact, spilling broth and potatoes across the wooden floor. He'd never heard that noise before, but he knew it could've only come from one thing.

An imp.

Errol rushed into the bedroom. Imps were creations of Necromancers. His blood chilled at the thought of a Necromancer so close to home. It was a good thing Elliot wasn't here.

He reached under the bed and pulled out a chest. He drew one of his daggers and used the hilt to break the lock off. Popping the lid open, he removed a bone flute. He rushed back into the kitchen, placing a hand on the front door before pausing to glance back at his wife. She was still sitting on the chair, lifeless. He would need to bring her to safety himself, but first he needed to send out a signal.

Errol stood on the porch. The imp's cry had been enough to send Mistfall into a panic. Villagers who had never heard anything so menacing were running. He needed to gather the scouts quickly so they could control the situation. He brought the flute to his lips and played. The signal was short, but it pierced through the night.

As soon as he finished the signal, Lyla was at his side. She must have rushed over as soon as she'd heard the imp. Relief washed over him.

"Elder Lyla," Errol said. "Please take Estelle with you to safety." He took Lyla's hand, hurrying her inside.

"Has she still not recovered?" Lyla asked, disappointment in her voice.

"I'm afraid not."

Lyla took Estelle by the arm, bringing her to her feet. "Estelle, come now, child. We must make haste."

Estelle mindlessly followed Lyla out of the cabin. That was one fewer thing to worry about. Errol trusted the elder elf to rush Estelle to safety in the Moon Shrine, where Alder had created a shield strong enough to contain the villagers with Vylantra's help.

When Errol returned to the porch, all his scouts were

already present. They were all dressed in their gear, ready for orders. Silas—his commander—and his oldest and most trusted scouts—Rowen, Ava, and Nile—stood front and center.

"Ava and Silas, I want you to control the evacuation to the Moon Shrine. Bring five scouts each to assist. The rest of you, we defend Mistfall."

"Sir!" they said in unison, then immediately dispersed. There weren't that many scouts, but he believed in their skills. It was unfortunate that Minari couldn't be present. He was one of the best he had. Lily's skill was close to his, but she considerably lacked stamina.

Wait.

Errol did a double take as he watched the scouts move.

Where was Lily?

Another shriek erupted. Errol covered his ears.

The imp flapped its large wings as it flew across the village. Its lanky arms dragged razor-sharp claws. Its long legs carried talon-covered feet. Its skin was gray, and its head had no hair. Its face was sunken in. The imp stuck its long tongue out as it clawed through the rooftops, splintering the wood. It grabbed torches from the square and scattered them across the broken homes. It landed on a cabin and roared, as if claiming its territory.

Errol cursed under his breath. He had hoped to have more time before the monster arrived. He used a railing to get on top of a cabin that wasn't ablaze. He wrapped his fingers around his dagger as he dashed toward the imp. The grotesque monster was smaller than he'd thought. Not counting its wings, it couldn't have been larger than an adolescent elf. He hoped that would give them the advantage.

Another scout reached the imp before Errol did. It was Rowen. His sky-blue hair flashed across the rubble. He had his longer dagger drawn, ready to bring it down on the imp's head.

In the blink of an eye, the imp's arm moved. Its claws wrapped around Rowen's neck. It swung its arm upward before flinging him through the roof and into the collapsed rubble. Rowen's body splattered across the debris. Crimson red splashed in random patterns. His eyes and mouth were wide open as he lay limp. Dead.

Errol couldn't move. His body was completely frozen. He wasn't sure what he'd just seen. One moment Rowen had been on the offensive, and the next moment Rowen was dead.

The cracking of bones sent shudders down Errol's body. The imp twisted its head completely around. Its bloodred eyes laughed at him, mocked him. Its lips curled, revealing rows of sharp teeth. Its slender tongue slipped through, and the imp waved it around as if tasting the fear in the air.

It spread its wings and took flight.

Errol snapped out of his trance when he realized where the imp was headed. It was following the shouts and cries of the escaping villagers. He saw a familiar head of green hair, and his blood ran cold. Estelle hadn't escaped yet. Lyla was having a difficult time trying to get her daughter to keep up with the crowd. He needed to get there. Now.

Errol climbed down from the cabin, but he was greatly hindered by the smoke and flames. The imp glided down with no issues. The imp lowered its arm, ready to grab an unfortunate elf in its clutches. And it was heading straight for Estelle. He wouldn't make it in time. "Estelle! Run!" he screamed.

Lyla turned. Fear overflowed in her eyes. She pushed Estelle out of the way, and the imp grabbed her instead. The imp continued to glide, dragging the struggling elf by her throat. It moved its arm up and slammed Lyla against a tree. It squeezed its fingers around Lyla's slender neck and tore her head from her body. It slid its tongue across its bloody fingers as Lyla's head rolled by its feet. Her decapitated body fell, turning the green grass red.

Errol sucked in a breath and gritted his teeth. Not another one. He tried to quell his raging storm of emotions. Lyla had been a harsh mother-in-law and elder, but he loved her as family all the same. Biting back tears and the bile that threatened to rise, he mentally thanked her. Lyla had given him enough time to reach Estelle, who still sat on the grass where Lyla had pushed her out of the way. "Estelle, get up. We have to go." He grabbed her arm, trying to pull her up.

Estelle's gaze was latched on her dead mother, and she was unresponsive to Errol's commands. Her legs refused to leave the ground.

"Estelle. Love, please. You have to get to the shrine," Errol said. Where were the other scouts? He'd only seen about three trying to keep the crowd moving.

The hairs on Errol's neck stood. Something was behind him. He turned and ended up face-to-face with the imp. Its lips were stained red, its gray skin splashed with blood.

Errol drew a dagger from his waist, aiming to slit the imp's neck. As if predicting his movements, the imp grabbed Errol's arm, stopping the attack. The elf then drew another dagger from his thigh and stabbed it into the imp's gut.

But its eyes were still locked on Errol; it was unfazed by the attack.

"Captain!" A familiar head of teal hair suddenly appeared. With one clean swipe, his dagger cut through the imp's wrist, releasing its hold on Errol. Silas's other hand came up to sink a dagger into the imp's skull. The monster fell to the ground, unmoving.

"Silas," Errol wheezed.

"Captain, we need to get out of here now. There are other imps. They were waiting in the forest. They forced us to take a detour."

Waiting in the forest? How would the imps know where to wait? Did the Necromancer who was pulling the strings know about the path? Only elves knew about it.

"Ava is with Lady Mayleen. She's keeping her safe, but Lady Mayleen plans on initiating the ensnaring trap. The scouts are trying to lure the imps away from the villagers. They'll arrive here any moment. We need to leave."

Errol's mind spun. This had to have been orchestrated by someone who had inside knowledge. But that meant there was a traitor amongst the elves. The race was already so small. They had yet to recover from the war. He couldn't believe one of his own kin wanted to wipe them entirely out of Etheria.

Silas's eyes suddenly widened. His mouth opened, wanting to scream something. Errol felt something push him forward, causing him to collide with his commander.

"E-Errol," Estelle whispered.

Errol turned his head.

Estelle had her hands outstretched, as if reaching out to him, but he knew. He knew she'd pushed him. She'd known what was coming, and she'd saved him. His heart shattered into pieces. It cracked, and he wanted to yell.

A blade had pierced Estelle's chest, barely missing where her heart was. The blade was pulled out, and Estelle fell to the grass. Errol's mind went blank as his eyes landed on a familiar face. His chest burned as if the blade had pierced him instead.

Red hair framed her pale face. Her body was clad in a scout uniform and daggers. There was a sinister curl on her lips. Her orbs were not the calming green he remembered. They were white—pure white. Her black pupils were a harsh contrast to her blank eyes.

"Lily," Errol said.

Lily slid the blade along her tongue. "Captain, Commander. Greetings. A lovely night we're having, isn't it?"

Lily.

Errol shook his head.

Lily was the one who knew the escape route.

Lily was the one who'd set the imps on the escaping villagers.

Lily was the Necromancer.

Errol was too dazed to realize Lily had moved. Silas grabbed his shoulder and pulled him back. Silas screamed as Lily's blade connected. He pressed his hand against the right side of his face. Blood spilled freely through his fingers.

Just like Lily had done with Estelle's blood, she licked her dagger. "Elven blood tastes so sweet."

"Captain, get out of here. I can deal with her," Silas said.

"Do you really think you can handle me, Commander? I'm not the same Lily you knew," Lily mocked.

"I'll be damned if I let you kill any more of Elliot's family," Silas sneered. "How could you do this to him? You two were friends!"

Lily pressed the back of her hand against her mouth, trying to stifle a laugh, but it escaped. She laughed straight from her stomach. It was a wicked sound. Her mouth grinned wide as she stared at Silas. "We *were* friends. I am no friend of the oracle. Rather . . ." She tilted her head. "I need him *dead*. It's unfortunate I didn't awaken to my memories and powers sooner, or I could've killed him myself, but I can't wait to see his face when he learns his entire family is dead and it was all his fault."

"You wouldn't dare," Silas said.

"I would." Lily twirled her blade. "Now, how would you like me to kill you? I guess I'm going to have to go through you before I can kill the deadbeat captain. Too shocked to even respond."

Silas elbowed Errol farther back before he moved.

Lily and Silas collided, blades clashing. Silas was extremely skilled. He wasn't the commander of the scouts off of merit alone. He had the ability to hold the position, so Errol couldn't believe it when Lily matched each attack Silas shot at her. But he was at a disadvantage. He wouldn't be able to see his right side with the gash that ran across his face.

Lily used that to her advantage, always steering herself to his right. Silas must have been so focused on accommodating for his blind side that he didn't see Lily strike from his left. She swept her foot under him, and he fell. She drove a dagger into his thigh, and Silas let out a strained grunt.

"You're sloppy, Commander. If we were sparring, I know you wouldn't have let me do that to you." Lily yanked the blade out and enjoyed the injured elf's blood.

Errol moved. He wouldn't let anyone else die on his watch.

Errol drew his dagger and flung it, aiming straight for Lily's neck. It pierced through, straight from the back to the front. Lily staggered, but she didn't fall. Her breaths came out in wheezes. She reached behind her neck and jerked the blade out.

Errol tackled Lily to the ground, his forearm pressed harshly against her wounded neck. Lily continued to take strangled breaths. She clawed at Errol's hold, but he only pressed down on her harder. She choked. Her struggles lessened, and her eyes rolled before she went limp. Errol released his hold and quickly stripped Lily of all her daggers.

"Captain . . ." Silas said. He had his hands pressed

against his wounded leg. "I'm sorry I couldn't protect—"

"Captain Errol! Commander Silas!" Ava rushed to their side. Her creamsicle hair stuck to her face, perspiration adamant on her features. "We attracted the rest of the imps. Please get out while you can. Lady Mayleen will activate the trap any moment now!" Ava's eyes widened when she saw Lily's unconscious body. "Captain! Lily. Why is she . . . ?"

"We're taking her with us. She'll be held underneath the shrine. Make sure everyone knows she's a Necromancer. She shouldn't be able to use any of her powers or abilities within the Moon Shrine, but better safe than sorry," Errol said.

"Necro . . . Necromancer?" Ava paled. She nodded. "Y-yes, sir."

"You help Silas. I'll take Lily."

Ava nodded.

Errol looked over his shoulder as the distance between him and Mistfall grew. A swarm of imps surrounded the village. Errol knew the scouts did their best, luring them and quickly making their escape. The ground rumbled. A black dome morphed around Mistfall before collapsing upon itself, destroying everyone and everything inside.

The once small and lively elven village became a pile of rubble devoid of all life.

40
MOVE

Chloé stood next to Bunnie at a large, round, wooden table. The table had a few chess pieces and the map of Etheria sprawled across the surface. They were in the Nighthawk's headquarters, which was inside the Red Walls Inn. There was a private dining room that was generally used for special guests, but that was only on the surface. In truth, the room was used for meetings amongst the Nighthawk members. There were no windows in the room, only a table and a few chairs.

Unlike Oasis, Nighthawk wasn't an official guild. They weren't given uniforms to wear to represent themselves. Instead, each member wore whatever clothes they had on their back. The only way for them to enter the meeting was for Bunnie to verify them herself. She had each member memorized.

It had been two weeks since Minari had left, and there had been no sign of him. When Bunnie had inquired about the elf's whereabouts, none of the members had been able to locate him. She could only hope he was all right. But that wasn't why she was here. She needed to focus. There was a good lead on Elliot, so they were finally going to move out.

"Nighthawk meeting number 254," Bunnie said. "Vivian, you may present your findings."

"Boss," Vivian said. The woman had short, brown hair and wore a simple coat and pants. Her clothes were functional rather than fashionable. Chloé recognized her as one of the violinists from Venin. Vivian placed the queen chess piece on the map. "We believe the hideout is here. After surveying the area for five days, we can confirm that we've seen Oasis members and a few captains enter what appears to be their secret base."

The queen piece was sitting in the desert area known as Pepper Zone. It was to the east of where Chloé had initially found Elliot and Minari. Few would consider going through there. If she thought summer days right outside the grottos were uncomfortable, she didn't want to imagine how it felt there.

"What does the outside of their hideout look like?" Bunnie asked. "As far as I know, Pepper Zone is just one gigantic body of sand."

"It is. They use magic to enter their hideout; that's why no one can find it. There is one specific location where the magic appears to work."

"Boss, if I may," a man said. He had black hair, was

dressed for functionality, and was one of the violinists.

"Go on, Deveran," Bunnie said.

"It appears each member has a stone they carry. The stone probably holds magic, and they're able to use it when entering the hideout."

"Magic, huh?" Bunnie tapped her chin. "How did Oasis get ahold of these magic stones?"

A flash of white appeared in Chloé's mind. "Ethereals," she blurted.

"Ah, that's right. The two captains you spoke with in Venin were ethereals," Bunnie said.

Chloé remembered them well. They hadn't shown any hostility toward Minari and had spoken to them with respect. They hadn't seemed like the kind to discriminate against chimeras, yet they were part of Oasis. They could have had an ulterior motive.

The proposal for Oasis had been submitted before Chloé's time in the council, but she knew what it was about. Oasis was to become an official guild, and their task was to bring unruly chimeras who entered towns or cities into their custody. There were a few mutual lands where the races could all meet. The outskirts of Pepper Zone was one of them, but hardly anyone used the area. If the chimera they took was well-behaved, they would escort them back to their chimerian lands. If they weren't, they brought them to the mutual grounds and reformed them to behave more like an appropriate chimera.

"If we can locate the hideout, we'll be able to see what they're actually doing," Bunnie said. "I doubt they're trying to reform chimeras there. If they were, they wouldn't be keeping it hidden."

"Miss Gemme, if I may?" Vivian asked.

"Yes?" Chloé said.

"If it's proven that Oasis is doing something unethical, will you be able to bring it to the council's attention?"

Chloé hesitated. Anything regarding giving justice to chimeras was a touchy subject for many, but she knew everyone in Nighthawk wanted to see chimeras treated fairly. It wouldn't be easy for her to bring it to the attention of the council, but she'd made a promise to Bunnie to do her best to disband Oasis. "I will do everything in my power to shine a light on the unfair treatment of chimeras. They obtained their freedom in King Valentine III's time, and we should uphold his wishes. Whether they were created and bred by humans or not, they are living beings and deserve as much freedom as we do."

The tension in the air dissipated. The members smiled at one another. They talked and hugged. Chloé blinked, utterly confused.

Bunnie smirked as she crossed her arms. "They were nervous when I said I was working with a council member. They weren't sure if our ideals matched up. They were skeptical when I told them we were looking for a council member's elven property."

A man's arm suddenly snaked around Chloé, pulling her against his body. "I'm glad we finally have someone from the council we can trust," he said.

Chloé did a double take. She looked up at the male, who was practically giving her a side hug, and then at Deveran, who was across the table. They looked identical, except the closer man seemed to have a more proper taste in fashion.

"I'm Oliver, Deveran's older brother."

"You're only older than me by ten minutes," Deveran said.

"Ten minutes is ten minutes, little brother." Oliver waved his hand. He released his hold on Chloé. "Sorry if I overstepped my boundaries. Just wanted to show you my appreciation. We've been wanting to prove Oasis is up to something, and this is our chance."

Chloé opened her mouth, but she was at a loss for words. The Nighthawk members were all looking at her with big smiles on their faces. She felt her body heating up and her cheeks flushing. They welcomed her. They trusted her. It was a fresh feeling. She always felt stuffed and congested when she attended the assembly meetings. The pink-haired nix hardly enjoyed being around the other council members, but with Nighthawk, she wouldn't mind having them as company.

"Did I stun you with my charming looks?" Oliver winked.

"Oliver, that's enough flirting for one day," Bunnie said.

"But I only started!"

"And that's already overkill. We need to discuss how to infiltrate the hideout."

Oliver straightened his back. His playful expression shifted. His brows straightened, and the curl on his lips disappeared. "Deveran and I can leave at a moment's notice, Boss. Just say the word, and we'll gather our ammo."

"You two are the best gunslingers I have. I would greatly appreciate it." Bunnie gathered the pawn pieces and the king. She scattered them across the map. There were three pawns around the king and a few pawns spaced out in the Pepper Zone and mutual lands. "Here's Mission Emerald's breakdown. Oliver and Deveran, you two come with me and Miss Gemme," she said as she tapped the top of the king piece. "We will head toward their hideout and stake them out. The rest of you stand on watch. Make sure we don't get caught. If you see any potential Oasis members, distract them. Those in the mutual lands, be prepared to receive chimeras. It's unknown how they behave after being reformed."

Chloé furrowed her brow. The twins were gunslingers? How violent was this mission going to be?

"Miss Gemme, we don't take lives unless we absolutely need to," Oliver said. "My brother and I are skilled, yes, but we aim to disarm before killing."

"Oasis is an official guild. The fewer casualties we have, the better," Bunnie said. "We don't want the council against us before they're with us." She slapped the table. "All right. Vivian, I want you in charge of receiving chimeras. Take nine other members."

"Yes, Boss."

"Victor and Yen, you each take one side of the hideout. Make sure you notify us if you see anything out of the ordinary. Take six members each."

"Yes, Boss," they both said.

"The rest of you act as normal. Tour different cities and towns and gather information. It'll take us six days to get to Pepper Zone. We'll move out tonight. Everyone meet at Point Z at eleven sharp. Anyone who isn't present will be left behind. Clear?"

"Boss!"

41
DETERMINATION

Minutes. Hours. Days. Weeks. Time was a figment of Elliot's imagination. There had once been a time when Elliot had smiled. A time when he could open his eyes and take in the beautiful world around him. When he was surrounded by people he loved and who loved him in return. A time when he was filled with warmth.

A time when he wasn't terrified.

Elliot's body was tarnished with cuts, gashes, burns, and scars. The only part of him that wasn't marred was his face. He didn't know why Charlotte hadn't laid a finger on him there, but he wasn't going to question it. She had moved him from the chained walls to just allowing him to lie on the floor. He was free to choose where he stayed, not that anywhere felt warm. He still couldn't see the room, but he was sure his blood stained the floor and walls. It surprised him he hadn't fallen ill from all the wounds.

The nutritional injections had stopped making him feel feverish, but he still couldn't feel his core. He longed to feel the rush of magic in his fingertips. He hoped he would still be able to experience the sensation. The burns on his hands didn't allow him to feel anything anymore.

The door opened. Elliot turned his head for a glimpse of the brief light that spilled into the room. It wasn't Charlotte. The unfamiliar figure was a man. His hair was pulled back, and he had small, gray wings on his head. Elliot scanned his memories. He'd seen drawings of the race before. They were called ethereals. He left the door open as he walked in and knelt beside Elliot. Elliot watched the unknown figure scan his mutilated body.

Elliot's heart was beating painfully against his chest. Blood rushed to his ears. He was sure the other man could hear how fast his heart was racing. Elliot flinched away as the man reached out.

He frowned. "Charlotte did a number on you, didn't she?"

Elliot shook his head. "N-no, we have fun when we play games." He couldn't keep his voice from quivering.

"Of course." He pulled his hand back. "Lady Namir sent me to see if you were still alive. She was afraid Charlotte had accidentally killed you, but seeing as you're still alive, I will take my leave." The figure left as quickly as he'd come, and Elliot was surrounded by darkness again.

Relief washed through Elliot. Maybe Charlotte was too tired to play games with him today. Sometimes she would come multiple times a day, sometimes only once.

The way he counted them was how often he saw her between the nutritional injections. It hadn't been too long ago that he'd last received one.

"What do you think about him?" she asked. She sat with her back against a tree. She held it out, tilting her head and squinting her eyes. The moonlight glimmered against her silver blades, illuminating her purple eyes.

Was this another dream? "Who do you mean?" Elliot asked. He played with the hem of her skirt. Again, he was wearing female clothes.

Elliot saw her lips move, but he couldn't hear the name she said, yet for an unknown reason, he knew whom she was referring to. "He saved me."

"I know he saved you. I'm asking what you think about him." She narrowed her eyes at Elliot. "I've seen the way you two look at each other."

Elliot felt himself heat up. He looked away, anywhere but at his skeptical elven friend. Friend? Yes, they were friends.

"Ah-ha! You do like him. I'm surprised you'd fall for someone like him."

"What do you mean by that?" Elliot puckered his lower lip.

"I'm not making fun of you. I'm just saying it's surprising. He's probably the last person I thought you'd have a crush on." She sheathed her dagger. She lifted her arms up in a stretch and let out a groan. She leaned her elbow against her knee and rested her chin against her palm. She tilted her head slightly, her laven-

der fringe swaying away from her eyes. "You're going to tell him?"

Elliot blew out his cheeks. He stuck out his tongue and turned away. The thought of the man made his heart flutter. His mind went to the time they'd shared a kiss. He pressed his fingers against his lips.

She gasped and pointed a finger at him. "You! You kissed him already, didn't you?"

Elliot buried his face in his hands, hiding his embarrassment.

She whistled. "Wait until I tell everyone about this."

Elliot gasped. "You wouldn't!"

"Are you still giving him the silent treatment?"

"I—"

Elliot couldn't breathe. His chested ached. He felt cold and wet. He tried to move, but hands around his wrists and ankles kept him still. He opened his mouth to scream, but another rush of water came.

There was a cloth over his face, drenched in the frigid liquid. Tears prickled in the corners of his eyes. Was this another game? Had Charlotte asked him a question, and had he not given her the right answer? Panic boiled in his stomach. Was she going to kill him?

The cloth was promptly removed from his face, and Elliot took in a gasp of air. He took deep breaths. His chest expanded painfully.

"I don't remember saying you could sleep," Charlotte

said. There were two others with her. They were large, probably chimeras like Sage. Their hold on him was bruising. "How long were you asleep for? Come on, take a guess."

Elliot was still heaving, delirious from waking up so suddenly. How long had he been asleep for? Minutes? Hours?

The wet cloth was placed over his face again, and Elliot was immediately filled with terror. His voice was muffled as another wave of cold water overwhelmed him. He tried to move his hand to get the fabric off, but it was held tightly over him. His lungs burned. He tried to move his arms, but the chimeras kept their grip on him.

It felt longer than last time. Elliot's head spun before the cloth was removed. He coughed, choking for air.

"I'm starting to think you enjoy giving me wrong answers, elf," Charlotte said in a singsong tone. "Let's review what you've learned, shall we? First, why are you able to use magic?"

"I was . . . born with it." Elliot felt light-headed. He battled to stay conscious.

"Correct! Next, why is it you were born with a magic core?"

"I'm defective. Since I was born . . . with a core . . . I'm the oracle." He repeated the lie he remembered giving her.

"Right again! Now, do you know what you are?"

"S-savage. Barbarian . . ." Calling himself a savage or barbarian had become second nature to him. That was what he was. It was why he was here.

"Why did you leave your cage in the mountains?"

"As the oracle . . . I wanted to . . . start a war." Elliot's eyes began to close. Was that the reason he was down here? To cause chaos and riot? He tried to recall the true reason he'd left the mountains in the first place, but he couldn't remember.

"Hey, no sleeping! Remember, sleeping is against the rules."

Elliot forced his eyes open. He had to think about how he blinked. If he did it too slow, his eyes would stay closed. If he did it fast enough, he could keep his eyes open.

"Good. Now, why did you want to start a war?"

"Overthrow the king." That was right. He needed to overthrow the king. If he did that, then the elves could re-gain power once more.

"Why do you want to overthrow King Valentine VI?"

"Because . . . we are savages. Barbarians. We are powerful."

"Powerful? Sure," Charlotte scoffed. "Do you believe your kind deserve to live?"

"N-no," Elliot whispered. He recalled what Chloé had told him back in the library in Blanc Grotto. How the elves brought forth destruction many generations ago. If that was true, then he didn't believe he deserved to live, but it didn't mean he wanted to die. It wasn't his fault his ances-tors had taken so many innocent lives.

"Say that again. I couldn't hear you."

"No."

"Good answer. Now the best question: Where are the

other savages? Tell me where your cage is."

The same question again. Charlotte always asked him that question. Where was everyone else? Where was the location of home? Elliot bit his lip, holding back a tremble that threatened to wrack his body. If he told her where they were, then she would stop. He wouldn't feel any more pain. He wouldn't fear her. Maybe they would even let him out of here.

He opened his mouth. "They're . . ."

Charlotte's lips curled, and her eyes widened. "Yes? They're . . . ? Where are they?"

"They're . . ." Elliot choked. He pressed his lips together and shook his head. He wouldn't answer that. No matter how many times Charlotte tortured him, it was a question he'd promised himself to never answer. Everyone was relying on him. The dark history of the elves be damned. He needed to protect everyone at home. There were still so few of them. He refused to be the reason for the extinction of the elves.

"Still no answer?" Charlotte's tone was full of disappointment. "All right then." Charlotte moved away. The sound of her footsteps reached the other side of the room. "Hold him up."

The two chimeras hauled him to his feet.

Then something tore through his left thigh. Elliot yelled, falling limp. The chimeras picked him back up. There was an arrow impaled in his leg. It had torn straight through the muscle. He watched as blood soaked through his pants.

A thwish of a bowstring reached Elliot's ears, and he

screamed.

Another arrow stabbed through the same thigh, right above the first one. Elliot took a labored breath. He did his best to avoid putting pressure on the leg. He closed his eyes, wishing his mind to be anywhere but here, hoping the pain would alleviate.

"Leave him. We're done here."

Elliot's support vanished. He stumbled, doing his best to break his fall and avoid adding pressure to his leg. He choked out a sob as the momentum from falling jolted his leg, causing waves of agonizing pain.

"Maybe you'll answer the question next time, hmm?" Charlotte made her way to the door and paused. "There was another elf with you, right? The one with purple hair. Maybe he could answer it." The door shut behind her.

Elliot pressed his hand against his thigh. His body was wracked with sobs. He didn't believe Charlotte had Minari. Minari was safe. Minari was with Chloé. Chloé was safe. He would protect them both. He would stay here in their place.

He had to stay here. This was going to be his new home. He would continue playing games with Charlotte until he took his last breath.

42
CROSS

The thick air was suffocating. Sage wiped the sweat off his forehead with his arm. His clothes had been replaced with a plain white tunic. It was worn and used, tarnished with stains and holes. His footwear had also been stripped from him. There were cuts and bruises on his feet from walking barefoot. His back and arms ached as he pulled a wagon full of stones. There were blisters on his hands from gripping the wooden handle. It had been three weeks since Oasis had captured him and Mimi. He hadn't seen the smaller chimera since. Sage's chest tightened at the thought of him. He longed to see him again, to know he was all right.

At night—or what Sage assumed was night—he was led down to the dungeons and locked up in a cage. The cages were small. It barely allowed Sage to lie down. He had to fold his legs and tuck his arms in if he wanted to sleep. During the day, he and the many other chimeras were forced out of the cages and led to a room where they hauled giant stones from one side of the large room to the other. He didn't know what the purpose was, and the other captured chimeras would look away whenever he tried to speak to them.

The room had an altar in the middle with candles along the edges. The surface was stained red with what he assumed was blood. During his first few days, he'd had the unfortunate experience of seeing a fellow ox chimera get chained to the altar and stabbed to death.

The guards had called it a sacrificial ritual.

Chosen chimeras were offered to Mykronos, the great god of darkness. Sage had never heard the name before, and he didn't care for it. Whatever greater power the humans, nixen, or ethereals believed in, it didn't affect chimeras. It was either kill or be killed. There was no savior.

After the chosen chimera had died, a figure had appeared next to him out of thin air. She'd had long, smooth, blonde hair. A gold dress draped in chains of jewelry had covered her curvaceous body. The moment he saw her yellow eyes, he knew she was a chimera.

A feline.

Sage's stomach dropped the moment he saw her. He recognized her from the village. She was Namir, a cat who'd been rejected by her family. She'd been born with a large birthmark on her face. It made her unattractive, opposite of what the cats were known for.

Cat chimeras were beautiful. Females had silky hair

and full bodies, while males had sharp, handsome features.

Sage had last seen Namir before leaving the village with Mimi years ago, but this Namir no longer had the defect on her face. Her skin was pure, tan, and clean.

Namir dug her claws into the dead ox and slathered her face in his blood. She ripped his body apart until she found what she was looking for. Her crimson hand pulled out his heart. She licked the organ before completely devouring it. It had been messy, and it had disgusted Sage. Thinking back to it made the chimera want to chuck up whatever food he'd had, which was practically none. He hadn't had a proper meal since Mimi's boar catch.

Sage was given injections each night. They soothed the hunger pains and gave him energy, but they were no substitute. He was left with a headache that felt like his head was about to split in two. It would sometimes last for an hour or more, and he couldn't sleep until it went away.

"Hey, no slacking!" the Oasis member sitting on the wagon yelled.

Sage heard the crack of a whip before he felt the familiar sting. He grunted as it connected with his back, and he fell onto his hands and knees.

"Lady Namir wants these rocks moved out of the way by tonight! If you don't finish, you don't eat!"

Sage rolled his eyes. It didn't matter to him if he ate or not. It wasn't like they gave him food. None of the chimeras received anything edible. But he found it off-putting that some chimeras seemed to *enjoy* getting the injections. They would sway in their cages and hum with enormous grins on their faces.

"Useless chimera," the member seethed. "Be grateful Lady Namir took you under her wing! Little shits like you don't deserve to live."

Sage heard the crack of the whip and braced for impact.

But it never came.

"Whip him again and he won't be able to work."

Sage had never heard that voice before.

It was another human, but instead of the brown blazer everyone else wore, there was a beige trench coat over his shoulders with a silver brooch on his left side. His dark brown hair was slicked back. He cocked an eyebrow as he looked down at Sage.

"This one is an ox," he said.

"Y-yes, captain Aiden," the member said, lowering his head.

"With the latest one sacrificed for the ritual, we don't have many left." Aiden narrowed his brown orbs. "Be more careful next time. They are valuable. One of them can lift as much as five of you."

"Of course, captain."

"Brother!" called a woman's voice. Sage was sure he'd heard it before.

The loud clacking of heels stomped through the room. Arms wrapped around Aiden's body.

"Charlotte," Aiden said.

"Luka said the snake chimera is taking the spell nicely." Charlotte's eyes were trained on Sage. She smirked before returning her attention to Aiden. "He should be ready to use soon."

"So it's confirmed he's the Colorless Snake?"

Charlotte nodded. "Luka and Owen tested the chimera's blood. It works just like we thought."

Sage froze. He stared at the two humans. Snake chimera. Colorless Snake. Those words repeated over and over in his head. They were talking about Mimi. He was sure of it.

"What did you do with Mimi?" Sage shouted. He brought himself off the ground. If it weren't for the chain wrapped around his neck and bound to the wagon, he would've marched over and slugged the disgusting grin Charlotte was sporting.

"Mimi?" Aiden asked. "I didn't know this one could speak common tongue."

The member yanked the chain, causing Sage to fall over. "I'm sorry, captains! I'll do a better job handling this chimera."

Aiden lifted his hand. "No, let me talk to this thing. I've never spoken to a chimera who can actually speak." He knelt down to Sage's level. "So, who is Mimi? Are you referring to the snake chimera?"

"Who else would I be talking about?" Sage said. "That wench behind you should know exactly what I mean."

Aiden's eyes narrowed. He gripped Sage's hair and pulled his head back. "You insult my sister again and I will slit your throat, shitty chimera."

Sage spat in Aiden's face. "I hope you both rot."

Aiden shoved Sage to the ground. He scrunched his face, wiping the saliva off his cheek with his sleeve. "Teach

this one a lesson, and make sure he remembers it. No injections for him for the next three nights."

"Now, captain? But he hasn't finished—"

"Did I stutter?"

"N-no, captain!"

"Get to it. Now." Aiden turned to leave. Charlotte
gave Sage another smirk before following her brother out.

Sage watched the member unlatch the chain from the
wagon. As soon as the chain unhooked, he ran. He wasn't
going to let those two walk away unscathed. They'd done
something to Mimi, and he was going to find out what. He
balled his hand into a fist and swung his arm back.

Aiden turned, meeting him head-on. There was a
broadsword in his hand, and Sage's fist met the metal.

Sage bared his teeth. "Where. Is. Mimi?"

Aiden's lips twitched upward. "Why not ask him
yourself?" He pushed the sword forward, and Sage stepped
back.

A gust of wind blew from behind Sage. He turned
right when Namir materialized behind him, a catlike grin
across her features. But it was *who* was in front of her took
his breath away.

Namir's hands were on the shorter male's shoulders.
She stroked his head, his sand-colored hair laced between
her long fingers. It made Sage's blood boil.

"*You were looking for little Mimi here?*" Namir asked in
their native tongue, her voice laced with seduction. "*He's a
little cutie.*" She caressed Mimi's cheek.

"*What did you do to him, you fiend?*" Sage seethed. His
entire body shook. He bit back the urge to force his fist into

her smug face.

"*Nothing he didn't already want. A cat's charm is desirable. He couldn't resist me.*"

"*Why you—*" Sage balled his fists.

"*Sage,*" Mimi said.

Sage paused. Their eyes locked, but there was something empty about Mimi's gaze. His gold orbs held no light. He looked at him as if he were soulless.

"*Namir told me the truth about everything,*" Mimi said. "*Mykronos is the god who will free us. Once we offer our souls, we will obtain freedom. Isn't that what you want?*"

Even Mimi's voice didn't hold its usual vigor. It was monotone. There was no warmth. No affection.

"*Cat got your tongue?*" Namir asked. "*I understand how much of a shock this is to you. But he didn't want to remember anything about his past life. He will reach salvation with us. With Oasis.*"

Mimi stuck out his hand. "*Come join us, Sage. Join me as I reach salvation. I'm going to take part in the ritual in four days' time, during the full moon. Tell me you'll be with me when it happens.*"

All the noise around Sage became muddled. The only thing he heard was the blood pounding against his ears and the quick breaths he took.

Mimi had to be bewitched. Whatever Namir had done to him, it had changed him. The smaller chimera wasn't aware of what he was saying or doing.

Sage needed to save Mimi.

He needed to find a way to break whatever spell Namir had cast on him.

And he needed to do it before it was too late.

43
BLAZE

The morning sunrise did little to warm Minari's cold body. He was leaning against the wall of the shrine with Redd on his head. The small bird had regained consciousness as soon as he'd stepped foot in the clearing of the Moon Shrine four days ago.

When he'd first arrived back, Stella had immediately run to him. She'd wrapped her arms tightly around him and sobbed. She hadn't been wearing her oracle robes any longer. A simple stringed, white blouse and dark pants had replaced them. Mayleen had been close by, deep lines across her features and shadows underneath her sapphire eyes.

The only ones living inside the shrine walls were the normal villagers, elders, Mayleen, and Stella. All the keepers and scouts were stationed outside in tents, ready to fight for their last line of defense if they needed to.

"Minari."

Minari looked up from the patch of grass he was staring at. "Stella."

"Can't sleep?" Stella asked. She was holding a mug in her hands.

Minari shook his head. "No." He took a deep breath. "I still can't believe this is happening." Stella moved the mug toward Minari, but he waved his hand. "No, thank you."

Stella blew into the cup before taking a sip. "Is it about Lily?"

Minari bit his lip. The oracle's task was to stop the Necromancers, ultimately killing them, and if Lily was one, that meant Elliot would need to kill her.

Minari knew it would tear Elliot apart, and he didn't want that to happen to the younger elf.

"She . . . isn't the same as you remember," Stella said.

"You've seen her?" Minari held his breath.

"I went to visit her with Mother. It was the night after the attack." She took another sip of her drink before continuing. "There was a stab wound on her neck that Errol had inflicted, but it was somehow fully healed when I went to see her. She was conscious, though Alder is keeping her powers locked away."

"Were there casualties?" Minari knew there had to have been some. He hadn't seen Rowen or Elliot's mother and grandmother since he'd arrived, but he didn't want to assume the worst.

Stella frowned. "Yes. Elder Lyla was killed during the attack."

Minari flinched. He sucked in a breath. "And Miss Estelle . . . ?"

"Yes . . . she fell too."

Minari let out his breath. His chest constricted. His stomach twisted into the tightest of knots that made him want to throw up. He covered his mouth. Because he'd grown up with Elliot, Elliot's family had always felt like an extension of his own. Although he was relieved his own blood had been spared from the casualties, losing Lyla and Estelle broke his heart. Fate was a cruel thing. He knew it was best if Elliot didn't learn about the fate of Mistfall and his family, but he promised himself he wouldn't keep secrets from his best friend. He couldn't sever the trust they had together.

"When will you see Lily?" Stella asked.

"Eventually."

"You need to go back to Elliot, don't you?"

Minari sighed. He ran his hand across his face. "I do. I never intended to stay here, but I can't leave without seeing her first." Minari's gaze wandered to his tent. Inside it were the saddlebags that used to be mounted on Xeno, and inside one was the pendant Lily had made for Elliot.

Lily had to have known Elliot was the oracle. Everything lined up: the night she sneaked around the captain's quarters, the morning she stopped him and Elliot at the gates. As a Necromancer, she probably had the ability to sense it. But why had she waited so long to strike? What had triggered her attack? Minari was unsure if he should keep the pendant with him, leave it here, or even return it to Elliot. He didn't know what Lily had done to it, and he'd rather play it safe. But if there was the slightest chance the pendant didn't hold any ill will, it would be the last piece they had of the Lily they'd once known.

"I should see her tonight," Minari said. His shoulders were heavy at the thought of confronting Lily. They were childhood friends, and he still had a difficult time believing she had caused all this mayhem. But the sooner he did it, the sooner he could return to Elliot's side.

"Why not rest until then? You don't need to keep watch. I'm sure the other scouts and keepers can manage."

Minari's eyelids felt heavy, but as much as he wanted to rest, he knew he couldn't. They were in a delicate situation. They would have nowhere to go if the Necromancers attacked. He should at least make himself useful. "I'm fine, Stella."

Stella placed a hand on his shoulder. It was warm. "Minari, I can see how exhausted you are. I know you have barely slept since you returned."

"I haven't had a chance to speak with Mother. How is she?" Minari asked, changing the topic.

"She spends most of her days by the basement door, and if not there then with the elders."

Minari grunted. That explained why he hadn't seen her. They had crossed paths the first night he'd arrived, but they'd neither seen nor spoken to each other since.

"It feels weird. Not being the oracle," Stella said.

"You never were one."

"I know, but I've been the oracle for the past four years, even if it was an act orchestrated by the elders."

"How did everyone treat you after finding out?"

"The villagers were . . . upset at first. Realizing they'd spent the last four years talking to a fake oracle about their wishes unnerved them. But they understood the situation. It was Errol who told them the truth, and the elders had no choice but to confess."

"They didn't try to hurt you?"

Stella's eyes widened. "Minari, why would they try to hurt me?"

Minari pressed his lips into a thin line. Was he beginning to think his own kin were untrustworthy? There weren't many of them, and they needed to work together, but knowing a Necromancer had been right under their noses . . . he didn't know who to trust.

"I'm okay. Honest." Stella smiled. "It just took some time to get used to the changes."

"If you say so." Minari couldn't hold back a yawn. Exhaustion was creeping in.

"Please, Minari, you need to rest. Even if you don't want to, do it for me," Stella said.

Redd chirped as if agreeing with the suggestion.

"All right. Fine." Minari relaxed his shoulders. Perhaps an hour or two of rest would be enough.

The next time Minari woke up, it was dark outside. Redd had his head tucked underneath his wing and was sitting next to Minari's pillow. Stella was sleeping soundlessly next to him. Just how tired had he been? He sat up and ran his fingers through his hair. Luckily, nothing had happened while he slept. He would've hated it if he'd failed to protect any more people.

Minari opened the curtains to his tent and jumped at

the sudden presence of Errol.

Errol's arms were crossed, and his eyes were stern, but they flashed in surprise when he saw Minari jerk. "I don't remember the last time I surprised you because you couldn't sense my presence."

Minari's heart was pounding against his chest. "I don't remember either."

"You probably still need rest if this is the case. You know how important it is to be alert."

"I can't be alert if I'm sleeping," Minari deadpanned.

"And you can't be alert if your senses are dulled because you lack rest," Errol countered.

They stared at each other, waiting to see who would concede first.

The crunching of the grass interrupted their stare down. Mayleen approached from behind Errol.

Minari didn't think it was possible for his mother to appear even more exhausted than before. Her sapphire eyes were dull, and her amethyst hair was ruffled. Stray strands escaped her bun, and her skin lacked its usual luster. She appeared small in comparison to the clothes she wore on her back, but she still emitted the aura of authority. That would never go away.

"Errol. Minari," Mayleen said.

"Lady Mayleen, how is she?" Errol asked, stepping out of the way.

"Nothing new. She refused to speak with me. We have learned nothing new since the beginning." Mayleen glanced at Minari. "Minari, how much longer are you going to stay here?"

Minari opened his mouth and closed it. He sucked in his bottom lip. He didn't know how long he was going to stay. He knew he needed to leave, but he couldn't leave without meeting with Lily.

"Visit Lily now, then take Xander and leave. I expect you to be gone before the morning sun rises." Without another word, Mayleen brushed past Minari, but she paused before entering the tent. "I've noticed you've been slacking on your scribe duties. See to it immediately. The prophecy needs to be fulfilled. Return to Elliot and your duties. You've wasted enough time here as it is."

Minari stepped out, allowing room for his mother to disappear inside. He bit the inside of his cheek. It was true—he was wasting time here. He knew Mayleen was right, but he wished the moment had never happened. He didn't want to see Lily and return to Elliot with devastating news.

"There's one thing I want to tell you before you see Lily," Errol said.

"What?" Minari's shoulders slouched.

"She isn't the same shy Lily you once knew. She's a Necromancer. Whatever history you three had with one another is gone."

Minari frowned. His chest tightened. He could feel the twist of his heart. He knew that was the truth, but being told it so bluntly hurt. Lily was his friend, and he cared for her. "Before I go," he squared himself to Errol, "I want to know why you brought me back. I'm practically useless here, and it doesn't seem like Mother wanted me here in the first place."

"I guess . . . I wanted some control back. A bit of normalcy," Errol said. His eyes softened. His lips had the slightest quiver. "I lost my family and a handful of scouts during the attack. Our numbers were small, and now they are even smaller. I defied Lady Mayleen's orders and left to look for you and Elliot. Alder helped. He gave me a stone that allowed me to travel quickly. But when I found you and you told me Elliot wasn't around, it relieved me. Strangely enough, I didn't want him to return, even if he was the only family I had left. There was a Necromancer in the shrine, and she was a threat to him." He covered his mouth and sucked in a breath. "Tell me, truthfully, Minari. How is he? How is my son? He's . . . alive, isn't he?"

Minari steeled himself. "He's alive. I promised to protect him. As long as I live, I will be by his side." Yes, that much was true. He'd pledged an oath to himself and Elliot. He would see Lily tonight and depart. Elliot was waiting.

Errol chortled and shook his head. "You've become a fine man. I know I'm not Melvin, but you are practically a second son to me. I'm proud of you, Minari." He gave Minari a smile.

Minari balled his hands into fists. Tears threatened to spill. His shoulders shook as he tried to bite down his emotions.

Minari had been afraid he had failed his duty as a keeper when he'd lost Elliot. He had been afraid he had failed his duty as a scout when Mistfall had fallen. Even after his failures, Errol, his captain and his father figure, was still proud of him.

Errol opened his arms, and Minari pressed himself against the older elf. He let his tears fall quietly. His breaths were muffled against Errol's shoulder.

Minari was a scout.

Minari was a keeper.

Minari was a scribe.

Ultimately, Minari was Elliot's confidant, a true friend he'd placed his trust in. He would be by the younger elf's side no matter what, no matter who stood against him and his destiny.

Elliot was destined to fulfill the prophecy, and Minari would be there to blaze a trail.

44

LILY

Minari's footsteps echoed off the empty walls. He descended the spiral stairwell. This was the first time he'd ever stepped foot in the shrine's basement. The purpose of the basement was to keep the oracle safe, away from any danger. But instead of an oracle, there was a Necromancer. And instead of keeping whatever was inside safe, it was to keep everyone outside safe. Ironic.

Minari finally reached the end. A wooden door blocked his path. It emitted a soft green light. He placed his hand against the surface, and a warm sensation filled his body, giving him goosebumps. Alder must have sensed him because the door clicked open.

There was a large earth spell circle in the middle of the room. In the middle of the circle was an upside-down triangle with a line that ran across the lower half. The white etchings glowed, illuminating the room.

Lily was sitting on the ground, her arms bound behind her back. Her eyes were closed, but Minari knew she was awake.

"You have finally arrived," Alder said. He was standing in the corner of the room. The branches on his head glowed a similar green color to the one around the door.

"How are you holding up?" Minari asked. It was strange asking a demigod that question, as if he were a mortal, but he didn't want to dive into the reason for the visit. Not quite yet.

"The Necromancer is responsive, but whether she will respond is a different story," Alder said, disregarding Minari's question. "You may speak with her, but do not enter the circle. That is where my power is the strongest, and since you do not hold any magical properties, it is best you do not step into it."

Minari nodded. He took a deep breath before making his way over. He ran through the questions in his head again. He could do this. He had to do this. The tips of his boots barely stood outside the edge of the circle.

Lily's head tilted up, and she opened her eyes. Minari sucked in a breath. Lily's bright green eyes were now white. They pierced through him, sending shivers down his spine. She curled her lips but said nothing.

"Lily," Minari said, deciding to speak first.

"Hello." Lily's voice resonated off the walls.

Lily's voice was cold. The way the word slipped past her smirking lips made Minari's skin crawl. The hairs on his neck stood, and chills ran down his body. His nerves were urging him to get away, telling him to get as far away from her as possible, but Minari stood his ground. He had to face his fears. "Who are you?" he asked.

"Lily."

"Was everything a lie? Our friendship? Your feelings for Elliot?"

Lily didn't answer. She simply kept the smile on her face.

"Why did you do it?"

The blonde elf tilted her head. "Do what?"

"Why did you . . . kill?" Minari choked. He still couldn't stand acknowledging the fallen scouts and Elliot's family.

Lily hummed. She rocked forward and backward. "They were delicious, and I was hungry."

Minari's stomach churned. He could feel the bile starting to rise. He took a step back, covering his mouth. This was not Lily. No. This Necromancer was prancing around in Lily's body, and it made him sick. Her eyes moved up and down his body like he was some sort of meal. He couldn't look at her any longer. He turned away. "You're not her. You're not Lily," Minari said. He couldn't hide the shake in his voice.

"Minari."

Minari's eyes widened. The voice that spoke to him was the same one he'd heard before leaving Mistfall. He slowly turned, afraid his hearing was playing tricks on him.

Lily's emerald eyes looked back at him. Her brows were pressed together in an arch. "Minari, is that you?"

"Lily," Minari whispered. What was going on? Why

was Lily inside the spell circle?

"Minari, it's really you! Please, before she comes back, kill me. I can't hold her for long!"

Minari's breath caught in his throat. Was Lily trying to suppress the Necromancer? If she was, then there was hope. Lily was there, alive. He could still save her.

"Minari, please," Lily whimpered. Her eyes pleaded with him. "Kill me while I'm still myself."

"Minari," Alder called out. "Do not listen to her."

"But Lily. She's . . ." He took a step forward.

"Minari," Alder warned. The demigod was by his side instantly. He grabbed Minari's wrist and pulled him away. "Lily is gone. That person is a Necromancer."

"But . . ." Minari shook his head. He could see Lily. Tears welled up in her eyes and fell down her cheeks. She looked frightened, scared to lose herself.

"Minari," Lily whispered. "*Please.*"

Minari ripped his arm out of Alder's grasp and rushed inside.

The circle disappeared as soon as Minari stepped foot within. Alder must have drawn his powers back. Minari would need to end it quickly, before he hesitated or changed his mind. He reached for his dagger. Lily closed her eyes and smiled.

Minari's back suddenly collided with the ground. His vision filled with stars. Lily—no, the Necromancer—was looming over him, her arms free from the binds. Cold and murderous eyes gazed upon him. Minari's dagger was in her hands. She stroked his cheek with the blade.

"I wonder how much praise Father would give me if

I killed you," Lily said. She licked her lips. "Unfortunately, now isn't the time. It wouldn't be fun killing an empty vessel."

Before Minari could respond, she vanished, disappearing into thin air. His dagger rattled when it hit the ground.

"Are you a complete buffoon?" Alder asked. "I warned you not to listen."

Minari didn't respond. He lay on the ground, allowing the demigod to scold him. He'd fallen for her trick. The Necromancer had used Lily, knowing he would reach out to her, knowing he would want to save her. And because of Minari's rash decision, the Necromancer had escaped. Now more than ever, Minari needed to find Elliot.

But the last sentence repeatedly played in his mind. What did she mean he was an empty vessel?

45
HOPE

Elliot's consciousness faded in and out. He was aware of the pain, then he wasn't. It was a constant battle—the push and pull, the rise and fall. The wounded elf was barely aware of the careful hands that handled him. Barely aware of the fingers that tapped his cheek, trying to keep him awake. Barely aware of the voice that soothed him.

Elliot slowly noticed a breeze that brushed past his exposed skin. There were gentle touches across his body, and something tight wrapped around his left leg. His eyes picked up the faint color of his flesh, so that meant he wasn't in complete darkness. He wanted to open his eyes, but he was afraid to find out what he would see.

He heard the door creak open, and heeled footsteps approached.

"Well?" A woman's voice.

"He's alive." This voice came from right above him. A male.

"Are you able to confirm Charlotte's report?"

A hand was suddenly pressed down on his chest. "He possesses a magic core."

"Perfect."

"Lady Namir, if you absorb his powers as well as the snake's, you'll obtain unmatchable strength and beauty."

Namir hummed. Elliot heard her walk around him, her pace slow. "This elf is quite pleasant on the eyes. Yes, perhaps it's because he has a magic core. Then again, I've never seen elves before, so I know not how they are." A pause. "Luka, you, on the other hand, are the epitome of beauty and elegance. Your skin is free of blemishes, and your hair is smooth."

"Lady Namir, please, an ethereal would be no match for you. You are a cat chimera."

"Of course." Elliot heard her walk away. "Make sure his wounds are healed on the next full moon. Both my goats should be in pristine condition when I perform the ritual."

"Yes, Lady Namir."

The door clicked. Elliot couldn't quell his racing heart. He was going to be sacrificed? He couldn't. He still needed to protect everyone in Mistfall. If he was gone, then Charlotte would find out where everyone lived. There had to be a way for him to change their minds. Maybe he could be a better player in the game. Was Charlotte getting bored with him? Was Luka the new member he had to play with? Surely Luka would realize he was awake with how loud his heart was beating. He wasn't ready to play another game. But what if this was a trick? What if they wanted him to stay asleep? The longer he slept, the crueler the punishment would be.

"You don't have to be so worried," Luka said, voice gentle.

Elliot held his breath as he cracked his eyes open. He squinted, not used to the bright light. There were torches on each wall of the room; it was more light than the elf had experienced in weeks.

Elliot realized he was lying on a wooden table, Luka hovering by his side. The man had silky, silver hair and light blue, feathered wings on his head. Another ethereal. He held a jar in one hand and a cotton swab in the other.

All the anxiety and fear bubbling inside Elliot disappeared. He relaxed onto the table. It was strange, suddenly feeling safe around the foreign man. He wasn't going to play another game.

Luka's lavender eyes fell on Elliot. "I'm sorry this is happening to you," he whispered. "You're the oracle, right?"

Elliot nodded. Yes, he was the oracle. Leader of the elves. A savage. Barbarian.

"There was no reason for you to get caught up in this mess." Luka continued to dab at Elliot's wounds. "Charlotte has a tendency to get her way though."

"W-we have fun playing games," Elliot said. He bit his lip, hoping Luka hadn't caught the way his voice shook.

"I'm not here to play any sick games." Luka frowned. "I'm a healer, not someone who inflicts wounds out of malice."

Neither of them spoke after that. Luka continued to treat Elliot's marred skin, and Elliot tried his best to lie still. Whatever salve Luka was using didn't sting, but he couldn't help but squirm when the man worked on his ticklish areas.

"A purple-haired elf," Luka whispered.

Elliot's eyes widened. His body stiffened. No. Did they have Minari here too? Minari was the only other person who knew where Mistfall was.

A curious elf suddenly flashed in his mind. The girl in his dream. She had purple hair too. Did Luka know who she was?

Luka continued his treatment. "He was looking for you, as was Miss Gemme."

Elliot had to strain his hearing in order to take in what Luka was saying. Luka had said "he," so that meant he wasn't referring to the girl in his dream, but Minari.

Luka closed the jar. "You and I are in the same boat," he whispered. "And neither of us will sink." He stood up. "I will come back to check on you. It's fortunate you didn't get an infection from all the wounds," Luka said, reverting back to his normal tone. He left the room.

Elliot released a breath he hadn't known he was holding. He ran a hand over his torso and felt bandages over the cuts and burns he'd received from Charlotte. Luka had also wrapped up his leg. Luka was a healer. As long as Elliot was with Luka, he would be all right. He wasn't going to get hurt anymore.

But what if it was all a lie?

Elliot chewed his lip. He recalled Namir's voice. She

wanted him in pristine condition for a ritual. He didn't want to die. There was something he still needed to do. He'd been tasked with the prophecy. That was why he'd left home. He needed to fulfill it at all costs. He needed to get out of here.

Elliot slowly sat up. His wounds didn't hurt as badly as they had before.

He felt a tug in his chest and held his breath. The tug happened again. He heard pounding in his ears. The veins in his body pulsated. There was a pressure and movement in his chest, like vines pulling together, intertwining themselves. They mended, wrapping around his core in a protective embrace. His chest was filled with warmth that radiated throughout his body. His fingertips tingled. It was a welcoming feeling.

Elliot looked at his palms. There were bandages wrapped around his fingers, but he ignored them. He tapped into his core, focusing on bringing out his magic. He gasped. The familiar sparkle of his powers glowed around his hands. But it disappeared as quickly as it had appeared. He clutched his hands. In time, his magic would come back. He was sure of it. He would get out of here and return to Minari and Chloé.

46

PHASE

If Chloé could've described how she felt in one word, it would be hot. Or perhaps a better word would be scorching. Even though night was upon them, it was still uncomfortably warm in the Pepper Zone. She glanced over at the humans and found it amazing they were trotting along like it was the middle of spring. How on Etheria could the three of them and their horses, Windfall included, handle the heat?

Chloé had found it surprisingly easy to adapt to the new mare. Windfall was fully grown, but she was smaller than the gray mare, making it easier for Chloé to ride. It was more comfortable for longer journeys. Windfall was attentive of Chloé's commands, having no issues with the new rider.

"And so I asked her for an evening out, and she rejected me," Oliver said. It was his tenth time explaining the same rejected love story. Chloé had learned that the flamboyant human enjoyed listening to himself talk, which was the opposite of his twin, Deveran.

"Yes, yes, and the fact you have to see Vivian every day breaks your heart," Deveran said.

"Oliver, surely you've learned by now that Vivian isn't interested in men." Bunnie laughed.

"A woman devoted to her work." Oliver sighed. "What have we Nighthawks done to deserve such an angel like her?"

"Oliver, don't tell me you haven't noticed," Deveran said.

"Noticed what?"

"When Boss said Vivian isn't interested in men, she literally means Vivian isn't interested in men."

Oliver furrowed his brow. He sucked in his lip and tilted his head. "What?"

Deveran sighed and shook his head. "Vivian fancies women."

Oliver gasped. He raised his shoulders and placed a hand over his chest. "Deveran! How could you withhold this information from me?"

Deveran rolled his eyes. "My dear brother, you wouldn't have listened to me even if I'd told you."

"Blasphemy. I would've listened to you."

"When it comes to matters of the heart, you wouldn't," Deveran deadpanned.

Oliver and Deveran continued to bicker. It made the travel lighthearted. Chloé nearly forgot where they were going and for what purpose because of the atmosphere the twins created.

It was already the sixth day of their travel. They should've been near the entrance of the hideout, but the vast desert was the only thing her eyes saw. The rise and fall of dunes would be etched in her memories forever.

"How are you feeling?" Bunnie asked.

Chloé bit her lip. "A little nervous, but the twins are helping to keep me distracted."

Bunnie chuckled. "Yes, they do have that going for them, though Oliver could tone down his gossip."

Chloé looked at the guns hooked on each side of the twin's hips. The barrels were cylindrical and longer than Chloé's own pistols. They used bullets instead of magic. The nix brushed a hand against her pistols. She hoped she wouldn't have to use them and that the situation would be quelled fairly quickly. Elliot was still publicly her property since she'd never removed the collar.

Bunnie pulled at Lightning's reins, bringing her to a halt. "This is where we'll wait. We watch out for any members and ambush them when they use the magic stone." She dismounted, and the rest followed suit.

Deveran and Oliver both popped open their guns, checking the contents inside before flicking the barrel closed.

"Legs?" Oliver asked.

"Legs," Deveran confirmed.

Bunnie crossed her legs on the sand, removing her crossbow and settling it on her lap.

Chloé settled down next to her. "I've never seen a red

crossbow."

Bunnie smiled softly. Her eyes were solemn. "It was my grandfather's."

"The one who adopted you?"

Bunnie nodded. "Yes. He taught me how to handle a bow and arrow, and ever since he passed away, I took it upon myself to learn how to wield this. I want to continue his legacy, in a way."

"It's well-known that Sir Alfred was legendary with the crossbow," Oliver said, joining them. "When hunting, he could shoot three birds with a single arrow or have a clean shot on a deer's head with one."

"Sir Alfred was the reason Bunnie formed Nighthawk," Deveran said.

"Sir Alfred . . . ?" Chloé had read that name before. She envisioned the list of human aristocrats she'd once reviewed out of curiosity. She nibbled at her lip. Alfred . . . Alfred . . . Chloé's eyes widened. She looked at Bunnie. "Sir Alfred Hawthorne?"

Bunnie gave Chloé a sheepish smile. She shrugged. "Caught me."

"If you're a Hawthorne, then are you related to Charlotte?"

"Not by blood, but we were siblings . . . once." Bunnie paused before continuing. "I threw the Hawthorne name away. Nothing ties me to that family other than this crossbow."

Oliver placed his hands on his cheeks and pouted, slouching forward. "Boss also changed her name, but she refuses to tell any of us what it was."

Deveran elbowed his brother. "If Boss doesn't want to tell us her name, then you should drop it. Stop pestering her. This is why Vivian rejected you."

Oliver gasped. "She rejected me because she's into women! You told me yourself."

"Right, right." Deveran waved his hand. "Forgot about that."

Bunnie cleared her throat. "I apologize on behalf of my men, Chloé. The older one is practically an idiot."

Deveran chuckled while Oliver made an expression of pure devastation. It was as if someone had just kicked his dog.

"But," Bunnie said, "a skilled idiot. One I would never replace. Now, as much as I would like to continue this conversation, we need to be on the lookout. Stay silent so we don't reveal our location. According to Vivian, Oasis usually takes a path from the northwest."

Chloé and Bunnie stationed themselves on one end of the dune while Oliver and Deveran took the other.

Curiosity chewed at Chloé. What was Alfred's ideology that had caused Bunnie to form Nighthawk? Taking a guess, she assumed it was related to Bunnie's and Charlotte's opposing views of chimeras. That would mean Alfred had been a believer in treating chimeras with kindness and had desired to give them fair rights. For an aristocratic family, it was practically unheard of.

Chimeras had first been created from a scientific experiment by the Rutherford family. The term "scientific experiment" was a mere cover-up. Anyone who was aware of what they'd been doing knew they'd meddled in magic.

She wasn't sure what kind of magic, but it had been enough to conjure an entirely new race. They'd somehow merged human and animal into one. They'd given them to other aristocrats and the royal family. Physically, the chimeras looked similar to humans, but they had specific physical traits that differed from humans. Those who desired a chimera used them depending on their animalistic abilities.

Rooster chimeras were born with bright red or orange hair. They were used for pit fighting, a type of entertainment. Families with roosters would pit them in a fight against one another, often to the death. The winning family would be deemed stronger. They gained nothing other than gloating rights.

Dog chimeras looked similar to humans, but their eyes tended to be rounder and more downturned. They were mostly used by the royal family. They had the ability to sniff out any poisons that may have been slipped into the meals. In most cases, they would be forced to eat the contaminated food to prove the accusation and would often perish from it.

Cat chimeras were born with luxurious curves and smooth skin. They were known for their alluring beauty. If a family was fortunate enough to own one, they would be used as a mistress or host. Cat chimeras were usually seen in whore houses.

Ox chimeras were taller and broader than any human could hope to be. They were used for their enormously powerful strength. They were able to lift and haul hefty objects and were used for construction work.

Snake chimeras had a pale complexion. They were

used for their blood. Their blood worked as an easy fix for illnesses and doubled as an antidote for poisons. They too were often kept within the royal family, but none of their blood would be given to the unfortunate dog chimeras.

There was one special snake chimera Chloé had read about. They called it a Colorless Snake because the chimera had been born with pale, almost colorless hair. A mutated gene gave the snake chimera special blood. The chimera's blood could heal wounds and bring someone back from the brink of death. The Rutherford family couldn't figure out how to create the mutated gene again, so only one of them had been born. The royal family protected the snake, and they always provided a mate. They couldn't risk losing the gene, and luckily it was passed down through their children.

But once King Valentine III freed the chimeras, the Colorless Snake went along with them. It was unknown if the mutated gene was still alive.

A hooting of an owl caught Chloé's attention. Had Victor or Yen caught wind of something?

Bunnie quickly slipped her glove on and raised her arm, allowing the bird to land. She furrowed her brow at the small package wrapped around the owl's leg. She unlatched it and untied the pouch.

"Well, looks like Victor and Yen outdid themselves." Bunnie handed Chloé the pouch.

Inside was a small note and a light blue stone. It was a teardrop shape with a few rough edges. "Is this . . . ?" Chloé looked at the pouch, then at Bunnie.

Bunnie nodded. "Yep. Looks like the Oasis members

took a different route. Victor and Yen were able to stop them and take this stone, then send it to us. Looks like we have our way in."

Chloé took the stone out and clutched her hands around it. Elliot was waiting. It would be rude of her to continue to dally right outside their doors. She took one last deep breath, exhaling through her nose. "Let's go."

47
WAY

Minari felt small as he stood in the middle of the tent. Mayleen was shouting at him, but nothing was registering. He could see her terrified eyes, her frowning lips, her arms as she waved them around in frustration.

Yes, he had defied Alder's warning. The demigod had been forced to pull back his magic so Minari wouldn't get crushed under the immense amount of power being poured into the circle. Because of this, Lily had escaped. No longer under a magical hold, she'd taken the chance and had disappeared. Now no one knew where she was.

Alder had readjusted his protection, creating a shield that spread across the clearing surrounding the Moon Shrine.

When Minari felt something smooth and warm touch his cheek, he snapped out of his daze. Stella was in front of him holding a mug.

"Mother just left," Stella said.

"Oh." Minari was at a loss for words. The hard realization that he'd just let a Necromancer free crushed him like a flood of boulders. It hadn't gone unnoticed by the villagers that Lily was now free. A patrolling scout had seen Lily suddenly appear right outside the clearing next to an unknown figure. The unknown figure wore a cloak of black feathers, concealing their identity. They'd vanished without a word.

It had taken a tiring amount of energy for Mayleen to calm the villagers, reassuring them that Alder would protect them and they would be safe from another attack. Both scouts and keepers would stand watch during day and night.

"Drink this before you leave," Stella said. She handed him the mug.

Minari inhaled the familiar aroma of peppermint tea. He was going to need the energy boost for the trip down. His mother had made it very clear he needed to leave as soon as possible. He gulped it down. It wasn't so hot that he needed to take his time, but was warm enough for him to enjoy. He handed Stella the empty mug. "Thank you."

"The next time you come home . . . it'll be you and Elliot," Stella said.

"Yes." Minari would make sure the next time he returned, he wouldn't be alone.

"We'll be waiting. For however long it takes, we'll be here."

Minari flashed his older sister a smile. "Hopefully I'll

still be this attractive when I come back. I'd rather not look like an elder when I should be the leader."

Stella playfully shoved Minari's chest. "I'm going to get wrinkles long before you."

Minari brushed his fingers through Stella's indigo hair and tucked a strand behind her pointy ear. "You'll forever be beautiful in my eyes, Stella."

Stella's cheeks went pink. She swatted Minari's hand away. "Stop it. That's something you would say to a lover, not your sister."

Minari chortled. "Since when is there a rule that I can't call you beautiful?"

"Since now, so don't call me that."

"What do I say then? Pretty?"

Stella moved to stand behind her younger brother and pushed him. "You need to leave."

Minari didn't resist. He allowed Stella to push him out of the tent, and they both walked over to Xander. The ovis's ears perked up. His saddle was already strapped on, and the saddlebags were secure.

"I prepared him for you," Stella said.

"Thank you." Minari grabbed Stella and pulled her into an embrace. He buried his face in her shoulder. His sister always cheered him up when he was upset, always found a way to ground him when he was lost. He was glad he could speak to Stella before leaving, but he knew this was only possible because of Lily. Because of the attack, Stella had been forced to confess her true identity: a fake oracle, a placeholder, a scapegoat. He wished this could've happened under different circumstances, but there wasn't anything he could do now. He needed to move forward.

Stella patted Minari's back. "Take care. I'll miss you. Mother will miss you too."

Minari pulled away. "You take care too. I'll be back." His eyes landed on Xeno. The animal was resting right outside Errol's tent. Minari had contemplated taking him along on his journey but had decided against it. Xeno was the only family Errol had left beside Elliot. He couldn't bring himself to separate the two, and Xander was more than capable of handling him and Elliot.

Minari mounted Xander. He had been gone from Elliot and Chloé for far too long. He needed to return to them. He recalled Bunnie mentioning she lived in a city called Lonin. He would check there first. He gave Stella one last farewell and departed.

There was no fog or maze as Minari proceeded down the mountain. Alder had lifted the illusion in favor of conserving his energy. Minari had also left Redd behind. The songbird would've been unresponsive just like before if he'd taken him out of the clearing.

The sun was cracking upon the horizon, and Minari entered the lower lands. He took a different path than before. He was more toward the eastern side of the base rather than the western. It should've been a shorter path to Lonin. At least he hoped it was, assuming his memory of the map Bunnie had presented while they'd been in Venin didn't fail him.

The area he ended up in was vastly different. Rather than fields of grass, the path forward took him through an extensive field of sand. The area was incredibly hot, and he felt the burn of the rising sun.

"All right, Xander, let's try to make this quick. I don't want to burn to death," Minari said. He gave Xander's neck a pat before urging him forward.

They traveled at a decent speed—not so quickly that Xander would wear out too fast, but also quick enough that a slight breeze brushed past Minari with each step. It was a slight relief from the heat. He couldn't afford to be picky, so he endured.

The elf was about to unzip his coat when he felt a sudden presence behind him. He brought Xander to a halt and turned. He squinted, the heat sending waves across his vision.

Beige coat. Feathered wings. Gray hair.

It was Owen.

Memories of the conversation with Bunnie and Chloé fired his nerves. Oasis was holding Elliot captive and possibly putting him through a reform.

Minari was about to shout when Owen lifted a hand.

"You are looking for the green-haired elf," Owen said. It wasn't a question but a statement.

Minari's eyes widened. His voice stuck in his throat.

"I'm here as a messenger for Luka," Owen said. "We wish for your aid, and you will receive it in return." The ethereal paused.

"What aid?" Minari asked, finding his voice.

"Free us from Namir's hold, and we will set him free."

Minari furrowed his brow. "Namir?"

"She is our leader." Owen glanced around, as if watching out for a change in their surroundings, but there was nothing around them except sand. "Luka and I have been tricked into joining Oasis. I cannot give too much detail, as I am crunched for time, but Namir has a hold on us, and we won't be free until she is dead." Owen patted the brooch on the left side of his chest. "She can track our whereabouts through this. Occasionally, she will force her black magic into it and make us behave in ways we normally wouldn't."

"If she can track you with that, then that means she knows you're meeting with me." Minari frowned. Was this a trap?

"Namir is undergoing preparations for a ritual. Right now, she doesn't know I am here, though being here still poses a significant risk. Luka, unfortunately, is compromised at the moment, thus I am here."

"What do I have to do?"

"I can bring you inside Oasis's secret base during the ritual. That is when you need to kill Namir."

"And how will I know who this Namir is?"

"Once you see her, you will know. If you want to save your friend, you will have to kill her. If you fail to do so, then it will be the end for the both of you."

Minari narrowed his eyes. "And how do I know this isn't a trap?"

"You will have to decide that for yourself. If I have your word, then I will help you. If not, then you will lose your comrade." Owen stared at him, waiting for an answer.

Minari knew full well that this could be a trap. Owen was part of Oasis, and he could've been luring Minari in because he was an elf. Whether he had Chloé's collar around his neck or not didn't matter to them. Returning to Lonin would be useless at this point if Elliot was still in Oasis's clutches. He knew this was his best bet at finding Elliot. It was a risk he needed to take.

The elf straightened his back and squared his shoulders. "You have my word."

Owen reached for one of the wings on his head and plucked a feather. He closed his eyes, and the feather emitted a soft silver hue. He opened his eyes, and the light disappeared. He handed the gray feather to Minari. "I just cast a teleportation charm. No matter what state of mind I may be in, the feather will teleport you into the ritual room. I warn you now that I may not remember our deal when we meet, but once Namir's hold disappears, my memories will come back."

Minari took the feather. "When is the ritual?"

"Tonight."

48
CHANCE

Sage was beaten the day Mimi came before him, just like Aiden had ordered, but the chimera hadn't expected Mimi to be the one to inflict the pain.

He remembered the way the smaller boy had held the whip, the way it had crashed down on his raw back, arms, and legs. Mimi had been ruthless, striking Sage continuously until he'd been called out of the room. Sage had lain on the ground. His body had ached, but what had ached the most was his heart.

It wasn't long before another member came to haul Sage out and shoved him back into a cage. He wasn't let out or given injections for the next three days. He silently watched the other chimeras receive their injections and get let out of their cages. His body cramped and burned from being held in the tight space for so long, but he couldn't find the energy to rebel. His body was wracked with cold shivers and tremors. He wasn't sure if it was a symptom of the wounds or if his body was going through a withdrawal from the lack of injections.

On the fourth day, the door to his cage creaked. Sage cracked his eyes open, and his breath hitched. Mimi was looking at him, thick handcuffs in his hands. They were the ones that locked onto the altar. Similar ones were around his own wrists, but they were not bound, allowing him to move freely.

"I came to collect you," Mimi said in their native language. *"Will you allow me to put these on you?"*

Sage hung his head. He didn't resist as Mimi clasped the heavy metal around his wrists. Mimi tugged Sage out of his cage, and he followed. Four days ago, he'd told himself he would be the one to save Mimi, but the younger chimera was still bewitched. He had done nothing to save him. Instead, he'd wallowed in self-pity.

Was this how everything was going to end? Was he to become fodder for Namir? He could think of a thousand different ways he'd rather die, but he tried to think of the positive. He would be with Mimi. They would be together when it happened. At least he had that. Together in life and in death.

The familiar bare hallways led to the same large room where he used to carry stones from one side to the other. At first, he hadn't understood what the purpose was, but he'd soon realized that it was just repetitive hard labor. He was an ox, so it hadn't been difficult for him to adapt, but for other chimeras who were here, like snakes or dogs, they had it the toughest. Their bodies weren't meant for hard labor, and their wills broke easily.

Was Sage's will broken? His eyes landed on the back of Mimi's head. Was he merely going to allow this to play out? In truth, he didn't want to. In reality, he didn't have a choice. What could he do? It was hard for him to walk. His legs trembled with each agonizing step, and he didn't feel any strength in his arms.

Namir was standing in front of the altar, but she wasn't alone. Elliot was by her side, on his knees with arms behind his back. His clothes were severely tattered and stained in blood that Sage was sure was the elf's. Elliot's complexion was sallow, and sweat beaded on his forehead. His pale green hair clung to his face.

On the other side of the altar were two ethereals Sage didn't recognize—one with silver hair and one with light gray. Their features were expressionless, but he could see the slight curl of their lips, the twinkle of malice in their eyes.

On opposing sides of the altar were the human captains, Charlotte and Aiden. Charlotte had a silver bow strapped against her back, and Aiden had tucked his coat away from his sword, revealing the weapon as it rested against his hip.

"So all the pieces are here," Namir said in the chimeran language, raising her arms to her sides. *"I've waited a long time for this moment. I will finally achieve true beauty."*

Elliot lifted his head as Namir spoke. His blue eyes widened, orbs landing on Sage and Mimi. Sage knew Elliot couldn't understand Namir, but seeing familiar faces had probably caught him off guard. Honestly, Sage was surprised to see Elliot here as well. He was an elf. What business did he have with Oasis?

"Luka," Namir said.

The ethereal with silver hair reached by his waist. He pushed his coat aside and drew a sword. He held the blade against his face, eyes closed. A deep crimson shadow morphed across the blade. He lifted his arm and pointed the blade upward. The shadow shot into the ceiling. The walls shook and rumbled. A small circle opened up in the ceiling and gradually grew. The opening spread across the corners of the walls, revealing the full moon in the night sky.

Namir wrapped her arms around herself, tucking them underneath her bosom. "The elf goes first. Then I will have the chimeras together as dessert."

Charlotte yanked Elliot up. His feet were wrapped in white bandages, concealing any wounds he had. She unlatched the handcuffs from around Elliot's small wrists and bound his hands to either side of the altar. The elf wiggled, but it was futile. He didn't have the strength to break free. His ankles were bound the same way, sprawling him across the stone slab.

Namir circled the altar. Her hand grazed across the surface, lighting the candles as she walked by. She licked her lips. Her hand caressed the frightened elf's chest. Elliot tried to shift away from the looming chimera.

Charlotte leaned toward Elliot and whispered something in his ear. The elf froze. Elliot bit his lip, but it wasn't enough to hide the quiver.

"*Sage,*" Mimi whispered. His voice sounded strained.

Sage turned his attention to the small chimera in front of him. "*Help . . . help Elliot.*"

Sage sucked in a breath. Mimi was fighting against the hold Namir had on him. He looked at his bound hands. How could he help? He couldn't break free even if he'd wanted to. Maybe . . . distract?

Sage glanced around. The sunken eyes of the captured chimeras merely looked forward. Their tasks had been put on hold because of the ritual. Could he use them? He tugged at his chains, nearly falling over. He hadn't expected Mimi to release the hold on him so easily.

Sage gritted his teeth. "*Hey! Are you all going to stand there and watch? Where is your pride? Where is your honor?*" There was a slight response. The chimeras' curiosity was now on Sage rather than Namir. Good. "*We are chimeras. We're strong and meant to be free, not bound by chains and ruled through fear by these humans and that pathetic excuse for a chimera.*" He glanced at Namir. Her eyes were narrow, a sneer across her features. The distraction was working.

There were murmurs amongst the chimeras. The Oasis members lashed their whips, threatening them. They flinched, but those brave enough to make a stand didn't back down.

A female ox chimera stepped forward. Her long, brown hair was matted, and random strands stuck out. Her skin was bruised and covered with grime, but she stood with confidence. "*Listen to him,*" she said. "*He has been here the shortest, yet he is the strongest. It puts the rest of us to shame!*"

More murmurs. Her voice seemed to rouse those

who'd initially hesitated. They were finding their strength.

A yelp came from across the room. One of the Oasis members was on the ground. His face and neck were being clawed by a male rooster chimera. The chimera's fingers were quickly dyed in the human's blood. He didn't stop until the man beneath him stilled. The chimera stood and spat on the floor. "*We rise.*"

Chaos ensued. The chimeran slaves rose and fought against the Oasis members. Screams and cries bounced off the walls and into the night sky.

"*You!*" Namir screamed. "*I will kill you where you stand!*" With a flick of her wrist, her nails elongated into black claws. She dashed toward Sage.

A gust of wind and light exploded between them. Sage lifted his arms, squeezing his eyes closed. Namir hissed.

"What's going on here?" It was a girl's voice.

The wind blew a familiar scent to Sage's nose. It was the same aroma as the collar around Elliot's neck. Sage opened his eyes, blinking away a few stray stars.

Three humans, a nix, and an elf stood where the blinding light had been.

49
DEFY

Elliot couldn't believe his eyes. Minari . . . Minari was here. And Chloé too. But why? What was going on?

He heard Chloé yell, then Minari was immediately by his side, fingers working on his binds.

"M-Minari?" Elliot whispered. He stared at the purple-haired elf. He didn't want to blink, afraid he would disappear. He heard a click, and his right hand was free. He pulled it close, glad for the small freedom.

"Don't worry. I'm here," Minari said. His voice was just how Elliot remembered. He wasn't dreaming, right?

Luka moved, the blade of his sword now pressed against Minari's neck. Minari narrowed his eyes at the ethereal, his hands freezing, but not before he freed Elliot's left hand.

No. No. No. Elliot wasn't going to let Minari get

hurt. He quickly pulled himself up and reached into his core. The strings had strengthened ever since Luka had healed his wounds. Elliot knew the ethereal wasn't in his right mind. He didn't feel the same comforting aura Luka had put off when tending to his wounds.

Elliot pushed his hands to the side, fully intending to protect Minari from harm. A blast of energy exploded from his hands, sending the Oasis members into the air.

Minari wasted no time and picked the locks on the remaining shackles on Elliot's ankles. Minari wrapped Elliot's arm around his shoulders and pulled him off the altar. Minari bit his lip but said nothing. Elliot knew he looked . . . repulsive. His once pale skin was now pink and red, marred with cuts and burns. There were bandages covering the damage, but he couldn't hide them from Minari.

"I'm okay," Elliot said, hoping it would soothe the older elf's worries.

"They're dead," Minari said. "All of them."

"Elliot!" Chloé rushed over, and her small arms wrapped tightly around his body. Elliot bit down a wince. It didn't hurt as badly as he'd thought, but it still surprised him. "I'm so sorry this happened to you. This should've never happened to you. The collar—"

"Miss Gemme!" Charlotte yelled as she pushed herself off the ground. Her face was scrunched, eyebrows sharp. "Please step away from the elf for your own safety."

"I think the only one who should be stepping away is you, Charlotte," a woman said. Elliot had seen her before. She was familiar. He bit his lip as he wracked his brain.

Back in Venin, he remembered being enthralled by Minerva's dancer. His eyes widened. *She* was the dancer, but why was she with everyone? "The elf is coming back with us, along with the chimeras." The dancer had her crossbow drawn.

Charlotte's eyes narrowed. She scoffed. "We found these chimeras trespassing in our towns and cities, and they refused to return to their land peacefully." Charlotte waved her hands. "As you can see, they are violent, attacking peaceful Oasis members. If we don't do anything, then—"

"Blah, blah, blah," a man said. He had black hair, and there was someone standing right next to him. They were identical. "Are you done yapping yet, Charlotte?" He twirled what looked like a gun in each hand.

"It's not polite to refer to a captain like that, Oliver," the other male said.

"Less talk, more shooting. You ready, Deveran?"

Deveran drew his guns from his hips. "On you. Legs?"

"Legs," Oliver said.

"Plan C.H., commence," Deveran said. They moved, splitting off in different directions.

Charlotte braced herself, but it didn't appear the twins were bothering with her. Instead, they were aiding chimeras who were struggling against the Oasis members.

The dancer looked over her shoulder. "Chloé, you take care of him," she said. "Leave Charlotte to me." And then she was gone.

"I'm not dreaming, am I?" Elliot whispered. He clung to Minari and Chloé. "Please let this be real . . ."

"It's not a dream, Elliot," Minari said. "We're here to get you out."

Elliot let out a sob. He collapsed to his knees, the two following him down. Minari rubbed Elliot's back. "I did my best . . . to protect you two. To protect Mistfall," Elliot said. He felt Minari's hand twitch, but the older elf didn't stop. His hands brought comfort to Elliot.

"You did well, Elliot," Minari said.

"We need to get out of here," Chloé said.

"Wait. The others . . . Mimi and Sage." Elliot looked around, hoping to find the two familiar chimeras. They were on the ground. Mimi was on top of Sage. The bigger chimera's arms were wrapped protectively around the smaller. Probably protecting him from the impact, but neither of them moved. Panic bubbled up in Elliot's stomach. His chest tightened. Had he . . . ?

"Elliot." Minari cupped his hand and Elliot's cheek, tapping him. "Elliot, focus. We need to get you out of here first, then we can get the others."

Elliot shook his head. "No, we can't leave them!" He tightened his grip on Minari's arm. He didn't want to leave them. If they just left, Sage and Mimi were surely going to get sacrificed. "We need to stop Namir."

"Which one is Namir?" Chloé asked. "If she's the leader, then I will talk to her."

Namir appeared behind Minari and Chloé. She gripped Chloé's hair and dragged her up. Chloé winced, reaching up to pull her pink locks out of Namir's hold.

"I don't have time to speak with a little girl like you," Namir said. Her opposite hand laced around Chloé's throat, and a black glow emitted from her fingers. It entered Chloé's body, turning her veins dark.

Minari quickly drew a dagger and lunged for an attack. Namir smirked before vanishing, taking Chloé with her and reappearing farther back.

Chloé's body convulsed, and her eyes rolled back in her head as her body went limp. Namir dropped her body, and she fell with a thud.

Elliot couldn't breathe. His throat closed. When Chloé's body hit the ground, something inside him shattered. It ripped him apart, and he couldn't move.

"You . . . what did you do to her?" Minari screamed. He dashed toward Namir, this time with daggers in both hands.

Namir curled her lips into a grin and disappeared in a puff of smoke. Another figure came out through the fog and clashed blades with Minari.

"You think a pathetic elf like you can fight Lady Namir?" he mocked. "As much as I would love to deal with you, I have other business to attend to." He pushed Minari forward. A bright beam came from his left, and Minari spun out of the way.

Chloé was standing. Her eyes were wide, and the whites of her eyes were now pitch-black. Black veins ran across her body. Her head was cocked to the side, shoulders hunched forward, and her limbs were twisted inward save for the one hand holding a pistol. She aimed at Minari.

Chloé was moving, but how was it that Elliot couldn't feel her? It was like she wasn't there.

And then the man was in front of Elliot. The elf

pushed against the altar, attempting to put distance between them.

"I'd ask if you have any last words, but little elf shits like you don't deserve any." He pulled back his sword. "As long as Lady Namir has your blood, it will be enough."

Elliot closed his eyes, waiting for the blow.

"Over my dead body!"

It was Sage's voice.

Elliot opened his eyes just in time to see the chimera ram his shoulder into the other male. The impact sent the man sprawling onto the ground, and his sword landed by Elliot.

"Elliot, take Mimi and get out of here," Sage blurted. He nodded his head toward the smaller chimera.

Mimi was slowly getting off the ground, the back of his hand pressed against his forehead. He gave his head a shake before groaning.

"I'll handle this human," Sage said.

Elliot nodded, still unable to find his voice. He scurried up and headed toward Mimi. He knew he shouldn't look. He knew Minari could handle himself. He trusted the older elf to be able to handle Chloé, to find a way to free her.

Chloé . . .

His chest tightened at the thought of the female nix. He couldn't bite down the urge to look.

His steps faltered upon seeing Minari's struggled movements. He held his arm. Blood streamed down the limp limb. Chloé was shooting at him, giving him little room to approach her.

When Elliot turned back to Mimi, a hand covered his eyes.

"Good night, elf," Namir said.

A rush of cold air filled his lungs before his world plunged into darkness.

50
BEFORE

Arrow after arrow. Bolt after bolt. Bunnie and Charlotte danced around each other's shots. They matched each other's tempo, but that was no surprise. They had learned how to shoot from the same master. Bunnie wasn't trying to bring harm to Charlotte, only trying to push her away from the group. Charlotte, on the other hand, seemingly had the full intention of killing Bunnie. Unfortunately for the Oasis captain, the Nighthawk captain was quicker both on her feet and her draws.

Bunnie was running out of bolts, and so was Charlotte. Charlotte's quiver had started out with more arrows, but the rushed attacks had dwindled the supply quickly. They eventually had only one left.

They walked together in a circle, each with their weapon drawn.

"Charlotte, stop this madness. You know this wasn't what Grandpapa wanted!"

Charlotte scowled. Her lips twitched into a frown. "Don't speak to me as if you know me. We were never friends, *Jasmine*." She let her last arrow go.

Bunnie was stunned upon hearing her birth name. She hadn't heard Charlotte say her name in so long, even if it was full of disgust. She narrowly dodged the attack, the tip grazing her left arm.

Charlotte threw her bow on the ground and reached for a fallen Oasis member's sword. Bunnie tightened her hold on her crossbow, ignoring the sting in her dominate arm. There had to be a way to make Charlotte realize her mistake. The younger woman had been close to Alfred. She knew the other woman wouldn't do anything that went against his beliefs, so why had she joined Oasis?

Eighteen years ago …

"Good job, you two. I'm proud of how quickly you've improved," Alfred said. He was kneeling at eye level as he stroked Jasmine's and Charlotte's heads. The older man had deep maroon hair with streaks of gray, combed sleekly back.

Jasmine giggled. "Really? Do you think we'll be able to become official hunters soon?" She and her sister had just brought a boar home. To them, it was their largest game yet, though probably still small in comparison to Alfred's if he hunted.

"Of course! I can probably stay at home and let you two hunt for our meals."

The blonde girl pouted next to her. "Grandpapa, you can't stay home. Who's going to watch us?"

"Aiden can watch you, Charlotte. Plus, Jasmine's here." Alfred smiled.

Charlotte shook her head. "No, Grandpapa, you have to stay!"

Alfred chuckled. The wrinkles around his eyes deepened at the joyful action. "Okay, okay. I'll stay until you two are old enough not to need me anymore."

"But we'll always need you." Charlotte frowned.

Alfred patted Charlotte's head. "One day you won't."

"Grandpapa, are you staying with us tonight?" Jasmine asked. "Are you going to help us cook the boar?"

"Of course. You know I haven't forgotten it's your eighth birthday today."

Jasmine grinned. She jumped into Alfred's embrace, wrapping her tiny arms tightly around his neck.

Jasmine and Charlotte had both been orphans before Alfred had taken them under his wing. They'd survived on food scraps and had stolen bowls of water left out for stray cats and dogs. They'd never stolen from anyone, but on one particular day, they'd been desperate. They hadn't eaten in two days, and their stomachs had been clawing at themselves, demanding to be fed.

The sky was gray, and rain poured heavily against the ground. Thunder rumbled in the sky. A small, tattered blanket was draped over Jasmine's and Charlotte's heads as they sat on the ground, backs pressed against a building.

Charlotte pressed her body against Jasmine's. The older girl wrapped her arm around her younger companion. She was shivering, and her body was warmer than it should've been.

"Don't worry, we'll have food today. It'll be nice and warm," Jasmine said. She rubbed Charlotte's arm, hoping to send warmth into the trembling girl.

"Am I going to die?" Charlotte asked.

"Of course not! I'll protect you."

Charlotte grunted, only pressing herself closer to Jasmine.

They sat in silence. Jasmine kept her eyes sharp for any leftovers the city folk dropped on the ground. Unfortunately, no one was eating out in the open because of the weather, but the market still bustled with people.

A coin pouch bouncing against a man's hip caught Jasmine's eye. It was exposed, right in the open, as if inviting a pickpocket to waltz by and steal it. Jasmine needed to get it. She knew food wasn't the only thing she and Charlotte needed. Charlotte was getting sick, and she would need to buy medicine too. They had no money, and the only way for her to get what she needed was to steal that man's coin pouch.

"Charlotte, wait here," Jasmine said. She gently pushed Charlotte off her shoulder.

Charlotte groaned. "Where are you going?"

"I'm going to get you some food and medicine."

"Medicine?" Charlotte squinted her eyes. "How are you going to get medicine? That costs money."

"Don't worry. Just stay here until I come back, okay?"

Charlotte bit her lip. She furrowed her brow and was about to shake her head when she nodded instead. Jasmine peeled the wet blanket off and draped the rest over Charlotte's body. She gave her one last look before rushing out into the crowd.

Jasmine weaved through the larger ones, determined to find the man who was dumb enough to leave his money hanging on his hip. It wasn't long before she spotted him. He was standing in front of a booth looking at vegetables. Jasmine scrunched up her face. Yuck. Vegetables were gross. Warm bread was definitely better.

The black-haired girl quickened her footsteps. She had to take his pouch while he was distracted. He had an umbrella in one hand and a potato in the other. She was close now. All she needed to do was reach up, grab it, and run away. She was a lot smaller than him, so it would be easy to hide within the crowd.

She was right beside him now. She wrapped her small fingers around the unattended coins. Hope swelled inside her. The pouch was larger and heavier than she'd thought. She and Charlotte wouldn't go hungry again.

Before she could make a run for it, someone suddenly grabbed her arm. Dread washed over her.

"What do we have here?" the man said. He had a tight hold on her.

"Let me go!" Jasmine thrashed around. "You're hurting me!"

The man frowned. "I would, but it seems you have something of mine."

"Sir Alfred!" A large woman ran toward them. Jasmine recognized her as the owner of the bakery shop she dreamed of eating from. The round woman was holding her skirt up, preventing it from getting wet. She held a hand over her eyes, guarding from the incoming rain. "Sir Alfred, this girl has been stealing food from us for weeks now! There's another one. She isn't working alone."

Jasmine's body ran cold. "You're . . . you're lying! I haven't been stealing!" She clawed at Alfred's hand, but his grip wouldn't loosen.

"Don't lie!" The woman raised her hand and slapped Jasmine across the cheek. "I would say your mother should've raised you better, but knowing a runt like you, your mother is probably a whore, off spreading her legs to some other man right now."

Jasmine pressed a hand against her hot, stinging cheek. Her vision blurred, tears threatening to spill. It wasn't the first time she'd heard someone call her mother a whore. She didn't know what a whore was, and she'd never met her mother, but it stung all the same. Someone who was meant to protect her had tossed her aside.

Alfred released Jasmine's arms. He knelt down and brought the girl against his chest. Jasmine gasped, body shivering. The older man was incredibly warm, and all she wanted to do was lean against him. "You have a sister?" he asked, voice gentle.

Jasmine bit the inside of her cheek. She couldn't risk Charlotte getting caught too.

"The other runt is over there, sitting outside Mo's Fabrics," the bakery owner said.

A large hand pressed against Jasmine's head, holding her closer to Alfred's chest. "I will take these two girls home."

The woman sucked in a breath. "What? But, Sir Alfred, these two are runts. Orphans of the streets! Children of some wench! Surely someone of your stature shouldn't dirty yourself with children as low as them."

Jasmine felt Alfred move. He tossed his coin pouch to the rambling woman. "Bring all your fresh bread and muffins to my manor. This is enough, correct?"

"Y-yes," she mumbled. "I will have them delivered with the hour."

"And make sure they're still warm."

"Of course." The woman scurried off.

Jasmine couldn't believe her ears. She and Charlotte were going home with this man. And he lived in a manor. Mykronos's luck must have been on her side.

"Now, where is your sister?" Alfred asked, giving Jasmine a warm smile.

Alfred took Jasmine and Charlotte home, where he cleaned them up and claimed them as his own. Charlotte bounced back, quickly recovering from the brief cold she'd had. The two inherited the Hawthorne surname and became part of the prestigious family. The older man took on the role as their grandfather and introduced them to his only grandson, Aiden.

Alfred was a renowned sharpshooter. There wasn't a single soul who could match his skill with a crossbow. His bolts were always clean, and he never used more than one to pierce an animal, giving them a swift end. Wishing to pass down his legacy, he trained both Jasmine and Charlotte in the art of archery. He provided them maps and showed them areas where they could hunt and areas they should stay away from. He warned them about the chimeras' lands and how they should never trespass. It wasn't uncommon for chimeras to show hostility if they felt threatened.

Jasmine was ecstatic when Alfred had her pick up a bow. She had always admired her grandfather and wanted to be as graceful as he was when hunting. While Jasmine picked up archery quickly, Charlotte fumbled. Her grip on the bow was never as strong as Jasmine's. The older girl could see how frustrated Charlotte got, but she always rooted her on. Jasmine reassured the younger girl that the difference in skill could've been because of their two-year age difference, and Charlotte believed her.

Aiden often teased Charlotte, telling her she should give up archery and pick up swordsmanship. The blonde refused, saying swords were too bulky and heavy, giving off an appearance that was too masculine. She wanted to be graceful like Jasmine and Alfred.

Jasmine was now fourteen, and Charlotte was twelve. They'd been with Alfred and Aiden for seven years. Long gone were the scrawny orphans, having been replaced by well-fed teens with bright, sharp eyes.

The four of them went on a family hunt. Jasmine was eager to try the new bow Alfred had gotten her for her birthday.

They spread jokes and laughed amongst themselves, unaware of the direction they were heading.

"Halt!" a voice called out.

Their laughter stopped immediately.

A figure stepped forward. He was tall and slim with a mixture of orange and red in his hair. The bronze cuff on his left ear glimmered against the sun. He had chains wrapped in one hand and a trident-shaped metal weapon in the other. They were right by the borders of chimeran territory—a grave mistake.

"Humans are not welcome here. Turn around and don't come back," he said.

"Ah, our apologies," Alfred said, raising his hands. He wanted to show the chimera he didn't mean any harm. "We were hunting, and it seems we wandered too far off from our original trail."

"I don't trust words, only actions," the chimera said. "Turn around and leave. Do not come back. This is my only warning to you."

Jasmine was in complete awe. She had never seen a chimera before, let alone one this close. She had only heard stories from the city folk, and she could only think of how wrong they were. The chimeras didn't look like beasts; they looked nearly as human as she did. Perhaps they did sport strange hair colors and eyes and had skills like immense strength and abundant stamina, but that was because they were part animal.

Jasmine itched for a closer look. *What was this chimera?* she wondered. Cat? Ox? Rooster? She slowly stepped forward, not wanting to alarm the chimera. Her foot suddenly landed on a twig, snapping it in two.

The sudden noise alarmed the chimera. He pulled the

trident back and swung toward Jasmine.

Alfred jumped in front of Jasmine, pulling her to the side and out of harm's way. A shuddered gasp left his lips as the three-pronged weapon pierced his flesh. The chimera pulled the chain, yanking it out of his body.

Alfred fell to his knees, gasping for air. The dried brown leaves beneath him quickly turned crimson, stained by blood.

"Grandpapa!" Jasmine was at Alfred's side. Her hands were on his shoulders as she tried to keep him from falling over.

"Grandpapa!" Charlotte screeched.

"Grandpa!" Aiden yelled.

"This is your last warning. Take him and leave. I will not ask you humans again." The chimera didn't move. His eyes stared at them intently.

Jasmine wiped her tears away. She was the oldest. She needed to be strong. This was her fault—she'd wanted to hunt, and they'd gotten distracted. "C'mon, Grandpapa . . ." She put Alfred's arm over her shoulders and tried to help him up.

Alfred wheezed. Blood splattered across the ground as he coughed. He sucked in a shaky breath. "Promise me one thing, children. Do not . . . do not fill your hearts with hatred. Learn to understand the chimeras. Learn to love and live with them . . . as if they were . . . brethren." His body went slack as his eyes closed.

"Grandpapa!" Charlotte cried. Tears stained her cheeks. "Wake up!"

"Charlotte, we need to get Grandpa back home to

Kletin," Aiden said. He wrapped Alfred's other arm over his shoulder, aiding Jasmine. "The doctor will know what to do. Grandpa is too strong to die by some chimera."

Night fell upon Kletin, and Alfred's soul passed. Even though the three children had rushed home as quickly as they could, Alfred had lost too much blood.

Alfred had made sure his grandchildren would live comfortably in the event of his passing. He gave them all of his wealth, dividing it evenly amongst the three, and the manor was now theirs.

Since that day, Charlotte had never talked to Jasmine the same way. The younger female shot glares and sneered whenever they passed in the hallways. Jasmine knew they blamed her for their beloved grandfather's death. Jasmine missed Alfred's smiles, his laughs, his voice, the comfort he'd provided when he was around. She could only imagine how much Charlotte missed him. She'd been more attached to the older man.

One year passed, and Jasmine still hadn't recovered from the guilt that weighed her down. She decided to leave the Hawthorne manor and discard her name. She was no longer known as Jasmine Hawthorne, but as Bunnie. Just Bunnie. She would start her life fresh. Before she left the place she'd once called home, she took Alfred's trusty red crossbow, determined to continue his legacy and fulfill his dying wish.

Bunnie danced around Charlotte's swings. The younger

woman must've had sword training during the eleven years they'd been apart. Bunnie used her crossbow to shield herself from a strike.

"What's wrong, *Jasmine*?" Charlotte spat. "It isn't like you to miss so much, let alone have me close enough so you can't shoot."

Bunnie grunted, struggling to push Charlotte's weight off the crossbow. "I don't want to hurt you. Please stop this, Charlotte."

Charlotte's eyes narrowed. "This crossbow should've been buried alongside him. How dare you use it?" She leaned in closer, and Bunnie was forced to take a step back. "You don't deserve it. *You* killed him." With one last push, she shoved Bunnie off-balance. Bunnie stumbled and fell on her back. Charlotte loomed over her. Her heels stomped down on either side of Bunnie's hips. "You know, I've always hated you. You were always better than me at everything. He loved you. He loved you more than me. I could see it in his eyes. All the attention and praise you got compared to me. I did everything I could to get him to notice me, but I was always behind you. Always second." She smirked. "But now I have my chance. I can finally one-up you. I will get my revenge upon the chimeras and bring Grandpapa back."

Bring him back? What was Charlotte talking about? There was no way to bring the dead back to life.

Charlotte held the hilt of her sword in both hands. The tip of the sword hovered over Bunnie's chest. "I will see him again, and this time there won't be a Jasmine." She lifted her arms and brought the blade down.

Bunnie quickly swung her crossbow against the blade, diverting its path. The force was enough to knock it out of Charlotte's hands. She pointed her last bolt at Charlotte.

And pulled the trigger.

A quick gasp left Charlotte's lips. Her mouth moved, but no words came out, only soft whines. Bunnie's last bolt had pierced the center of Charlotte's chest. The blonde staggered backward, eyes wide at the silver jutting from her body.

"Charlotte!" Bunnie yelled. She tossed her weapon to the side and took Charlotte into her arms before she fell over. She eased Charlotte down, cradling her in her arms. Bunnie's vision blurred, and she let the tears fall. Drops fell onto Charlotte's face.

"You . . . you're crying," Charlotte whispered. "Why? You shot me . . . you won." Crimson trickled from the corner of Charlotte's pale lips.

Holding a quickly fading life in her arms was all too familiar to Bunnie. She shook her head. "No. I didn't win. There is no winner here." Bunnie sucked in a shaky breath. Her lips wouldn't stop quivering. "Charlotte, I am so sorry."

A small twitch appeared on Charlotte's lips. "Sorry? You've been saying that . . . ever since Grandpapa . . ." Charlotte coughed and wheezed.

"Don't talk anymore! Save your strength. I'll . . . I'll save you."

"Save . . . ?" Charlotte's eyes softened as they met Bunnie's. "I wanted him to . . . come back. I miss him so much. When I met Lady Namir . . . she said she could save him . . . bring him back. She needed . . . the snake chimera to do it. So Aiden and I . . . we devoted our services to her, did everything she wanted . . ." Her eyelids began to close. Bunnie tightened her grip around Charlotte's shoulders. "Maybe the four of us . . . can be together again. Do you think . . . Grandpapa will forgive me . . . for hurting chimeras?"

Bunnie couldn't swallow the lump in her throat. She bit her lip as she nodded.

Charlotte smiled. "Tell Aiden . . . I'm going to see Grandpapa first." Charlotte's eyes closed, her head rolling to the side. Her body went slack against Bunnie's.

Bunnie held Charlotte—no, her sister—close, burrowing her face into her neck. "You've always been a kind and skilled person, Charlotte. Never forget that." Her chest ached, and her heart tore in two. Sobs wracked her body as she let her tears flow freely.

Aiden was her only family now.

And deep down, she knew her younger brother would face the same fate.

51
SAVE

Minari gripped his arm. The wound wasn't deep, but for some reason he couldn't move it. He had no idea what kind of powers Chloé's magic beams had, but getting hit had showed him they probably had some sort of paralysis effect. He had been momentarily distracted when one of the Oasis captains had approached Elliot. Minari needed to return to his side, and the distraction had been enough for him to get hit. His arm had grazed the edge of the magic beam just enough to burn his skin and draw blood.

At first, Minari had thought Namir had killed Chloé, stripped her of her life force. At least, that was how it had appeared to him. He didn't know what she was capable of and quickly realized she could use magic. She was neither nix nor ethereal, so she had to have gotten her magic elsewhere. Was she a Necromancer? Was that the reason she wanted Elliot?

If Namir was a Necromancer, that meant Minari had run into two so far—two out of the five. This time he wouldn't let her go. He would kill her. Now he understood why Owen had warned him if he failed to kill Namir, then he would also fail to save Elliot.

Black magic flowed inside Chloé, and in order for Minari to free Chloé, he would need to finish Namir off.

Minari turned, scanning the room for Namir. His eyes widened as he saw her appear out of thin air in front of Elliot. She pressed her hand across his eyes, and he fell limp against her.

"Elliot!" Minari yelled. He wanted to run toward the fallen elf, but a magic beam shot in front of him, stopping him in his tracks. He mentally cursed. He would need to deal with Chloé first, but how?

He shifted his attention, now focused on the possessed nix. He knew there was a limited amount of stamina within a magic core. She wouldn't be able to keep shooting at the rate she was using her stamina.

Chloé pulled the trigger, but nothing shot out of her gun. It was an opening. Minari lunged toward Chloé and grabbed her wrist. He twisted her body, bringing her arm behind her, and pulled the pistol from her hand. "Chloé, snap out of it," he said.

The nix stayed quiet. Her head hung forward, pink hair covering her face. He couldn't see if she was responding to his voice or not.

"Chloé?" Minari leaned forward, attempting to see a reaction beyond the curls.

Chloé jerked her head up, ramming the back of her skull against Minari's face. Minari yelped, letting go of Chloé, and pressed his hand against his nose. It was hot, and Minari could feel the rush of blood oozing down.

Chloé turned. Her small hands reached for Minari's waist and stole two of his daggers. They were his smaller ones, meant for throwing, but they appeared larger in the hands of the small female.

She moved her arms, brandishing the daggers. It was evident she didn't know how to use the weapons, but she could still do damage if Minari wasn't careful. He sidestepped, dodging the random swings Chloé threw at him.

Minari tried to force his left arm to move, but he still couldn't feel anything. He needed to disarm Chloé. He ducked down as Chloé swung her arms again. Minari swung his foot across Chloé's feet, knocking her onto the ground. The daggers fell out of her hands. He hovered over her, grabbing one wrist and putting it above her head. "Chloé, snap out of it!" he yelled. There was a slight reaction in Chloé's eyes, but she still stared at him with ominous orbs.

Chloé's mouth opened and made a strained gargling noise. Her lips curled upward.

Then she snickered.

And shrieked.

The noise was ear-piercing. Minari closed his eyes and bit his lip. He tried to block out the offensive noise. It dulled his senses. He wasn't able to feel or hear Chloé, but a sudden burst of pain pulled him out of the daze.

Chloé had drawn another one of his daggers and had buried it in his side. Minari let out a strained groan as Chloé twisted the blade before yanking it out. He rolled off of Chloé and onto the ground, applying pressure to the deep wound. He gritted his teeth and tried to steady his breathing. Crimson liquid seeped through his fingers.

Chloé's gaze locked on Minari, the menacing grin still plastered across her features. Minari quickly stood, hunching over. He couldn't let it end here. He still had so much to do. But his head spun, and he had a hard time keeping his eyes steady.

Chloé lunged at Minari, and he moved to the side. He reached for Chloé's wrist and twisted the dagger from her hold. It dropped to the ground. Minari kicked it away, not wanting it to be used against him again.

"Chloé, snap out of it," Minari said through clenched teeth. He saw white specks across his vision. He released Chloé and reapplied pressure to his side. He was losing blood. Fast.

Chloé's head stayed tilted to the side. Her smile had disappeared. She looked at Minari curiously, but her eyes were still black. Her head creaked to her other shoulder, and her lips curled once more. She moved quickly, stealing another dagger from Minari. This time it was one of his longer daggers, the ones he kept strapped to his thighs.

The two danced. Chloé waved the weapon around while Minari could only move out of the way. His movements were considerably slower, and his body was starting to feel cold. The world spun as he tried to get away from Chloé.

Minari's heel caught a crack in the ground, sending him sprawling back. He let out a pained grunt. Chloé crawled over him, the dagger still in her hand. She lifted her hand and forced it down.

Minari quickly grabbed the blade. The sharp edges dug into his fingers. Blood dripped onto his cheeks, and he struggled to push the blade away.

"Chloé," Minari said. "Chloé . . . fight it . . . I know you can." With the last bit of strength he had left, he pushed the blade to the side, sending Chloé sprawling against his body. He grabbed Chloé with his bloodied hand and rolled them onto their sides. Even if he couldn't pull Chloé out of whatever hold Namir had on her, he could at least prevent her from going after anyone else. If he couldn't get Elliot out, then hopefully Bunnie could.

Chloé attempted to escape his hold. He shifted, tightening his grip around her middle.

A sharp pain pierced his hand. He grunted. Chloé had sunk the dagger into his hand. Warmth spread across his fingertips. Blood drenched the front of Chloé's dress. The blade had sunk through his hand and into Chloé's stomach. He tried to pull away, but Chloé kept the blade pressed deep. She must have tried to free herself, and the logic in her mind was to stab the thing that was holding her down.

Minari's head fell to the cold ground. If Chloé didn't draw the dagger out, then she was stuck with him. That was enough for him.

Black danced around the corner of his vision. Sounds became muffled as he let his eyes close.

52
REALIZE

Mimi blinked and furrowed his brows, attempting to clear his mind. He remembered being bound to a table, then the next moment he saw Elliot getting strapped to an altar. There was nothing in between. He struggled to find his voice, struggled to even move. He felt a familiar presence behind him and knew it was Sage, so he asked him for help.

The ox shouted for the other chimeras to rise and fight for their freedom. He mentally smiled, knowing that was something Sage would do. Namir, who Mimi suddenly remembered as an outcast chimera from the village, ran toward them, fully intending to kill Sage for interfering with her plans.

A blinding light blasted between them, and a group of people instantly appeared: three humans, a nix, and someone just like Elliot—an elf.

The elf rushed to Elliot's side and tried to free him. The white-haired ethereal held the elf at sword point, but the elf had freed Elliot's hands. A sudden blast of magic sent them flying, Mimi and Sage included.

Mimi felt strong arms wrap around him before they collided with the ground. Sage had broken his fall. Mimi's head spun vigorously. He couldn't tell up from down, forward from back. His brain felt like it was about to explode, but the pain eventually settled down to a mere throb.

Mimi felt Sage shuffle out from under him. Mimi staggered to his feet and gripped his head. The blast from Elliot must have jostled his head and forced forgotten memories to return. He recalled the moment he'd been alone in a room until now. He remembered getting impaled by a fang. He remembered being taught he needed to sacrifice himself for the greater good of chimeras. He remembered . . . hurting Sage. A pang of remorse rooted in his heart, but he swallowed it down. Sage was now fighting one of Oasis's captains. He recalled him being called Aiden.

Mimi was about to go to Sage's aid until he realized Elliot was coming toward him. "Save Elliot." That was what Mimi had told Sage. With Elliot now free, it was up to Mimi to get him out of here. He played back his memory of the building they were in. There were many hallways, stairs, and different rooms. It was a maze, and Mimi couldn't remember if they'd taken him outside, but at least he knew where not to go.

Mimi was about to reach for Elliot when Namir suddenly appeared between them. Elliot collapsed against her body, and they disappeared. Dread filled Mimi. He looked around frantically, seeing if they'd possibly appeared elsewhere, but he didn't see them. Had Namir taken him to perform the ritual somewhere else?

He needed to save him, needed to get him out. Something inside Mimi urged him to get Elliot to safety. Elliot was important to him, but he couldn't explain why. It was a different kind of importance compared to Sage. Mimi wanted to be with Sage and protect him because they had a mutual understanding of each other and shared the same feelings. Their love brought them together. With Elliot, it was more instinctual. He needed to follow him, aid him, protect him in any way possible.

Then he sensed something. Down the hall, down the spiral staircase, beneath the floor. That was where Elliot was. It was like his spirit was calling out to Mimi.

And he answered.

Mimi raced out of the large room, ignoring the shouts and screams around him.

He ran through the dim halls, ignoring the feeling of déjà vu as he descended the stairs. He ran past the empty cages. There was a door at the end of the room, and he yanked it open.

It was a circular room, smaller than the room with the altar. Namir was in the middle, hovering over Elliot. Her hand had somehow disappeared inside his chest, but there was no blood. Elliot's hands clawed at Namir's arm, trying to get her out. He arched his back in agony, a scream ripping through his throat.

Namir moved her eyes, her golden gaze landing on Mimi. She licked her lips. *"Back to me so soon, my little dessert? You will have your chance soon enough."* The cat chimera's arm twitched, and Elliot froze. A small whimper slipped from his lips.

Mimi charged forward.

Namir smirked. A puff of black smoke appeared before Mimi, and he collided with a hard body. Luka and Owen emerged. Luka's eyes were unfocused, while Owen's were sharp and alert.

"Take care of him," Namir said. "But don't kill him. I need him for later." She returned to the task at hand.

Elliot continued to squirm. He was growing paler as the seconds ticked by.

Mimi needed to get to Namir, but how? He'd rushed down without thinking of picking up a weapon, and his rapiers had been confiscated.

Owen grabbed Luka's wrist, but his blue eyes remained on Mimi. "Go."

Mimi raised his eyebrows. Were they not under Namir's control anymore? Thinking back, they'd been hit with Elliot's outburst. That was it. That must have been why Mimi had been able to regain himself. Whatever magic Elliot had, it was able to nullify Namir's magic. With Namir's hand inside Elliot's chest, Mimi knew she was trying to rip the elf's magic core out. He wasn't going to let that happen. He brushed past the two ethereals and ran straight to Elliot.

Namir frowned. Her eyes narrowed at Mimi. With her other hand, she snapped her fingers. A large, black shadow formed in front of her. It was airy, yet it took the physical shape of a leopard. Its red eyes glowed in contrast with its dark body. It lunged toward Mimi.

He barely had time to react. The shadow leopard sunk its teeth into Mimi's arm, knocking him to the ground. Even though it didn't appear to have a solid body, its teeth tore through his flesh.

Mimi cried out. He tried to pry the animal off, but it didn't let go, only tightened its jaw. Pain traveled up his body. It felt like his arm was getting ripped off.

A silver sword speared the leopard's head, and it disappeared.

Mimi slowly sat up, keeping his injured arm close.

Luka had his sword drawn. Two gray feathers hung off the hilt of the sword. "Let him go, Namir."

Namir's lips curled. "You think you can stop me after breaking free from my hold?" She moved her arm slightly, and Elliot gasped. "I have my hand wrapped around his core. One wrong move and I will tear it out and crush it."

Luka scoffed. "As if you weren't already going to do that."

"This elf is interesting." Namir traced a finger across Elliot's cheek. "With my hand around his core, I can feel it sting, as if it's sending me a warning. His core has a mind of its own. It is not like the other magic cores I've taken."

Luka's fingers twitched against his sword. "Maxwell," he whispered.

Namir tilted her head. "Ah, Maxwell. His was the most . . . *delicious*."

Luka lunged toward Namir. He slashed his sword, severing her arm from her body.

Namir shrieked. She pulled away and teleported back.

She held on to what was left of her arm. No blood dripped from her body. A dark cloud formed around the wound.

"You will not harm our oracle," Luka said.

"Such a change of heart," Namir said. "But I guess it was to be expected from you." She moved her hand over what would be her other arm. Her severed limb grew back at the same time the arm that was still jutting from Elliot disappeared. She straightened her back. "The chess pieces are all together, yet here I am, early to the party. I suppose it wouldn't be fun if I overstepped and changed the tempo of this dance." She gave one final smirk. "Until next time."

Namir disappeared.

Mimi didn't bother to consider Namir's word puzzle. He made his way over to Elliot, ignoring the heavy throb in his arm.

Elliot's eyes were glossed over. His eyes skimmed over to Mimi and then to Luka. He was still pale, and his breathing was labored.

Luka sheathed his sword and ran his hands over Elliot's chest. He furrowed his brow. "She left a piece of herself inside him," he mumbled.

Mimi's eyes widened. If Namir's dark matter was within Elliot, then she could take ahold of him and manipulate his memories, just like she'd done to him. He was sure Luka and Owen had dealt with the same experience.

Luka's aura was the exact opposite from when he'd stabbed Mimi. It was calm, peaceful.

Mimi's ears picked up Owen's footsteps. The feathers on his head glowed but then quickly dimmed. The ethereal placed a hand on his brooch. "It seems this elf's powers nullified Namir's." He ripped the metal piece off his coat. "We are free, Luka."

"Finally," Luka said. "But now he's . . ." He pressed his lips into a thin line. "We cannot leave him, Owen. I do not know how to extract Namir's powers from him, but I should be able to ground him when his mind starts to wander."

"Is he . . ." Mimi bit his lip. "Will her dark magic stay until she is killed?"

Luka nodded. "Destroy the source, and it will destroy everything that came from it."

"That's the reason we risked ourselves finding the other elf," Owen said. "We trusted him to kill Namir, and in return it would destroy the hold she had on us, but this elf somehow had the power to do it."

"He is the oracle," Luka said.

Mimi frowned. "What is the oracle?"

"An oracle is a warrior of sorts, someone chosen by the goddess of light, Vylantra," Luka said. "It's something a chimera wouldn't be aware of. Your kind are not acquainted with the divine powers of Etheria. I will not go into much detail." He held out his hand. "Give me your arm."

Mimi hesitated at first. Moving it even the slightest sent his body into a fit of tremors. He had thought his own regenerative abilities would be enough for the wound to heal, but the animal must have punctured him deeper than he'd thought. He stepped toward Luka and held out his arm, biting down a hiss.

Luka placed a hand delicately underneath Mimi's

palm. The other hand hovered over the wound. The silver-haired ethereal closed his eyes, and the feathers on his head glowed. A warm, white light emitted from his hand, and Mimi's body was filled with warmth and immediate relief. The ache and throb disappeared as the bite mark receded. His arm was fully healed.

Luka let go of Mimi's hand. "Before I forget . . ." He reached into his coat and placed something in Mimi's hand. "This is yours, I believe."

Mimi sucked in a breath. It was his earpiece. "You kept this?"

"I was under Namir's hold when I took it from you, but I was able to piece together my missing memories and retrieve it. I know this is of importance to you." Luka brushed his hand across Mimi's left ear. Mimi felt a brief flow of warmth. "Why not put it on?"

Mimi hooked the snake earpiece back on. It didn't make him feel any different physically, but he felt more like himself. Proud. Brave.

"There, now we should get back to the others," Luka said.

Mimi gasped. *Sage.* He hoped he was all right. If Sage were in tip-top condition, Mimi knew he could take Aiden down. But with the lack of food and the injuries he had . . .

Mimi shook his head. No. He had to believe in him.

Owen knelt down and wrapped his arms around Elliot. He had an arm underneath the elf's knees and shoulders. "Let's return to the others. Hold on to me or Luka."

Mimi pressed a hand against Luka's elbow.

The air was sucked out of his lungs, and the ground

disappeared from underneath him.

53
SAFE

Sage dabbed the sweat off his chin. The adrenaline that had kept him going against Aiden was growing thin. He had fed off the surrounding energy of the rioting chimeras, but it seemed the fight was nearly over. The ones left in the room were Oasis members, either knocked out or killed in the brawl.

Sage tried to steady his grip on the sword he'd stolen from Aiden when he'd knocked the human over. The weight of the metal seemed to grow heavier as time went on. His arm trembled, forcing him to grip the hilt with both hands.

Aiden threw Sage a cocky smirk. "Tired already? Typical for a worthless chimera. Taking our resources and giving nothing in return. The lot of you are better off left to rot."

Aiden swung the sword he'd taken from a dead Oasis member, and Sage brought his up. Metal clashed, and the force reverberated across Sage's exhausted body. Aiden's lips curled. He pushed forward and down, bringing the points of the swords toward the floor. He swung his foot out, knocking Sage onto his back.

Sage lost his hold on the sword, and it was quickly kicked out of the way.

Aiden hovered over him. "I'd ask if you have any last words, but, frankly, I don't give a damn if you do." He placed the tip of the blade against Sage's chest. "Now *die.*"

Sage closed his eyes and forced an image of Mimi into his mind. If he was going to perish, he wanted his last memory to be of his lover. He imagined the softness of Mimi's hair, the cute pout Mimi would give him whenever he teased him for his height, the warmth of his body when they embraced.

The sound of Aiden's surprised grunt forced him out of his reel.

"Aiden! Stop!" It was a woman's voice.

Aiden cursed under his breath. There was a silver bolt lodged in his arm. It had been enough to stop him from striking Sage down.

Sage grabbed one of Aiden's ankles and yanked him to the ground. Aiden yelped, winded from the sudden pull.

Changing their positions, Sage ripped the sword from Aiden's hands. He pressed the blade against his chest. "I'd ask if you have any last words, but I don't give a damn if you do." The other human's voice urged him to stop as he sunk the sword home.

The sparkle of life in Aiden's eyes disappeared, and his head lolled to the side.

Sage pulled the sword out and threw it to the side. He panted. Whatever force had flowed through him and kept him running was practically gone. He struggled to keep his eyes open, let alone stand. His legs started to give out.

Sage was about to let himself fall into unconsciousness when he heard the familiar sweet sound of his beloved. His eyes snapped open, and a pair of small arms wrapped around his torso. They both sank to their knees.

"*Sage!*" Mimi said, burying his face against him.

"*Mimi . . .*" Sage brushed his fingers through Mimi's hair. It was as soft as he remembered.

Mimi looked up at Sage. "*Are you all right?*" he asked in their language. "*Are you hurt?*"

Sage shook his head. "*I'm okay.*" He cupped Mimi's cheek, and the smaller chimera leaned into the touch. "*Are you okay?*"

Mimi bit his lip. His yellow eyes scanned Sage's body. He pressed a hand against Sage's chest. "*I did this to you. I . . . I hurt you.*"

Sage leaned his forehead against Mimi's. "*No, you weren't yourself. It was Namir who did it.*"

Mimi frowned. "*I couldn't stop her from getting Elliot. She got away.*" He sucked in a breath. "*She left a piece of dark magic inside him.*"

Sage creased his brows. "*Is he . . . ?*"

"*He's all right for now, but he isn't conscious. Not yet. He's with Owen and Luka.*" Sage opened his mouth, but Mimi pressed a finger against Sage's lips. "*They were under*

Namir's control as well. They didn't mean to hurt us."

"How did you break free from her control?"

"Elliot."

"Elliot?" Sage thought back to when Mimi had brought him out of the cage. Mimi had somehow been able to break free from Namir's hold when he'd seen Elliot. And then after the magic blast . . .

If the two ethereals had been under Namir's hold and weren't anymore, then it made sense Elliot had freed them.

Mimi nodded. *"Luka mentioned he's the oracle. Something about a warrior of Vylantra. I don't really understand it myself, but that must be why Namir wanted him, and that was how he was able to free us."*

Someone cleared their throat. "I apologize for interrupting your . . . intimate moment, but are you two severely injured?" a human asked.

"Oliver, did you even consider whether they can speak common tongue?" an identical human asked. "You should use your head more when dealing with things besides flirting."

Mimi quickly scrambled away from Sage, a pink blush creeping across his cheeks. He helped Sage up, steadying his shaky legs.

"We can speak common tongue," Sage said.

Oliver smiled. He turned to his twin. "See, Deveran? I knew they could understand me."

Deveran rolled his eyes. "Pure luck."

"I'm fine, though I'd like to rest," Sage said.

"Are you sure?" Mimi whispered. "I didn't hurt you too much?"

Sage gave Mimi a reassuring smile. "Don't worry. As if you could do lasting damage to me."

Mimi puffed his cheeks. "And Aiden?"

"No human can best me."

"Some of our members are leading the chimeras who escaped during the brawl to the mutual area. If you two have sustained no major injuries, then would you head over there?" Deveran asked.

Mimi shook his head. "We-we're together with Elliot." He glanced around, trying to spot Luka or Owen.

"Ah, the elf Miss Gemme was looking for . . ." Oliver said, trailing off at the end. "It seems Miss Gemme and the other elf they were with sustained some injuries though. We aren't sure if the elf is going to make it."

Deveran elbowed Oliver. "That's not something you should say."

Mimi's eyes widened at he spotted the two ethereals. He separated himself from Sage and made his way over. Luka was kneeling beside a purple-haired elf and a nix. Owen stood nearby, Elliot still in his arms, and a female human was by their side.

Oliver and Deveran looked at each other, shrugged, and made their way over. Sage followed.

The purple-haired elf and the nix were lying side by side on the ground. The elf's arm was wrapped around the nix's torso, but what was troubling was the amount of blood surrounding them. A dagger was impaled in the elf's hand and into the nix's stomach.

"He's still alive, but just barely. He's lost too much blood," Luka said. "I'm afraid I can't heal him, but I can save

Miss Gemme." He brushed his fingers across her pink fringe. "The dagger prevented her from bleeding out, but it appears the elf sustained a stab wound."

"I can save him!" Mimi said. "I . . . I should be able to."

Sage raised his brows. Was Mimi going to expose his identity to these random people? Sage knew the two ethereals were aware of Mimi's Colorless Snake abilities, but the other humans weren't. Sage wasn't so keen on letting the humans know. They were quick to exploit chimeras, and he wasn't about to let Mimi go again.

"*Mimi,*" Sage warned.

"*It's fine. I trust them,*" Mimi said in their language. "*And this elf . . . he's an elf like Elliot. They must be close friends. You'd do the same for me, wouldn't you?*"

Sage bit the inside of his cheek and clenched his fists. It was true. If Sage had a secret ability to save Mimi, he would risk exposing himself for him, but this wasn't Sage who was dying. It was another elf. Yes, it was probably true the elf was friends with Elliot, but why go the extra step?

"If you can save him, then please do," the female human said in common tongue. "Minari is important to Elliot. He's been searching for Elliot since they got separated." She paused. "And Chloé Gemme, this nix . . . she is part of the council, but she is doing what she can to disband Oasis. She is on your side."

Mimi nodded. "I'll save him."

"I will cast my magic on Miss Gemme. Shall we work together?" Luka asked.

Mimi moved over and knelt in front of the nix. He wrapped his fingers around the dagger. "I need to use my blood to save him. I'll use this dagger, but we need to act quickly." He looked at Sage. "Sage, can you help me?"

Sage relaxed his shoulders. As much as he was against this, he wasn't going to go against Mimi's wishes. He nodded. "I'll turn him onto his back." Sage looked at the female human. "I don't know your name, but when Mimi takes the dagger, can you take Chloé off the elf . . . Minari?"

"Yes, he's Minari, and my name is Bunnie." She smiled. "And sure, I'll move her away. Luka, you will be able to heal her, yes?"

"Yes. If you hold her, I can use my healing magic."

"Got it," Bunnie said, shuffling over. She slid an arm behind Chloé.

Sage held Minari by his shoulders. The elf was extremely pale. Mimi was going to have to use more of his blood than usual to bring him back.

"On three," Mimi said. "One . . . Two . . . Three!"

Mimi pulled the dagger out. Bunnie shifted Chloé away from Minari, holding her close, and Sage turned the elf onto his back. Mimi held his arm over the stab wound. He sliced his forearm with the dagger. Blood flowed freely from the deep cut. It fell onto Minari's wound and seeped inside. The crimson liquid flowed from Mimi as if it were alive.

Chloé moaned, and her eyes fluttered open. She looked around, disoriented. "Where . . . ?"

"Welcome back, Chloé," Bunnie said.

"How do you feel?" Luka asked, retracting his hand.

"Like I just woke up from a very long nap," Chloé mumbled. Her eyes began to close, but then they snapped open. She leaned away from Bunnie. "Elliot? Purple Hair? Where?"

"Elliot is all right. Owen has him. As for Minari . . ." Bunnie frowned, and her gaze shifted to Mimi.

Chloé followed Bunnie's gaze. Her eyes widened. She looked at Minari and then back to Mimi. "You're . . . you're the Colorless Snake."

"He is," Sage said, answering for Mimi. He didn't want Mimi's focus to break.

Chloé bit her lip. "There's so much blood . . ."

"He can save him," Sage said.

Chloé pressed her lips together and gave a small nod.

Sage kept an eye on Mimi. Blood still dripped from his arm, and Minari still wasn't showing signs of recovering. "*Mimi, you need to stop,*" he said in their native tongue. "*You're losing too much blood.*"

As if understanding Sage, Luka placed a hand on Mimi's shoulder. "Let me heal you," he said gently.

Mimi was starting to sway. His arm had dropped, his hand resting on Minari. "But . . ."

"If you lose any more blood, I won't be able to do anything for you," Luka said.

And then Minari stirred. He furrowed his brows, and a groan left his lips.

Chloé gasped. She covered her lips with her hand. "Mi-Minari!"

Luka took ahold of Mimi's arm and healed his wound. Mimi had brought Minari back. There wasn't a need to spill any more blood.

Minari's eyes cracked open, but they remained unfocused. "C-Chloé?" He let out another groan before closing his eyes again.

"He must be tired," Bunnie said. "Let him rest."

"Boss," Deveran said. There was an owl on his arm. "Message from Yen. Whatever magic made this hideout invisible is gone. They can see it now, and all the chimeras they saw leaving are now in the mutual area." He looked around. "The only ones left are the ones . . . here."

"The cleanup is going to suck," Oliver said. "How are we supposed to explain the dead Oasis members and chimeras?"

"I don't suppose the kingdom is going to care about the chimeras, but we will need to make up a story about the Oasis members," Bunnie said. "And their two dead captains."

"Technically, Owen and I are still captains," Luka said. "We can make something up before resigning."

"It's going to be one elaborate lie." Oliver shrugged.

"Let us leave this place for now," Luka said. "Is there a place you'd like to meet?" he asked Bunnie.

"Our headquarters is in Lonin, but that's too far to travel. We have a smaller base in Ruglow."

Luka looked at Owen before turning back. "Owen and I are able to teleport two people each. I'd suggest letting us bring the two elves with us, so that leaves room for two others."

"I-I want to go with you," Chloé said.

"How about you two?" Bunnie asked, attention now on Sage and Mimi. "I know you come in a pair, but the small one here looks like he's going to pass out. Travel won't do him any good."

Sage gritted his teeth. The mere idea of being separated from Mimi irked him. He still wasn't sure if he could trust them either. One glance at Mimi told Sage he needed immediate rest. A comfortable bed would suit him well. With the ordeal he'd just gone through, he deserved it.

"We meet back in Ruglow?" Sage asked.

"Yes. A day's travel. We have horses waiting outside."

Sage didn't *need* to ride another animal—he was part ox—but he knew he was pushing his body to the limit. In actuality, he wanted to fall on his back and just sleep off the exhaustion.

"There is a carriage you can ride in," Deveran said. "We had them prepared for the possibility of injured chimeras, and I think you fit the description."

Mimi reached for Sage's hand. His breathing was slightly labored, his eyes unfocused. "*I trust them,*" he said in their language. "*Go. I'll meet you in Ruglow.*"

Sage took a deep breath. He clutched Mimi's hand and leaned forward. His lips pressed against Mimi's forehead in a chaste kiss. The message was simple. "*Wait for me.*"

54
MEND

The group was seated at the round table inside one of the private rooms in the Ruglow Inn. A week had passed since they'd first arrived. Chloé listened idly as Bunnie and Luka discussed the success of resigning from Oasis. As promised, Luka and Owen had written an official letter to the council explaining the events that had happened in the hidden hideout. They'd confessed Namir had been secretly collecting chimeras for her own personal gain rather than leading them to the mutual lands. Charlotte and Aiden had been a part of her plan. The chimeras had eventually rioted against their captors, which had ended with the deaths of many Oasis members, as well as the two captains. Namir had escaped and was nowhere to be found. In order to keep this scandalous news from reaching public ear, the council had agreed that Luka and Owen had no part in Namir's personal agenda and had allowed them to part from the guild.

Chloé wasn't surprised the council didn't want the public to know. It would've tarnished their reputation, especially Licht's. Licht was the one in charge of overseeing Oasis's tasks. He was the one who spoke to Namir regularly, so for this to have slipped past him must have shocked him immensely.

Chloé ran her fingers across the top of her cup. The tea had long gone cold, no longer pleasant to drink. She hadn't had an appetite as of late. She'd been anxious when they'd reached the small town, hoping no one would recognize her. The group she was with was an odd bunch: two elves, two chimeras, two ethereals, and a human. Anyone would stop and give her a stare. When the town remained quiet, she'd realized she wasn't anxious because she was afraid someone would recognize her—she was anxious because Minari hadn't regained consciousness. He'd remained asleep for five days, only waking up two days ago. It had brought her great relief when Luka had informed her Minari had finally awoken. She wanted to see him desperately, to see if he was all right.

But memories of what had happened at Oasis's hideout stopped her.

Chloé remembered losing control of her body, the feeling of her joints popping and her muscles spasming. Her body was on fire, and she couldn't do anything about it. Her mind felt like it was being torn in different directions. One side of it felt far away, and that was the side controlling her body. No matter how much she willed herself to stop, she kept firing at Minari, moving around him, intending to cause him harm. And even after she felt the cold drain of her core, her body didn't stop. It kept going as if her existence had only one person. Only after stabbing him and feeling his body turn cold did she feel the waves of release. Her mind mended together, becoming one again. But it was too late. She was too weak to move. Too tired to keep her eyes open. She'd plunged into darkness soon after.

Chloé would never forget the moment she'd opened her eyes again. The sight of Minari's still body. The sight of Minari's blood all over his body. The sight of Minari's blood all over *her body*. She'd thought the worst. She'd thought Minari had *died* because of her. She would never have been able to forgive herself or face Elliot. How would he have reacted if she had killed his best friend? He would have definitely left her. And if he'd left, then she would've been alone. She would have been forced to return home to Blanc Grotto and resume her mundane life.

Even though it had been two days since Minari had woken up, Chloé still hadn't been able to bring herself to speak to him. Her chest tightened whenever she thought of going up to him. To even pass a greeting made her stomach fill with anxiety.

"Chloé."

Chloé squeaked. She jumped, nearly knocking her cup over. She looked up, meeting Minari face-to-face. She quickly turned away. She had been so deep in thought that she hadn't realized the room had emptied out. It was only her and Minari now.

Minari crossed his arms and leaned his hip against the table. "You've been avoiding me."

Chloé chewed the inside of her cheek. She had hoped Minari wouldn't notice, but she supposed turning away every time Minari looked at her or tried to get her attention had seemed obvious.

Minari sighed. "Did I do something to offend you?"

"No," Chloé blurted.

"Then what?"

Chloé felt small next to Minari, like she didn't deserve to be next to him. Not after everything she had done.

"I can hear you thinking. The gears turning are surprisingly loud."

Chloé puffed up her cheeks. She stood, and the chair scraped across the wooden floor. "I'm sorry."

Minari cocked a brow. "What are you apologizing for?"

Chloé felt her cheeks flush. She turned away, trying to hide her reddened face. Why was Minari pretending not to know what she was referring to? It should have been obvious. "Back in Oasis's hideout . . ." she whispered.

"Oh."

The silence that stretched between them created a heavy atmosphere in the room. Chloé knew Minari wouldn't forgive her. It was foolish of her to even try. She clenched her fist and tried her best to keep from shaking.

"You were . . . aware of what was happening?" Minari asked, finally breaking the silence.

"I saw everything. I . . . I tried so hard to break free from Namir's hold, but I couldn't. And because of that you almost died." Chloé choked. Tears started to well in her eyes. Saying how close to death Minari had been was hard.

Her chest twisted in pain she hadn't known was possible.

"But I didn't die."

"If not for Mimi, you would've," Chloé whispered. She kept her gaze on the floor.

Minari tilted Chloé's chin up. "Are you crying?"

Chloé swatted Minari's hand away. "Of course I am! You almost died, Minari!"

Minari's eyes widened. He opened his mouth, then closed it and opened it again. "Did you just call me by my name?"

Chloé felt her ears heat up. She stuttered before taking a few steps back and turning away. "Don't get used to it! I just . . . I was just . . ." She pressed her hands to her chest, trying to keep herself from shaking.

"It would be nice if you kept calling me by my name instead of Purple Hair." Minari chuckled. "I accept your apology, but you have nothing to apologize for. We were in the midst of a battle, and anything goes in one. I'm just glad you're alive. You're a dear friend, after all."

Chloé fell to her knees, tears finally flowing from her eyes. Her shoulders felt lighter, and she took a breath of relief. Minari had not only forgiven her but had admitted he was happy she was alive. He didn't blame her for what had happened. He didn't resent her or wish she was dead. Instead, he'd accepted her with open arms. He'd accepted her as a *friend*.

Chloé had promised herself to do whatever it took to keep Elliot and Minari safe from prejudice. She vowed to prove elves and chimeras deserved respect and the same rights as the rest of the lower lands. She vowed to overturn the inaccurate writings in the historical books across all of Etheria.

As long as Chloé was with Elliot and Minari, she felt like she could do everything. As long as she had the support of the others, she would make a change.

55
AGAIN

"What are you?" Namir asked. She circled around Elliot. The room was dark, empty. Her voice reverberated around him.

"I'm the oracle," Elliot said.

"What are you doing here in the lower lands?"

"I'm here to start a war with the kingdom." Those words echoed in Elliot's mind. He furrowed his brow. Was that the real reason he was down here? It was the answer Charlotte had accepted, so it had to be true.

Namir chuckled. "A war? Is that what you're truly down here for?"

"I . . ." Elliot hesitated. Had he given her the wrong answer?

"What is the true reason you're here, Oracle?"

"To . . . to find . . ." What was he here for again? He was sure it was to start a war. He was an elf, a savage barbarian who

enjoyed killing and eating the flesh of the dead. But was that the true reason? How come he couldn't remember?

Namir stopped in front of him. She placed a hand flat against his chest, right over his heart. "Do you want to play a game, Oracle?"

Elliot sucked in a breath. A game. Charlotte's smile flashed before him. Fear wracked his body. He didn't want to play a game.

"Tell me, are you afraid of pain?"

Namir's hand suddenly sank inside Elliot. He choked. He could feel each of her fingers moving inside him. It sent hot pain through his body. He couldn't breathe. Each breath caused a sharp pain.

"What is your purpose, Oracle?"

Elliot's eyes shot open. He gasped for air, relieved to feel it flowing through his lungs. His eyes darted around. He'd been expecting to see pitch-black darkness, to be back in the room, to feel the cold, stone floor against his back. But what he saw was the opposite. Sunlight spilled through a window. A soft blanket was draped over his body. Had he woken up from a dream only to end up in another one? There was something warm wrapped around his hand, and he felt it move.

"Elliot! Elliot!"

Elliot turned his head. Tears immediately welled up in his eyes, blurring his vision. Minari was by his side, a hand clasped over his. Chloé was right next to him.

"Thank Vylantra you're awake," Minari said. "You've been asleep for two weeks."

Elliot's eyes widened. Two weeks? What had happened? He tried to sit up but sank back down as the world spun. "What . . . ?" he croaked. His throat felt dry.

"Try not to get up too quickly." Another voice. It was Luka's.

Elliot turned his head to the other side. The ethereal was no longer in his Oasis coat. His attire was comprised of a white robe with accents of purple, and there was a sword on his hip. He held a mug in his hands. "Try getting up slowly."

Elliot moved to prop himself up on his elbows. Minari rested his hands against Elliot's back, easing him into a sitting position. He still felt dizzy, but it was manageable.

Luka handed Elliot the mug. "Drink this. It should help clear your mind."

Elliot sipped it. The drink had no flavor, tasting just like water. He emptied the mug of its contents before handing it back to Luka. His body instantly felt light. The dizziness was gone, and his mind felt clear. His throat was no longer parched.

"What . . . what happened?" Elliot asked. "Everyone . . ."

Chloé stood. "I'll go get them." She left the room, closing the door behind her.

"We're in Ruglow," Minari said, returning to his seat beside the bed. "Everyone escaped Oasis's hideout. Luka and Owen helped."

"Owen?" Elliot furrowed his brow.

"Owen is my partner," Luka said. "Do you recall a gray-haired ethereal visiting you while you were in the hideout?"

Elliot blinked, thinking back. "Owen was the one who checked up on me . . . to see if I was alive?"

Luka nodded.

"He was the one who told me where I could find you," Minari said. "He gave me some magic feather that teleported me inside the room you were in. After everything was over, I learned he'd given a stone to one of Bunnie's men, which allowed Bunnie and Chloé to teleport inside. That was how we got in together."

"Bunnie?"

"Ah, do you remember the dancer back in Venin?" Minari smiled. "She's Bunnie, the captain of Nighthawk. This inn is one of their bases."

Elliot frowned. He felt like he'd missed so much after being separated from everyone for so long. He clenched his fists against the blanket. His heart felt empty. He felt useless. While he'd been playing games with Charlotte, Minari and the others had been desperately trying to find him. It was his fault for being so weak. If he hadn't been, then he wouldn't have been so easily captured. Tears pricked the corners of his eyes.

"Hey." Minari placed a hand over Elliot's, giving it a reassuring squeeze. "What's wrong?"

Elliot bit his lip, biting back a sob. He lowered his head, unable to face Minari. "I . . . I let you all down." He sucked in a breath before letting it out slowly. An overwhelming amount of guilt crushed his chest. Had he done anything right since leaving Mistfall? He was struggling to even remember why he'd left in the first place. "I don't remember . . . I don't remember why we left. I don't remember why we are here. Minari, I—"

Minari moved off his chair, taking a seat beside Elliot on the bed. He placed a hand behind Elliot's head before pressing Elliot's face gently against his chest. Minari's fingers ran through Elliot's hair. Elliot felt himself relaxing against his best friend.

"I'll return in a moment," Luka said. He left the room with an audible click of the door.

Sobs wracked Elliot's body. He couldn't keep the tears from falling.

"Shh," Minari cooed. "It's okay. Everything is all right." He continued to stroke Elliot's head.

Elliot clung to Minari as if his life depended on it. He couldn't wrap his mind around the simple fact that Minari and Chloé were here with him. It felt like an eternity had passed since he'd been together with them. All he knew was the cold dungeon with Charlotte, the torturous game he'd played with her. He was the oracle, yet he didn't have the power to do *anything*.

Minari moved his hands onto Elliot's shoulders and gently pushed. Elliot reluctantly sat back, already missing the warmth Minari provided. Minari cupped Elliot's cheek, his thumb stroking his tear-flooded eye. "What's wrong?"

Elliot pressed his lips together. He knew he had to tell Minari what had happened. He knew Minari would be with him no matter what. He choked back a sob. It was just so hard to tell him what had happened. Minari would surely be agitated at Elliot's inability to defend himself. He was the oracle. He had the ability to use magic, yet he'd allowed a mere human to capture and torture him.

"Elliot?" Minari's voice was soft. He wasn't pushing Elliot for an answer but was waiting patiently for Elliot to be ready.

Elliot took a deep breath. He placed his hand over Minari's, relishing the heat the palm provided before pulling it away. "I was captured by Charlotte." Elliot paused, wondering if Minari would ask questions, but he stayed silent. "She held me captive in a dungeon. There were no windows. I didn't know how much time had passed." Elliot shut his eyes. Images of Charlotte's cruel expression replayed in his memory—the way she'd toyed with Lily's dagger against his skin, the way she'd made the flames dance across his body. Elliot let out a gasp, pressing his hand over his mouth. His stomach churned. It threatened to empty, but he knew there was nothing for him to purge.

Minari rubbed circles across Elliot's back. "You don't have to tell me now. I'll always be here for you, Elliot. You can tell me when you're ready."

Elliot shook his head. He didn't know if he was ever going to be ready to tell Minari. He was afraid Minari would laugh in his face and leave if he knew the truth. He was sure Minari wouldn't want anything to do with him once he knew how incredibly *useless* he was. Elves were supposed to be strong. They were savages, strong barbarians who paved the path without fear.

Elliot blinked.

No.

No.

No.

That wasn't right. Elves weren't anything like that. They were peaceful. Back home in Mistfall, everyone lived in peace, and they were happy. They didn't need to pave a path to show how strong they were.

A sharp pain shot through Elliot's head. He gasped and clutched his hair, pulling at it to help relieve the pain.

Images of peaceful days merged with images of a burning village. Charlotte's questions echoed in his mind.

Why was he able to use magic?

Why did he have a magic core?

What was his purpose in leaving the mountains?

The questions repeated themselves over and over again. He could hear Charlotte laugh and scoff. He wanted to scream. To yell. He pulled at his hair, harder this time. "Stop . . . please . . ."

Warm hands wrapped around his wrists, urging his hands away from his head. He let the hands move his own, and they fell on his lap. He looked up, and his eyes met with Minari's worried gaze.

"Elliot, it's okay. You're safe now. Do you know where we are?"

Elliot looked around. The room was warm and well lit, the opposite of the cold, dark dungeon. And Minari was with him. He could feel his nerves relax. "Ruglow . . ."

Minari smiled. "Right. You're in Ruglow."

Elliot looked around the room again. "She's not here?"

Minari shook his head. "No. You won't see her ever again."

Elliot grasped Minari's hands. "You're sure?"

"Yes, you have my word. You'll never see Charlotte again."

Elliot relaxed his shoulders. "Sorry."

"Do not be sorry, Elliot. You have nothing to apologize for."

Elliot bit his lip. He couldn't bring himself to believe those words. Not yet. Not until Minari knew the truth. "The others?"

Minari smiled. "Are you ready to see them?"

Elliot nodded. "Yes."

Minari stood. "Then I will go get them." He paused at the door, taking one last look at Elliot. Elliot gave him a single nod, telling him that he was ready. Minari gave a small smile before opening the door. He poked his head out, saying a few words before swinging the door open.

Chloé entered. Following behind her were Mimi, Sage, Luka, and who Elliot assumed were Bunnie and Owen. The female human had black hair tied back in a ponytail and wore a black, leather coat. The male ethereal also had a ponytail, but it sat higher, and his hair was light gray. He wore a robe similar to Luka's, but the sleeves were tight at the wrists rather than loose.

"How are you feeling?" Mimi asked, rushing to Elliot's side. "You look like you've been crying."

Elliot chortled. Of course his eyes would be puffy, his cheeks stained with tears. But he couldn't let that stop him from meeting everyone. "I'm better now."

"We haven't properly met. I'm Bunnie." The woman stuck out her hand.

Elliot met her halfway, and they shook. "Elliot."

"Pleasure." Bunnie smiled.

"Hello again, Elliot. It is nice to properly meet this time," Owen said as he stood by Luka.

Elliot gave Owen a nod.

"Now that everyone is here and acquainted, I'm sure we have some explaining to do," Bunnie said. She placed a hand on her hip and shifted her weight onto one leg.

"Explaining?" Elliot tilted his head.

"Well, it turns out Luka knew you were the oracle," Minari said.

Elliot furrowed his brow. Yes, he was the oracle, leader of the elves . . . right? But what was his purpose again?

"We ethereals keep *accurate* documentation in our libraries," Luka said. "They are technically open to the public, but hardly anyone travels to the Snowy Hills."

"Accurate? What do you mean by accurate? Does the rest of Etheria not have accurate documents?" Elliot asked. He leaned forward. If what Luka said was true, then had everything he'd admitted to Charlotte been a lie?

"Purp—" Chloé cleared her throat. "Minari explained to me what an oracle actually is, along with the prophecy you tried to tell me about. I'm sorry I didn't believe you at first."

Prophecy? The word rang a bell. Elliot wracked his brain, forcing himself to remember the meaning behind the prophecy. Vylantra's words suddenly coursed through his mind. Elliot had left Mistfall to fulfill a prophecy. He needed to find four warriors and the lost hero. Right. That was his purpose. That was why he'd left Mistfall.

"We've discussed it, and it seems Mimi, Miss Gemme, and I all share a unique connection with you," Luka said. "So we are the warriors you are looking for."

Elliot frantically looked between everyone, mouth agape. "What? All three . . . ?"

Chloé smiled. "Well, you already knew when we met. It was like meeting a long-lost friend."

"I had an instinct to protect you," Mimi said.

"And I was drawn to your magic. Something within you was calling out to me, and I responded. When I first saw you in the dungeon, that's when I knew. I knew you were the oracle and I was a warrior."

Elliot placed a hand against his chest. He closed his eyes and focused. He could see thin colored strings coming out of his body. They led to the different figures in the room. A pink one wrapped around Chloé, a golden one wrapped around Mimi, and a light blue one wrapped around Luka. They were all connected to him and to one another by a green string. There was one last string. It was black and thinner than the rest, but it didn't lead anywhere. It was cut short, barely traveling past him.

Elliot opened his eyes. The three warriors looked at him, smiles on their faces.

"If Mimi is coming with you, I'm coming along," Sage said as he crossed his arms.

"Wherever Luka goes, I will follow," Owen said.

"I'm not tagging along on your epic adventure, but I

know you guys may need my help," Bunnie said. She reached into her pocket and flicked a coin at Elliot. He reached up and caught it. It was a single bronze coin with an owl's head etched on it. "Keep that with you, and our owls will be able to locate you. If I gather any information that may be useful in your journey, I'll definitely write." Bunnie winked.

"Do you feel well enough to travel?" Minari asked. "We can take another day to rest if you need to."

Elliot shook his head. "I've already wasted enough time as it is. Vylantra entrusted me with the prophecy, and I need to fulfill it."

"There's one issue I need to tend to," Chloé said. "I need to go to Valquent. I've already missed two assembly meetings. I cannot miss another one."

"Heading to Valquent may not be a bad idea. There are plenty of people there. One of them is bound to be a warrior," Bunnie said.

Chloé chewed her lip. "The problem is . . ."

"Us," Mimi said. "Sage and I are chimeras."

"Until I can persuade the council and King Valentine VI that chimeras should have the same rights we do, there is nothing I can do," Chloé said, frowning.

"Could you do what you did with me and Minari?" Elliot asked. He reached for his neck but found it was bare. There was no collar.

Chloé shook her head. "I refuse to have any more property. It's not right, and it would go against what I believe in. If I truly want to see the chimeras free, then I need to show it."

"It will be as difficult as it is traveling with two elves," Luka said. "Luckily, Owen and I can use illusion magic. We can disguise you four, but only when we enter cities or towns. However, it's strenuous on us, so we can't do it for long. The first thing we should do when we reach the capital is search for an inn."

"Then it's settled." Elliot nodded. "Tonight we depart for Valquent."

The End